THE
QUEEN
OF
BRIGHT
AND
SHINY

THINGS

ANN AGUIRRE

FEIWEL AND FRIENDS
NEW YORK

A Feiwel and Friends Book
An Imprint of Macmillan

Feiwel and Friends books may be purchased for business or promotional use. For information on bulk purchases, please contact the Macmillan Corporate and Premium Sales Department at (800) 221-7945 x5442 or by e-mail at specialmarkets@macmillan.com.

Library of Congress Cataloging-in-Publication Data

Aguirre, Ann.
The queen of bright and shiny things / Ann Aguirre.
pages cm
Summary: "Sage has learned to substitute causes for relationships, and it's working just fine . . . until Shane Cavendish strolls into her math class. He's a little antisocial, a lot beautiful, and everything she never knew she always wanted"—Provided by publisher.
ISBN 978-1-250-04750-2 (hardback)—ISBN 978-1-250-07810-0 (ebook)
[1. Dating (Social customs)—Fiction. 2. High schools—Fiction. 3. Schools—Fiction. 4. Conduct of life—Fiction. 5. Single-parent families—Fiction. 6. Social action—Fiction.] I. Title.
PZ7.A26877Que 2015
[Fic]—dc23
2014042423

Book design by Anna Booth

Feiwel and Friends logo designed by Filomena Tuosto

First Edition: 2015

10 9 8 7 6 5 4 3 2 1

macteenbooks.com

For my daughter, Andrea.
Every word of this book is for you.

CHAPTER ONE

I KNOW WHAT THEY CALL ME. THE GOTH GIRLS STARTED it, all ripped black fishnets and heavy kohl, with chipped black nail polish and metric tons of attitude, like any of that makes them cooler than anyone else. It so doesn't, but high school is full of people who think what they wear matters more than who they are. But I should talk. Before I came to stay with Aunt Gabby, I was worse than those girls. But she's taught me a lot in the years I've been living with her, mostly how to stop being angry about things I can't control.

Like my mom. My dad. And especially the nickname.

It echoes as I walk past the burners, which is what I call the pot and pill heads, who cluster near the emergency exit. They disable the alarms after each inspection, so they can slip in and out for a smoke. A bleary-eyed guy who's failing to rock a soul patch says, "What up, Princess?" and holds up two fingers in what's supposed to be a victory sign . . . or maybe peace, I dunno.

I ignore him, though it's not easy. There's always a part of me that wants to make people sorry when they piss me off, but I've swallowed her whole, wrapped the shadow me in plastic, and I'm waiting for her to stop breathing. I walk on, brightening my smile through sheer determination. I've heard if you pretend long enough—or maybe wish hard enough—faking normal becomes real. I'm counting on that. Until then, I'll carry on.

Everybody at JFK has a thing. For the drama dorks, it's huddling up in the auditorium, singing or running lines every chance they get. They all have big Broadway dreams, fattened by watching *Glee*. Since we're also in a podunk Midwestern town, they figure the show speaks directly to them. I don't mind the concept, but it's ironic that they get twenty-five-year-olds to play high school students. Which explains why all the performers have such poise and polish. I'd like it more if they looked real, if they occasionally had zits or bad hair.

The burners take pride in not doing *anything*. Most of them have a 1.2 GPA, barely attend class, and are heavily into recreational drugs. The preps are all about grades, sports, and pretending to be awesome in front of adults. Ironically, they also drink the most; a few of them do it binge style and suffer from blackouts on a regular basis.

I fit in with the crunchy granola do-gooders. I'm involved in eco-related clubs, partly because it looks good on your college application, and I don't intend to stay in a crappy Midwestern town. When I graduate, I'm getting out of here, where everything feels small. Maybe that sounds like I don't appreciate Aunt Gabby, which is the opposite of true, but I can love her without thinking this is the best place ever.

"Is she ever gonna stop with that?" one of the goth girls asks.

"Whatever. Let Princess Post-it do her thing," says a dude with a safety pin in his ear.

I wish they'd listen to him; it's not like I'm hurting anyone. Basically, my thing is this—and it started freshman year—I had a pack of pink Post-it notes with me on the first day of school because I was so scared I'd forget something important. Before I started at the junior high here, it had been years since I attended a normal school, and I felt pretty sure that junior high wasn't the same as high school. So yeah, reminders. Inside my locker. On my notebooks. Everywhere.

There's this girl, Becky, who has great hair, bouncy and red, but she's . . . big. Not like me, with a small chest and a big butt, but all over large. So that day, first day of freshman gym, they didn't have shorts or a tee that would fit her. So she's sitting in the bleachers in her school clothes, red-faced, shiny-eyed, fighting tears while she hears people saying stuff like "orca" and "lard-ass" as we run laps. I can tell by watching her that she's about to cry, which will just make her humiliation complete. But the bell rings before she breaks, and we go back to the locker room. The other girls treat her like she's invisible, and I see her register that *this* is how high school is going to be; her place in the social strata is already cemented from one bad day. And I couldn't change that. So I don't know why I did it—just an inexplicable impulse—but later that afternoon, I wrote *You have amazing hair* on a pink Post-it and stuck it on her locker, where everyone could see it.

I waited for her to read it, and after she did, Becky looked around to see if somebody was punking her. So I made eye contact to be sure she knew I meant it, smiled, and gave her a thumbs-up. Maybe it was stupid; maybe it didn't help at all, but from the way she lit up, I feel like it did. She gave me two thumbs back, and we went our separate ways.

However, I liked the feeling. I enjoyed cheering her up. High

3

school is hell and I'm trundling around passing out ice water. Maybe it doesn't end the torment but if the nice balances out some of the crap, then I feel like it was worth my while. So that's how Post-its became my thing. Hence the nickname.

I do this daily, scope for somebody having an awful day, and look for a bright side. Sometimes it's lame, but at least I'm trying. Aunt Gabby says if you put positivity out into the world, it will come back to you tenfold. I don't know if that's true, but I want it to be. I'm trying so hard to build up good karma, like when you can't see how furiously a duck is paddling beneath the placid surface of a pond.

Aunt Gabby is actually my half aunt because she was my dad's half sister. Apparently she and Dad weren't raised together; they have the same father, and he was the kind of guy who thought it was awesome to impregnate multiple women and then wander off. I don't remember my grandma. She passed on when my dad was young . . . and *he* died when I was seven. That doesn't bode well for my potential lifespan, I suppose. But bad ends run in my blood, not genetic disorders or congenital health problems. So whatever goes wrong, at least it'll be quick.

"Sage!" My best friend, Ryan, wanders out of Mrs. David's classroom, falling into step. "You going to Green World tonight?"

That's our eco-awareness group. Supposedly, we'll come up with ways to save the planet, brainstorm green technologies, and sponsor community cleanup projects. So far, one month into the school year, we've only managed to order pizza and screw around.

"Yeah. I hope we actually *do* something soon."

"Ditto that. I signed up to pad my college apps, but this failure to launch is becoming problematic."

"You sound like you already work for NASA," I say.

"I try."

Ryan is over six feet tall with black hair that refuses to lie down, regardless of how it's cut or combed, and he's a total string bean. He wears hipster glasses to disguise how much of ginormous dork he is, but so far, this strategy has fooled no one. Not that it matters to me how he looks.

He was the first friend I made when I moved here three years ago. That day, I forgot my lunch; I was a huge mess, and I sat down in the corner of the cafeteria at a broken table, or at least, it was half broken, because it almost collapsed when I leaned my elbows on it. Everyone else at the school knew not to sit there, but after I plunked down, I was too nervous to move. To this day, I have no idea why Ryan came over. I had terminal new-kid disease, which can be mad contagious, but I guess Ryan was vaccinated—or lonely. That day, he gave me half a peanut butter sandwich and the courage not to drown myself in the girls' toilet. We've been inseparable ever since.

"Seen anyone who needs a pick-me-up?" I've got my Post-it pad in hand, purple glitter pen at the ready.

It's super girlie, I know, and faintly ridiculous, but I was into that two years ago, and since that's what I did the first time with Becky, who has since lost weight and joined the volleyball team, I'm still doing it. I don't claim I'm the reason she got motivated to change her life, but I believe in the power of ritual. So if I have any positive mojo to give to people who need it, maybe it comes from my pink Post-its or the purple glitter pen. Also, this is how people know the message comes legit from the Princess herself.

Occasionally, there *are* pretenders.

Ryan groans. "Are you seriously doing that again this year?"

"I'm doing it until I graduate. There are plenty of people who go around being dicks. Not enough go around being nice."

"That much is true." He hugs me around the shoulders, then dashes into history class.

This period, I have Mr. Mackiewicz for math. The Mackiewicz math class is the ninth circle of hell, and I'm currently failing. Everyone thinks I'm super smart, but I can't get geometry. This was a huge revelation, as prior to this year, I skated through the rest of my classes. I made dioramas and participated in discussions; I did extra credit and gave my all in group projects. I'm a good test taker, too. I don't get nervous or anything, have no trouble memorizing stuff.

But geometry? It's a foreign language. So the first test of the year is still in my bag. I haven't been brave enough to show Aunt Gabby yet, but that big circled F haunts me. If I close my eyes, I can see it, along with the smear of red sauce and the grease stain at the edge of the paper. I suspect Mr. Mackiewicz was eating pizza when he graded my exam. Somehow that makes it worse. He's cramming cheese and dough into his face while decreeing my epic failure? So uncool.

I trudge to the back of the class, wishing somebody would write something nice on a Post-it and stick it on *my* locker for a change. The classroom hasn't been updated in forty years, I bet. The globe probably still has Persia and Constantinople and other places that were dissolved prior to 1900. The math trivia cards that have been posted around the room are yellowed at the edges, starting to fray. Mr. Mackiewicz's desk is crooked.

The jocks have a bet going—every day, they nudge it back an inch, and they're running a pool to see how long it takes for Mackiewicz to notice that it's majorly askew. So far that's half a foot. It doesn't speak well of the cleaning crew that it stays that way, even less of Mackiewicz that he hasn't spotted a problem. But the guy's fairly myopic: thick bifocals, a white monk fringe, and a wispy mustache. If that doesn't sound enticing enough, he's also all about baggy cardigans, plaid, and corduroys.

I take my seat, wondering if this is the day when math lightning strikes, and suddenly all of the theorems will make sense. Since fakery seems like the only answer, I get out all my supplies, notebook, pencil, iPad. One cool thing about JFK, we aren't using textbooks anymore. They're all available electronically, and the school subsidized iPads. Of course that meant cutting metal shop and drivers ed from the budget. Doesn't affect me, as I refuse to drive on principle until affordable electric cars are widely available as an alternative; I'd prefer a solar one, but Ryan says I should keep dreaming. As for metal shop? Well, I tried to build a birdhouse in eighth grade. It didn't end well. God only knows what would happen if I attempted to weld.

I'm fiddling with my supplies when Mackiewicz shuffles into the room. He's wearing the gray sweater with the red stain. People reluctantly settle down, folding into their desks like grumpy origami dolls. Geometry is the only class where I sit near the burners, who slouch in the back, letting sunglasses and hair hide their bloodshot eyes. Most of them, I suspect, doze off before Mackiewicz sits down at his crooked desk.

The bell rings. Anyone who enters at this point is officially tardy.

Before the teacher can numb my brain with an hour of droning, the door creaks open, and a new kid slides in. New Kid is kind of a big deal because people don't move to Farmburg, Illinois, by choice; you can guess what's around here by the name of the town. He's almost as tall as Ryan with a mop of brown hair, not curly, but messy and hiding most of his face. Though it's late September, he's got on an old army surplus jacket, which pretty much hides any sense of chest and shoulders. His legs are long, though, feet encased in battered boots. They're not Docs, more like something soldiers would actually march in. His jeans are faded, torn up and down one leg, but in his case, I don't think it's a fashion statement. You can tell intentional grunge from pure wear. He keeps his head down as he hands a slip to Mackiewicz.

The math teacher skims it, then drops it on his desk. "Please welcome Shane Cavendish, transferring in from Michigan City. Take any empty desk."

What Mackiewicz hasn't told New Kid Shane is that he'll be stuck wherever he sits for the rest of the year. I wish I could warn him. Shane never looks up entirely, his shoulders hunched like this is a horrible ordeal. Though I was thirteen when I first hit JFK, I still remember that awful feeling, like a pit in my stomach, because starting over just sucks so hard, especially when other stuff is bad, too.

Shane skims the room and then he's coming down the aisle one over from me. He drops into the desk with the uneven leg. It rocks a little, making it annoying to write, but he doesn't move even after he discovers the fault. It's like he just wants to disappear, but people watch him get his supplies out like it's fascinating.

Finally, Mackiewicz gets started on the lesson, and I tune out. Fifty minutes later, my brain switches back on. My notebook is empty. As the bell rings, I scrawl the assignment, which I'll make a mess of, into my work diary. I'd like to say something to the new kid, but before I can, he's up like a shot. At the door, Dylan Smith, one of the jocks, shoulder slams Shane into the jamb, and his buddies do the same on the way out. Yeah, I guess they've decided where he fits in the pecking order. Because he doesn't have the right haircut or the right clothes, he's an auto-reject? It totally sucks.

"You all right?" I ask, but if he heard the question, he's ignoring me.

He doesn't turn. I tell myself it's because if he acknowledges my concern, then the bad junk is real. To face the day at the new school, he told himself, *This time it'll be different.* You can lie to yourself about all kinds of things. Until you can't, anymore. Until reality pounds a hole through your fantasy castle and the reality check must be cashed.

But he must be fronting because nobody ever *wants* to be lonely. You just pretend not to care if anyone talks to you because otherwise, you're the desperate loser begging for friends. Whatever, Shane's gone, long strides eating up the hallway, and he's not even rubbing his shoulder, like he's used to pain.

For some reason, that bothers me.

CHAPTER TWO

AFTER SCHOOL, I STICK A POST-IT ON EMILY FRANKLIN'S locker. Seeing as she dumped her lunch tray everywhere in the cafeteria, I figure she could use an ego boost. I don't always stick around to watch people read like I did that first time. Sometimes I have places to be.

Like today.

I unlock my bike from the rack out front. My house is two and a half miles from school, not an easy distance, but I'm determined. Riding five miles daily should keep me fit, but it's bulked up my thighs while doing little for my butt. There are probably other exercises I should try, but I don't care enough. Pedaling doggedly—while responding to the occasional greeting—carries me home.

Aunt Gabby is still at work when I arrive. She manages a new age place, where they sell healing crystals and hand-dipped candles. You'd think there wouldn't be much market for that in a small Midwestern town, and mostly, you'd be right. Which is why she spends a lot of time filling Web orders. There's a light walk-in business, but mostly she parcels things up and takes them to the post office.

Home is a two-bedroom bungalow, the exterior painted a cheerful robin's egg blue. The house has pine-green shutters and a fanciful menagerie of statues in the front yard. Now, in early fall, the garden is bright with orange and yellow mums, an explosion of color curling around the side of the house. The lawn itself is browning around the edges, as we're in a bit of a drought.

We live in a western subdivision, not far enough from the town center for the farms to take over. Once you leave Farmburg, drive four miles in any direction and fields are all you'll see. It's a fair drive to the interstate from here, so we don't get highway traffic often. In the spring, there's nothing but fertilizer and in the fall, there's the scent of cut hay. This is a peaceful place, I suppose, better than where I've been. Most of the houses around ours are bigger, but they lack the quirky charm my aunt has cultivated. I imagine our neighborhood looks like a patchwork quilt from above, but since I've never been on a plane, I wouldn't know.

After parking my bike in the shed out back, I let myself in, passing the hand-carved umbrella stand and driftwood coatrack. Aunt Gabby has a thing for primitive arts and crafts and natural furnishings, so our place looks like a roadside museum. The result is bright and cozy. My room is nestled at the back of the house, past the bathroom. It's small, so I've got a battered bureau, a bookshelf made of reclaimed lumber and cinder blocks, painted scarlet and yellow for cheer, and a daybed that we bought at the thrift store downtown, and then sprayed a shiny gold. I've piled the bed with tons of throw pillows in all manner of fabrics, mostly inspired from watching *Arabian Nights,* as there's lots of satin and sparkle. I never crafted or sewed before coming to Aunt Gabby, but she taught me, so I made the pillows myself. My closet is tiny, too, but that's fine, as I don't have many clothes. I hide that fact by rotating my skirts and leggings with different tanks and shrugs.

I spend two hours doing homework, and then leave a note, advising her I'll be home by nine thirty. Then I haul my bike out of the shed. It's not dark yet, so I don't worry about reflectors; I'll put those on later. I have plenty of time; I don't kill myself peddling to the library, where we hold our monthly meetings. This isn't a school club, so we had to find someplace else to host our group. It's open to all ages, but so far, it hasn't taken off. Only six members have joined.

I wave to Miss Martha, the librarian, as I push through the doors into the air-conditioning. The public library is one of my favorite places in the world. It's an old building, two-story and historical looking, with marble floors, full of nooks and crannies where people can curl up to read. The books are organized by subject and then via the Dewey decimal system. Back near the reference desk, there are a couple of ancient desktops that people can use to check their e-mail. Fortunately, I don't need those. I saved enough money this summer to buy myself a laptop. I'm pretty stoked about that.

Since I'm fifteen minutes early, I drop off my books at the front desk and pick out a couple of new titles. I carry them to the conference room upstairs where we hold our meetings. To my surprise, somebody's already sitting there, reading, arms propped on the table. I recognize the green Army surplus jacket before I place him— Shane Cavendish, new kid.

How did he hear about Green World?

"Hey," I say, as I sit down. "Good to see you."

His head jerks up; he was totally into the book and didn't hear me at all, which makes me like him instantly. I know all about the transportive power of fiction. Back in my old life, there were plenty of days when I wouldn't have made it if I didn't have an exit into the pages of somebody else's life. My breath catches as his gaze meets mine. No joke, it's like the whole world pauses for that second. Because Shane Cavendish has the most beautiful eyes I've ever seen, aquamarine flecked with darker blue and green, fringed with long dark lashes that actually curl up toward his brows. Eventually, I notice he has a nose with a bump in the bridge, like it's been broken, a pair of sharp cheekbones, a faint scar on his left temple, and a layer of scruff at his jaw. His mouth . . . no, I can't even.

But it's incredible, too.

Though I could probably stare at him for another five minutes in awed silence, he's not on board with that plan. His brows pull together as he shoves his book into his bag. "What're you talking about?"

I thought "good to see you" was self-explanatory. It's a universal greeting and expression of welcome, isn't it? "I'm happy the group's adding a new member," I offer cautiously.

"Oh." Shane pushes out a breath. "Is there a meeting in here?"

I check my watch. "In five minutes."

"I'll clear out then."

"You're not here to join?"

"Unlikely," he says.

That tone tells me what he thinks of people who organize and try. He's probably a nihilist or something, who thinks it's a waste of energy because nothing will ever get better. I admit, there are some days when I understand that philosophy. But without people agitating for change, there's only the awfulness of the status quo.

"You're welcome."

"What am I supposed to be thanking you for?" His expression is outright puzzled, but he's paying attention to me, his eyes trained on my face like he really sees me for the first time.

Which is cool, except . . . "I didn't mean it that way," I explain awkwardly. "You're welcome to check out Green World."

"Let me guess. You sponsor recycling drives and bug people to stop using plastic grocery bags."

I guess that breathless moment where our eyes made contact was a one-way circuit. It's a good thing I have a sense of humor or his attitude might bother me. "So far, we haven't achieved even that much. Mostly, we argue and order pizza."

Shane laughs, surprising me. His fingers relax on the edges of his ragged backpack. It was like he thought I was setting him up. In some respects, he seems like a kindred spirit, as if life has taught him to expect the worst.

"I could eat."

"Then stay," I say.

My heart pounds crazy hard, like, I can hear it in my ears. I've never said anything like that to a guy before. I wonder if he knows how bad I want to keep him here, just so I can look at him. His mop of chestnut hair has a hint of curl, and it's pretty adorable the way it falls around his ears. In geometry, he used it to hide, but he's not doing that now. He's letting me see him.

"Okay." It's apparently that easy.

Before I can figure out where to go from here, Ryan bounds into the room, tossing his backpack onto the table with a *thunk*. He flings himself into the chair next to me, beaming, and then launches into a convoluted story about why he couldn't get a burrito. I must admit, while I usually love Ryan's stories, I'm not riveted by this one. It *feels* like he interrupted something, though maybe that's just wishful thinking. At the end of the epic saga, I laugh because that's what he expects of me. Shane goes back to reading.

The other four file in, some of them late, so it's ten past before we're all assembled. In Green World, there's Kenneth, aka Kenny Wu, Gwen Reave, Tara Tanner, and Conrad Loudermilk—two freshmen, one senior, and one other. Conrad is in his twenties, but for reasons known only to him, he hasn't gone off to college yet. Instead he putters around his mom's house and hangs out with high school people when he's not working at the local supermarket, the P&K. Which is like an A&P, I guess, only crappier.

Gwen is the senior, which means she has a car and the sense that she's in charge, so she orders the pizzas—one cheese, one veggie, from Pizza the Action. The main thing you need to know about this town is, it's a small place, so the biggest name restaurant we have in town is the Dairy Queen. The whole downtown can be traversed in five minutes on foot. There's a strip mall toward the highway, but there's nothing shiny in there, either, mostly low-rent shops and stuff like the dollar store, only it's not even a national franchise; it's called Bang for Your Buck.

Anyway.

Once Gwen gets off the phone, she calls the meeting to order while studying Shane through her bangs. I can tell she's wondering who he is. I don't clarify. It's not like I own him.

But he does the talking. He cants his head at me and mumbles, "She invited me. I'm Shane Cavendish."

He doesn't even know my name, I realize. *Smooth.*

"Sage Czinski."

Nobody ever spells my last name right from hearing it pronounced, and they rarely get it when reading off a list. It's not that hard, really: suh-ZIN-skee. But I'm prepared for a career of correcting people as I go through life. My first name is kind of strange, too, but my dad always said that when I was born, he thought I had wise eyes for a baby, so that's why he called me Sage.

"Good to have you, Shane." Gwen sparkles at him. She's pretty, with blond hair and blue eyes, and good teeth from three years of orthodontia.

I'm self-conscious about mine, as I have a slight overbite, and they're a bit crooked. Not bad enough to merit braces, but not perfect. My canines are a little too long, too, which means I get vampire jokes at Halloween. Better than every day, I suppose.

The rest of the members introduce themselves to him, too. Then we go around the room as we wait for the food, offering our presentations for the first Green World project. Each week for the past month, we've done this and not gotten anywhere because everyone wants his or her idea to be implemented first. It's starting to feel like a waste of time, but Wednesday is two for one at Pizza the Action, and I've gotten used to bickering with these people.

We've just completed the pitches when Steve the delivery dude taps on the door. This is old hat for him, too, as he knows to come upstairs if he wants a decent tip. For a few minutes, we scramble, scraping together his payment from crumpled ones and pocket change, then I add a little more to keep him happy. I don't look at Shane, who hasn't reached for his wallet. Based on the state of his jacket, jeans, and backpack, I bet he doesn't have any cash on him. The promise of free food might even be why he agreed to stay.

He goes for a couple of slices of plain cheese while I pounce on the veggie. I'm not horrified by the idea of eating meat, but Aunt Gabby is, and since she was kind enough to take me in, I feel like I should conform to her values for solidarity. So for the last three years, I've been on tofu and vegetables. Fortunately, she's not vegan because I don't think I could live without cheese. Seriously. I'd die.

Eating takes up ten minutes of the meeting, and then Gwen calls us back to order. "Now we just need to decide which idea to go forward with."

This is where everything usually breaks down. We'll spend the last half hour arguing among ourselves. But before we can get started on that, Shane says, "Why not just vote? If you're worried about hurting somebody's feelings, do a closed ballot. Write down the idea you like best."

Gwen looks like he just gave her a tiara. "That's *genius*. Make sure you vote for the idea you truly think is best. Because if everyone votes for himself, nothing will get done."

I don't point out that since Shane didn't present an idea, he has to vote for somebody . . . and that means his support will carry the day, even if everyone *does* vote for his own project. After digging a scrap of paper from my backpack, I jot down a name, not my own. I actually like Ryan's idea better.

The slips of paper go into Kenny's Mario hat, then Gwen reads them out.

"Gwen. Kenny. Tara. Ryan. Ryan. Sage. Sage." A frown. "We have a tie."

"We can't do both." Conrad is staring at me with a happy smile, which makes me think he voted for me.

It occurs to me that Ryan probably voted for himself, so does that mean . . . Shane chose my plan? That doesn't *mean* anything, I tell myself.

Tara offers, "We should vote again, now that we've narrowed it down to two. Pick between Ryan and Sage."

Gwen nods. "Good idea."

The atmosphere is surprisingly efficient without the usual garbage. I wonder if they're showing off for Shane. I understand why Tara and Gwen would want him to think well of them, but what's up with Kenny, Conrad, and Ryan? My bestie's been wearing a faint scowl for the last ten minutes, and he hasn't said much since Shane suggested the vote.

"Okay, round two."

Just to be consistent, I vote for Ryan again, but when the vote comes up, it's four to three in favor of my idea. Which is to clean up a vacant lot downtown in preparation for planting a garden in the spring. I'm not clear on the legalities of using land you don't own, but maybe I can get permission. I say as much to Gwen when she proclaims the project a go.

"That's your top priority," she tells me. "Next meeting won't be here. Let's go directly there after school next week. Dress comfortably and bring biodegradable bags to hold the garbage."

"Sounds good."

The meeting breaks up thereafter with everyone mumbling good-byes. Like I always do, I start cleaning up the room. The others are used to my routine, so they don't stop to help. They all have curfews or other places to be, apart from Ryan, who musters a smile when he sees me looking at him.

"You've won this round," he says, pretending to twirl an imaginary mustache. "But I'll be back with another nefarious plan next week."

God, he's a dork. And awesome.

"See you tomorrow," I answer.

"They just leave you to deal with the mess?" Shane asks, after Ryan bails.

Since I've hardly looked at him since the others arrived, I'm surprised that he's hanging around. Surprised but glad. I finish breaking down and folding the pizza box before replying. "I'm the library liaison. I talked Miss Martha into letting us use this room, and they don't usually allow food in the building." I hesitate, wondering if I'll sound crazy anal if I try to make him understand. I settle for, "So it's on me if the room's not clean enough at the end of the night."

It's not that I'm a total neat freak, just that this falls under the heading of keeping a promise, something I *am* fanatical about.

"I get that."

I pick up the second box. "There's one piece of veggie left if you want it."

"Sure you don't?"

"I'd have suggested we split it if I was still hungry." I flip open the second pizza box, offering him the final slice.

"Okay," he says slowly. "Thanks."

He picks off the mushrooms, then devours it in six bites, not that I was counting, and afterward, he helps me clean up the room, though he laughs when he sees I've got wipes in my bag, which I use on the table and the arms of the chairs. Shane Cavendish is even better with humor shining in his eyes. I can't stop looking at him, whereas, to him, I'm sure I'm the weird girl trying to hide a big butt with a flouncy skirt.

"Do you have a vacuum cleaner in there, too?" he asks, tapping my backpack.

"That's where I draw the line." Though I have considered bringing a hand broom and dustpan to sweep up crumbs. Not that he needs to know that. "Does it look all right?"

"Fine."

He follows as I head out, pausing to pull the door closed. It locks automatically, so we're good to go. That thought depresses me. Oblivious to my chagrin, he trails me downstairs; it's ten minutes until closing and Miss Martha has started turning off the lights. I wave at her as I go out the front door; she smiles back. She's a pleasant woman in her mid-fifties with short salt-and-pepper hair and a fondness for beads, reflected in the bedazzled top she's wearing.

Outside, he gets to watch me put on my reflectors. Clearly, there's nothing hotter than a hygiene-and-safety-obsessed girl. But part of my deal with Aunt Gabby involves this gear; she said she could only allow me to ride my bike after dark if I agreed to her terms. Which means this stupid helmet with a light on it, and glow strips all over my body, like I belong in a bizarre off-Broadway show. My cheeks heat as I get to work while Shane studies me in horrified fascination.

"You can go," I tell him through clenched teeth.

"What are you *doing*?"

"My aunt makes me. It's the cost of nocturnal bicycle freedom." At his blank look, I explain, "She thinks I'll get run over if I don't wear it."

"Ah. Well, you're pretty hard to miss."

I have *no idea* what that means, if it's a compliment, or a crack about the size of my butt, or a reference to my awesome light helmet; I could totally go spelunking in this. When I buckle the chin strap, I'm wishing for death.

"Think you'll come back next week?" I ask.

"Unlikely," he says.

So it was the free pizza. Well, that's to be expected.

"See you tomorrow," I say, and then I wish I hadn't because it makes me sound like I'll be looking for him.

"In geometry, right? You're next to me, one seat back."

"Yeah." I'm so absurdly pleased that he saw and recognized me that I offer a ten-thousand-watt smile. Then I remember my teeth are a little crooked and I have suck-your-blood canines.

Shane doesn't seem to mind. Or notice. "Be careful out there. How far are you going?"

"Two miles, give or take."

If he offers to drive me home, I'll have to pass, as I don't ride in cars. Not that the automobile industry has been noticeably impacted by my boycott. Aunt Gabby says it's good that I stick to my principles even if they're inconvenient for other people. For the first time, I wonder if my principles would mind shutting up for a minute. But it's not *only* that. My dad died in a car wreck when I was younger, and I'm still skittish.

"Which way?"

God, he's totally going to ask to drive me home. I brace for it. "West."

"Ah."

The euphoria drops like a brick. There's nothing from him but a chin jerk in acknowledgment. I misread everything. At least I didn't show any of it—I don't *think* I did. His face would be full of embarrassment if he realized. I take the trash bag from the meeting around to the side and sort everything into the recycling containers. It took me six months to convince the town council to adopt this measure, but it was worth it. When I turn, Shane's still there, which leaves me feeling weird. Doesn't he have somewhere to be? It's almost eight, not full dark, just saturated in shadows; the air is cool with a gentle wind sweeping through. This is my favorite part of the year, after the heat of summer dissipates, but still some warm weather before the first cold snap. I say I'll be back by nine thirty, but the truth is, I'm always home before nine. I build a buffer into my promises to Aunt Gabby so there's no chance I'll break them.

"Night," I say, shouldering my backpack with both straps.

Then I swing onto the bike, careful to wrap my skirt so I can ride. I try not to think about what he's seeing, but I have on leggings, so it's totally fine, even if it's not pretty. I realized a long time ago that some guys are assholes and they'll do anything to peek at your underwear, which makes a skirt hazardous.

Shane doesn't answer. When I turn the corner, he's still standing in front of the library watching me ride away.

CHAPTER

THREE

AT SCHOOL THE NEXT DAY, SHANE PRETENDS HE DOESN'T know me. When I spot him in the hall before lunch, his gaze slides away; he's back to playing the invisible boy. I understand why . . . the jocks have targeted him as their latest victim. Since JFK is a small school, serving a number of rural communities, the sports program is streamlined. There's no fluff—no lacrosse, rugby, field hockey, certainly nothing European like soccer or fencing. We have football in the fall, basketball in the winter, then baseball and track for spring. That's it. That means the athletes often double and triple letter, participating in more than one sport. This creates a tight clique and when a new guy drops into the mix, he better find a crew in a hurry. Otherwise, he's fair game. Dylan and his cronies blow by; and it happens so fast, even I'm not sure what went down.

Shane hits the ground, his backpack smacking open. His iPad doesn't bounce out, but everything else does: dog-eared notebooks, nubs of pencils, and what looks like sheet music. Only it's not the professional preprinted kind. This is blank white paper with lines, notes, and bars drawn in. I've never known anyone who wrote music before. I break away from Ryan and Gwen, who're talking about logistics for the cleanup next week. Shane doesn't even glance up as I help him gather his stuff; he snatches his music, shoves to his feet, and strides away.

Ryan watches with a faint frown. "He seems pretty antisocial."

"It's hard being the new kid." I remember how hard I tried to hide my desperate fear that people would sense that I wasn't like them . . . and how much I wanted to make friends, but I couldn't show it, not like grade school when you can hand over a juice box and seal the deal. By high school, there's so much judgment.

"You did okay," he points out.

"Because of you."

Ryan laughs. "It wasn't a hardship. In case you didn't notice, in junior high, I had exactly one friend, who was sick that day."

I remember. "Then Phillip moved to Cleveland. Do you talk to him much?"

"Online sometimes." Ryan slings an arm around my shoulders. "Let's get to lunch."

People act like we've been dating for two years, but in fact, he's never asked me out. Early on, I obsessed over it, trying to decide if he *like* liked me, but eventually we settled into a comfortable routine. Now he's my best friend; since I got my laptop, we're always on Skype when we aren't together, but I can't imagine making out with him anymore.

We stand in line, so I can get what passes for a veggie entree at this school, macaroni and cheese with a side of withered green beans. I'm offered Jell-O, but that has pig parts in it, so I pass and follow Ryan to our table. Gwen from Green World doesn't eat with us, but the freshmen do, and we let them because we remember how much it sucked. Sometimes Ryan's other friends join us; he's a Renaissance man these days, so in addition to all the academic clubs and the debate team, he also takes pictures for the yearbook and the school blog. Which doesn't sound cool, maybe, but everyone knows who he is. I'm definitely the sidekick in this relationship.

As I take my first bite, Ryan asks, "So what's with you and the new kid?"

I can't place his tone, but I'm feeling squirrelly. "Huh?"

"You invited him to join our stuff?" He says the last two words like some people say "our song," as if it's private and privileged, just for the two of us. But he's never been exclusionary.

"He was there when I showed up," I say, puzzled. "So I told him about the meeting. Was I not supposed to?"

Ryan snaps, "He's a grunge kid. Like he *cares* about the environment. Right now he's probably writing song lyrics about how nobody understands him."

Wow. He seems to have it in for Shane, which is *so* not like him. I frown while Tara and Kenny glance between us, wide-eyed. They're not sure what's going on, and neither am I.

"Maybe we could talk about this later?"

"Come on," he says, gathering up the remnants of his lunch.

I'm not sure I want to, but following Ryan has become second nature at this point. So I trail him into the hallway. I fold my arms, waiting for an explanation.

"I just . . ." Here, Ryan pauses, at a loss for words as he never is. "He doesn't seem like our type, that's all."

"How can you tell, just by looking?" I ask incredulously. "You've hardly talked to him."

I can't believe I'm hearing this from him. He should know, better than anyone, how it feels to be picked on and excluded, based on factors beyond one's control. Until the summer after freshman year, he was five foot four and routinely got shoved inside lockers. So Ryan knows damn well how Shane must feel; apparently he just doesn't care.

"Well, I'm not letting you decide who I can be friends with," I tell him.

"You don't know—" he starts.

"Does he kill kittens? Sell drugs?"

"One of the secretaries talked to my mom, okay? She said he's got a thick file. I'm not supposed to know about it, but . . . that's never good, right?"

I almost get mad at Ryan then, but that—*no.* For a few seconds, I'm woozy and scared; this can't happen. So I take four deep breaths, mustering a smile and a polite tone. "Did Dylan's mom talk to yours?"

Ms. Smith might be Mrs. McKenna's source; she works in the school office, which should make Dylan an outcast. Instead, he manages to be popular, probably because he's hot and plays multiple sports. He's also the asshole leading the crew that picks on Shane, who's supposedly a bad guy. I could laugh at the irony.

"It doesn't matter. Do what you want." Ryan falls silent then.

This feels weirdly like an argument, but I have no idea what it's—and then it dawns on me. "Are you jealous?"

Possibly not in a romantic sense, but Ryan's used to being the only star in my firmament. Maybe he's worried the Sage and Ryan Show can't withstand Special Guest Shane. Who is totally uninterested in the role, believe me. Besides being the new kid, he's got other problems, most of whom wear lettermen jackets.

"Do I need to be?"

Huh. That's not a no.

"You'll always be my best friend, no matter how many others I make." Is that what he wants to hear?

Maybe I'm paying more attention than I usually do, but his face falls a fraction, and then he pulls on a goofy smile. "Obviously. Who could ever replace me?"

"Nobody."

Ryan slings an arm around my shoulders on the way to chemistry. It occurs to me that people are used to seeing this because it doesn't earn us a second glance. In chem, we're lab partners, and if I'm honest, Ryan does most of the work. I'm not good with hard sciences or math; this frustrates me because I feel like I'm letting women down all over the world by feeding existing stereotypes. I wish I rocked at physics and could do differential equations, but I don't have that type of intelligence. In fact, it's likely I'll never even get to physics or calculus.

Mr. Oscar teaches all the advanced science classes. You'd think that's a first name, not last, but in his case, you'd be wrong. He's thirty-something, and he thinks he's cool, which means he's always telling people, "Call me Tom," but he doesn't notice that everyone still calls him Mr. Oscar and only laughs at his jokes to be polite. I laze through a lab experiment while Ryan does all the measuring, mixing, and pouring. I pull my weight with excellent note-taking, however, and then I log our result. Chemistry is boring, but since it's after lunch it means there's only three periods to go.

The rest of the day, every time I see Shane, he's getting a different kind of crap from the jock squad. At this point, if he was anybody else, I'd have already put a pink Post-it on his locker, but it feels like it would be too personal now. I mean, I could totally write, *Your eyes take my breath away,* in purple glitter pen, and I'd mean every word, but that would be so weird now that I've hung out with him. He'd probably take it wrong, not realizing this is what I do, and other people would see it, Ryan would hear about it, and it would become a thing—

No. I'm definitely not writing about his eyes. That's a quiet truth, just for me, hugged to my chest like the hitching breath I can't control when I glimpse him. He's like a hunk of chocolate cake slathered in frosting that I'm not supposed to have, but can't help wanting.

When I walk past the music room, I hear something that stills me in my tracks. People push past; I've become a rock in the middle of a rushing stream, but I can't move. Then someone shoves me from behind, not on purpose, but the result is the same. I slam into the lockers past the classroom and bounce. The underclassmen who were wrestling don't even notice that my brain has stopped firing.

Shane Cavendish plays like it's his reason for living.

I don't write that on the Post-it, of course. That would just get him beaten up even harder. Instead I scrawl, *You're awesome on the guitar,* because the jocks might think that's cool and leave him the hell alone. It's a long shot, as I don't have any particular cred with their crew, but being a musician is pretty spectacular. I can't breathe for how good—how remarkably talented—he is. And I suspect that if he found out anyone was paying attention, he'd stop playing.

Backtracking to his locker will make me late for class, but it's worth it. I stick the note just below the vents, as I always do, but this time it feels weightier, *more,* somehow, like this is a turning point. Shaking off the odd sensation, I dodge into econ with a mumbled excuse. Sadly, it holds no weight with Mrs. Palmer. Unlike the male teachers, she isn't impressed with talk of "female problems," so I get my first detention of the year, only the second I've ever had.

Since tomorrow is Friday and I have standing plans with Ryan, I ask, "Can I just get it over with tonight?"

I calculate; school lets out at two forty-five. An hour of sitting in silence, and I'm supposed to be at work at four. If I hurry, I can still make my shift at the Curly Q. Which sounds like a diner, but it's actually a salon. I'm not qualified to do anything but shampoo hair, sweep up, and answer the phone, but it's better than fast food. I work two afternoons a week from four to eight, which earns me spending money for the week. Since I'm under eighteen, I get paid fifty cents an hour less than an adult; that makes me a bargain. After detention ends, I'll just need to pedal hard to keep Mildred from yelling at me.

Mrs. Palmer glances up from scribbling down my doom. "Can you get a ride home?"

"Yeah."

I've always got my bike out front, and the town is small enough that I can ride anywhere I need to go from school. This is the one positive aspect of living in a tiny burg like this, especially given my opinion of privately owned fossil-fuel-burning vehicles, which covers nicely for my lingering fear

"Then it's fine with me. I'll let Mr. Mackiewicz know."

The math teacher is on detention duty? Awesome. Math sucks, but I might learn something if Mackiewicz wasn't such a black hole for hope. With such a good time ahead, economics drags even more than usual. I'm feeling bummed about the afternoon's prospects as I take my place in Mackiewicz's classroom, right up until Shane slips in. There are other people, too, mostly burners who cut class more than they attend. The room fills up, but I watch as he comes down the aisle toward me and settles in the desk next to mine.

Questions clamor in my mind, and before I realize it, I've blurted, "Why are you here?"

His brow goes up in quiet amusement, which is when I notice his black eye. "For fighting, of course." Sardonic tone.

"You mean when those assholes jumped you?"

"The athletic department needs them. I'm superfluous. So, obviously, I need to work harder at getting along with my peers." Though he's trying to be cool, bitterness seeps through his flat tone like rain through a crack in the roof.

"That is *so unfair.*"

Shane shrugs. "Welcome to life. What're *you* doing here? Doesn't seem like your kind of place." He offers a smile that makes me feel . . . I don't even have the words, but it's a longing that curls my toes.

"Mrs. Palmer has no tolerance for tardiness," I answer.

"Harsh."

"Not really. I was late, so I'll do my time." With him sitting beside me, it doesn't even feel like punishment anymore.

Until Mackiewicz shuffles into the room and demands that we quiet down and do our homework. I do . . . for the ten minutes it takes him to doze off. The burners are already asleep, which leaves Shane and me alone for all intents and purposes. He digs into his backpack and produces the pink Post-it I left him. I guess he's heard about the Princess.

"You left me this?" he asks.

I nod, feeling heat wash my cheeks.

"When did you hear me play?" He studies me through those thick, curling lashes, giving me the I-see-you look. I could curl up in that expression like it's an afghan.

"Just before last period."

"Explain to me why this was worth a tardy."

So he knows, then. It sounds stupid when I try to articulate it; my reasons come out in a whispered jumble, about making somebody's day better when things are total crap. I talk about silver linings and being the queen of bright and shiny things. He's listening, but I sound crazy. I know I do. It's pointless, possibly even pretentious, to think I could make a difference. I end my rambling recitation by saying as much.

To my surprise, he shakes his head. "No way. I'm sure there are people who are glad that you pay attention to them, who need to know someone gives a shit."

"But not you?" I ask softly.

"This is a cakewalk compared to what I'm used to dealing with on a daily basis." The moment the words are out, he looks like he wishes he hadn't spoken them, but it's too late.

I'm left wondering what's so bad at home that being beaten up is a welcome change. His tropical eyes dare me to ask, dare me to pry into his business, but I'm not brave enough. If he wanted me to know more, he'd tell me, right? Otherwise it's just me being nosy.

"My aunt Gabby is pretty great," I say. "But . . . it was bad before."

Shane makes a scoffing noise. "What do you know about 'bad'?"

He sees the image I've cultivated for the last three years. I went to therapy; I learned how to be good, how not to be angry. But every day, there's an underground river inside me, and I'm trying not to drown in it, every second of the day. This smile hides so much. It hides everything.

Part of me wants to tell him the truth. But I don't. Instead I duck my head, dodging his slow realization that my life hasn't been sunshine and rainbows. I rarely let anyone see Shadow Sage; I've done my best to bury her. Now she's just a thin hand reaching up from a fresh grave.

"Hey." He touches my forearm briefly, and in those scant seconds, I register the heat of his fingertips, the calluses on his skin. "I didn't mean to be a dick. I don't hold the trademark on crappy deals."

He's looking at me *that way* again, and the pretext of dispassion falls away. We're twin counterweights on a scale, hanging in a moment of perfect balance. I hardly dare to breathe for fear the air will shift, and the hunger I'm seeing in him will disappear. Though he's pretending otherwise, he wants somebody to notice him. I recognize it so fast because I've been there. *Hey, world, please acknowledge my existence. Please care.* On my end, nobody has ever seen me before. Not like this.

Until this moment, I didn't realize I was walking around all this time with a Shane-shaped hole inside of me.

CHAPTER FOUR

I LOVE WEEKENDS.

Most teenagers probably feel the same way, but I *adore* them. Friday night belongs to Ryan. Since there's so little to do in this town, he comes over with a DVD and I make popcorn on the stove. Aunt Gabby doesn't own a microwave oven; she says they're dangerous and can give you cancer. I don't agree with all of her opinions, but I'm so grateful to be here that I don't argue with her. This is heaven, compared to where I've been, and I'll do anything to stay, anything to keep her happy.

She's four years younger than my dad would be, if he were alive, which makes her thirty-seven. Gabby was married once, but it didn't stick, and she's been single for five years. So that means she's bustling around the bungalow, trying on various accessories. I can't remember when her last date was, so she's probably nervous.

"How does this look?" she asks from her bedroom doorway.

Outfit number four is a simple black dress with wedge heels and silver accents. "Good."

She makes a face. "You said that about everything I've had on."

"It's impossible for you to look bad."

She has smooth blond hair that falls just below her shoulders. While some people might argue that she needs to lose weight, I think she looks soft and feminine. Like me, she tends toward narrow shoulders and wide hips. It looks better on her. She's a little shorter than I am, which makes her five three. We share the shape of our faces and eyebrows, but that's where the resemblance ends.

"What're you and Ryan watching tonight?" she asks, buckling a belt around her waist.

"I dunno." We didn't talk today like we usually do, so there was no chance to ask him.

"I want him out of here by midnight."

I laugh. "Absolutely. But you realize, even if he slept in my bed, nothing would happen."

"I've always wondered what his deal is. Is he gay?"

"I have no idea," I admit. "But it would explain a lot. I mean, I understand why he wouldn't want to come out, here. JFK isn't the most progressive of schools."

Of course, that would mean I'm functioning as his beard. I'm not sure how I'd feel, if that were true. During year two of our friendship, I developed an unfortunate crush, but since he never showed any sign of returning it, I smashed all such inclinations. I figured it was better to keep him as a friend than embarrass myself by pushing for a relationship he didn't want. In retrospect, I'm glad things worked out like this. My aunt warned me that high school boyfriends rarely carry beyond graduation, so this way, I have some hope of keeping him in my life, even after he goes to MIT.

"Still good?" she asks, shaking back her hair.

"You look fantastic. Tell me about this guy?"

34

"He works for UPS." Aunt Gabby makes a face, like there's some shame in that.

I grin. "Does that mean you're gonna inspect his package?"

"Sage!" Her tone is faintly scandalized, but she smiles back at me, eyes crinkling at the corners. They're a pretty shade of hazel, flecked with gold and green. She relents. "Probably not tonight, but maybe someday, if things go well."

Ryan and the UPS man, whose name is Joe, arrive at the same time. There's a confusion of introductions and greetings, then Aunt Gabby goes off in her date's truck. It's silver, shiny, looks new, so that tells me he's fiscally solid. I'd like for her to find someone and be happy, but it also scares me because bringing a new person into the life we've built together could be pure chaos. I imagine Joe the UPS man telling me what to do, and I get a little queasy. But I'm jumping too far ahead. There's no way Aunt Gabby would let him move in here after one date. Like me, she's slow and cautious, so by the time she gets serious enough for such a big step, I'll probably be off to college anyway.

So yeah. Things are fine.

"Hey, you okay? I feel like I lost you for a minute there."

While I don't share all my thoughts with Ryan, he knows enough about me to understand this. Sheepishly, I confess my moment of mini-panic. He settles me against him with quiet surety because we've done this a hundred times. Maybe he isn't interested in romance, but he's a world-class hugger. I put my arms around his waist and lean my head against his chest. Ryan McKenna is safety.

"Better?" he asks after a few seconds.

"Yeah, I'm good. I was just being dumb."

He lifts a shoulder. "We all have moments where we wig out over nothing."

Like you did over Shane? But I don't say that out loud because Ryan and I seem to be back on the old footing, and I want to enjoy the night. I make the popcorn and bring a huge bowl out to the soft gray sofa, where he's already waiting with the movie on the menu screen.

I recognize the title immediately and cut him a surprised look. "*Crazy, Stupid, Love?* I thought you hated romantic comedies."

"I hear it's not just a romantic comedy. And I remembered you really wanted to see it."

The movie . . . is awesome. I'm so riveted by Ryan Gosling, Emma Stone, Steve Carell, and Julianne Moore that I don't even notice when the dynamic changes. There's usually a comfortable distance between us, some kicking, maybe, or a popcorn fight, but the next time I look up at Ryan, he's right next to me and his arm is around my shoulders. This is *not* standard operating procedure; while Ryan hugs, he doesn't cuddle.

I'm cuddling with Ryan McKenna.

What does this mean? If I knew crap about boys, I'd have some clue how to play this. But they're a giant mystery to me, so I'm frozen. Eventually, my heart stops thundering, and I decide he's still in comfort mode because I was freaking out over the idea of UPS Joe ruining my life. Ryan can be pretty protective. So I take this as a gesture of friendship and lean against him.

By the time the credits roll, I'm laughing and crying at the same time. It's messy, but I can't hold it in. "I wanted them to get back together so bad. Do you think they will?"

"You *do* know it's a movie, right?"

I scowl. "Don't interrupt my emotional ramblings with relentless logic."

This is one game he won't play with me. He doesn't talk about book or TV people as if they're real, speculating about their lives after the story ends. In my opinion, if Ryan has a fault, it's his lack of imagination. He's practical to the point of pain sometimes. At least, it bothers me a bit when he reins me in and reminds me this stuff's not real. It's not that I don't *know* that but sometimes I like a world somebody has created so much that I want to stay in it a little longer, dreaming of the possibilities.

He doesn't reiterate his position—that a work of art is exactly what it is, nothing more or less. You can't add to it any more than you can draw mustache on the *Mona Lisa*. To which I say, *Yeah, but you can wonder why she's smiling.* You can write a story about it. But this is a bridge that Ryan can't cross; his brain just isn't wired that way. It's also probably why he rocks at chemistry, and I do not.

"Hey, I liked it," he says, smiling. "You could tell he's still crazy in love with her, regardless of how many women he slept with."

"You'd think if he really loved her, he wouldn't want anyone else."

"Sometimes sex is just about wanting not to feel alone. Or it can start that way, anyhow."

I feel like I'm about to fall into the deep end of a pool without a swimsuit. Ryan and I have never talked about this stuff. Ever. Obviously, I'm a virgin, as I've never even had a boyfriend. Which means I'm sixteen and never been kissed, let alone . . . other stuff.

"You know that how?" Grinning, I add, "If you say she lives in Canada, I'm calling bullshit."

He searches my face, brown eyes serious behind the hipster glasses. "No, not Canada."

So there is *somebody. Why didn't he tell me?* Shock rockets through me with hurt hot on its heels. A normal person might get mad, but I'm *afraid* of anger, so I never let myself go there. My therapists don't realize they've trained me to suppress it, but I feel better that way. Safer. I'm really, really determined to be good. Positive. Worthy of a second chance.

So I manage a smile, shoving away the bad feelings. "Who? Where? When? Damn. I sound like a journalism lead." He laughs, as I intend him to, and it eases the tension. "Seriously, Ry, you can tell me anything. I won't judge."

"Her name is Cassie."

So he's not gay. There's another little pang, as I remember how much I liked him last year. Strangling that, too, I put on my attentive face, encouraging him to continue.

"And she's twenty-one."

Holy crap. What do I even say? I mean, it's kind of skeevy. Why is this Cassie messing around with someone Ryan's age? Not that he isn't awesome. But still.

I'm guessing he interprets my expression correctly because he explains, "It's not her fault. When we met last year, I told her I was eighteen."

"So she thinks you're nineteen now? Why aren't you in college?"

"I'm saving up."

"Wow. So your entire relationship is based on lies. And sex, I assume?" He looks so miserable that I don't say more, even though I so could. I thought Ryan was better than this—he'd never lie to a girl to get her to sleep with him. But as it turns out, that's exactly what he's done. Hurt and discomfort pushes up toward my throat. I really want to yell at him.

But I won't. I can't.

"That wasn't why," he starts, but it's a weak effort, and he gives it up.

"I don't understand at all, Ry." Then something horrible occurs to me. "Why do you put your arm around me so much at school? And walk me to my classes?"

"I never said we were going out," he tells me quietly. "I just didn't deny it when people asked."

"To hide this . . . whatever it is. Did it ever occur to you that if you have to cover it up that maybe it's not okay?"

"*Yes.*" He runs an agitated hand through his hair.

This . . . this is huge. It was one thing when I thought the misunderstanding about us just happened. Knowing he did it on purpose—and for such a shady reason—makes my stomach cramp. *I can't get mad at him.* So I embrace pain and sadness instead; I can deal with that duo better. That only ever hurts me. And that's fine. I'm used to it.

I swallow hard. "Why involve me? What's the point?"

His dark eyes are pools of hurt. "You know how they are at JFK. If you're never seen with a girl, they assume you're a closet case, and you saw how that turned out for Jon Summers."

"Damn," I whisper.

Jon killed himself last year. He came out at school, which was a brave thing to do, but people didn't take it well. They bullied him until he eventually left to be homeschooled, but that didn't fix it. His house was vandalized repeatedly, until he got ahold of some of his mom's pills. When I found out, I felt so horrible. I wished I'd done more, but he refused to see anyone after he left JFK, and sometimes, it's impossible to know how bad somebody feels until it's too late.

Ryan goes on, "Best-case scenario, they assume I'm *not* gay, but I'm such a loser that I can't get anyone to go out with me. That doesn't end well for me either, Sage. Or I can choose to be a douche and brag about the older girl I'm banging. Provided anyone believes me, that would hurt Cassie a lot."

"So you threw me under the bus instead?" Maybe it's wrong, but I don't care at all why Ryan did this. Fury boils like acid in my throat. But hurt and anger war within me, so I choose the pain again and hug it close. The barbs sink in. Ryan has been my best friend for three years—the one person I trust. And now this.

"How did you see this playing out, exactly? You string her along until you actually *are* eighteen and then say, 'By the way, baby, funny story, I'm actually five years younger than you'?"

Ryan can't even glare at me, though I suspect he wants to. "It seemed simple at first. Age is just a number, right? But then we were hooking up, as she has time, because she works two jobs and she thinks I do, too. Then there was the sex—" He trails off, seeing that's not a good tack to take with me. "And I thought I was in love with her, okay?"

"Thought?"

"It's complicated. At first, it seemed harmless to let people think we're together, Sage. It was easy. It gave both of us some cred, you know?"

The rage pushes. I shove it down, trembling as I listen.

"At school and on Friday nights, you feel like my girlfriend. Most people think you are. So the line started to blur. It's just physical now with Cassie . . . and everything else . . ." Ryan takes both my hands. "Sage, you're everything else."

I'm so angry I can hardly speak. The feeling is fire, and it'll burn me up if I don't lock it down. I'm so scared. I can't feel this. I close my eyes and breathe, willing it away. It's better to be sad and hurt. I'll take the damage rather than inflict any.

When I finally speak, my voice is quiet and calm. "Are you

asking me to be with you? While there's a girl who still thinks her hardworking, nineteen-year-old boyfriend loves her?"

To make matters worse, I *know* why he's moving on me now. He was fine keeping Cassie and me in our respective roles, until it looked like I might be interested in someone else. Now, suddenly, Ryan wants to promote me to full girlfriend status. I guess he doesn't want to lose the "cred" he mentioned before. He's my best friend, but at the moment, I don't like him very much.

"Did it ever occur to you that I wondered if something was wrong with me?" I ask quietly.

His eyes widen. "What—"

"You never made a move, but nobody else asked me out, either. Other girls date all the time. But not me. *Of course* I worried about why. I try to be positive, but sometimes? It felt pretty crappy."

I can see the pain in Ryan's eyes, but it doesn't make mine go away. "I'm so sorry. That's a hundred percent my fault."

"Because it was easier for you. That's really selfish."

"Let me make it up to you." He leans in, but I turn my face, so his mouth glances across my cheek. Ryan McKenna will *not* be getting my first kiss.

"If you're unhappy with this girl, you need to break up with her. She'll probably be furious and ashamed, but that's better than letting her think the relationship failed because of something *she* did." I pause, weighing my next words. But, yeah, I mean them, though it means I'll effectively be alone. "Once you do that, plus some hard thinking, I could consider being friends with you again. But right now? I need some time."

His mouth twists. "Are you breaking up with me?"

Since I didn't even know we were dating, that strikes me as funny. "I guess I am."

"You promised you wouldn't judge me," he says softly.

"That was when I thought you might be gay. I can't support you being a liar."

He flinches, but doesn't dispute my assessment. When Ryan leaves, he takes a chunk of me with him. We've been through so much together, shared everything—I thought—but he had this whole other life that I never even suspected. It makes me feel stupid and disposable, like a paper towel he used to clean up his mess.

I don't sleep much that night, and it's not because of the Dream.

CHAPTER FIVE

MONDAY MORNING SUCKS SO HARD, I HAVE NO WORDS.

Somehow I managed to hide my colossal bad mood from my aunt. She makes a point of doing stuff with me on a regular basis, which is more than my mom ever did. This weekend, we made falafel and flatbread, then gave each other pedicures. Which might sound boring, but it was exactly what I needed after the drama with Ryan.

To distract her from my life, I asked all kinds of questions about UPS Joe. The date went well, I guess, and they'll be doing it again. I joked, "Tell me if you need me to have a sleepover some night," and to my amusement, Aunt Gabby turned bright red. The teasing carried us until bedtime.

Then I overslept this morning and didn't have time for more than a ponytail. No makeup. And I'm in my usual Crappy Weekend outfit: pink-and-black-print skirt, black leggings, pink tank, black shrug. The idea is that the pink will cheer me up. Mostly I remember Ryan saying I look like a hydrangea in this. My life has Ryan McKenna's stupid size 13 shoes all over it. I'm realizing I don't have many other close friendships; I let him eat up all my time, though we weren't even dating. God only knows what would've happened if we had been. We might've merged into a mecha-something or fused consciousness like the Borg.

So, yeah, Monday morning, and I'm alone. There's no Ryan waiting for me at the double doors. Though I know this is the right move, it still sucks. Which makes me even surer this is the best decision because maybe we've gotten codependent. But this feels like the first day of school all over again; in my head, I'm thirteen, nobody likes me, and they're going to find out where I lived before, what I've done. *Crap.* Ryan isn't the only one keeping secrets, but I guess it doesn't matter now. I ride past the students milling in the parking lot, the few perched on cars, and lock up my bike along with a couple already secured to the rack. Come winter, I'll be the only one still riding. It doesn't get easier inside the building. The usual groups are clustered around their lockers, but now they look like aliens with their craning necks and curious eyes. It's like they've never seen me before. I slide past them, heading for my locker, where I pull up short. I glance to either side, wondering if this is a joke. Then I imagine this is how other people feel when they find my pink Post-it. But this one is bright blue and it's written in black Sharpie. It says, *You are the silver lining.*

I love that phrase and the fact that it came from John Milton. "Was I deceived, or did a sable cloud / Turn forth her silver lining on the night?" So somebody out there thinks I'm the bright side of a dark cloud. I take down the note and stick it inside the cover of my binder. Feeling someone's gaze, I glance around, hoping to catch the person who wrote it, but there's only Ryan, watching me from his locker across the way. From his expression I can tell he saw the Post-it, maybe even *read* it, but he didn't leave it there.

I turn away without speaking to him and the girl next to me

notices. Lila's not goth, but she wears a lot of black, and she's a pro at rolling her eyes. She thinks everyone except her has an IQ of seventy-five. "So, are you two done?"

God, I don't even know how to answer that. It isn't what she thinks, but I still care about him, and I won't dump his secrets in the lap of the first person who asks. Soon enough, gossip will hit that we're "over." *Awesome. All the break-up bullshit, none of the making-out.*

"For now," I say finally. "Sometimes it's good to take a break, get some perspective."

"Somebody cheated." She smirks. "But you both look so squeaky clean that I can't guess who's the injured party."

"Good talk, Lila. See you later." Though we've been locker neighbors for two years, this is the most she's ever said to me.

She laughs. "That was almost sarcastic, Princess. I didn't know you had it in you."

She doesn't mean it in a bad way. I get it; I'm a joke to most people. The people at JFK think I never get down—that I don't have shitty days and dark thoughts. I've just learned not to follow them down the hole. I've seen what lives in there, and it's pretty awful. Depression threatens. I can't bail on all my activities, but I'm no longer enthused about the meetings because it will be beyond awkward, dealing with Ryan. I'm just grateful I have a few things of my own, like my part-time job at the Curly Q.

My classes blur together, until it's time for geometry. Despite my emotional turmoil, I resolve to pay closer attention, except there's no point. Because Mackiewicz slaps a pop quiz on the front desk in each row.

He's smiling; that's never good. "Let's see how well you can apply these theorems."

Right. The day only needs this.

The quiz is OMG-hard, so that means I'll soon have another circled F. *Awesome.* Even failures should have a friend. I'm *sure* when I explain to Aunt Gabby that I only failed the second quiz for symmetry, she'll be good with it. I read over both pages, but it makes no sense to me, so I wind up writing nonsense in trying to "show my work." For all the good this quiz will do me, I might as well be doodling penguins all over the paper. When I walk out at the end of the period, I hear the doom song from *Star Wars* in my head—and that's *totally* Ryan's fault. Before I started hanging out with him three years ago, I didn't know Han Solo from Luke Skywalker.

"Tough one," Shane says.

Huh? I'm faintly astonished that he hasn't bolted in trying to beat the jocks acting like they aren't waiting for a chance to screw with him. I could've told him there's safety in numbers, but he seemed to be in full-loner mode. Maybe he wouldn't have listened. But he's here now. Talking to me.

"Yeah. I'm not dumb, swear to God, but this stuff . . ." I trail off.

"He just doesn't explain it well." Shane tilts his head toward Mackiewicz's classroom.

The man's got tenure and he's coasting. He gives us pages to read, rambles for an hour about Pythagoras, and then expects us to figure this stuff out from the text.

"You mean at all," I mutter.

"If you're struggling, I could help you."

I'm surprised speechless.

Misreading my silence, he goes on quickly, "I know I don't look like a math geek, but—"

"When?" I cut in. "I work Monday and Thursday afternoons."

"And you have your green thing on Wednesday night."

I'm ridiculously thrilled he remembers. "I'm not sure if I'm continuing with that."

He falls into step as I glimpse the jocks already moving down the hall. They don't have long attention spans, so they're probably thinking about lunch or the next kid who needs to be taught a lesson.

"How come?"

I shrug, not wanting to get into it.

But he does, apparently. "I heard you broke up with your boyfriend. Is that why?"

We're outside the cafeteria, other students pushing to get their tater tots. I consider letting the lie stand because it makes me sound cooler, less stupid, but if I'm mad at Ryan for lying, then I can't start that way with Shane. Because gazing up at him now, just glimpsing the magic of his eyes through his tousled curls, I want this to be the start of something.

"Eat lunch with me," I say then. "And I'll tell you about it."

Not everything. I won't betray Ryan's secrets, but I want Shane to know I'm not on the rebound; it's not like that. It's knottier and more complicated in some ways, but in others, it's dead simple. I've been looking Shane's way since he strode into my geometry class.

He hesitates. "I usually hide out behind the school."

"With the burners. Do you smoke?" It's a general question, but I mean weed more than tobacco. In my opinion, either is gross.

"No. Can't afford it, even if I wanted to."

"Do you?" I ask, joining the end of the lunch line.

"Sometimes. It might be nice not to care."

Being numb is good for a while, until it's not anymore.

"They're fooling themselves," I say. "It's better to deal with your shit head on. Life doesn't get better if you look away."

Shane swivels his head sharply toward me. "No joke. Sometimes you absolutely have to stare it down." But he seems astonished I *know* that.

Yeah, I'm full of surprises.

Waiting in line doesn't offer the usual annoyance because I'm standing with Shane. But there's going to be an awkward moment soon; the way he dresses makes me suspect that there's not a lot of spare cash at home. So I put a few extra things on my tray, food I'm pretty sure he'll eat, and pay the cashier. He's frowning as he follows me to the table. Not the one I usually sit at with Ryan and the rest of the eco crew. Farther down, there are some random sophomores, but they won't tell juniors like us to screw off.

"You don't eat meat," he says, staring at the burger.

I'm shocked he remembers me mentioning it at the Green World meeting. "This hardly qualifies. It's probably eighty-five percent soy anyway. But it's not for me." I slide the paper plate toward him.

Shane shakes his head. "Thanks but I'm not hungry."

"It'll make me feel weird to eat alone. Plus, I can't afford to pay you to tutor me. The least I can do is get lunch now and then." A guy's pride is a delicate thing—I know enough from dealing with Ryan not to say more.

I just start eating. A few seconds later, he digs into the undelicious burger, as if he was damn near starved. I down a few more bites of limp salad before saying, "I guess I promised you a story."

"Somewhat."

The sophomores can't hear us down the table, as it's loud in here, but I pitch my voice low just in case. "Basically, Ryan was never my boyfriend. He just let people *think* we were together. Because I'm an idiot, I didn't guess why." Those last words come out bitter.

"So why *did* he do that?" I hear all kinds of nuances in his voice, questions, doubts.

Here's where it gets tricky. "It's complicated. He lied to me, though, and that's what I can't just get over. Maybe someday we'll be friends again, but for now . . ." I shrug.

"Friends?" he repeats.

"Yeah. Friends."

"So he didn't break your heart." He sounds relieved.

"Did you want him to?"

"I was afraid he had. That maybe you were talking to me . . ." His eyes cut away from mine.

"Because I was trying to make Ryan jealous? Not my style."

I want to say, *OMG, Shane, you think I'm a dude magnet?* I've been Ryan's sidekick, his not-girlfriend so long, that I have no idea what *this* is or what I'm doing. But I love it.

"I'm not looking for drama," Shane tells me.

I understand the reason for the pronouncement immediately. Ryan's watching us from across the cafeteria, but he won't be shoving Shane into any doorjambs or cornering him in the boys' toilet. In some ways, his silent, wounded eyes are worse. I can tell he feels horrible and that he misses me, but what am I supposed to do? After what I've learned, I don't *want* to be his girlfriend, which is what he was shooting for when he made his big confession. I feel like I hardly know the guy, and that hurts most of all.

"There won't be any."

"I just . . . I can't afford any trouble," he says softly, not looking at me. "Any more, and I'm off to juvie until I'm eighteen."

Possibly he thinks this will scare me off. But I have my dark side, too. The staff at the group home pulled me off an emotional ledge years ago, so I know what it's like to feel completely out of control, doing stuff you know deep down is a terrible idea and yet you *cannot stop*. I study the rigid line of his shoulders. "Did you put that Post-it on my locker?"

He's dead silent, but his eyes answer where his lips do not. I see the *yes* written in aquamarine.

In this moment, I want to kiss him so bad it hurts.

CHAPTER

SIX

I DON'T, OF COURSE.

This is still the JFK lunchroom, and I'm not that brave. In the end, I let him get away with not answering. It's enough that he's here with me and not hiding out with the burners. I finish my food, just shoveling it down, so I can say I did. I'm too nervous to enjoy the salad, especially with Shane studying me so intently. I'm suddenly worried I have lettuce in my teeth.

Afterward, Shane walks me to my next class, even though he's not in it. Instead of saying good-bye, he brushes my hair away from my face and gives me a smile that makes me forget what subject I have this period. Then he lopes away, hopefully to make his next class before the bell. I melt into my seat before remembering where I am . . . and that Ryan is already sitting in the desk next to mine.

As I sit down, he glances over, but he doesn't say anything. Around us, three girls are whispering behind cupped hands. It's so weird to be the subject of gossip over a relationship that never existed except in other people's minds. I heard the speculation before, but it's different, knowing that Ryan encouraged it behind my back—that he was using the rumors. I mean, he knew his parents wouldn't approve and that I'd be upset. Who wants to be the girl somebody pretends to date while secretly going after someone better? Yet he did it anyway. My anger kindles fresh, and I tamp it down. Rage tastes like burning in the back of my throat. Once I'm calm, I bend my head to my paper, taking copious notes that I'll probably never look at again. Afterward, I linger over packing up my stuff to give him a chance to leave.

The day passes at the speed of snail.

Before last period, I leave a Post-it for a freshman kid the football goons are harassing today instead of Shane. They call him Alexa instead of Alex, and that has to suck. Since I don't know him, I compliment his taste in sneakers, which are awesome old-school Chucks, just the right amount of grunge. Alex does a clumsy karate kick as I go by, showing off the shoes, and I laugh. The beautiful people think I'm an idiot, but their scorn is worth it for moments like this. It's like everybody I tag could be a potential friend.

"Hey," Alex calls. "I hear you're on the market again."

. . . Wait, what? He's a freshman.

I stop. "I'm not seeing anyone."

"Does a younger guy have a shot?" he asks, flashing me a grin.

He's short and skinny, like Ryan used to be. Alex has a goofy sense of personal style, plus bad coordination and unpredictable skin. His hair looks like his mom cuts it by trimming around a bowl. But I don't want to hurt his feelings.

"Only if said younger guy can pick me up in his G6." I figure he'll know that's a joke since I don't approve of fossil-fuel burning cars, let alone absurdly wasteful private planes.

He grins. "I'll get right on that."

By the time I get to the bike rack, the initial after-school scramble has passed. The buses are loaded and leaving the parking lot. Most people who drive take off as soon as they can, clogging the road leading away from JFK. Still, even now, there are a few stragglers in the parking lot. Two guys wearing knit hats practice skate tricks until Mr. Mackiewicz runs them off. It's pretty funny how he makes time to be a buzzkill even on his way out to his car.

I have fifty minutes before I need to be at the Curly Q for my shift, so I'm in no real hurry. But I'm surprised when Lila hails me. She breaks away from a pack of mostly goth posers, who are piling into a gray van. Lila is tall, five ten or so, and she might look like a supermodel, if she wasn't so into death fashion. Her long legs eat up the distance between us.

"Where you headed?" she asks me.

I can't figure out what her deal is today. We *never* talk. "Work, eventually."

"Want to get a frap?"

Oh. I think I know what this is about, so I mumble, "There's no dirt. Nobody cheated."

"I'm not interested in that anyway. I'm sure the story's tedious."

"Then what?" I don't mean to be rude, but seriously, we barely live on the same planet.

She shakes back her super-vibrant dyed red hair. "Since you want me to lay it out, well, you're *way* short on female friends. Most of mine've killed too many brain cells, so I'm in the market for someone with whom I can use polysyllabic words."

"I'm flattered. I think. And, yeah, I have time for a frap." The tiny café that serves as a substitute for Starbucks is two blocks from the salon.

"Sweet. Can I ride on the handlebars of your bike?"

"No. You can run along behind me like a spaniel." See, I can be sarcastic, too.

Lila grins. "I could seriously get to like the new you."

"I'm still me. Same princess. Same nice. Just . . ." Something *has* changed, but I can't put my finger on it.

"With an angry breakup edge?" she offers.

"That works." *Anger* is the wrong word, though, because I don't permit that feeling anymore. The cost is too high when I unleash.

I wasn't kidding when I said she could run after me. Conversation over, I swing onto my bike and head for the coffee shop, which is cunningly named Coffee Shop. There was a sign that said ANDREA's above it at one point, but she sold the place, and the new owners took that part down. They just never mustered up the ambition to dub it anything clever. The pastries are pretty good, however, and the décor is cute, belying the uber-utilitarian name.

By the time Lila arrives, I'm already settled and sipping a latte. I smile at her as she pushes through the door, jingling the bell. She places her order, then joins me; the barista will bring her drink when it's ready. There are a few other people in here, mostly artsy types. They like the ambiance better than the fried meat grease and dull roar over at DQ. A couple of them double-take at the sight of me hanging with Lila, as we're not really from the same social strata.

"So why don't you tell me what this is about," I say, sipping my drink.

"I can't put anything past you, huh?"

"Unlikely." After I say it, I realize that's Shane's word, and a goofy-happy feeling sweeps over me. It's absurd, but it makes me feel like he and I have a thing.

She cuts her eyes to both sides, as if there are spies from JFK nearby. "Sophomore year, I broke up with Dylan Smith."

"Rings a bell." Now that she's mentioned it, I remember. "He's such a tool. You were spirit squad, weren't you?"

"Yeah."

After the breakup, she hung a sharp left away from the beautiful people, swapping her dance routines and pom-poms for thick eyeliner, lots of black, and a bad attitude. Dylan went around with his crew talking about what a druggie whore she'd become without him. Personally, I thought she was better off, especially given the way he treated people he saw as lesser beings.

"At first, my old friends were all, 'OMG, are you insane? He's *so hot,* you two are *the* power couple.'" She shrugs. "They didn't care that he was a controlling asshole. When I refused to 'see reason,' they just cut me off. I had like a month where I just didn't talk to *anyone.*"

I wait, guessing there's a reason she's telling me this. The waitress brings Lila's frozen mocha, which delays the story for a few seconds. Then she carries on as if there'd been no interruption.

"So in the middle of this, I get a Post-it on my locker. I don't even remember what it said now."

Oh. "I do. I said I loved your black corset top." It wasn't something I'd be brave enough to wear, but it looked stunning on Lila.

"Right." She smiles at me, the look untouched by her usual cynicism. "I was trying to show Dylan what he was missing at that point. I really needed somebody to be nice to me. It helped that you were. So now that you're basically in that same situation, I want to return the favor. I'm not the Post-it type, and that's your thing anyway. So . . ."

"Hence, the fraps." Although I'm not drinking one, she is.

"Exactly."

I'm no longer worried about the potential pitfalls, but I mentally go back over something she said. "Same situation? You mean Ryan's talking shit about me?"

If he is, I don't even. Everything freezes inside me. *How* can he? I'm not the one who lied on so many levels. I was just there.

"Not that I've heard. I just meant . . . you can't hang with your usual crowd anymore. I know how awkward that can be. And I really am in the market for a new best friend. My current crew keeps me from being forever alone, but they're not . . ." She taps her temple and grimaces, conveying that they suffer from stoner brain.

I can't believe she's just *telling* me this. It seems so unlike Lila, but then I realize I really don't know her. For the first two years, I saw the side she showed while running with the beautiful people, and then the new version she created to fit in with the goth crew. Maybe neither Lila was exactly the person she wants to be; that thought is kind of revelational. It's probably true of me, as well.

"I'm definitely willing to hang. I might be quitting a number of my clubs." That thought pains me, as I joined them for my college application, but I just can't see working with Ryan at this juncture.

"What's your cell number?"

I give her the number without my usual spiel it's for emergencies only. When I check the time, I see I need to get moving. "Work beckons. Want to set something up for this weekend?"

"Do you ever go to the Barn?"

That sounds like it would be a club, but it's actually a barn. Oh, the joys of rural living. There's a kid who graduated last year, still famous for hosting parties. Which strikes me as a little sad. Why does he want to be the Man to a bunch of minors? I mean, maybe that's all he has.

"I didn't last year." But maybe it's time to change it up.

"There's a bash on Saturday. You want to check it out?"

"Sure." Then I realize that transportation will prove a problem. "Can you text me the address? I'll meet you there."

Parties are always hosted at night, so I'll need to ride out to the farm, which could take a while. It also means I'll be gross and sweaty when I arrive. I'll also be covered in reflectors. I close my eyes and sigh. Maybe this isn't the best idea.

"I can give you a ride," she says.

I shake my head. "It's not that. I have a thing about cars."

"Are you scared of them?" She sounds worried, like if this is true, I'm 100 percent weirder than she banked on, and I've already lost her.

Fortunately, I have a valid reason to cover the deeper motivation behind my dogged avoidance. "No, I just don't ride in them. They're killing the world."

"Oh, it's like a protest?"

"Pretty much. I know it's not getting media coverage or anything, but *I* care. I'd know if I broke down just because it's easier."

"That's cool," she says, visibly relieved. Then I see an idea register. "My dad restores golf carts as a hobby. Don't ask. If I picked you up in one of those, would you go?"

"Totally." I can't believe she'd do that for me. It's so dorky and she hardly knows me. "But is that even legal?"

"They're allowed on back roads, as long as I yield to faster moving traffic. It'll be faster than a tractor at least."

I laugh, but she has a point. Country roads are often clogged by farm machinery this time of year. So I offer a quick nod. "Then I'm in. I really appreciate it."

"Where do you live?"

I scribble my address on a Coffee Shop napkin, then groan at the time. "Now I really have to jet. Mildred will eat my face if I'm late."

That's the owner of the Curly Q. She's a hundred years old with thinning, dyed-orange hair. From the look of her, you'd be scared to let any of her employees work on you, but the stylists are great. They like practicing on me when it's slow. Usually, I don't let them do anything permanent, but tonight, I'm feeling reckless. It's just hair, right? Since I'm going to a party at the Barn with Lila Tremaine *in a golf cart* it seems like I need to update my look.

I have forty seconds to spare when I burst through the doors. Mildred gives me the side-eye, but since I'm not technically late, she just says, "Get your smock on, girl. There's cleaning to be done."

Though it's not strictly legal or sanitary, I'm pretty sure they save the hair for hours. The stylists just sweep it away from the chairs and pile it out of the way. So by the time I arrive, there's a small Sasquatch on the floor. It takes me an hour to get the shop pristine. Customers come and go, mostly walk-in haircuts. Around six, it slows down, and Grace beckons me to the chair.

"When are you gonna let me give you some highlights?" She asks this often.

This time, however, I say, "Tonight, if you have time."

Grace gets excited. "Mildred, get the camera. I'll do it free if you let me take a picture for the before-and-after wall."

I eye the wall, not sure I want to be immortalized up there, along with all the eighties hair and prom refugees, but eventually I shrug. "Why not?"

My hair is a dark blond, mousy and forgettable. I mean, it's decent hair, neither straight, nor curly. Left to its own devices, it falls in messy waves. That's why I wear a lot of ponytails and braids. Aunt

Gabby has similar problems, only she gets it lightened and high-lighted so it looks bright and flirty, and she spends forty-five minutes a day straightening hers, so it's sleek and smooth by the time she goes to the shop. UPS Joe seems to like the results anyway.

Grace fastens me into the plastic smock, then snaps a Polaroid. I still don't care that much how I look; I mean, it's so superficial, but a small part of me would like to be prettier, at least maximize what I'm working with. I tell myself this is more of a social experiment, and I can evaluate how people react to the new me. But that's not it.

I'm totally doing this to see if Shane notices. Sometimes I hate being a girl.

CHAPTER SEVEN

IT'S DUMB TO BE SO NERVOUS.

This is a Tuesday. Nothing earth shattering ever happens on a Tuesday. It doesn't even have a catchy nickname, unlike Wednesday, aka Hump Day. Still, I can't shake the butterflies in my stomach. Instead of my usual leggings and skirt, I'm wearing jeans, an old pair that miraculously still fits; and I try not to think about how much of my butt they reveal. I didn't discard my sweater shrug for unavoidable reasons, but instead of wearing an ordinary cotton tank, I borrowed a lace-trimmed cami from Aunt Gabby. Why all the effort? I want to be worthy of my new hair.

This morning, when she saw the highlights, my aunt insisted I let her use the straightener on me. It only took fifteen minutes, but I admit it was worth it. My hair's never looked this sleek and glossy, and the delicate golden streaks brighten the darker part until it's positively pretty. I don't know that I've ever thought that about myself before. It's kinda nice.

Lila waves as I come down the hall toward her. "Wow. You look fab."

"Thanks. I let one of the stylists work on me last night." I dial my combo and pop open my locker, getting the stuff I'll need for first period.

"Trying to show him what he's missing? Good plan." She cuts her eyes toward Ryan, who is standing with one hand on his locker. He can't seem to look away.

This time last year, I would've given a kidney to see him look at me like that, but he was oblivious. *And no wonder,* I think with a touch of bitterness. *He was sleeping with somebody else.* At this point, however, that's not why I changed things up. My reason isn't here yet.

"I've got to admit," Lila says, still studying Ry. "I'm surprised. I would've thought he was fundamentally decent. He *seems* like a good guy."

Crap, I don't want her to think he's a cheater. Technically we weren't together, so the mess with Cassie isn't that. "He is. He just . . . made a mistake. Lied to me. And I can't handle it."

"Oh. So we don't hate him?"

I shake my head. "Mostly, I'm sad. I wish he hadn't done it, but some lies change everything."

"Absolutely, they do." From the ferocity of her tone, I'm guessing Lila has some personal experience with this, but I don't pry.

Privately I wonder if Dylan lied, and that's why they broke up. Once we get to know each other better, maybe she'll tell me. It's pretty cool to have somebody who wants to hang out with me, not because of Ryan or because we're in the same club. Just . . . because. Since moving here, I've avoided that kind of closeness, mostly because the more friends you have, the harder it is to keep secrets. More people mean more questions. And I wasn't ready. My first year here, I was barely functional, so it's no surprise I imprinted on Ryan and let him drive my social life.

"I have to get to class," I say then.

"Sucks we don't have any together. See you at lunch, though?" It's a question, not an assumption.

"I brought mine, so I'll get a table."

Lila acknowledges the plan with a jerk of her chin, then she dives into the stream of students, letting them carry her toward her class on the opposite side of school. I haven't seen Shane this morning, but maybe he's running late. I wander through my morning classes hoping for a glimpse of him, but still, nothing. Geometry confirms it; he's not in today. The desk diagonal, one up from mine, seems more than usually empty; I'm so disappointed, and I hate that I am. To put the cherry on the crap cake, I get my quiz back. As expected, it's another circled red F. That clinches it—I have to tell Aunt Gabby. It's not that she'll be mad at me; I can't stand her *disappointed* look. Maybe the news that I have a tutor lined up will help. Kind of, *I see there's a problem and I'm working to solve it.*

"Miss Czinski, I need to see you after class." Mackiewicz levels a serious business stare on me while the rest of the class goes "ooooooooooooooh" in that super-annoying way.

"Yes, sir."

As anticipated, he lectures me on how poorly I'm doing and tells me how he expects better from someone of my academic stature. Seriously, that's verbatim. I listen meekly until he's finished, and then offer, "I'm definitely struggling, but I'm taking steps and getting help. My performance will improve."

Mackiewicz seems mollified. "Good. I know you can do better."

Glad somebody's sure of that.

On impulse, as soon as I escape from his class, I head to admin. Ms. Smith is the only one around at this time. She looks young, to the point that I suspect she was my age when she had Dylan. I imagine her wanting to be a dancer or something; I doubt her dreams included working in the school office.

"I was wondering if you could get me a copy of Shane Cavendish's schedule. He's out sick today, and I'm taking his homework to him." My voice doesn't reveal that I happen to know a juicy secret about her.

"Not a problem. That's sweet of you."

"Y'know," I mumble, when this is actually kind of stalkerish.

I've never been so interested in a guy before, certainly not to the point that I'd go out of my way to learn his class schedule. When she takes a page from the file and trots off to copy his classes, I take it a step further. Rocking up on my toes, I peer at the folder she left on the counter. His address is in the upper-right-hand corner of the form he filled out during registration. Upside-down reading is one of my weirder skills, so I can see the address. I memorize the house number and turn away, like I haven't just crossed a line.

I hope he doesn't think I'm crazy.

"Here you are, hon."

"Thanks." I take the paper and figure I might as well visit Shane's classes now. Teachers who aren't stuck on monitoring duty will be in their rooms, working on stuff for the afternoon or writing a novel, or in Mr. Johannes's case, possibly cooking meth, whatever floats their boats.

In short order I get five of his seven assignments. Not bad for a spur-of-the-moment plan. By the time I get to the lunchroom, Lila has already made it through the line and is obviously looking for me. Her face lightens with relief when she realizes I didn't ditch her. *As if I would.* Making an executive decision, I head over to the sophomore table where Shane and I sat yesterday. There's only four of them, so there's room. This time, I wave. To my surprise, they wave back, looking pretty happy to see me. *Hm.* When Lila joins me, they're surprised, but they say "hey" to both of us as we sit down.

"Who're your friends?" she asks.

I glance over at the four: three girls, one guy. "I have no idea."

A red-haired girl smiles. "Kimmy, Mel, Shanna, and Theo." As she performs the introductions, I memorize their names and faces. If we're sharing their table from now on, we should be social.

Mel is a freckled, athletic blonde while Theo is small, brown-skinned, and fond of sweater vests. Kimmy is a pale redhead with an infectious smile whereas Shanna has long black hair caught up in Lolita pigtails, and her makeup enhances almond eyes. She seems like the rebel of the group.

"Sage and Lila," I say.

"We *know*." Theo stresses the last word in a weird way.

I exchange a look with Lila, who shrugs. "Should I be afraid to ask?"

"Maybe," she says.

Mel offers, "We think it's really cool of you two. Brave."

"What?"

"You know. Being out."

What the . . . "Let me get this straight . . . People think Lila and I are dating?"

"Dylan Smith says that's why Lila broke up with him. Cuz she's a big dy—"

Kimmy claps a hand over Theo's mouth before he completes the word. I'm glad; otherwise, I'd have to smack him. "First, that's crap. But if it were true, Lila's out of my league."

She laughs, cocking her head. "I dunno. You're looking pretty cute today."

Theo looks like this is a dream come true while the girls stare, wide-eyed.

I sigh. "Don't encourage him."

"True. But this is exactly why I broke up with Dylan. I mean, he told everyone I slept with him when I did *not*. Then when I got fed up and dumped him, he said I was a lesbian. Because, obviously, only a chick who's into girls would let go of a prize like him."

"What a douche," Mel says.

"That explains the looks I've been getting all day, though," Lila adds. "I'm sorry, Sage. I should've guessed Dylan would invent some shit about your breakup the minute we started hanging out."

I shrug. "I don't care what people say about me. To be honest, it's kind of novel for it not to be related to the Post-it notes."

"I think that's pretty cool," Shanna volunteers.

I smile. I'm a little surprised, however. Of this crew, she dresses the darkest, but I should know not to judge a book by its cover. I look squeaky clean, innocent even. What I don't tell her is that I'm beyond doing stuff because someone else thinks it's a good idea. These days I do things to fill craters inside, filling up the bad echoes with goodness. God knows I need it.

"Do us a favor, though," I say to Mel, who seems the most sensible of the four. "Spread the word that it's just gossip, okay?"

"Not a problem," Kimmy says, already texting.

We make general conversation after this, and midway through lunch, I look up to see Tara and Kenny standing by the table. They both look awkward, so I try to make whatever it is easier with a smile and a friendly "hey, guys."

"Is it true?" Kenny asks. As usual, he has on his cherished

Mario hat. Kenny is really good at two things: math and video games. He'll probably make a million dollars before he's thirty.

"What?"

Tara bites her lip. "That you dumped Ryan to be with Lila."

Ha-ha, OMG. I feel a burning desire to put my head down on the scarred table and laugh. This has been a busy week, what with the fake boyfriend and the fake girlfriend, when I've never had a real date. Somehow, I restrain the mild hysteria. I hope people aren't as mean to us as they were Jon Summers. But maybe it's only horrible to be gay in this town if you're a guy. Two girls together, on the other hand, might be considered hot. I hate that double standard *so much*.

"Nope. Don't tell me you bought into the rumor mill." I cock a brow at them.

"I knew it was crap," Tara says.

"So . . . we were wondering," Kenny adds.

"Yes?" Lila looks tremendously amused.

"Can we sit with you, every other lunch period?" Tara asks in a rush.

"Not every day?" I wonder aloud.

Kenny grins. "Nah. Even if he's been a grumpy ass lately, we're not ditching Ryan. We thought you guys could share custody."

"This is so adorable, I could barf." Lila is choking on her fries.

"It's cool with me if Mel, Kimmy, Theo, and Shanna don't mind." I cast an inquiring look at the sophomores who have first claim on the table.

"Not a problem," Mel decides.

Lila sighs. "This is starting to feel like a babysitting job."

"You can walk away anytime. My broken heart will mend." I grin at her, seeing the ridiculous in our situation.

She laughs.

"It's not that I mind people thinking we're together," I say later, walking with Lila back to our lockers. "On principle. But you might like someone, and if they think you're taken . . ."

That's *exactly* what Ryan did to me.

"They won't ask me out," she finishes. "There *is* someone, but he's emotionally unavailable at the moment. So, not a big deal."

"This crap is so complicated," I mumble.

She grins. "Should I put my arm around you to fuel the rumors?"

"Only if you want them *never* to die."

In a school this size, she and I will be lesbians forever to some people, even now, just from a mean joke Dylan Smith made to some football buddies. Man, what is wrong with people? If Lila and I were really struggling, the looks, snickers, and whispered jokes would be unbearable. High school really is hell. I think of Jon Summers and I want to get back at the ones who drove him to it. I know how. It's hard not to imagine all the ways I could make them sorry.

But I'm not like that anymore. I don't do bad things.

They can hurt me only if I let them, right? And I'm used to people laughing at me. If I didn't have a certain level of fortitude, I'd have given up on the Post-its long ago.

I head to chem, leaving an encouraging note on a locker along the way. Ryan's already there with the day's project ready to go. He looks tired, eyes red behind his glasses, like he's not sleeping well. Because I'm mad at him, I don't *want* to feel a pang of remorse. If

I forgive him now, I can stop flailing around looking for a new life. But looking at him hurts. I'm not ready to spend Friday nights watching movies, pretending nothing's changed. When everything has.

"You look beautiful," he says, as I sit down.

I push out a pained breath. "Thanks. Can we focus on the work, please?"

"I miss you." He ignores my request, like I don't know what I need. It's only been since Friday, one weekend, two school days. Only in his mind is this a long time.

"Ryan, don't make me ask for a new partner." I totally will; it's not a bluff.

"Right. Sorry." His face shuts down, and this time, I participate fully in the experiment.

I can't sit and watch because that's not okay anymore; since I'm not giving him the support I used to, I can't coast on his work. Probably, I shouldn't have done that before. I've let Ryan handle *too* many things for me in the past few years. I told myself it was fine because we were like two sides of a coin or something, but it was really just me letting go of the reins.

After school, I hit Shane's two last classes, and then I have a full list of his assignments, plus his address. *Are you really gonna just show up at his house?* It's so unlike me. I don't know what I'll say, how I'll explain it so I don't come off like a total headcase, but I don't even care. Hopefully he'll be glad to see me, or happy not to fall behind on his homework. He said he couldn't afford more trouble and bad grades qualify for most people, though it's not the kind that gets you sent to juvie.

Lila's not at her locker when I get to mine after making my rounds. She probably got a ride home in the gray van today. Just as well. I'd hate to explain why I look like I'm about to vomit all over my shoes. Shouldering my backpack, I head out to the bike rack, where mine is the last one still chained up. Feeling like a spy, I ride over to the library to check the directions. I have his address, and I know it's out in the country, but I'm not sure how far.

Five minutes later, Google gives me an answer.

Holy crap. Five miles. Do I want to see him that bad?

CHAPTER
EIGHT

YEAH, I TOTALLY DO. I'M WORRIED HE'S SICK. I'M concerned he'll fall behind in his classes and his grades will suffer. I'm . . . I'm . . . insane. Maybe I've caught some bizarre virus that causes unpredictable and uncharacteristic behavior. I don't print out the map because clearly that's *too far* when everything else I've done today is totally normal.

I just make a mental note of the route and jog to my bike. Before getting on, I text a message to Aunt Gabby, telling her I'm studying at a friend's this afternoon. She'll assume I mean Ryan, and I squelch a frisson of guilt over that. I'll explain things to her soon. I *will*. Just as soon as I figure out how much to tell her. And how.

I swing by the Coffee Shop for snacks and drinks, then stow them in my backpack. Since I don't want to arrive dripping sweat, I ride at a leisurely pace, so it takes me thirty-seven minutes to get to his place. And at first, I think the school must've gotten it wrong, but I recognized Shane's handwriting on the form. So no. This is it. Nerves assail me as I walk my bike down the rutted drive, over-grown with curly dock, chickweed, and quack grass. I can't even *see* a house from here, but I'm committed. At the end of the lane, there's a decrepit trailer; the thing looks so run-down that I imagine it's cold in winter, leaks during a hard rain, and must be an oven during the summer. It was once cream with brown trim, but that's hanging off in rusty strips and the weather has discolored the lighter metal. The underpinning is loose, flapping in the breeze, and I'm nervous as I start forward.

Cinder blocks have been stacked up in lieu of steps long since rotted away. I lean my bike against a pile of tires out front, climb up, and knock. My heart thunders in my ears. I must be crazy for showing up uninvited. Now that I've seen where Shane lives, though, I'm more worried, not less. I'm scared he might be mad at me for barging in like this, but I have to make sure he's okay, echo of a time when I desperately wished somebody would've checked up on *me*.

Mustering all my courage, I tap lightly on the door. Immediately, I hear movement inside and I brace for one of his parents to yell at me. Instead, Shane cracks the door, then freezes, staring at me in utter astonishment. The first thing I notice is that he has a second bruise, a newer one, to match the black eye Dylan gave him a few days back. And he didn't get it at school.

"What're you doing here?" he demands.

Yeah, he's not happy. I decide only absolute honesty will serve. "I was worried about you. And I brought your homework."

"Thanks." His anger blurs into confusion. Shane looks like he can't decide what he wants to ask next, a series of questions flickering on his face, but eventually he steps back. "You may as well come in, now that you're here."

Inside, it's cleaner than I expected. The kitchen has old linoleum and there's scratched paneling all over the place. Everything is worn, old-fashioned, and threadbare, but somebody looks after this place. I'd bet money that person is Shane. A small living room adjoins the kitchen. I imagine there's a bath down the hall, which ends in two small bedrooms.

"Your parents won't mind?" I ask, stepping in.

"My mom's gone. And my dad isn't here."

By which I presume "gone" means for good and "not here" indicates at the moment. So he lives with his father, who's probably the one who messed up his face. Otherwise, he doesn't seem sick, so he must've skipped to hide the evidence. I close the door behind me, then dig into my backpack. First I produce his list of assignments, as promised. Next, I get out the drinks and food I brought, not much, just some chicken soup sealed in a cup, bottles of juice, and two pieces of fruit. He watches with an expression of blank astonishment.

Finally, he gestures. "Is that for me?"

"The soup and juice are. And the orange. I thought you were sick."

"God," he whispers. "What am I supposed to do with you?"

I try a smile. "I hope that's a rhetorical question."

"Seriously, how did you find me? And why did you ride all the way out here?" His jaw ticks and he glances away. I barely hear his last mumbled question. "Why do *you* care when nobody else does?"

"I already told you."

"You didn't answer anything," he points out.

I really don't want to admit that I skulked around the school office to find his address, so I respond to the last thing he said. "I remember how hard it was when I moved here." I hesitate.

He's quiet, and I can't tell if he's mad, if he believes me. We eat in silence while I try to decide if I should mumble an excuse and leave. There's a darkness about him, a shadow in his eyes, and he doesn't look at me while finishing the soup and peeling the orange. I take my time with the apple, conscious of how much noise I'm making as I chew. I can't tell him that I'm slightly obsessed because he's hot, and I'm intrigued because he's a musician, and all the *girl* reasons behind why I'm here. So maybe—

"So you came because you were worried?" He asks like it's never happened before. "Not because you feel sorry for me. I don't want to be a . . . project."

"Well, yeah."

For another long moment, he's quiet. Then he seems to come to some conclusion.

"Thank you." Those are the most heartfelt words anybody's ever spoken to me. Sincerity burns in his blue, blue eyes, and he's beautiful, despite the bruises. I want to ask, but for now it's just enough he's not making me go.

"Since you're here," he adds, "want to work on some geometry?"

Not really. I'd rather stare at him or make out on the couch, but those options aren't on the table. "Sure, thanks. But that's not why I came. I mean, I don't expect you to help me just because—"

"I know," he interrupts. "I want to."

An hour later, I'm totally awed by Shane's brain. He has this way of simplifying the theorems so they actually make sense. With his guidance, I've successfully managed to solve two problems on my own. I still can't imagine why I would ever need to be able to figure out the length of one side of a mystery triangle, but if I'm ever kidnapped by a geometry-obsessed madman, maybe I won't die.

"Make sense now?" he asks.

"Yeah, I think I got it. I'd love to pull my grade up to a C before midterms."

"I'll get you to a B by the time the grading period ends."

I say without thinking, "If you do, I'll love you forever."

It's the sort of joke I'd make with Ryan, just hyperbole, but with Shane, it gains layers. He gives me that look again, the one that x-rays through my skin down to my bones, until I feel like he can view my heart. That should be a terrifying, creepy feeling, but it's more of a relief, like I don't have to hide; there's nothing about me that could scare him because he's been through so much himself.

God, how I want that to be true.

"Then I better apply myself," he says softly.

To what? Geometry? Or making me love you forever? Oh God. My stomach swirls.

"I never do this," I tell him.

"Study?"

I huff out a breath. "No. Show up at someone's house uninvited. It's so rude."

"I was just cleaning up a little."

The place is already as spotless as it can be, given its condition, but I spot a shimmer of broken glass in the trash can. So his dad's a drinker. I don't say anything, but I register him noticing. Shane may not say much, but he's the most observant person I've ever met. Which is why it's odd that he hasn't said anything about my hair. I mean, it's stupid and self-centered to want him to, given the mess he's dealing with, but I'm not 100 percent enlightened. I want him to think I'm pretty, and I wish he knew I'm fighting my way out of the fog for *him*.

"I should go—" I start, before it gets awkward.

But at the same time, he asks, "Would you—"

Then we both break off. Does he feel like I do? I hope he's nervous and excited and scared, and it feels like the start of something he wants desperately. I wait for him to go on, urging with my eyes.

Finally he murmurs, "You want me to play something for you?"

Oh God, yes. Please. Because I'm afraid my voice will reveal pure breathless glee, I just nod.

Shane goes back to his bedroom and returns with the battered guitar he was playing in the music room. He tunes it with a few expert thrums and I focus on his hands: long fingered, scars on the knuckles, hard but graceful. I'd imagine lacing our hands together but I might hyperventilate.

The song is haunting, and he plays with his eyes shut, head tilted back. After a few bars, I recognize it as one Aunt Gabby plays sometimes—"Collide" by Howie Day. I've never listened to the lyrics so closely before, but when Shane sings it, I find it impossible to do anything else. His acoustic cover is quiet and slow, a hint of melancholy, so it feels like a breakup song, though I don't think that's what it's about. The line about being tangled up with me? *Yes. Please.* By the time he strums the final note, holding it until it feels like a touch, I suspect I'd agree to anything.

"You're really good," I say.

Understatement.

"Think so?" And he's not asking for an ego boost. For a moment, his heart shows in his eyes. I've seen yearning before, but never so raw, and this isn't for me. He *wants* to be good, probably for the same reasons I push for good grades and lots of clubs. Like me, he needs to get out of here; he's running toward something bigger and brighter.

"The best I've ever heard, who wasn't already getting paid for it." That's actually not saying much. My car issues mean I don't go to many concerts. But I'm *sure* he's talented.

"I've got some original songs, too, if you'd like to hear one sometime."

"Sure," I say, as if I'm not inwardly screaming that he wants to see me again. On purpose. But the last thing I want is to get him in trouble. "Do you need me to head out? What time's your dad—"

His fingers clench on the neck of his guitar and he gives me a measuring look, before apparently deciding to spill. "I won't see him again for a while."

"Where is he?" That's not what I want to ask, and he knows it.

"He's a truck driver. He didn't even have a place until the court dumped me on him. He just put up at short-term motels between long hauls."

Judging by the crappy accommodations, Shane isn't close to his dad, as the guy didn't go out of his way to provide. "I shouldn't even say anything, but—"

"Don't say it. I'm not reporting him."

"Why?" I demand. "He can't get away with hurting you."

"I made him a deal," Shane says, surprising me. "He bought this place . . . and signs off on any paperwork. In return, I look after myself."

"But . . . your face . . ." I really thought his dad had hit him. But he's not even here?

"You've seen the front porch. Try going out the door when you have an arm full of stuff."

"You're trying to convince me you fell."

He smiles. "I really did. I promise. After I broke my history project, I said screw it." *So it's the project in the trash, not liquor bottles?* "I didn't feel like going today. My dad is many things . . .

76

and a good father isn't one of them, but he doesn't punch me in the face. He'd just rather not see me."

"Why not?" I ask, despite my resolution not to pry.

He shrugs, but the careless gesture reveals a world of vulnerability. "I remind him too much of my mom. It hurts, I guess."

"Because she's gone." I have no idea what that means, though. Did the woman move to California to find herself, or—

Before I can speculate, he says softly, "Yeah. Her funeral was the worst day of my life."

Wow. So, forever gone.

Without even thinking about it, I move over beside him on the sagging couch, gently nudging his guitar aside to cover his hand with mine. This is new to me; I'm more familiar with distant kindness, leaving Post-its and moving on. I don't know much about making real connections, but for Shane, I'll crawl out of my comfort zone. He wraps his fingers around mine, and I think, *I could live in your eyes.*

"What happened?" Belatedly, I realize he might not want to talk about it, but if he doesn't, he can say so. I won't back off the bravery with a babbling disclaimer.

"Things were okay when I was younger. My dad was never around a lot. He's always driven a big rig, as long as I can remember. But when he came home, my mom would light up and it was like Christmas. He always brought presents . . ."

"That sounds nice." I don't remember a time when my mom and dad were together and happy. She left right after I was born. Things were better when my dad had custody, but I've never been part of a typical family unit. I know how it feels to lose a parent, though. Later, I'll tell him so, but right now, I don't want to interrupt.

"I was always closer to Mom for obvious reasons."

I nod.

"She got sick when I was twelve."

There should be some words in the world that could make it better somehow, but if they exist, I don't know them. So I just cling to his hand, gaze locked on his bruised face. His eyes are just swimming, not in tears, but sadness. His chin drops.

"We went through rounds of radiation, aggressive meds, chemo. Year after year. She had two remissions before it finally got her."

No wonder the football team didn't have the power to bother him.

He goes on, "My dad bailed when I was fourteen. He couldn't stand watching her die."

"That was a pussy thing to do," I say. That's not a word I normally use, but it applies.

Wry smile. "You're telling me. But my mom forgave him. Said he just loved her too much to let her go. And that's what I had to do . . . so she could finally, y'know."

"Rest?" I supply, unsure.

"Yeah," he says tiredly. "Dad wouldn't come back to Michigan City, said he couldn't. I was on the verge of going into the system for the last time when I cut this deal with him."

"The last time?"

He hunches his shoulders. "I didn't handle it well after my mom died. A friend of hers let me stay with him while he looked for my dad, but I wasn't . . . cooperative. Or law abiding." I can see that he regrets it, probably feels like he let his mom down.

"You went a little crazy. It's understandable." I'm guessing whatever he did, like get into fights, shoplift, drink, maybe drugs, it isn't as bad as what I'm hiding.

"So I'm lucky I avoided a permanent stay in juvie," he concludes. "My dad came through."

"And bought you all this."

My disdain must've penetrated because his brows draw together. "It's not much, but it's mine. It's all he could afford. My mom's medical bills . . ."

"I am such an asshole. I'm sorry."

"It *is* a dump. But it's better than foster care. I just . . . I couldn't deal with a new family right now. I just wanted to be by myself."

I wonder if that's really what he needs, but it's not my place to judge. I had years of court-mandated therapy and I don't feel fixed. I just feel like a different kind of broken.

He goes on, "Promise you won't tell anyone. I'm not sure if this is strictly legal."

Most likely it falls under the heading of neglect, though if he's been looking after his terminally ill mother for years, he's not a kid in the usual sense of the word. I respect his desire for privacy.

"I promise."

His silence makes it clear he'd prefer not to say more.

Then it dawns on me. "I've been pestering the crap out of you." I should've known there would be a reason he avoids people, but I only thought about how he made me *feel*. It's been a long time since I was so selfish, since I let myself be. Ryan was right after all when he dubbed Shane antisocial. "I'm sorry."

"It's okay." He's smiling. "I haven't had friends the past few years. It was too hard. I was taking care of my mom, no time to hang out. Most of them got tired and went looking for fun."

Friends? Well. If that's what he needs, what he sees in me . . . I die a little inside because this feels like Ryan all over again. Maybe I'm just destined to play that role. I muster a smile.

"*I* think you're fun," I say.

"You pick up garbage for a good time."

I shake my head. "That's giving back to the community."

If Ryan taught me anything about friendship, it's that hugs are acceptable. And I could use one after hearing Shane's story. So I reach for him, winding my arms around his neck. At first he's stiff, like he doesn't know what to do, then he gets it, softening into me, and his arms curl around my back. It feels so good I almost moan.

Friend. He wants a friend. I'll get right on that.

He murmurs into my hair, "I came here looking to finish school quietly. Stay out of trouble. Maybe write some new songs. I never expected you."

CHAPTER NINE

COME WEDNESDAY, I'M STILL WONDERING WHAT SHANE meant. Today, when I get to my locker, the Post-it isn't blue; it's green, and it's written in normal ballpoint pen. *I told her. You're still everything.* Despite my best intentions, I glance over at Ryan. He looks worse than he did yesterday; I can tell the conversation with Cassie wasn't easy. I'm glad he manned up, but I'm not sure what he expects from me. It would be easy and safe for me to walk across the hall and into his arms, just slip into the relationship he let everyone think we already had.

But that doesn't feel like the right choice. I mean, it's not that I want to hurt him, but this isn't as easy as Ryan wants it to be. Quietly, I take down the Post-it and stick it inside my binder. I don't know if I'm keeping this one, but I won't throw it away in front of him. Despite what he's done, he was my best friend for years.

Lila joins me, her gaze following mine. "Ouch. I think he's really in love with you."

"Maybe he should've realized that sooner," I mutter.

"Hey, I'm not advocating a reconciliation. Do what you need to."

He shapes the word *please* as we stare at each other across the hall. *Please, what? Forgive you? Talk to you?* Deliberately, I turn away.

"See you at lunch," I say to Lila, heading off to class.

Shane's in Geometry today, a fact that makes me happy. He smiles at me as he takes his seat, but there's no chance to talk. Mackiewicz dumps another quiz on us, but this time, I can do some of the work, possibly even enough for a passing grade. If I can show something other than an F, dated later than the prior two, Aunt Gabby will be less disappointed. When I hand forward my paper, I'm relatively confident that I didn't fail.

Shane waits for me after class. Dylan and his crew linger for a few seconds, but when they see he's not forever alone, they move on. They're cowards like that. It's one thing to pick on a kid, another to deal with his friends. While the teachers will look the other way in some instances, when you start involving lots of other parents, that becomes impossible. Which is why Shane shouldn't wander the halls by himself until the jocks lose interest in him.

"Lunch?" I ask.

"Sure. Just let me stop by my locker."

"Not a problem."

I tell myself it's for his benefit that I follow him around the corner; he's situated in the opposite corner of the school from me. He stows his backpack, then turns. "Ready."

Today I banked that he wouldn't have anything with him, so I packed enough food for two. I get the feeling his dad is so underwater with medical bills that he's not sending much living allowance. That would be why Shane's perpetually hungry. I stop at my locker, too, on the way to the lunchroom. When we walk in, Theo waves, like he was watching for me.

"Friend of yours?" Shane asks.

"Not exactly. He's the kid we sat with the other day."

"Oh, right. Seems like he's into you."

"Maybe." I suspect it's more that he enjoys the attention they're getting due to our presence at their table.

At the moment, people are talking about Ryan and me, Lila and me. The lesbian rumor seems to be dying out, at least. Soon, somebody will get drunk or pregnant, crash a car or steal one, and then that'll be the new focus. It can't come soon enough for me. I head over, smiling, and the girls, at least, seem truly happy to see me. I introduce Shane to Kimmy, Mel, and Shanna. He's polite, but I see he's feeling a bit WTF about the whole thing. As he said, his master plan was to lay low, write songs, and get out of school unnoticed. Between Dylan Smith and me, that's becoming impossible. I can't control Dylan, but I'm not letting him pick on Shane anymore if there's anything I can do about it. And I *do* have one card to play but I'd rather not, unless he forces me to it. We'll see.

I set lunch on the table, daring him to protest when I portion out his half. Today it's apple raisin salad, peanut butter and jelly sandwiches, carrot sticks, and two brownies. He doesn't protest in front of the sophomores; they're talking about a movie they're seeing this weekend. When Lila joins us a few minutes later, followed by Tara and Kenny, Shane's mouth quirks into an adorable smile.

I see why he's amused. Our table doesn't have a single free seat, and it's heretical in that it has freshmen, sophomores, and juniors all mixed up. We don't have any seniors; we're not that cool, but we're the most integrated of the lunch crowd. By comparison, Ryan's table looks a little sparse.

"I'm Lila," she says, taking a bite of what passes for an enchilada in this school.

Oops. I should probably have done that myself. If I'm honest, maybe I didn't want to because she's pretty striking. I'm happy when he doesn't seem wowed; he's low-level friendly, nothing else. Let's see, Shane met Tara and Kenny at Green World, so that's handled. Part of me wishes I had him to myself, but this is better. The more people know who he is, the less likely the jocks can get away with harassing him.

"I'm pretty excited about the cleanup tonight," Tara says.

By looking at her, you'd never guess; you'd think she's afraid to get her hands dirty. Her nails are always perfectly manicured, and you can tell her family has money, so I find her participation in Green World fascinating. Past experience with rich kids tells me most of them are spoiled and don't care about giving back. Today, her designer outfit is pristine; she's spent hours on her personal grooming. Tara is pretty, but she wears more makeup than she needs. I saw her without it once, and her mahogany skin is flawless.

Kenny, on the other hand, is a total gamer geek. All of his clothing has the logo of some game franchise, and he never goes without his Mario hat. He's also got a crush on Tara the size of Texas, which explains his interest in the environment.

"What cleanup?" Theo asks.

I glance at Shane. This is a chance to evangelize, but he might think I'm weird. Then I remember that he's already been to one of our meetings. It's not like this information will surprise him, so I explain the purpose of the group. By the time I finish, the sophomores look interested.

Mel asks, "Is it something that would help on a college app?"

"Absolutely." I'm smiling.

"What time today and where?" Kimmy wants to know.

Wow, did I just recruit four new members? The flyers I posted at the start of school got defaced and torn up. Until now, I'd considered ditching tonight's cleanup, though it was my idea. Frowning, I abandon that plan; it's chicken, and as long as there are other people around, there will be a buffer between Ryan and me. I can do this. I *will* do this.

"I can help," Lila says unexpectedly.

"That would rock. We'll get done a lot faster with more bodies."

"Anything for my college app," she mutters, like she's embarrassed to be seen caring.

I write down the place and time in a grid I draw in my notebook, then fold the paper until it tears neatly into multiple squares. When I glance up, Shane is watching me with a riveted expression, a carrot stick hovering halfway to his mouth. I want to say, *What?* But that will ruin the moment because he's not going to tell me what he's thinking with everyone else sitting here.

Friend. He needs a friend. Well, I'm doing my best to surround him with people.

I summarize the plan and add, "If you can't get a hold of biodegradable trash bags, that's all right. I have extras."

"Of course you do," Lila says, grinning. "I bet you were adorable riding in with all the boxes balanced on your bike."

I glare at her. "Hey, that was *not* easy."

"I'm not mocking you, Princess. I like your determination. It's . . . odd." That shouldn't sound complimentary, but somehow, between her warm eyes and her sincere smile, it does.

The remainder of lunch is spent on logistics with the sophomores texting their parents to explain they've gotten involved in a community cleanup project and will need rides later. Shane doesn't say much, nor does he volunteer to help. I'm a little sad about that. But he does walk me to my locker.

"Why did she call you 'princess'?"

Awesome. Sighing, I mumble an explanation about the nickname and conclude, "So yeah, the Post-its. I should probably stop with that."

People whose names I don't remember wave to me as I go down the hall. This is strange. I mean, the ones I've tried to cheer up have always acted quietly pleased, but they never go out of their way when they see me. *What's changed?*

Before I can puzzle on that too long, Shane says, "I hope you don't."

Huh. Ryan always found it silly and slightly embarrassing. I mean, not enough to complain about it, but he also never got the point; he told me once it was a huge waste of time and paper. Obviously I disagree.

"Unlikely," I say, smiling as I parrot his word back to him.

"Cute. Uh. I'd like to come tonight if you could use another pair of hands."

"Wear gloves," I say, touching his fingers. "These are guitar-playing gold."

His smile melts me. "I'll see what I can do."

"But I thought you weren't interested in coming to another meeting?"

"That was before I realized how relentless you are."

My cheeks flush, burning with heat. I can't meet his gaze, so I stare at his battered army boots instead; yeah, these are totally tan. "I told you I was sorry about that."

"Hey." He tips my face up with warm fingers, and for a crazy moment, I think he might kiss me. "I was kidding. I mean, you *are* hyper-focused, but not in a bad way. I probably need someone who won't let me hide." Shane runs his other hand through his tousled curls. "God, somehow you got my life story out of me in one afternoon. I never . . . I don't talk to people like that. I just don't."

I didn't even realize it was rare; that's how right it felt. But maybe he needed to open up . . . and I was there. Could've been timing more than anything to do with me. Still, the glow of satisfaction starts in my toes and radiates all the way up to my neck. I've never felt this way before, not this exact combination of giddiness and abject terror.

Shane drops me at my classroom, then takes off for his. Down the hall, I see Dylan and crew lying in wait, but Shane's smart this time. He spots Mr. Johannes walking ahead and falls into step with him. I can't hear what they're talking about, but he'll get to class without being harassed.

Chemistry is boring but bearable, and luckily, Ryan is all business this time, though at the end of the period, he asks, "Are you coming to the cleanup?"

"Of course. It was my idea."

"I'm glad." That's all he says, but there's more trembling on the tip of his tongue. He swallows it as I pack up my things and hurry toward the door.

"Sage." It's the science teacher, who I never call Tom.

"Yes, sir?"

"I just wanted to tell you I've noticed an improvement in your participation in the experiments. Your grade will reflect the additional effort."

I smile at him. "Thanks."

"Carry on."

To my surprise, Shane is already waiting for me outside

chemistry. That's . . . unprecedented. He must've persuaded his teacher to let him out a few minutes early; that's some impressive smooth talking. God, I hope I'm not beaming the way I feel.

"You can't continue feeding me every day," he says.

Wow, *not* what I'm expecting.

He goes on, "I don't want you to see me as a stray dog."

"I don't!"

"Well, you're always feeding me. It's nice, but . . . things will pick up. Dad's paying on the hospital bills, and I'm looking for work to help with my daily living expenses."

"Maybe I can help you find something."

A frown knits his brows together. "Don't worry about it, I can handle my own business."

"But—"

"You can be annoyingly persistent, you know that?" Yeah, he's aggravated.

I can't just drop it, though. Seeing Shane now reminds me of when things were the worst for me. My skin itches over at the idea of offering the same indifference I got.

"I've kind of been there," I explain quietly. "I wasn't old enough to work, but it would've been nice if somebody . . . cared."

Shane sighs, but there's a faint softening to his impatience. "Fine."

"Is there any kind of work you won't do?" Relief brightens my voice.

He shakes his head. "I can't afford to be picky. I'd like to buy some groceries."

"Don't you get lonely out there?" I ask.

The pause tells me he's thinking about his answer as we walk. Finally he says, "I've been alone a long time. Lately I just have time to notice."

I guess he means his mom wasn't much company toward the end and he was run ragged taking care of her. He doesn't seem to be angry, not like I was. Or maybe he burned it out back in Michigan City when he was staying with his mom's friend. I ponder whether this guy was her boyfriend, if he loved her after her husband left. It would take a lot of courage, I decide, to fall for someone you *know* will leave you, sooner rather than later.

He adds, "That's why I was in the library the other night. I wanted to be near people. It's really quiet out in the country at night. And, yeah . . ." His voice drops. "Lonely."

That feels like big admission. Warmth swells in my chest over the fact that he trusted me with it. As I recall, he was hiding in an upstairs conference room for privacy, but I understand what he's saying. It's different knowing folks are nearby, even if they're not in the room with you. That trailer in the middle of nowhere must be super-creepy at night. And that's the difference between an empty home and one that houses somebody who loves you.

I nod. "Do you know where we're going?"

"Not exactly."

"You can come with me." Then I realize I have the same problem that I had getting a frap with Lila the other day. I have a bike; Shane does not. So I make the ultimate sacrifice. "Do you know how to ride?"

"A bike?" He looks at me like I'm crazy. "Well, yeah."

"Sweet. Then we can double up. We're going to a vacant lot downtown, not too far. I hope you have good balance."

"I don't trip over my own feet. Generally."

"How do you get to school?" I ask.

"Bus, usually. But if I stick around to do something in town and miss it, then I walk."

"That must take forever," I observe.

"It's not so bad."

"So I'll meet you outside after school?"

Shane nods. He drops me at my next class, and I spend the next two hours daydreaming. If there was a quiz in econ, I don't remember. I hope I didn't write my name on a blank paper. I join the throng streaming toward the front doors. *Do I need anything from my locker? Trash bags.* So I stop, load up, then head out. The crowd has thinned a little by the time I get outside.

Shane's already waiting for me. I could so get used to this. "Hey. You ready?" I ask.

"Yeah. I can't wait to go serve the community."

"Hey." I aim an admonishing finger at him. "Caring's cool."

He laughs, as I intend him to. Trying to act like I'm not nervous, I climb on the bike first and take the seat. Shane's obviously done this before, as he swings on and pushes into motion. I hang on to his waist, trying not to stare at his butt as he pedals. Okay, that's a lie. I'm totally looking. My backpack, stuffed with biodegradable trash bags, wobbles madly until I'm afraid we'll tip. We're both cracking up by the time we arrive at the lot, but he's not even out of breath.

"I haven't done that since junior high," he says.

"I never have."

And I thought I never would.

Normal pleasures like this are reserved for girls without a shadow staring back at them in the mirror. But whether I deserve this or not, I don't care. It's too sweet to stop.

CHAPTER

TEN

SHANE HELPS ME OFF THE BIKE, AND I'M PRETTY SURE I'M not imagining the intensity as he gazes into my eyes. We're having a moment.

Which is promptly interrupted by Gwen blowing a whistle. "Awesome, everyone's here. I'm dividing you up into pairs, and the team who fills the most bags wins a ten-dollar gift certificate from the Coffee Shop."

She points at people seemingly at random, and I end up with Lila. I'm not sad about it. This gives me a chance to recover from riding behind Shane. At this point, I suspect Gwen of being the devil because she puts Shane with Ryan. The four sophomores are paired among themselves, which leaves Tara with Conrad, who looks more than usually stoned. Gwen gets Kenny, and the moment he finds out he's not working with Tara, he exhales a sigh audible all the way over here. I think Gwen crushed his dreams.

Lila nudges me, a grin slowly spreading. "You and New Kid, huh? That was fast."

"I don't know. I don't want to talk about it."

"You let him ride your bike." Somehow she makes this sound absolutely filthy. "I bet Ryan never did."

As a matter of fact, she's right, but mostly because he's uncoordinated. Most guys eventually master their arms and legs, but he's still struggling. I used to find his awkwardness adorable. Cassie probably did, too. I wish I didn't feel bitter, but last year, I had *such* a crush on him, after his dorkiness crossed some kind of line until he was cool. The hours I spent wondering why he didn't see me that way . . . I shake my head and sigh.

"Shut up," I mumble.

"Are you blushing? Oh my God, you're totally blushing."

"Pick up some trash already." I curse my fair complexion.

In the sun, I don't tan. Ever. With enough exposure to daylight, I will freckle over every inch of my body. Since I worked inside most of the summer, I've got them down to a sprinkling on my cheeks and shoulders. It's bright today, though, so I can expect a fresh crop just in time for fall. And nothing says hot like an uneven distribution of melanin.

Gwen thought to bring her iPod along with a dock that has a couple of small speakers. She blasts Black Veil Brides, which is supposed to make us rock out and work faster. It actually is pretty fun. Lila and I race to see who can get the most plastic bottles. This lot is absolutely disgusting. Even if I can't get permission to plant a garden here in the spring, just getting the trash hauled away will make a huge difference.

It takes three hours, but eventually we have eight full bags, plus some random junk. I'm amazed when a truck pulls up. Gwen grins at me. "I bothered my dad to make some calls for us. And *voilà*! Phil is taking everything to the junkyard today."

"Thanks. This is really impressive," I say.

Gwen doesn't answer; she's counting piles before Phil can take them. Looks like Tara and Conrad gathered the most. He punches the air when he gets his five bucks, which is basically a latte or a frap. Still, it's better than nothing. She's more restrained, but she beams at Kenny, who cheers up a bit beneath his drooping Mario hat.

"That's it," Gwen announces, then she beckons to her dad's friend.

Ten minutes later, when the truck pulls away, the lot looks fantastic. I can imagine how the garden will look. It would be awesome if we could do three different types: herbs, vegetables, and flowers nearest the sidewalk, adding both beauty and purpose to the wasted space. There are shops to either side of the lot. I think Aunt Gabby told me there was an inn here, a long time ago, but it burned down, and nobody cared to rebuild as this isn't a tourist destination. There's a motel out near the freeway, but this isn't the kind of town that gets the bed-and-breakfast crowd.

"Good start," Conrad says in his slow, dreamy way. "But we probably need to keep an eye on the place, make sure it doesn't get junky again before spring."

"Seconded," Ryan murmurs.

That's the first thing he's said in my hearing this afternoon. I wonder what he and Shane talked about, if anything. Lila and I kept too busy for me to stare at them, but I was tempted. Gwen makes plans for a weekly watch program, and while I register my day to walk by, I'm only half paying attention. The meeting is breaking up by the time I tune back in again.

"Some of us are heading over to the Coffee Shop to wait for our rides," Theo says.

I take that as an invitation, but I'm not interested. "I need to get started on my homework, but thanks. Next time?"

"Totally," Kimmy says.

"That wasn't horrible," Mel is saying as the four of them stroll off.

"Next meeting's at the library, usual time," Gwen shouts and gets random finger gestures from people who are so done for now.

"So what's next, Princess? Can we save a kitten from a tree?" Lila opens her eyes obnoxiously wide, so she looks like an anime character.

"Not tonight. I have to get home. And please don't call me that."

"Sorry." She actually sounds it. "Old habits."

I surprise myself by asking, "You want to come?"

She pauses, cocking her head in apparent contemplation. We've never done that, but she said she wanted us to be better friends. That means hanging out, right? Since I'm new at this, I'm winging it.

Finally she says, "Why not? Let me call my mom." The conversation that follows is reassuringly normal. I hear Lila's side, answering typical parental questions, then she hands me the phone with a sigh. "She requires corroboration that I'm running with a new crowd."

"Hi, this is Sage."

"Nice to meet you. Well, sort of." Lila's mom sounds friendly, curious, and desperately hopeful. "Did Lila really participate in some kind of project?"

"Yes, ma'am. We cleaned up the vacant lot between the dry cleaner's and the hardware store. You can drive by and check it out if you like. I think it looks great. I've invited her to dinner at my house. If you want, I can have my aunt call you when we get there."

She's a little choked up. "No. No, that's all right. I'm so happy she's making some new friends."

"Bye, Mrs. Tremaine." I hand the phone back to Lila, who leans her head back in the classic Why-God-why pose.

"Well, that ranks among the more humiliating moments in my life. She doesn't trust me at *all* anymore."

"How come?" I ask.

"I got busted with some weed a while back. The stupid thing is, it wasn't even mine. And I know *everybody* says that, but it really wasn't. It was just stupid. Everything I've done in the last two years is stupid, starting with Dylan."

"Dating him or dumping him?"

She cuts me a look. "What do you think?"

"The first thing."

"Brilliant."

When I turn, I nearly run into Shane, who's come up behind me. His cheeks are flushed from wind and sun, his hair tumbling into his eyes. My fingers itch to brush it away, like he did for me once, but I'm not brave enough, especially with Ryan and Lila looking on. I tell myself that his smile warms just for me as he gazes down, that his so-blue eyes gain sparkle, but that might be wishful thinking. I wasn't kidding when I said I don't know anything about guys. If I did, surely I'd have figured out Ryan's not-so-cunning scheme long before he told me.

"I'm heading home," Shane says, like he needs to tell me.

"See you tomorrow." It's a nothing of an exchange, but I'm smiling when I include Ryan in that statement, offering a parting nod.

"You want me to walk you home?" Ryan asks as Shane moves off down the sidewalk.

Lila takes half a step forward. "We're fine."

I know Shane has a five-mile walk ahead of him, and there

might not be anything to eat. Dammit, I know too much about him now, and it bothers me. He doesn't want me to feel sorry for him; and I don't. I just desperately want to take care of him because, from what he's said, it's been a long time since anybody did. Since his mom was sick, she couldn't, and his dad bailed. Plus, it will be dark soon—before I can think better of it, I run after him, leaving Lila and Ryan staring.

"Wait!" I'm digging into my backpack as I run. "You need some tape."

"I do?" He's adorable in his bemusement.

"Yes, it'll keep you from getting hit at night."

"You realize there will be four cars on the road, maybe, the whole way home?"

"I don't care. Please wear it?" If he makes me admit I'm worried about him, I will melt into a puddle of embarrassment. But I seem to have internalized my aunt's fears.

"Okay, damn." But there's a fond note in his exasperation. I hope. Muttering, he takes the reflector tape and sticks it on his army jacket. "Better?"

"Yeah. Thank you."

"G'night, Princess." Somehow, when he says it, I don't even mind . . . because he doesn't mean it as a jab. Shane touches my nose lightly, then goes, glimmering, down the darkening street.

"That was kind of adorable," Lila observes when I retrace my steps.

Ryan doesn't seem to think so. In fact, he looks like I punched him in the stomach. He makes a good recovery, though, pasting on a smile. If I didn't know him so well, I'd think he was fine. This is how his face looks just before killing a bug. Ryan *loathes* insects.

"So, taco night."

I hope he's not expecting an invite. My aunt's chipotle seitan tacos are delicious; and he won't be having any for a while. "Yep. Have a good night."

Lila takes my arm in case I'm tempted to linger, but I'm not. I push my bike for a block before saying, "It's over two miles. I'll pedal. You can ride."

"Seriously?" She shakes her head, but climbs on it.

This is less fun when I'm doing the work, but it's good for me. It's half past seven by the time we get to my house. The lights are on inside, which means Aunt Gabby is home and cooking. I push through the front door, calling out a greeting, and wipe my feet. She comes to the kitchen doorway, wearing her cute sunflower apron.

"Oh, you didn't tell me we were having a guest." But she's glad.

Though she never says anything, she worries about my socialization. She thinks I try too hard to be positive and she's afraid I don't put enough effort into making friends. But she doesn't realize how tough it is not to backslide after a bad day. I keep my temper under lock and key and, *mostly,* I'm okay. I treat rage like an alien that hides in a corner of my brain. My aunt is devoted to ensuring my life is as normal as possible—and I'm happy I'm done with therapy, finally. If I lose it, even once, I'll have to go back, which is why I take such care never to lose my temper.

"This is Lila."

Who says, "I'd shake, but we've been garbage picking. Is there somewhere I can wash up?"

"This way." I show her to the bathroom, decorated in Aztec style, with orange and yellow accents. In the middle of winter, it's a burst of much-needed warmth.

"Cute house."

I beam because my aunt and I spent hours picking out things

together; she said it would make me feel more at home—and she was right. I love this house. It's pretty much the only real home I've had since I was seven years old.

"Dinner's done!" Aunt Gabby calls.

At first, Lila is skeptical of seitan tacos, but once we load them up with peppers, onions, cheese, pico de gallo, and sour cream, her eyes say, "yum."

"I'd probably eat a shoe, prepared like this."

My aunt grins. "You'll love it, I promise."

"You should try her lasagna," I say, three tacos later. "She makes it every other Sunday because the cheese poundage she uses is a sin somewhere."

Lila laughs. "I could be down with copious amounts of cheese. Huh. Why does that sound so wrong?"

I make the I-can't-even face at her while snarfing the last of my black beans and corn.

Smiling, Aunt Gabby starts to clear the table, but I jump to my feet. "No way, it's my turn."

Though I don't say so, it's *always* my turn. I have to earn my keep. Lila raises a brow at me; I guess she's never seen anyone so eager to clean up. I have my reasons.

My aunt relaxes back into her chair with a tired, appreciative smile. "Thanks."

It's nice listening to them talk while I work. My aunt seems to like Lila, who's on her best behavior, though she's still a little sharp on some notes. She wouldn't be herself without a little sarcasm. Their laughter is warm, contented, and I enjoy the feeling. It occurs to me that this is the perfect time to talk to my aunt, while there's a witness.

"Uhm. I have good news and bad news," I say at the next pause.

Aunt Gabby comes over to the sink, propping a hip beside me. "Bad first."

This is SOP for us. "I got two Fs, both in geometry. One was a test, the other a quiz."

Through clenched teeth, she asks, "What's the *good* news?"

"I found a tutor, and I think I did a lot better on the quiz I took today. He said he can help me bring my grade up to a B by the end of the term."

"That *is* good news. Okay." Aunt Gabby exhales, pushing the stress out of her body. "I'll spot you a couple of bad grades, but you better not bring me a D or an F on your report card."

"I won't, I promise."

"I'll have to get medieval." She tries to maintain a stern look but she just can't do it, and we both burst out laughing. "So, a he-tutor? A not-Ryan he?"

Oh, crap.

"Yeah." Hopefully I'm not the color of a Christmas ornament right now.

"Hot?" she asks Lila.

Who tilts her head and asks, "Shane?"

I nod.

"Then yeah," she tells my aunt. "A little grunge, a little emo, but a hundred percent cute."

"He is *not* emo."

"Sorry. Dreamo." She's not sorry at all; she's loving this, and so is my aunt.

Who asks, "Is that a thing?"

"No," I say at the time Lila answers, "Totally."

"Dreamo is not a thing."

Lila has an argument ready. "Sure it is. Dreamy plus emo equals dreamo. Shane."

Aunt Gabby laughs. The worst part is, if she means it, like, he daydreams a lot and doesn't talk much, then yeah. Well, whatever. I'm not bickering with them. Muttering, I finish up the dishes, and by this time, it's almost nine.

"Where do you live, Lila?" my aunt asks. "I can run you home."

"It's not that far. I could walk—"

"Forget it," I say. "Unless you plan on letting her cover you in reflective tape." The irony of me coming across protective with Shane doesn't escape me.

"Never. Not in a thousand years." Lila shakes her head repeatedly.

"Then get in the car."

While my aunt gets her keys, Lila hugs me unexpectedly. "Thanks. Your aunt is great. I mean, seriously great. You're so lucky."

"I know."

"The way you two are together, it's seems so easy. You can actually talk to her without worrying she'll rip your head off or give you an hour lecture."

"Yeah. I'm lucky all right."

But I wonder if Lila would still think that if she really knew me. I wonder if she'd still want to be my friend.

CHAPTER

ELEVEN

WHEN MY AUNT GETS BACK FROM DROPPING LILA OFF, I remember to ask, "Do you know of any place that's hiring?"

She cocks her head. "Aren't you happy at the Curly Q?"

"Not for me. For my friend. Shane."

"The dreamo guy who's tutoring you in geometry?" She knows perfectly well who he is.

But I nod anyway. "Yeah, he could use a part-time job after school."

"I saw a sign that they were looking for somebody over at the P&K."

"Better than DQ. I'll let him know. Thanks."

"Not a problem." She sinks down onto the couch with a weary sigh.

I head to the kitchen to make tea; it's our nightly ritual, one we started early on, so we'd always have a few minutes a day to catch up. Prowling through the cupboards, I look at all the interesting and exotic choices. Tonight seems like it calls for some green matcha, so I boil the water and prepare the cups. There's something calming about the process, and by the time I bring the cups back to the living room, she's already curled into the pillows.

See how helpful I am? There's no reason to send me back to state care. I'm an asset. I don't cause trouble. I make your life easier. I hope she thinks that when I do nice things. I hope she keeps me.

She takes the mug and warms her fingers around it before taking a sip. "So tell me."

"How do you know there's anything up?"

"You just confirmed it."

I have to smile. It would be impossible for me to put anything over on my aunt. She's ridiculously smart. So I dump the whole mess with Ryan in her lap, hoping it will distract her from Shane. I am *not* ready to talk about him. Maybe there's nothing to say, anyway.

"So," I finish, "do you think I'm overreacting?"

She looks positively astonished. "Ryan? We're really talking about Ryan."

"Yep. Apparently he's got game."

"I suppose this explains a few things," she says thoughtfully.

I summon a smile. "I kinda wish he was gay."

Aunt Gabby ticks the points off her fingers as she considers. "Let see if I have this straight. You're hurt because he went after some older girl when you kind of liked him. You're upset that he used and lied to you . . . because that's not the way you treat a friend."

"That's the gist."

"Do you still like him?"

"Not as a boyfriend. But . . . I'll probably forgive him. Eventually."

"Then you need to ask yourself why you're punishing him. Is it ego or are you trying to teach him a lesson?"

"I'm not—" I start, but I totally am.

I'm changing my life, hoping he'll see how awesome I am and be sorry he went after this Cassie person instead. Which is so immature since I don't even want to be with him. Sometimes I hate how perceptive my aunt is. She's also incapable of being mean to *anyone*, even the hyper-querulous Mr. Addams, who gets in line with four things at the P&K and then argues for half an hour about the price of three of them. Gabby says he's just lonely.

"You think I should forgive him, don't you?"

"Is it worth damaging your friendship permanently?" she asks. "Everybody makes mistakes, sweetheart. But if you can live with the possibility that this silence between you might last forever, if that's what you want, then go ahead."

"No," I say softly. "But I also don't want the whole school thinking we're back together."

"Make it clear you're not."

"How?" I demand.

"Post it on Facebook."

Sometimes she just doesn't get it. "It's not like the whole school sees my wall. And it would be so lame to write, 'Dear World, I have forgiven Ryan McKenna, but we are *not* dating.'"

"I see your point. Then let him squirm a little longer and see what you come up with."

"Thanks." I finish up my tea and lean down to hug her.

When I pick up my backpack, I can feel that it's vibrating. I don't let on as I carry the bag down the hall. Once I'm in my bedroom, I pull out my cell and check. Four texts from Ryan. Before

I read them, sadness suffuses me. Even after I forgive him, things will never be the same between us.

Text one: **its been a rly long time since i felt this bad**

Text two: **i miss u, i hate this**

Text three: **so do u like him?**

Text four: **just tell me what to do**

That's the problem; I have no idea. But my aunt's words echo in my head, and I work my thumbs over the tiny keypad on the phone. Once I type the reply, I hesitate before hitting send.

i dont know

His answer comes so fast that he must've been watching for a possible reply. **at least ur talking to me again, thats a start**

I leave it there because I don't know what else to say. After plugging in my phone, I head to the bathroom to wash my face and brush my teeth. Peering closer, I see that my cheeks are positively aflame with new freckles from the lot cleanup. *Awesome*. I spit and rinse, exhausted by this point.

Unlike some nights, I have no trouble whatsoever sleeping, which means I wake up late. I get ready in a hurry, then gulp a quick breakfast of oatmeal and fruit. Aunt Gabby is running around with one shoe, but I don't have time to help her look for it. I aim a kiss at her, but she darts off, so I only hit the back of her head. Close enough.

"I'm gone," I call, grabbing my phone and my backpack.

My bike is in the shed around back, so I run for it. At this point I'm not even sure if I match, but hopefully, the outfit's not horrible. I grabbed the first three things I found in my clean laundry basket, so this could be interesting. I pedal like crazy for the first mile, and then—because I'm tired—I slow down. If luck's with me, I made up enough time so I won't catch a tardy.

When I coast into the parking lot, a few people are still milling around, but not many. So the warning bell's already rung, leaving me about a minute to get to class. No time to stop at my locker, but I have everything I need in my backpack. I go through the hall at a dead run, ignoring the teacher who yells at me. I manage to dive into my chair as the second bell rings.

With a start like this, I figure the day's going to suck.

Only it doesn't work out that way. Classes are fine; or at least, I don't get in any major trouble. I sit quietly, turn in homework when requested, and once, I even make eye contact with Ryan and give him a half nod. He still looks exhausted and sad, and I don't notice *anybody* who looks worse, which makes me feel good. So I leave him a Post-it on his locker; I can't tell him he's everything, but . . .

You tell the best stories.

He's already reading it as I pass by. I don't know what he expected to see, but he seems happy I reached out. Maybe forgiveness won't take as long as I thought. I'm smiling when I get to Mackiewicz's class, where I get my quiz back . . . and it's a C+. I can't wait to show Shane. He's already looking at me expectantly, so I flash my paper, and a huge grin spreads across his face. The bruises are fading, finally, so he's even better looking in that quiet way.

Once we're in the hall, he says, "I knew you could do it."

"It never would've happened without you." Before I can think better of it, I spring onto my toes to kiss his cheek.

Shane stills. I don't know what he would've said because Dylan Smith shoulders him as he swaggers out of the classroom, just in time to catch the kiss. "You dated Dorkenna for two years, and this is what you dump him for? Even *you* can do better, Princess."

"What's it to you?" I ask. "Unless you want to date me. If that's the issue, it's not happening. So move on already."

He laughs. "In your dreams, fat ass."

That's such a lame insult that it doesn't even bother me. I gesture in response, and Dylan doesn't know his history well enough to understand what I just invited him to do. But when I turn to Shane, his expression says he's about to go nuclear. Quickly, I take his hand and pull him away, before he can use that balled-up fist. A quiet thrill ripples through me; he can put up with any abuse these guys offer, but the minute they start on me? He can't deal.

"No trouble," I remind him.

"He shouldn't get away with treating people like that." Usually, he's so low-key, all about blending into the background, but right now, Shane is vibrating with outrage.

For me?

"I don't care what he thinks. He's an asshole."

As he cools down, we walk to our lockers together, no need to talk about it; in just a few days, this has become the new normal. When he lets go of me to stow his stuff, I realize we held hands all the way here. I have no memory of our fingers lacing together after I grabbed him to keep him from starting a fight with Dylan, one Shane would be blamed for, but it happened. I process that while we continue to my locker, where I dump my backpack and grab lunch. Today I've brought enough leftover tacos to feed the whole table. Including Shane. I suspect he'll guess what I'm up to, but if everyone else is eating them, he can't complain. I hope. For once, we're the first ones to arrive, and I start setting the food out. As the others come in, I wave them over before they get in the cafeteria line.

"Lunch is on me today," I say.

"Oh my God," Kimmy squeals. "I *love* tacos."

After everyone's eaten several, Shane murmurs, "Tell your aunt she's a fantastic cook."

"You should come over sometime."

The whole table looks interested, and I *think* I might've just invited everybody for Sunday lunch. "Do you guys have plans?"

"Nope," Theo says without hesitation.

"I have to ask my mom," Mel tells me, "but it's probably cool. And I'll bring lunch tomorrow, if you guys want. This was fun. I'll make sure to bring some veggie stuff, Sage."

"Wow. Thanks." Lila looks about as surprised as I feel.

These four sophomores are *really* nice. I mean, I never would've gone out of my way to meet them because they're . . . average. Normal. And I always feel self-conscious with people who don't have any baggage . . . because I'm deceiving them, and they deserve better. But maybe I need to make friends like this to stop feeling that way.

Kimmy and Shanna say they'll let me know tomorrow. I wonder how Aunt Gabby will feel about our Sunday afternoon being invaded by a bunch of teenagers, then I decide she'll be happy; she'll think my *wanting* to have people over is a milestone. I hope she doesn't make a huge deal of it . . . but apart from Ryan—and now Lila—nobody has ever been to our place.

After lunch, on our way back to class, Shane asks, "You want to hang out Friday night?"

"Sure." I'm not ready to bring him home for a night like I used to spend with Ryan. "We could catch a movie at the Capitol."

There's no multiplex here. Instead, we have an old-fashioned theater built in the 1890s. It's a little run-down and the roof leaks during a hard rain, but the current owners are working on restoration. The only problem is that they can't afford to shut down, so there's always random construction going on, something roped off or covered in plastic. But I like the charm of the ornate moldings and the worn but fabulous carpet. The concession stand is covered in gilt, and there's a heavy crystal chandelier on the domed ceiling. Upstairs, the Capitol even has a balcony, which is usually closed; that doesn't stop couples from sneaking up there to make out. Since the place is understaffed, they usually get away with it.

"That sounds good," he says.

I expected he might make an excuse due to money and suggest hanging out on the square instead. That's the low-rent option for weekend fun in this town. Those who don't have cars or can't afford DQ, Coffee Shop, or a show will buy a drink at the convenience store near the courthouse, and then just wander around the square until the cops run them off. Sometimes they bring music and dance on the front steps, but that's mostly drama dorks trying to start a flash mob of four. People don't pick on them, though, because all the beautiful people are out at the Barn getting shit-faced.

"There's only one show on Fridays," I tell him. "At eight."

"Then I'll be at your house at seven thirty."

"Do you need the address?"

"That'd be good." I scrawl it on a piece of paper, which he sticks in the zip pocket on his backpack. "Thanks."

"Not a problem. Oh," I add, remembering. "You might want to swing by the P&K after school. My aunt said they're looking for help."

Shane's relief is a tangible force, warming the air between us. "I definitely will."

When he slides a hand beneath my hair—unstraightened and I didn't even have time for a ponytail—I think he's going for a kiss, right in the hallway. But he just cups his palm around my nape, fingers strumming slowly like I'm a tune he's trying to learn. Chills start on my neck, roll down my shoulders to my arms, until I have goose bumps. I'm wearing a shrug or he'd *see* them. Reflexively, I tug at the sleeves, making sure they're all the way down.

"Class," I mumble, unable to string two words together.

Shane lets go, and I manage to get to chem without stumbling over my own feet. Today, I actually beat Ryan, so I get our supplies from the back table. The beakers and things are already at our lab station, so I start setting up as best I can. The teacher watches me take the initiative, then scribbles a note in the grade book. Ryan barely reaches his stool before the final bell, looking more rumpled than usual. Since his head is one enormous cowlick, that's saying something.

I listen while we get the instructions for our experiment, then I turn to Ryan. "You ready?"

"I got your note. About my stories."

"Yeah." It's true; he can make a trip to the QwikMart sound like an epic adventure.

"I guess . . . you have plans tomorrow night?" He says it with such awful resignation, like he can't imagine a worse fate than *not* hanging with me.

"I do. But . . ." The invite slips out in response to his puppy eyes. "You can come to lunch on Sunday if you want."

"I'm there."

"I invited a bunch of people, apparently. We're girl heavy, so—"

"Tell me you *didn't* just invite me for my Y chromosome."

I don't think I've ever seen him this angry. Ryan doesn't have a temper; at least, not that I've ever seen. Until now. His brown eyes practically throw sparks behind the black frames of his glasses.

"I'm trying, okay? I can't handle just the two of us yet. I mean, I want us to be friends, but—"

"Last week, I was trying to tell you I'm *in love* with you. I broke up with my girlfriend for you. Don't friend-zone me."

"Your girlfriend . . . ? The one you were *lying* to? Don't even try for the moral high ground." I can't believe that he's acting like the injured party.

"Ryan and Sage, less 90210, more chemistry, please," the teacher says.

"That's their problem," somebody cracks. "Not enough."

Oh God. How did my life end up this way? So much pointless drama, and Ryan's just making it worse. Tired of it, I put my head on the lab counter and wait to be struck by lightning.

Sadly, this never happens. I'm forced to finish this class and two more, then make my way to work. By comparison, my shift at the Curly Q is a marvel of peace and quiet. We get two new customers, which is cool for Mildred. The second girl comes in half an hour before closing. She's small with long brown hair and shaggy bangs. Her blue polo shirt has a pharmacy logo on it—along with the khaki pants, this looks like a work uniform. Just inside the door, she chews her lips nervously as I walk toward the front desk.

"Can I help you?" I ask.

"I just need . . ." Her voice is tiny, hesitant.

Wow, she's shy.

"My bangs trimmed. Maybe the split ends on the rest."

That won't take long, so I call to Grace, who did my high-lights, "Do you have time?"

She nods. It's ten bucks more than she would've made fiddling with her own hair.

"I have to shampoo your hair first," I explain. "It's the law. This way."

I notice she's actually shaking when she sinks into the red reclining chair. Maybe she's never had a haircut in a salon before? Pondering why that would be, I run the water so it's nice and warm and then go about my business of wetting, lathering, rinsing, and conditioning. Water speckles the lenses of her red glasses, the one pop of color about her. I usually throw in a little head massage if there's time, but she has a lot of hair, and Grace needs her in the chair to get it done before eight.

"There you go," I say, helping her sit up.

The customer follows me over to Grace's station, where I settle her with protective cape. "Do you want a magazine? Some water?"

"Water would be nice," she says softly.

I head back to the tiny employee lounge and fill a paper cone for her. When I get back with the drink, Grace is already at work with the comb. That accomplished, I go back to work cleaning the rest of the salon. The other stylists are all gone; Grace and I are closing up together tonight. Windex and towels in hand, I do all the mirrors by the time she finishes the trim.

"I don't have time to blow it out," Grace says, then shows the girl how it looks it in back.

"I like it. Thank you." She digs into her purse and slips Grace a few bucks.

That makes me smile; some people seem opposed to tipping

their stylists. I head over to the front desk to ring her out. A full haircut is twelve bucks, so I charge her eight for the partial. Her eyes look so sad as she counts out the singles that I can't help but ask:

"Are you okay?"

"No," she says softly. Then she squares her shoulders, like she's about to drink some medicine. "See, I'm . . . I'm Cassie."

CHAPTER TWELVE

OH. CRAP.

I feel weirdly like the other woman. What am I supposed to say? "Ryan mentioned you."

"Yeah . . . he talked about you all the time. I thought you were a coworker."

"At which of his fictional jobs?" This is so awkward it hurts. To make matters worse, Ryan's family has plenty of money; he's never needed to work. They're against it, focused on him getting good grades and participating fully in high school in order to get the best possible start. They've been looking at college brochures at the McKenna house since Ryan was fourteen.

Her pained gaze sparks with humor. "The one at the credit union."

"So he was a bank teller in his secret life?"

I wonder why she never went to see him at work. It seems like there would've been some natural moment in the last year where it all fell apart. Can it be that easy to live a double life? I mean, obviously I've heard about men who manage to have two wives, two families, but it sounds like an awful lot of effort. But if anyone could make it work, Ryan could. He's diabolically smart; I just never expected him to use his brain for evil.

"That's what he told me."

"I don't mean to be rude, but . . . why are you here? I'm guessing not just for a trim."

Cassie shrugs, looking upset and angry at the same time. "I told myself I'd just come in for a haircut—that I wouldn't even tell you who I was."

"Why did you?" In a way, I wish she hadn't.

"Because you're not like I thought you'd be."

I'm confused now. "Did he tell you something about me when he . . ."

"Broke up with me? Yes, he said he had feelings for you. That things between us hadn't been right in a while." She sighs softly. "And I knew that. I thought he might be cheating on me, or that the relationship was just dying from lack of time. I'm at the day-care center from nine to five, and then I work midnights at the pharmacy."

"Wow. You don't get much sleep, huh?"

"I usually pass out between six and eleven. Ryan and I were lucky to see each other once every couple of weeks. We'd Skype in between, send texts, but it wasn't the same."

"No." That explains why she never stopped to see him at work, however. No time. And really, if you trust someone, it never occurs to you that they could be inventing their whole life.

"I know he's a liar, but . . . did he cheat on me, too? It probably shouldn't matter, as I could do jail time for being with him, but I swear I didn't know." Tears stand in her big eyes, and I feel a fierce pang of pity for her.

114

"Hey, he lied, not you. You thought he was a bit younger, but not jailbait. It would've been weird if you'd carded him."

"I will, going forward," she mutters.

"And to answer you, no. He didn't cheat. At least, not with me. If there's someone else, I don't know about her."

"Where would he find the time?"

I laugh. "I have *no* idea. Learning about you shocked me, that's for sure."

"It's none of my business, but . . . are you . . . will you . . ." Cassie trails off, obviously embarrassed that she still cares about the jackass.

"No. Ryan can't have everything he wants, and that includes me."

She actually smiles. "I'm a bad person, but that makes me happy."

"Yeah, well. Nobody wants to break up with someone and then find out he's with somebody else a day later."

Grace calls, "Are you about done? It's time to lock up."

"Yes, she's squared away," I answer. Then dropping my voice, I ask, "Aren't you?"

She nods. "Thanks for your time. You're not like I thought you'd be."

I raise a brow as I gather up my belongings. "How's that?"

"Big hair, bright red lipstick, lots of spandex. Classic man stealer."

This is so far from the truth that I laugh. "I don't know any high school girls who look like that."

"I wasn't in a rational mood."

"Night!" I call to Grace.

Cassie walks out with me as the stylist turns out the lights behind us. My bike is chained to the rack nearby. There are only a few cars parked at the meters, as the businesses downtown close pretty early. I assume one of them belongs to her. With a smile in parting, I dig into my backpack and start taping my sleeves, so I will annoy as many drivers as possible on the way home.

"Night," I say, moving to unlock my ride. There's no way I'm saying it was nice to meet her.

"This might be totally out of line, but maybe you'd like to get a coffee sometime, just to make Ryan profoundly uncomfortable?"

I smirk and give her my cell number. "I could be persuaded."

"It won't be for a while. Like you said earlier, I don't sleep much. Which kinda makes it hard to have a normal social life."

"I'm finding it impossible to imagine Ryan as a booty call."

Cassie smiles slowly. "We had our problems, but . . . never that."

Uh. Wow.

Since I don't want to imagine Ryan having sex, I end the conversation by swinging onto my bike. With a wave, I take off down the sidewalk. I don't look back. Cassie wasn't like I thought she'd be either; I figured she must be sophisticated, but in fact, she didn't seem much more together than me. She's just a person, working hard, trying to save for college. On bad days, I imagine she's sad and exhausted; on good ones, she probably sees the light at the end of the tunnel, where she'll have enough cash to attend classes full time for a while. It's kind of revelational to realize that graduation doesn't also mean receiving all the answers. This is also depressing. I imagine being fifty-eight years old, still with no idea what the heck is going on.

As I ride home, I consider. Some of my friends, like Ryan, know what they want; he has his future all mapped out. He's going to

MIT, where he'll major in computer science. Others, like Conrad, are still living at home, three years after graduation, and he doesn't seem to have any plans at all. I fall somewhere in between. I definitely intend to go to college, and basically, my decision will be driven by the school that offers me the best scholarship. There's a college in Maine that I would love to attend; I've crunched the numbers and if I keep my grades up, I could earn a presidential scholarship at Unity, plus if I factor Aunt Gabby's income, I'll be eligible for some financial aid, too. We're doing okay, but we're not rich. If I do well on the SAT, it'll probably cost around eight grand a year, which would be sweet. I'd *love* to finish college without any student loans.

Before I know it, I'm turning down the drive to my house. Two and a half miles isn't that far, and it's still before nine. By this point I'm starving, though, so I can't wait to see what's for dinner. *Oh my God, yum.* She's made one of my favorite dishes, stuffed peppers.

"I'm home," I call.

"Good day?" My aunt's already eaten, judging by the plate beside her on the coffee table. I grab it and take it to the kitchen, then pull my plate out of the oven.

With a contented sigh, I plop down at the end of the sofa and then eat about half of my stuffed peppers, before remembering to praise her cooking. I'm afraid if I don't, she'll start doing takeout all the time. "This is so good. Uhm. Just so you know, we're apparently having a small party on Sunday."

"*How* small?"

"Like seven guests. We're having lasagna."

She cocks her head, thinking. "I have plans on Friday, but if you do the shopping on Saturday, we can put a couple of pans of lasagna together that night, and then bake them right before your friends come over on Sunday."

"Plans, huh? UPS Joe strikes again?"

Her cheeks color. "Just call him Joe."

"Noted. It's awesome you're letting me do this. I'd hate to tell everyone tomorrow that it's not on, after they ask their parents and everything."

"Next time, I'd appreciate more notice, but . . . this is a momentous occasion."

"It is?"

"You've never wanted to invite people over before." I hear the *ping* of happiness in her voice—that I'm doing normal things, making new friends, and having them to our house to eat pasta. If I'd known it would thrill my aunt this much, I'd have rounded up some random people to feed earlier.

"I guess not." It seems like a bad idea to tell her that this was a conversation that got away from me, not some master plan to come out of my shell. "I'll make sure to give you more than two days next time . . . and of course I'll do the shopping. I can get some salad stuff, too."

"Sounds good."

While my aunt watches TV, I finish my dinner, then take my plate to the kitchen and clean. I have to prove that I'm not more trouble than I'm worth. Life with my mom was hell, and the group home was just as bad—in a different way. Everything was regimented, and I had no privacy. The first month, I shared a room with a girl who kept trying to smother me. Eventually, the housemother caught her during a random bed check and she was relocated. They were always searching our rooms for contraband and taking away our scant privileges, but sometimes I couldn't *help* fighting. Sometimes it was self-defense.

I wash the dishes, wipe the counters and stove. The floor looks okay, so I'll leave it.

"You don't have to," she calls, but she hates cleanup.

Since I can't cook like she does, this division of labor makes sense. I'm learning, though. I can do a few of her recipes. Hopefully by the time I move out, I'll have a respectable number of dishes, so I don't wind up living on Maruchan. I had enough of that in elementary school, and I'm not looking to repeat the experience. Without noodles and gas station burritos, I probably would've starved. It's hard to imagine sometimes; there's such a demarcation between then and now, but once you've been truly hungry you never forget the feeling. And it's hard not to think about where the next meal is coming from.

It's ten, so I spend an hour on homework, and then fall in bed. It's one before I finally drift off, and even then, my sleep is sporadic, plagued by the Dream. There are half-empty liquor bottles everywhere. I break one. Another. The glass sprinkles over me. I walk on it, but there's no pain. I'm crying, but I can't feel it; my face is numb. The tears taste like salt in my dry mouth, and my feet are bleeding. The red stains crushed packs of cigarettes, and my toes nudge a bright yellow lighter. Yellow on a stoplight means caution, but I pick it up anyway.

Smoke and licking flames, and there's only my heartbeat pounding in my ears, my ragged breathing. I jolt upright in a pool of sweat. My aunt doesn't know the Dream is haunting me again, or she might insist I go back on meds. But I hate how they screw with my brain. I want to feel things, even if they're bad. I have to learn how to deal.

At six, I'm wide-awake, so I get up. Scramble some eggs. I do everything I can to be a good niece, a good kid. She's the only thing standing between me and the system; and on days like today, I feel irrationally scared that my good, safe life could inexplicably implode. It's the kind of fear that my old therapist would pick apart with a fine-tooth comb, asking me endless rounds of *why, why, why.* Then he'd offer me a new prescription.

I suspect I'm so nervous because I have a date with Shane tonight. I think.

School is school. There's no quiz in geometry, but I did my homework right. Now we're moving on to a new set of theorems, so I need more tutoring from Shane. I love that he waits for me after class, and that the jocks seem to have forgotten about him, mostly. Dylan gives us both a look, but he has bigger fish to fry, as from the loud convo, there's a senior walking around in a sweater vest and bow tie. Clearly that challenge cannot go unanswered.

Shane smiles as we step into the hall together. "I put in an application at the P&K."

"And?"

"When they found out I could work any hours, they hired me."

I hug him to celebrate the awesome, and when his arms go around me, I swear my heart skips a beat. He smells of laundry detergent, sunshine, and fresh air, no cologne, no body wash. And that works for me in a big way. I imagine pressing my lips to the curve of his jaw. In helpless reaction, I curl my fingers into his army jacket, hoping he won't notice my unsteady breathing. *His eyes are so, so blue . . .*

When somebody bumps us, I break away and head toward his locker. Shane is a few steps behind me, looking thoughtful. As he dials his combination, he says, "You know, it would save time if we just picked one and shared it."

I know some couples do this, but I've never—does this mean we're a couple? I wish I had a clue what's going on between us. If I was brave, I'd just kiss the hell out of him and see what happens. I lack the confidence for that maneuver. Also, I'm not exactly sure how to kiss.

So I just say, "Sounds good. Which?"

"Yours," he says.

"Okay. When do you want to move your stuff?"

"Might as well take care of it now."

So while I wait, astonished, he packs up his stuff and sticks most of it in his backpack. I carry a few odds and ends, and then we're at my locker. My hands shake as I dial the combination, so I need to do it twice. "Did you catch what it was?"

"No. Can you tell me?"

I raise up on tiptoe to whisper it, and I swear his eyes fluttered closed briefly, like he's really into me exhaling right there. It gives me a weird feeling to realize that Shane might be as into me as I am him. Or maybe I'm reading him all wrong because I so want him to be.

In two minutes, he's all moved in. My locker has more personality than his, as I've had the same one for two years, going on three. It's a desirable location as well, located in the main hallway, equidistant to all classes and departments. Shane pauses, examining the pictures I've cut out and stuck in the door. Unlike most girls I don't have a mirror, snaps of hot guys, or tiny plushies. He's seen the décor before, obviously, but he feels more investment now that he's sharing it, I guess.

"What are these places?"

"Pictures of countries that have better conservation and recycling programs than the U.S. I want to visit all of them and bring back ideas we can use here."

"That's pretty cool. How did you get so into this stuff?"

Nobody's ever asked me that before, and I struggle for an answer that won't give away too much. I'll tell him about myself . . . I owe him some answers after how open he was with me, but not here, not in school on the way to the cafeteria. So I eventually say, "I lived in a bad area when I was younger. I guess . . . I want to fix the world for other kids. Well, try anyway."

His expression reveals pure surprise. "I thought you'd been here longer. You seem really at home."

"No. I moved in with my aunt three years ago."

Questions stir in his eyes, but we're at the lunchroom, and our crew waves with mad enthusiasm. I can see that Mel already has lunch set out, and as we approach, they're all saying how awesome it is that we're hanging on Sunday. Operation Lasagna is a go.

Shane gives me a look that says he'll ask later. Tonight, probably, and I dip my head in silent acknowledgment. I don't know if I'm excited that he wants to know me or terrified about how he'll feel once he does.

CHAPTER
THIRTEEN

TONIGHT, AUNT GABBY HAS ANOTHER DATE WITH UPS
Joe. This time when he picks her up, I notice that he has kind eyes,
and he takes the time to chat with me while she putters in the bathroom, pretending to put the finishing touches on her face, but really
she's just making him wait. With some women, this would be a
power play, but with my aunt, it means she's nervous.

"You have plans tonight?" Joe seems like a good guy. I mean,
he's trying to make conversation.

"Yeah, we're seeing a movie."

"Which one?"

"I don't even know what's playing. It's not like we have a
choice."

He makes a face. "Small town."

"Pretty much."

Eventually, my aunt comes out, looking beautiful. I don't know
why she worries. Unlike their first date where she went for cool
sophistication, tonight she's wearing a bold pink-and-purple-print
dress with kicky retro shoes, chunky gold jewelry, and her hair up

in an adorably complicated twist. They must be going to dinner in a neighboring town, or possibly even the city, a fifty-five-minute drive on the highway.

"Where you taking her?" I ask Joe.

Some men might get irritated, but he answers me in a quiet, polite tone. "To Rudolfo's. We have reservations at eight."

Yep, he's taking her to the city. Rudolfo's is where the rich people eat before prom. Then they take a limo back to be dropped off at the country club in style.

"Have fun," I tell them both.

"Ryan's not coming over tonight?" My aunt knows I'm talking to Ry again, but things are still awkward between us, made more so by his quiet jealousy.

"Actually I'm going to see a movie with Shane."

Things have been so crazy, I forgot to tell her, but this works out better for me. In front of Joe, she won't go all hyper-protective and ask a million questions. She can't implore her date to stick around so she can meet mine without looking anal, plus it would ruin Joe's reservations. Aunt Gabby gives me a look that says we'll talk later.

"I can't wait to hear all about it," she says pointedly. "Be home by eleven."

"The movie will be out by ten or so, and there's nothing else to do. So . . . definitely."

I give Joe a smile as he sets a hand in the small of her back. It's not a gesture that casts aspersions on her competence, more a quiet assertion that he'll help if she needs it. After all, the driveway is rocky and she's wearing heels. She kisses my cheek on the way out, then I scramble to finish getting ready. Shane will be here in an *hour*, and I don't even know if this is a date.

Please let it be a date.

His comment about not expecting to find a friend echoes in my head. I can't glam up too much or it'll look like I'm trying too hard. Plus, I'll probably burn my hair off if I try to use my aunt's flat iron without supervision. In the end, I settle for jeans, a lacy sweater, and a T-shirt with sparkles on it, then it's time to decide what to do with my hair. The usual ponytail doesn't seem like a solution, so I brush it out and then aim the blow dryer at it for a few seconds. It's a little fluffy but not too big. I tame it with a squirt of product from Aunt Gabby's stash. She won't mind if I borrow some earrings to go with my silver key necklace, so I dig into her jewelry box and find some hoops.

That leaves makeup. I don't do foundation because to cover my freckles, I have to use too much and it looks caked on. Which leaves me with eyes and lips; I'm pretty good at those, though I don't bother for every day. Five minutes later, there's a knock. I scrub sweaty palms against my thighs as I move to answer, swinging the door wide to find Shane waiting. He looks as nervous as I feel; that makes things easier.

"Wow. You look beautiful. Not that you don't always." He's about to stammer something else, and I feel like kissing him.

I don't, obviously. That would take way more swagger than I possess.

He's wearing the usual boots and jeans, but he traded his T-shirt for a blue button up and he has on a black jacket instead of the army one. It's big on him, which makes me think it might be his dad's. But he made the effort, and I can't help thinking this means tonight counts as a date.

"Thanks. Ready to go?" I ask.

"Yeah. I hope you don't mind walking. My limo's in the shop."

I smile at that. "I wouldn't get in it, even if it was out front."

Shane tilts his head, looking surprised. "Come to think of it, I've never seen you in a vehicle of any kind."

Glad of this conversational opener, I explain my stance on the decadence of private cars burning fossil fuels. Cars also have pretty awful associations for me; my dad died in one. They took me away in one to foster care. When I was with my mom, I never rode in one, but afterward . . . well. That kind of stuff is too dark for a first date. Fortunately, Shane seems interested in the constructive reasons behind my boycott. This discussion carries us halfway downtown, mostly because he asks smart questions about how I cope in a small town with limited options for public transportation.

"It's not easy," I admit. "But I can ride my bike most places, and if I can't, then I just don't go. My aunt and I have taken the train to the city a few times, though." I add the last part so he doesn't think I advocate traveling by wagon.

"I admire your dedication," Shane says, smiling.

My weirdness probably also takes the pressure off him to have a car. Since he knows I don't want any part of that, he can't imagine the date would go better if he had a sweet ride. A few minutes later, he takes my hand in a casual gesture. Did he think about it at all or reach for me instinctively?

At night, the Capitol looks cool with the white bulbs surrounding the marquee. Darkness softens the dilapidated lines, lending the old building a certain grace. Ryan and I came here occasionally when there was a show we wanted to see, so I'm used to half the town turning out to buy tickets. Tonight, according to the misspelled title on the sign, there's a horror movie playing. I have no desire to see it, but I do want to sit in the dark with Shane. Somewhere in front, Ryan's laugh rings out. I stretch up on my tiptoes

126

and spy Gwen, Kenny, and Tara, along with my former best friend; I can't tell if they're on a double date, but I smother a laugh. *At least it's legal for Ryan to date Gwen*. Given Tara's general indifference to Kenny's interest, I figure they're just all hanging out. Shane's brows draw together, probably wondering why I'm laughing, then he spots the group ahead of us.

"They're funny for some reason?" he asks.

"It's just ironic to see Ryan here when I'm trying to avoid him. But it's a small town." I shrug, wishing I could explain fully.

Shane nods, like this makes perfect sense. But if he can accept my other off-kilter ideas and my refusal to ride in a car, he likely thinks this is just a postscript to strangeness. We move up as the cashier processes others ahead, then it's our turn at the window.

"Two, please." He speaks for both of us before I can even touch my wallet.

"Eight dollars."

Shane passes the girl a crumpled bill and she gives him back some change. So I murmur my thanks as we pass through the gilded doors into the faded luxury of the lobby. I nearly bump into Gwen, who doesn't register anything odd about the fact that she's with Ryan and I'm not.

She beams a Colgate smile. "I didn't know you guys were coming. You want to find some seats while we get the junk food? We can settle up inside."

Ha, this could be awkward. I'm *not* having my first date with Shane while Ryan looks on from three seats over.

"Thanks for the offer," Shane says, surprising me, "but we're fine."

Since Gwen tends to boss people around, she likely gets that response a lot, so she just smiles and waves. Ryan watches us walk away, and I'd be lying if I said I'm not happy that Shane's still holding my hand. The theater is already half full as we step into the aisle. He glances up and down before leading me to the left side of the theater. These rows are short—only four seats—compared to the ones in the center and we sit in the middle two seats, which should make it awkward for anyone to join us.

"Do you want popcorn or anything?" Shane asks, as we sit down.

I shake my head. "We can have a snack at my house after the movie."

There's no way my aunt will be home before eleven, and it'll be more like ten for us, even with the walk. That gives us some time alone, which makes me nervous and excited at the same time. With some guys, I'd worry about the message I'm sending, inviting him back to my house with nobody else around, but Shane won't pounce on me like a leopard. I've already been alone with him at his place, and he only touched me when I hugged him.

"Is that the plan?"

"If you want," I add, hoping I haven't assumed too much.

"Sounds good."

He's still holding my hand, and I'm aware of how much longer his fingers are than mine, slender and graceful; he has a musician's hands, with calluses that aren't just from playing guitar. He has those, too, but his palms are hard as well. I feel like fidgeting in my seat, but since he's calm, I pretend I am, too. I wonder if he has any idea how new all of this is to me. His comment about needing a friend echoes in my head. Still, a guy doesn't act like this with a girl unless he's dating her. Right? I study him out of the corner of my eye, trying to decide.

The previews start before I get too nervous, giving us something to look at besides each other. There's the usual product placement and trailers for flicks not yet released. Eventually the scary stuff starts, and I remember why I hate this kind of movie. I'm really susceptible, so I'm always the first one to jump or scream, but it's not all bad because halfway through the movie, Shane puts his arm around me and his thigh bumps against mine. My heart's not racing from the creepy noises anymore.

Forty-five minutes later, it turns out the nerdy guy was the killer, which surprises no one, but I have the shivers as we file out with the rest of the audience. I can stand monster movies better because they aren't real, but you never know when an actual psycho could be lurking in the bushes.

"What did you think?" Shane asks. "Worth the price of admission?"

"I was confused as to who was doing it until I realized that Reggie knew too much about the crime scenes. Overall it wasn't bad."

He grins down at me. "You hid your face through all of the murders."

Yeah, I did. I regret nothing. I can still feel the warmth of his shoulder against my cheek and the smell of his freshly washed shirt. The night is chilly, and I wish I'd worn a heavier coat. But that just makes me walk faster, putting distance behind us. It's half past nine by now, and I'm hungry, as I was too nervous to eat dinner before Shane picked me up.

"I'm a wimp," I admit.

"It's sweet. Will your aunt mind my coming over so late?"

"No." That's probably true, though she would prefer to meet him before leaving us alone together. "But she's on a date."

"So no awkward introductions tonight?"

"You dodged that bullet," I tell him. "What're you doing tomorrow?"

Belatedly I realize he might think I'm trying to lock him in for a second date and I stutter-step. I don't want him to think I'm desperate or anything. Luckily Shane doesn't notice my nerves. The sky has clouded over while we were inside and a light drizzle sprinkles down on us. I hope it doesn't pour before we get to my house. I walk faster; this is the downside of my vehicular limitations.

"It's my first night at the P&K. I'm working three shifts a week to start. The manager said I might get more hours if I'm reliable."

"Will that be enough to help?"

"Hell yeah. It's close to two hundred bucks a week, before taxes." In the moonlight, relief shines from his blue eyes.

"Do you get a store discount?"

"I wish," Shane says. "But no. Though I can have first pick of day-old pastries from the bakery, once they're marked down."

"You will live on donuts," I predict.

He laughs. "Watch. I'll get real food after I cash my first paycheck."

Shane teases me about the way I flinch at night noises and jump at shadows. Before I know it, we're outside my house. The lights are all off; Aunt Gabby's car is parked out front, but since she went to Rudolfo's with Joe, that doesn't mean anything. I let us in and slide the bolt behind us; I lived in scary places too long to feel safe with the doors unlocked, even in a town like this. I go around flipping on lights, not just because of the movie. As I look out, the drizzle turns into a downpour, rain coming down in sheets that I see rippling in the wind.

Shane looks around, admiring pictures of my aunt and me while I go into the kitchen. I don't ask if he's hungry. I just start making grilled cheeses. And these aren't ordinary sandwiches; I use sourdough bread, butter, and three kinds of cheese. While those are in the pan, I also open a can of tomato soup and start stirring, so it'll be ready around the same time. By the time he realizes I'm making food, it's pretty much done. I set the table for two, not wanting to deal with the stress of eating on the sofa. There's a zero percent chance that doesn't end with my shirt covered in red splotches.

"This is so good," he says, after the first bite.

No point in false modesty. "I *do* make a mean grilled cheese."

"I was talking about being here with you."

I have no idea what to say, but I feel heat creeping into my cheeks. Fortunately—or unfortunately—depending on your point of view, my phone rings. It's my aunt checking in, so I have to take it. I hold up a hand at Shane, motioning him to silence.

"How are things?" I ask Gabby.

"Good. But it's raining pretty hard and Joe's worried about the drive back." My aunt's never indicated she wanted to stay out all night before, so this feels oddly like she's asking my permission. The weather is an excuse.

"Don't take any chances," I tell her. "It's bad here, too."

"Are you sure you won't be scared?"

I glance at Shane. "No, I'm fine. I'm home already. The movie was fun."

It's not lying if she doesn't ask, right?

"Okay, Sage. Make sure you lock up and check all the doors and windows. I won't make a habit of this, I promise."

It's okay, I think. *You deserve a life.*

"I'm fine," I repeat. "Have fun. I expect all the hot, sweaty details tomorrow."

This is a safe joke because I know Aunt Gabby will never open her bedroom door to me. Proving me right, she makes a horrified noise, and I laugh, disconnecting the call. Shane has paused, waiting for me before he continues eating. This strikes me as incredibly polite.

He gives me a questioning look as we go on with our meal. "You're on your own tonight?"

"Apparently," I answer. "Do you want another sandwich or more soup?"

"If it's no trouble."

CHAPTER
FOURTEEN

I'M GLAD HE'S NOT COMPLAINING ANYMORE ABOUT how I feed him like a stray dog. That's not it at all; I just can't stand anyone going hungry, mostly because I had my share of it, growing up. Shane's not a helpless kid like I was, but I can't change how I respond to his situation. Efficiently, I fry another grilled cheese and pour the rest of the tomato soup into his cup.

"At school, you said you lived in a bad area before." It's not a question.

I get that he deserves to know more about me, but I can't spill everything. Not yet. The whole truth will probably change how he sees me. But . . . this is the first time I've wanted to let anyone else all the way in—and it's fairly terrifying.

So I nod. "Before I moved here, I lived in a scary part of Chicago with my mother."

"Where is she now?" he asks.

Sickness roils in my stomach. "Gone."

All kinds of questions percolate in his gaze, but this isn't something I can confide over bowls of soup. In fact, nobody here knows about my life before I moved. At first it was because I was struggling so hard to keep my head above water, and then my silence came from shame. I didn't want anyone to know the girl I was before. In order to survive, I had to reinvent myself. I glimpse the moment he decides my mother abandoned me . . . and she did, when I was a baby. But the whole truth is *so* much worse.

"What about your dad?"

That's simultaneously easier . . . and harder. "When I was seven, he died in a car wreck."

"Oh God, Sage."

This, I can talk about with him, an offering out of respect for what he shared the other day. "I was in second grade . . . the police came to school."

In halting words, I tell Shane how I sat outside the principal's office after the teacher pulled me out of class, wondering what I did, why I was in trouble. Up until that point, my life was pretty normal. Like other people, I had one parent at home. My dad had a mail route; I took the bus to after-school daycare, where he picked me up around four thirty. But that day, I sat for half an hour outside the main office waiting for someone to explain all the whispering and sad looks. Eventually, a policewoman came and said, "I'm sorry, honey."

I stayed at school for a long time while they tried to figure out what to do with me. My dad didn't have any near relatives on file, so I ended up with a foster family in the district. The courts thought it was best not to disrupt my routine any more than necessary, but I'd just lost my dad. Everything was messed up, and it got worse when the system located my mother.

I stop talking then. This feels like a fair distribution of facts; he knows one of my secrets and I know one of his. I take a deep breath because it's hard talking about my dad. He was a good guy, who made pancakes with smiley faces on Sunday mornings. He took me to the park and he helped me with my homework. But when your whole world hinges on one person, it's like a house of cards that collapses at the first gust of wind. Yet when things were at their worst with my mom, I clung to those memories. In the end, they weren't enough to keep me from the flames.

"Wow," he says softly. "You really *do* understand."

I'm glad he didn't offer sympathy for my loss. That's bullshit. Most people who spout platitudes have no idea how you feel, the way loss chews at you until you're a bottomless hole. They just want to fill an awkward silence.

"Maybe not exactly." I've never nursed anyone I cared about, but I know the feeling once they're gone.

"Closer than anyone else." Shane's got this look in his eyes, like he's about to open some door between us.

"Are you done?" I ask.

He nods, so I take our plates and stack them in the sink. The rain patters on the roof, but it's warm and cozy inside. I head back into the living room and turn on the TV. There's never anything on—we don't have cable since Aunt Gabby thinks it's a waste of money—but we have a decent DVD collection. I drop onto the sofa and wave toward the shelves.

"Pick something."

Shane puts in a slightly campy movie filled with aging action heroes. Then he sits beside me, though I didn't leave him much choice by picking the middle of the couch. I'm glad when he puts an arm around me, so I can settle against him. We watch for a few minutes in silence, but I'm too conscious of his fingers on my shoulder to pay much attention.

Trying to seem relaxed, I turn my head to say something about the plot and realize he's really close. In fact, I've caught him smelling my hair. He freezes like it's not okay, and embarrassment raises red flags in his cheeks.

He pulls back with a mumble. "Sorry. I didn't mean to—"

"I don't mind." I'm trying to tell him so much more than that, but I don't have the words.

Neither of us is watching the movie. He's just staring at me through his tousled curls. Shane shakes his hair out of his face, eyes intent on mine.

"So this is definitely a date?" I ask.

"What do you think?"

"I wasn't sure. You said you needed a friend—"

"And *I* wasn't sure what your deal was. Everyone thought you'd just broken up with your boyfriend of two years, but *you* claimed you were never together. So what was I supposed to say when you showed up at my house?"

Put in that context, it was surprising he hadn't suspected I was crazy. You don't get over a long relationship and move on that fast, unless there's something messed up in your head. "I'm glad you gave me the benefit of the doubt. I mean . . . you did, right? You believe me or you wouldn't be here." I remember how he suspected I might be using him to make Ryan jealous.

"Yeah. But I have to ask. Do you go after *all* guys you like this way?"

"All I did was bring you some soup," I say, indignant.

"And multiple lunches. You also got me involved in your environmental group, then invited me to Sunday lunch with your other friends and your aunt. Plus, you found me a job indirectly."

Put that way, it does sound like I've made a project of him, but it wasn't a conscious endeavor. As far as the P&K goes, I only wanted to *help*, plus it's not like I ran around town. Big deal, I asked my aunt if she knew of anything, then Shane got the job on his own. The other stuff just kind of happened.

"I had nothing to do with you coming to help clean up the lot," I mumble.

Which is true. I didn't invite him; he volunteered.

Shane smiles. "You had everything to do with it. I wouldn't have been there if you weren't. And you still didn't answer my question."

The heat in my cheeks actually burns, and I can't meet his gaze. "*No.* I've never liked anyone before. I mean, last year, I had a bit of a crush on Ryan, but he didn't seem interested, so I left it alone. It seemed better not to ruin our friendship." I lift my chin to check if he believes me.

His eyes darken at the words *crush* and *Ryan*. "You need to explain exactly what happened there. I know he's not happy with me, but I don't understand the problem. If you liked him last year and people thought you were already going out . . ." He's getting tense, I can tell, and he said he doesn't want any drama.

"You have to promise not to tell anyone," I whisper.

"I'll keep it off my vast gossip network." The irony in his tone doesn't escape me.

So I give him the rundown on everything that's passed between us: how we were the best of friends and then I bailed, after learning how he used me to keep anyone from suspecting his real secret. When I finish, Shane looks as shocked as my aunt Gabby.

"That tall, skinny kid? Really?"

I nod. "And I've *met* Cassie."

"So where do I fit in all of this?"

I realize then; he doesn't understand that I'm just . . . drawn to him. He's trying to figure out the reasons. "You don't. Ryan has nothing to do with why I'm hanging out with you."

"Then I don't get it. I'm nothing special."

"You are to me."

There's no way to explain why some people like coffee and others prefer tea. And that's how I feel, frustrated because Shane thinks I have an agenda. But it also tells me he's insecure, too, which is reassuring. With all my other issues, trying to date would be worse if he was all smooth and experienced.

"I'm not used to this," he says softly. "I was pretty invisible at my old school . . . until I started causing trouble. Then I became That Kid. Everyone saw me after my mom died, but nobody wanted to. I was just another problem to solve."

"I *do* want to help, but only because I'm wired that way. I'm not trying to fix you." I hesitate before adding, "I don't see you as broken."

Not like me. And I'm so afraid that if I tell you everything, you won't see me as more than the pieces they swept up after.

Shane lets out a shaky breath, running a hand through his hair. "At this point, I should probably say, stay away from me. I don't have anything good to give you right now, but then I think about not talking to you anymore and my chest hurts."

"I can't," I point out. "You moved into my locker. Look, we'll take it one day at a time. It's pretty clear I don't know what the hell I'm doing. So . . . relax."

"I don't know how to be a boyfriend," he warns me.

I cock a brow at him, smiling. "That's too bad . . . since I have a PhD in girlfriendology from the University of So Many Feelings."

He laughs, as I intend. Then he's leaning toward me. I have a panicked moment when I worry that I won't know what to do, but when he tilts his head, I go the other way automatically, and it's pretty natural when our lips meet. He kisses me tenderly, and it's everything a first kiss should be. I sink my hands into his curls as his arms go around me. Shane's so warm, his lips moving on mine in slow, gentle glides. It's a sunbeam of a kiss, all delicious heat and lazy pleasure. When Shane pulls away, I can't restrain a ridiculous smile. He seems pleased with himself, cuddling me close so we can pretend to watch the rest of the movie. By the time it ends, it's after midnight and the storm has worsened.

"You're not walking home in this," I tell him.

"I wasn't looking forward to it. Are you asking me to stay over?"

"Not for sex." It seems best to make that clear.

"Damn." Obviously teasing, he makes a mock-disappointed face, as if he really thought that was on the table. "I can take the couch—"

"I'd rather have you with me." This is a unique opportunity to be close to Shane, so I can't look a gift horse—or storm—in the mouth. We can probably make do in my bed. It's a daybed, but if we curl up close, it should work. Aunt Gabby has a bigger one, but it would be too weird to sleep in there with Shane. It's odd as I go about the nightly check, which my aunt usually performs. She looks at all the windows and doors, making sure everything is fastened and bolted. Two women living alone can't be too careful, she says, and I appreciate that she doesn't call me a kid.

"Do you do this every night?" he asks.

"My aunt does."

After I'm sure the house is as safe as we can make it, I turn out most of the lights and lead the way back to my bedroom. Then I find Shane a large University of Michigan shirt that my aunt stole from some past boyfriend and never gave back. I'm wondering, *Do we have spare toothbrushes in the bathroom? I think so.* Aunt Gabby buys stuff when it's on sale. So I pull a new blue one from an open package and hand it to him.

"You can wash up and change in the bathroom."

This isn't a normal date; I know that much. They usually end because somebody has a curfew, or people waiting at home, but the way things have worked out, nothing is ordinary between us. And maybe that's how it should be.

While he's occupied, I put on my pajamas quickly. I'm grateful they're long-sleeved because I don't want to have that conversation with him tonight. Most people don't notice, but I've always got on a sweater, shrug, or hoodie, covering my arms. For some girls, it might be the fact that their biceps aren't toned enough, but I'm hiding something else entirely.

Shane grins when he sees me in the green thermal jammies. Clearly I've dressed for seduction. But he's still wearing his jeans, though he's barefoot now and I can see he's washed his face. I still need a turn in the bathroom.

"You can take them off," I say, embarrassed. "You have on boxers, right?"

He nods. As I head off to brush my teeth, I tell myself it's no different from shorts and a T-shirt and I'm wearing enough clothes for both of us. I putter, taking more time than usual. When I get back, he's already in bed. He's left the cushions behind him, pressed up against the back of the daybed to leave me more room. It's a good idea and if I sleep on my side, too, we should manage. I flick off the light, then walk toward him, wondering if he's as nervous as I am. What if I snore or drool? We don't know each other well enough to get past that. *Do we?* In some ways, it feels like I've known him forever, as if I've waited for him twice that long.

Crazily, it feels like this is exactly where we're supposed to be.

CHAPTER
FIFTEEN

LYING IN SHANE'S ARMS IS THE BEST THING IN THE
world.

I mean, it takes us a while to work out the perfect position—
and there's some awkward squirming—but once I settle against his
chest, I feel like a bomb could go off and I'd still be safe. I'm not
used to that feeling. The last time I had it, I was with my dad. When
I was little, he'd always take me to see the Fourth of July parade
and he'd toss me up onto his shoulders, so I could see better and I
never once thought he'd let me fall. Snuggled up against Shane,
that's exactly how I feel right now. Well, the security part, not the
dad part. Not even close.

"Can I ask you something?"

He stirs against me, moving his hand over my back. "I think
you just did."

"What was it like with your mom?" Maybe the question is too
personal, but I want to understand him, and this seems like the
obvious place to start.

"There were good days and bad days. When she was in

remission, I could pretend everything was fine. She did more then. Worked on her songs."

"She was a musician, too?"

"Yeah. She's the one who taught me to play the guitar. I can't remember a time when she wasn't singing . . . except at the very end."

"Alto or soprano?"

"Alto. When I was a kid, I thought all moms made up songs about broccoli."

"She sounds like she was wonderful."

Shane nods; I feel the movement against my head. That's how close we are. Maybe it's easier for him to talk about her because it's dark and he can't see my face. "It's been nine months, but sometimes I forget. Like, I wake up in a panic because I can't remember if she's had all her meds."

"I have bad dreams, too." Hopefully he won't ask about them. I also hope he doesn't think I'm saying that for attention. I just want him to know that he's not alone.

"Not tonight," he promises. "Not when we're together."

"You either."

"I feel okay," he says.

That's enough to make me smile. "Night," I whisper.

I expect to have trouble sleeping, but the next thing I know, it's morning with light shining through my window and birds making a racket outside. (Did I ever mention that I hate birds?) Shane looks cute, even at this hour. He's grown faint scruff on his jaw and his lashes are tangled, giving glimpses of his blue eyes like glimmers of sky through a canopy of leaves. He's smiling, I think, as I roll out of bed. I'm a little stiff from staying in the same position all night, but nothing serious.

I'm weirdly nervous and excited at the same time. I've never slept with anyone before, not even girls at sleepovers because life with my mom didn't permit anything like that . . . and I didn't have any close girlfriends before this year. Besides, I don't think Lila would want to spoon in my bed even if she did stay over. I picture her camping out on the floor instead.

"You want some breakfast?" I ask.

According to my alarm clock, it's 8:10. I can't imagine Joe will bring my aunt back too early, so we have time. It's nearly an hour from the city, too. Shane rolls out of bed and scrambles into his jeans so fast that I don't see much, then I'm left thinking about morning wood. He was holding me away from him, so I wonder—

He interrupts my blush-inducing thoughts with, "Yeah, that'd be nice. Then I need to get home. I have some things to do before my shift."

As I look on, Shane swaps the U of M tee for his button-up and I suddenly have butterflies in my stomach. His bare chest is . . . delicious. He's lean and strong without being too muscled. I don't let on that I've never seen a half-naked guy up close and personal before. It's my private opinion that I should win an Oscar for being *so very cool* about all of this.

I search my brain for reasonable response. "When do you work?"

"Three to eleven, Saturday, Monday, and Tuesday."

I'm pleased to hear he'll have Fridays free, though I can't assume he'll want to do this every week. And he certainly can't stay over all the time. "Noted."

In the kitchen, I whip up some scrambled eggs and toast. He eats quickly, but I think it's a sign that he's worried about being here when my aunt gets home. Afterward, he leans down to kiss me. For a few seconds, I forget my own name.

I'm dazed when he says, "See you tomorrow?" like that's a question.

"Yeah. That reminds me . . . I told my aunt I'd do the shopping for tomorrow's lunch. So when I show up at the P&K, don't assume it's because I'm stalking you."

"If I was going to think that, it would've been when you showed up at my house, out in the middle of nowhere."

He has a point—and it's closer to true than I'd like to admit. "Then see you later, maybe."

"Do you want me to help you clean up?" I shake my head, but he totally gets twenty gold stars for offering. "Later, Sage."

Shane shrugs into his jacket and he's out the door at a quick jog. I'd like to say I don't stand at the window to watch until he turns off my street. That would be a lie. Eventually I get motivated enough to clean the kitchen and hide the evidence of my sleepover. I feel so awful; this is the first truly bad thing I've done since I got here. So I work like crazy all morning to make up for it. The house is spotless by the time Aunt Gabby sweeps in at ten; she doesn't have time to do anything but change her clothes before work. I'm glad Joe doesn't come in. Though I like the guy well enough, I'm not eager to make conversation on a Saturday morning, especially when I suspect he boned my aunt the night before.

"You have enough money to buy stuff for tomorrow? If not, there's some cash in the coffee can," she tells me as she sweeps out the door.

"Bye!" I call, feeling guilty that she trusts me and here I let a boy spend the night.

She can never find out. She thinks you're better, that you're good.

I do a couple hours of homework while ignoring the *ping* of texts from Ryan. Once I finish, I check my phone, still in my bag from the night before. To my surprise, they're not just from Ryan. I have messages from multiple people, including Lila and the sophomores.

Text from Ryan: **did u have fun last night**

Text from Lila: **will pick u up at 7:15, ok?**

I realize then that I haven't asked my aunt if I can go to a party at the Barn. She thinks we're making lasagna tonight. *Crap.* Having a social life is complicated. The other messages are confirming the time for lunch tomorrow. Quickly I send replies: **yes, yes,** and **2:30, see you then.**

If I do some prep work, we can probably put together the pasta before I leave with Lila. So I head to the market to do the shopping, then I get to work in the kitchen.

Later, when Aunt Gabby calls, I say, "All we need to do is finish up when you get here."

"This much ambition means you want something."

She's sharp, my aunt. "Y'know. I forgot to ask earlier, but . . . is it okay if I go with Lila to a party out at the Barn tonight? Transportation is covered."

"No drinking to excess," she says. "And be home by midnight."

It's cool that she doesn't ask if there will be liquor or parental supervision. Since my aunt grew up here, she knows what goes on out at the Barn, and I'm sure she partied out there a time or two, back in the day. Instead she trusts me not to drink until I vomit or do anything ridiculous.

"Done," I promise.

"And I expect to hear about Shane while we fix the lasagnas. Those are my terms."

"I accept."

Just then, I hear the bell jingle, which means she has an actual customer, not an order from the interwebs. "Gotta go. See you in a bit."

I spend the rest of the day getting ready for the party. This is my first time, but I figure nobody dresses up, so I go with jeans and a sparkly cream sweater. In the dark, I doubt anybody will notice, but I think it's pretty. Then I put on an apron in case I manage to get red sauce on me. I'll do my hair and makeup after we finish.

When my aunt gets home, I have everything set out with military precision. She laughs at how prepared I am. "You really want to go, huh?"

"Yeah," I admit. "I'd like to see what it's all about."

"I'm really glad to see you branching out, making new friends. I'm looking forward to meeting them all tomorrow."

"Should be fun."

"So . . . Shane," she prompts, filling the bottom of the pan with lasagna noodles.

Aunt Gabby is a pro at putting all of this together, so I stand back. I've done my share by getting it all ready and I'll handle the salad tomorrow, plus cleanup. Taking a seat at the table, I watch while she spoons in the veggie and soy filling, cottage cheese, mozzarella, then the next layer of pasta.

"He's phenomenal."

"Two words aren't getting you to a party tonight."

I grin . . . and recount how the date went. Pretty much the only things I leave out are the kissing and the fact that he spent the night in my bed. I tell her that he's a gifted guitar player and that he applied at the P&K after she told me about the HELP WANTED sign and that he got the job to help out with family expenses. I don't share that his dad is a long-haul trucker who doesn't even live with him. *Asshole.*

"A musician, huh?" Her smile seems extra curvy. "I dated one in college. Just wait until he writes you a song. That's a guaranteed panty-dropper."

"You *did not* just say that. In fact, I'm pretty sure you're not allowed to use that phrase."

She shrugs as she puts the lasagna in the fridge. "You're sixteen. Get over it."

So Aunt Gabby only gets awkward and embarrassed when discussing *her* prospective sex life. Mine is apparently fair game. I mumble something about doing my hair and makeup and escape to my bedroom. As I'm getting ready, I wonder if there will be a bonfire out at the Barn—what it'll be like exactly. This is what cool people do on weekends instead of seeing movies or hanging out in the square.

Just past seven thirty, Lila pulls up in the promised golf cart. I laugh when I see it because the thing is totally decked out with running lights. It looks like somebody featured it on an episode of *Pimp My Ride*. Aunt Gabby stares out the window, eyes wide.

"Are you two kidding me with this?"

"How did you think I was getting there?"

"Eh. I figured you probably caved on the car thing."

I shake my fist, making a supervillain face. "Never!"

Then I shrug into my vintage faux-leather jacket. It has a nicely grungy look to it and a vaguely military air. Overall, I look pretty good, so I'm feeling confident as I peck my aunt on the cheek, grab my bag, and run out to join Lila before she reconsiders this idea.

"How many people honked at you on the way over here?" I ask, climbing in.

"Six."

"Seriously?" I want to ask if it bothers her, but she's grinning, so that would be a no.

"Yep. But this thing's fun to drive. I kick it up to the highest setting and it gets pretty close to thirty miles an hour." I have no idea if that's fast, and I guess she can tell. "Normal ones do fifteen."

I wave to my aunt as we pull away. Lila is careful to take back roads as we leave the subdivision and head out into the country. A few cars honk at us as they pass, but since the drivers are smiling and waving, it doesn't seem like a big deal. The cops might be less amused, but the farther we get from town, the less likely it is anyone will bother us. Since the golf cart is open, it's cold as hell, but worth it when the alternative is riding in a car. It takes about half an hour to get to the Barn, and by that time, it's pretty late. There's a fire crackling away, sending orange sparks up toward the dark sky. I'm glad to see it, as I wish I'd worn a scarf and gloves. Beyond, there are a bunch of cars parked in the field. Lila picks a spot where she's not likely to be blocked in. Somebody must be in charge of the music because it's blasting from one of the trucks.

"This is it," she says. "Impressive enough for you?"

"I guess." I hop out of the golf cart, ready to be amazed.

"Let me give you the grand tour. Here, we have the social types." Lila gestures.

The ones she indicates are clustered around the fire while others run around. By the stumbling, it seems like they're already pretty wasted. I follow Lila across the uneven ground, glad I opted for boots instead of Chucks. She points at the drunken game of tag.

"Those are the hard-core drinkers. They were probably toasted *before* they got here."

"Note to self—avoid the pro drinkers to keep them from hurling on me."

Lila grins at me. "In some cases, you'll have to be quick. That guy's kind of a ninja barfer."

"Why, God, why?" I mumble.

"Hey, you wanted to come."

I answer her smile with a smirk. "I feel like Jane Goodall, studying apes in the wild."

"Take good notes. Maybe you can publish your findings later." She continues by pointing at the open barn doors. "Inside, you'll find couples doing things they should reserve for seedy hotel rooms and the backseats of cars. Beware the hayloft."

"Do you *know* how scratchy hay actually is?"

"Not firsthand. But I'm not the kind to put out in a barn, regardless of what Dylan says."

I touch her shoulder lightly. "He's an asshole. Let's go see who's here."

She ignores the kegs and the coolers full of beer. Luckily I spot some Cokes mixed in with the Budweiser and grab two of them for us. I'd prefer hot chocolate or tea, but this is strictly low-rent. A few people have brought bags of marshmallows and packs of hot dogs. I take the former from a guy who might be in my chemistry class. Because I have nothing better to do, I focus on toasting my marshmallow to the perfect shade of light brown. This feat requires absolute patience.

I'm about to eat the perfect marshmallow when Dylan Smith says, "Wow. I can't believe you have the nerve to show up here, Lila."

In the flickering firelight, her face is pale and tense. Given how much he hates her for breaking up with him, there's no way this doesn't get ugly.

CHAPTER SIXTEEN

"YOU NEED TO LEAVE HER ALONE," I SAY QUIETLY.

Dylan doesn't even notice when I join them; he's too focused on Lila to see anything else. She wasn't kidding when she said he was abnormal about their breakup. It's like he can't accept that anyone would leave him. I'm unsure if that makes him conceited or insane.

"Fuck off, you fat bitch. This doesn't concern you."

The people in our immediate area quiet, not wanting to miss a minute of this. But there's no way I'm letting this go further. He has no right to screw with Lila when we're here like everyone else, hanging out on a Saturday night. Dylan Smith has been making Lila's life hell since she had the nerve to dump his loser ass, but she's my friend, and I'm not having it. I grab Dylan's arm.

"Actually it does. Come on." Shadow Sage surges to the front of my brain, all darkness and destruction. She knows exactly how to break this little shit, and for the first time in three years, I'm going to let her.

"Looks like the Princess is hot for you," one of his friends calls.

"It's to be expected." Surprise colors his tone, despite the cocky words, and he follows me more out of curiosity than anything else.

Once I get him away from the others, I drop his arm like it's a snake about to bite me. "So here's the deal. You leave Lila alone. You don't talk to her. You don't talk *about* her. You don't look at her. You don't even think about her. Matter of fact, that goes for all my friends. You and your crew just steer clear from now on, got me?"

"You're crazy—"

"I'm not." I cut off his bluster with a hard look. "See, even though you're a complete dickhead, I suspect you love your mom. Even if she's banging Principal Warick . . . the very married Principal Warick. I'm sure you get tired of people telling you what a MILF your mother is. Imagine how much worse it could be, if people found out she's having an affair—"

"Shut up." Dylan lunges at me, clamping a hand over my mouth.

There are enough people in view that I'm not worried he'll do more. If he tries, I'll show him all the ways I can make him hurt. Because I'm only playing the role of nice girl; I've spent a portion of my life as something else entirely.

In a small town like this one, Tamara Smith, the hot school secretary, draws censure for how she dresses, the amount of makeup she wears, and for the way she'd allegedly cheated on her husband— and that's why he left. Whatever the truth, she's definitely doing Principal Warick. I've seen them kissing, but I never would've brought it up if Dylan didn't made a career of screwing with two people I care about: Lila and Shane.

He applies more pressure, almost enough to bruise my jaw. So I bite him.

Dylan lets go, hate warring with unease in his eyes. He stumbles back a few steps, then he yells to his friends, "These bitches aren't worth it."

I take one breath, another, watching him walk away. Time to put the scary back in the box. The athletic crew disappears around the side of the barn, then Lila heads over, looking astonished. "What the hell did you say to him?"

By the time, I turn to face her, I've got my mask back in place. I shrug. "I just made it clear he can't mess with you anymore."

"I hope you don't regret this. Dylan isn't known for letting shit go."

"Maybe he's turning over a new leaf."

Lila still seems doubtful but I don't reveal anything. If I tell her, she might repeat it, and then I'll lose my leverage. My anger at Dylan writhes like a snake twining and tightening around my intestines, but this is where I stop. It takes all my willpower to smile and eat my marshmallow, which has cooled off nicely. The rest of the party is quiet compared to the beginning. I play a game of beer pong, set up on two sawhorses and a plywood board; my team loses, mostly because I suck. After that, Lila and I dance by the bonfire while various guys try to hit on us. That's . . . different.

Eventually, I get bored and by that point, Lila's ready to head out, too. The golf cart is easy to maneuver around the cars, so we set out for my place.

"Is it okay if I stay over?" she asks as we pull up outside my house. The lights are still on in the living room, which means my aunt is probably dozing on the sofa.

"If it's cool with your mom, I'm sure my aunt won't mind."

"I already asked her." She's been weird and quiet on the drive home. Now she sounds subdued, like she's thinking about something else.

I grin. "Glad I could conform to plans you already made."

As she hops down from the golf cart, she says, "Seriously, Sage, I hope this doesn't blow back on you. While I appreciate the way you stood up to Dylan for me, I have a bad feeling."

"Don't worry about it. Whatever Dylan thinks he can do, I guarantee I've been through worse." I don't mean to tell her so much, but Lila's gaze sharpens.

"You never talk about what it was like before you moved here."

Instead of answering, I dig into my bag for my key, then step inside. Sure enough, my aunt is crashed out on the couch, her head back, while the TV is stalled on the DVD menu. I turn everything off quietly and then kiss my aunt on the head.

"I'm home. Lila's with me. You can go to bed now."

Aunt Gabby's bleary gaze finds the wall clock. "Thanks for getting in before midnight."

"No problem. The party was kind of boring anyway. I don't know if I'll go to another."

"Not your thing, huh? Well, at least you tried something new." My aunt flashes a sleepy smile in Lila's direction, then pads toward her bedroom.

"She's so cool."

"Agreed," I say.

I unroll an old sleeping bag and set up on the floor. The rug on the wood floor is fluffy enough that it should serve as another layer of padding. While I'm doing that, Lila heads for the bathroom, and when she comes back, she looks much younger without makeup. The red hair seems extra bright against her pale, clear skin.

I point at the bed. "You sleep there. My aunt will kill me if I put a guest on the floor."

"I guess since you're my bodyguard, I have to listen to you."

"At some point, I'll remind you that you said that."

She smirks.

Laughing, I go brush my teeth. By the time I get back, she's settled in my daybed, and I wonder if the sheets smell like Shane. This is the most traffic my room has ever seen. I'm unsure what the deal is, if we're supposed to whisper until we fall asleep or if the night's basically over. I make a show of snuggling down into the sleeping bag, letting her decide.

"You don't have a TV in your room," Lila says softly.

"No, we just have the one. My aunt got it so we can watch movies. No cable. It's supposed to motivate me to read more." Though I don't say so, I need little encouragement to stick my nose in a book. I've loved fiction since I was a kid in need of rescuing.

"I hope she doesn't talk to *my* mom."

"She's not like that. She doesn't proselytize."

"Somebody's dropping her SAT vocab words."

"Bet you don't get that from the burner crowd."

Lila laughs. "That's why I'm here on Saturday night, not watching them smoke."

Her mention of the lack of a television clues me in; she isn't used to falling asleep when it's quiet. "I can turn on some music. I have an iPod."

"Go for it."

I rummage in the dark until I find my nano, then I set it on shuffle and click in place in the dock on my alarm clock. "Better?"

"Yeah, thanks."

"Night."

To my surprise, Lila seems in no hurry to leave the next morning. Instead, she helps with breakfast, then the three of us watch an old romantic comedy about losing a guy in ten days. Before long, it's time to straighten up the house and get ready for our guests. My stomach is a mass of butterflies, not only because Shane's coming over, but also because he's meeting my aunt for the first time and Ryan will be here too, maybe.

I've dropped my hairbrush for the third time when Lila says, "You okay?"

"Not really," I mumble.

She's pretty good at getting the truth out of people; with pointed questions, soon she knows exactly what's on my mind. "Is that all?" she asks, once I'm finished talking. "If you want, I'll take Ryan off your hands."

I stare at her. "What does that even mean?"

"I'll keep him from fixating and making things awkward, promise."

Now I have visions of Lila draping herself across Ryan's lap, but I'd pay to see his face if she does, so I nod. "Go for it."

It's a last-minute scramble to get both the lasagnas baked, and I'm pouring the salad into a big wooden bowl when the doorbell rings. Aunt Gabby trots down the hall, calling, "I'll get it."

Kimmy and Shanna arrive together, followed shortly by Theo, Tara, and Kenny. Mel's dad drops her off next, and she's brought homemade rolls, which Shanna says makes everyone else look bad.

Everyone is kind of milling around—God, how did I get into this—when Shane knocks. Maybe it sounds dumb, but I recognize his tap: *bum-bum, bum-bum-bum*; it's more musical and rhythmic than anyone else's.

I manage to be cool as I swing the door open. But my first sight of him since he left yesterday morning steals both my breath and my good intentions. He's wearing black skinny jeans with black sneakers, a white shirt, and a black faux-leather jacket. His tousled hair falls into his eyes as he smiles at me, then bends to kiss me. His lips brush mine, soft and warm, carrying the faint tinge of mint. Shane acts like it's easy, but I'm tied in knots, hardly able to move, because I don't know if my knees will hold me or I'll end up against the wall, grinning like a reject. Ryan comes up the walk then and, judging by his expression, he saw the kiss.

"Hey," I say to both of them.

The guys step past me into the house. Since our kitchen can't accommodate this many people, Aunt Gabby has set up a couple of card tables, but they're covered with red-and-white-checkered cloths. The white vases with red silk carnations make it look like we're running an Italian bistro. As I run around, I perform breathless introductions. For a few minutes, it's a constant rush of getting plates out, serving this and that, but pretty soon, we're all seated, devouring the veggie lasagna and salad, along with the rolls Mel donated to the cause. True to her word, Lila manages to get Ryan next to her, and from his puzzled expression, he has no idea what's going on. But he seems okay with the attention.

Lunch is loud, which gives me no chance to talk to Shane. Mostly, I enjoy Aunt Gabby's pleasure in being a hostess. After everyone's done eating, I carry the plates into the kitchen and close the galley door, so nobody can see the mess. I have no idea what to do with these people now that we've fed them, but Lila is good at this kind of thing. She finds a terrible SF movie in our collection, which encourages everyone to shout commentary at the screen. Soon Ryan is replacing all the dialogue with his own improv, delivered in a Russian accent. He's supposed to sound like Borat, but given how bad he is, I'm probably the only one who knows this.

Around six, parents pull up out front. Eventually, it's just Ryan, Lila, Shane, and me. Ry puts his hand on my arm and says in a subdued voice, "This was fun."

"Yeah. You can have the party at your place next time."

He gives me a hopeful look. "Would you come?"

"If it's a bunch of us, sure."

Just then, his mom leans on the horn and he hurries out with a general good-bye and a call of "Thanks!" for my aunt.

"No problem," Aunt Gabby yells back.

At last, Lila decides she should head out, too, and she hugs me. Her eyes are yelling, *Text me as soon as he leaves.* "This was really fun. See you tomorrow."

"So . . . that was nuts," Shane says as the door closes.

"Yeah. But on the plus side, my aunt didn't have a chance to interrogate you."

"Is she likely to do that now?" he asks, looking faintly alarmed.

I shake my head. "You want to go for a walk? I could use some fresh air."

"Sounds good."

After heading down the hall, I tap on Aunt Gabby's door. "Shane and I are going out. Don't worry about cleanup. I'll take care of it when I get back."

"Where are you headed?"

"Probably to the Coffee Shop." It's not like there's much to do here on a Sunday night.

"Be back by nine," she says.

"Not a problem. I still have homework . . . and Shane probably does, too."

He nods at this. "Plus it's a long walk home."

If I could think of a way for Aunt Gabby to drive him that wouldn't end in a bunch of awkward questions, I'd ask her. "Come on. The weather won't be warm enough for us to do this much longer."

CHAPTER SEVENTEEN

ONCE WE'RE WALKING DOWN THE DRIVE, I ASK, "HOW was work?" With so many people around, lunch didn't give us much chance to talk, and I'm wondering how he did at the P&K.

"It sucked about as much as I expected. I opened boxes. Priced and put cans on shelves. Twice, I mopped up stuff that other people broke."

"But you can deal?"

Shane nods. "I'm looking forward to my first paycheck."

There are a lot of questions I want to ask him, like if he misses his dad and whether he likes living alone, but it seems too soon to poke around in his head that way. I'm full of blazing curiosity about how he dealt with something so big by himself. My control slips, and I think of my mother. I start to shake. Somehow, I lock it down before it turns into anything worse. I imagine melting down in front of Shane and my cheeks fire up.

He seems to think the tremors mean I'm cold, though it's in the sixties today, unseasonably warm for this late in the fall. Not that I mind. Life gets downright uncomfortable in the winter. Because he's sweet, Shane takes off his jacket and drapes it around my shoulders. I've seen this move a hundred times in romantic movies and, until this moment, I always rolled my eyes. But now I've got his warmth wrapped around me, his smell enveloping me, and this is pretty close to the best thing ever.

"Better?" he asks.

"Yeah, but you'll be cold now."

"It's worth it if I am."

This is me, melting like butter on the sidewalk. Somehow I keep my knees from turning to total jelly. I'm not sure what we talk about the rest of the way, only that Shane is murmuring and I'm nodding at whatever he's saying. It's wrong to zone out, but I can't help it. His coat feels and smells *so good*. I wonder how he'd respond if I don't give it back.

Knowing Shane, he'd be nice about it, even though he doesn't have anything to spare. We have that in common. I can't relate to people who get whatever they want, just by asking. Aunt Gabby would do more if she could, but our budget doesn't allow for it. She pays the mortgage, utilities, and buys our food; she says it helps that we don't eat meat. Anything extra, like my clothes, comes out of my paycheck. I'm trying to save for college, now that I've bought a laptop, but it's tough sometimes.

Shane's scuffing his feet on the leaves littering the sidewalk; sometimes they crunch and sometimes they quietly dissolve. "It's hard to believe things can be this way. Like nothing happened."

"I don't know how you coped."

"Mike helped. He was a friend, someone she met in group." At my blank look, he explains, "She was in a support group for cancer survivors. Mike beat the odds. My mom didn't."

"He went into remission and it didn't come back?"

162

"I think it's been seven years. And at the end, I was just so mad. Mike has no close family. No people. No reason to stick around, you know? But my mom, she had me. So why her and not Mike?"

"Did you say that to him?" I ask softly.

"Shit, I screamed it at him, afterward. He tried so hard to help me, and I pissed all over it." He pauses, gazing down at me, looking torn. "My mom had papers drawn up, appointing him as my legal guardian. She was trying to look out for me, even at the end. If I hadn't been such an asshole, Mike would've been there for me, just like he was for her."

"He sounds like a good guy."

"Yeah. He helped me with all of it, picking up prescriptions, the special diet, and he relieved me sometimes, near the end. He even helped me take care of the funeral arrangements."

"I'm sure he doesn't blame you, Shane."

"I keep thinking how disappointed my mom would be. But back then, I just kept thinking, *There's no reason for anything anymore*. Screw it all."

Touching his arm, I say, "I bet she'd understand. It was a lot to deal with."

"Wow. I didn't mean to unload so much at once." He appears shaken.

"I don't mind. I'm glad you can talk to me." To be honest, I want to hug him hard and refuse to let go, but then we'd never get to the Coffee Shop.

"You're a good listener. You make it easy."

"Thanks." That might be the best compliment I've ever received, especially coming from a guy who says he never opens up to people. Shane makes me feel like I'm special, if only to him. We keep walking. His hand wraps around mine, warm and sure.

"Here we are," Shane says, shoving the door open.

The bell jangles as we step inside. There are, like, twenty middle-aged women in here, sitting in threes and fours. I'm guessing they wanted to get away from people after church. It's cozy in the Coffee Shop, padded furnishings in complementary colors; I love how they've mixed patterns for an inviting impression. There's a line and only a couple of chairs vacant.

I offer, "I can get our drinks if you'll grab those—"

"Sit. What do you want?" Normally, I'd be a little irritated at the interruption, but I don't mind if Shane takes charge. He's probably used to that, under the circumstances. Given what he told me on the way here, he doesn't *know* how to let people look after him anymore.

"Chai latte, please. Soy milk."

"Be right back."

I slide into the seats just before a couple of girls my age can claim them. If they were old women, I'd feel guilty and cede my ground, but these two can stand. I ignore their glares and drop my bag on Shane's spot. I wish we'd gotten a love seat, but it's pretty hard to talk on those anyway. You have to turn sideways and worry about whether you look weird with one leg bent up at an angle.

At this point I notice there's a mic to the left of the barista counter and the chairs have been pushed back, giving the room a slightly off-kilter feel. A wooden stool sits in front of the microphone, but nobody seems to be setting up to play. A flyer on the bulletin board tells me what's going on:

EVERY SUNDAY! 6pm. The Coffee Shop is proud to present a showcase of local musicians.

Only it's six fifteen now, and I hear the women next to me

complaining. "I missed my hair appointment for this, and the Curly Q is closed now."

And they have been for over two hours. Mildred only opens the place from noon to four on Sundays; she doesn't want to obstruct anyone's religious practices. Which is good of her, and the kind of thing you rarely see outside the Bible Belt.

Soon Shane returns with our drinks; I can't tell what he has, but it's not a frap since it's in a hot beverage cup with paper guard around it. He drops into an adorable sprawl across from me, long legs taking up the space between us. If I had more confidence, I'd prop my feet on top of his, but this thing has just gotten started between us, even if we're already sharing a locker. Just . . . for the first time, I want so bad for someone to like me back. Don't get me wrong, I've had crushes before, guys I'd never meet or ones I knew would never look at me like that. Sometimes it's safer to pin your dreams on somebody who's never going to see you. While it's sad, it's also safe. Because there's no chance he'll ever break your heart for real.

Shane? Could crush me.

To cover the thumping of my heart, I sip my chai latte. He didn't sweeten it, which is perfect. "This is great, thanks. What's yours?"

I ask because the next time we come here—and I hope there *will* be a next time—I intend to get his drink. While I like that he wants to buy things for me, I can't let him do it all the time.

To my surprise, the tips of his ears go pink. "Hot chocolate. I don't like tea *or* coffee. I realize that makes me sound like I'm nine."

"With whipped cream or without?"

"Without."

"Cinnamon?"

He raises a brow at me. "Are you writing a paper on this?"

"Maybe."

"Yes, cinnamon."

I memorize his preferences, so I'll get the right drink when it's my turn to buy. Before I can reply, the door bangs open, ruffling the papers tacked to the walls. A guy dashes in carrying a battered guitar case; the thing has all kinds of stickers on it, some ancient and peeling off, others from bands I recognize, some of which I even like, including Paramore and All Time Low. He's out of breath and cradling his hand against his chest.

The counter girl yells, "You're late, Jace! This is the third time . . . which means you're out of the showcase for good. I'm calling the manager."

Customers respond poorly to this, grumbling. Jace heads to the front of the shop.

"Come on, it wasn't my fault. I had a tire blow out, and then I slammed my hand in the car door after changing it, and I dropped my phone—"

"Whatever," she interrupts. "These people came down to hear you play. Now what?"

"I don't know," Jace says miserably. "But please don't call the boss."

He's pretty cute, if you like black hair and dark eyes. Jace's probably in his early twenties and he's failing to grow a goatee. I'm interested in the drama unfolding before us; this is almost as good as live music. It's entertainment anyway. But the older women don't seem to agree, bitching as Jace argues with the barista. The injury isn't fake, though. His hand is swollen, black and blue across the knuckles. If he really had a flat, then broke his phone, he's on course for the worst day ever.

Shane cuts me a look that I can't interpret. So I'm just looking at him when he puts down his hot chocolate and heads over to the counter. Because I'm straining, I hear him say, "I could fill in for him, just for today. Should be better than nothing."

He's incredible, I want to say, but I register how much of a big deal it is that Shane's volunteered at all. Just a few weeks ago, he was talking about how he wanted to lie low and graduate. Now, he's willing to play music in public. If I know anything about him, I suspect he's doing it to help the guy out more than from pure desire, but he's not backing off as the barista looks him up and down.

"Are you any good?" the girl asks.

Shane shrugs. He's not going to sell himself to them.

But Jace hands over his beat-up guitar case. "The picks are in there, too." Then he faces the room, raising his voice to carry over the complaints of multiple coffee klatches. "We have a special treat today at the Coffee Shop. One show only—" Jace glances over at his replacement, and Shane fills in his name in a low voice. "We have Shane Cavendish, live and unplugged."

The applause that follows is mostly mine, though a few girls brighten up as Shane arranges himself on the stool, long legs propped to support the guitar. Jace collapses where Shane was, right next to me, and he looks both exhausted and relieved. His hand looks like he might have broken fingers, and that can't be good for a musician.

As Shane settles in with the pick, strumming the guitar experimentally, I whisper, "Shouldn't you see a doctor?"

Jace shushes me since Shane's short warm-up has concluded and he's playing the opening chords of a song. At first I can't place it, but then I realize it's an arrangement of "The Reckless and the Brave"; I really like All Time Low's version, which rocks, but this is . . . more. You know how sometimes an acoustic version brings out things you didn't notice before? Yeah. That. Plus, Shane's *voice*. When I heard him in the music room before, he was only playing. *Only*. That's like saying Michelangelo was just a guy who liked to carve shapes in rocks.

I'm not alone in going breathless, however. All the talking stops immediately, just as soon as Shane sings the first lines. He's got rich tone with just a hint of a growl, and it underscores the aching strains he evokes in a melody I'd previously considered pugnacious, defiant even. But somehow, the way he plays the song, along with the slower melody, he elicits a touch of pathos. The girls behind me let out a collective sigh when he sings the line, *"I don't think I want to be saved,"* because he sounds like he's drowning, and I'm pretty sure everyone in the room wants to rescue him.

I do, too.

"Wow," Jace breathes. "This is a badass cover."

I can only nod.

Without a single word of segue or explanation, Shane sings the last notes and immediately begins the next song. This one takes me even longer to identify; the Pretty Reckless isn't my favorite band, though I like Taylor Momsen's voice. If the first song was soulful, this one is a broken heart; it's every bad marriage that ever fell apart, every family splintered, and everyone who's ever seen somebody they love drive off in the middle of the night. As he sings, I can imagine a couple fighting in the street—she's drunk and he's broken. Oh *God*, Shane does broken so beautifully.

I can't stand it.

I never cry in public, but I can feel the tears starting, a hot burn in my eyes. *Shit.* At least I'm not wearing mascara. Beside me, Jace stirs, but I only have eyes for Shane. Suddenly I can't breathe, can't figure out what the hell he sees in me, but I can't look away, either. And that's when I realize, his eyes are locked on mine. Until this moment, I didn't notice; I thought he was off in music land, but he's lost in me instead. Though he's not letting on, he's scared and I'm holding him steady. I wonder if he's ever performed in public before. Somehow I manage an encouraging smile.

That's it. Sing to me. Just me.

When he sings the question, *"Do you understand who I am?"* I nod because the answer to any question he asks me will always be yes. Maybe I'm in too deep, too fast. I haven't known him for very long, all things considered, but I'm falling in love, song by song. The room is dead silent when he finishes this one, like the audience doesn't dare breathe, let alone applaud, but Shane doesn't need motivation to continue. He's already strumming the next number.

I'm surprised to recognize a song by an Australian band, one I'd swear few people in the U.S. know about yet. I found them on YouTube, so I guess it makes sense that Shane did, too. And this song. OMG. It breaks my heart because I could be singing it to him, asking these questions. *"Why, why me? When you could have had anybody."* I ask myself if he's singing this for a reason, if he saw how much I doubt belonging with someone like him, someone hot and talented.

I'm so not enough. I can't be. I smile, and I act happy, and I *pretend.* I'm the queen of bright and shiny things, eternally looking for the positive and seeking a silver lining in the dark. He's dating a girl I invented three years ago because the real me is horrible, and I wanted to leave her behind, along with the group home and the court-mandated therapy sessions. I want so bad to be normal, but I never can be.

I can't. Not after what I've done.

The tears slip down, but I'm not alone. Other women look misty, but this number isn't as sad as the others. He infuses this one with a sweetness that melts the females in the audience, regardless of age. Shane cradles them all in long, graceful fingers; he has them hanging on his every word, every note. The women are all breathless and smiling by the time he winds the song down, ending on a sexy flourish.

The next one, I don't know at all, but as I listen, I know I'll be looking for it online to compare the original with Shane's version, which is somewhere between melancholy and bittersweet. To me, it feels like he's singing about endings, letting go, and saying goodbye. We both know too much about that, he and I. I listen and dry up my tears, eyes half closed with the sheer power of Shane's voice. He should have his own channel online, where he posts videos of himself singing. I suspect he'd have a million views and record companies wanting to sign him. I see that future stretched ahead of him like a strand of pearls, and I don't see a place for me there. Sometimes when you meet someone, you can glimpse the future around them like swirls of smoke, and he's like that, marked for greatness. Someday people will watch him on TV and onstage; and they'll marvel they knew him, even for a little while.

I'm marveling now.

Finally, he speaks, pausing in his performance. "This is actually meant to be a duet, but I like the song so much that I'm going to try it solo. Be gentle, okay?"

Soft laughter greets his words, which tells me he's won the

room completely. From there, he flows right into a dreamy-folksy number, more upbeat though still with plenty of heart. This song feels like it's about healing and new beginnings, and I memorize a few of the lines, so I can Google them later. When I get home, I'll discover some new band. I can envision how it would sound sung in harmony. *Beautiful.* That could be my theme, and I'm smiling along with the rest of the listeners when he finishes.

Good Charlotte is up next, one of my favorite bands. But Shane picks "Wondering" instead of a more popular choice, like "The Anthem." His arrangement is unique and masterful, using not just the strings of the guitar but thumps on the body as well. He's confident now, and he seems to be having fun. Music is such a personal thing, but it lights him up when he plays. I've never been to the ocean, but I imagine Shane's eyes look exactly like sunlight on the Caribbean, and in this moment, they're shining just for me. His hair tumbles over his forehead as he plays, rocking a little. I could watch him forever.

Apparently the audience agrees because when he tries to stand up and take an awkward bow to indicate he's done, someone shouts, "Encore!"

"I never get asked for an encore," Jace mumbles.

"That's my whole set list," Shane says.

"Not even one more?" a girl from our school begs.

Yeah, this performance will probably change his status at school a lot. He won't be a nobody that Dylan Smith can easily push around; and that makes me happy, even while I wonder how it'll affect us. I mean, I don't think that Shane is so shallow that he'll ditch me for the first hot girl who flips her hair when he walks by. Still, I'm nervous. My life has already changed so much, so fast.

I don't know if I can handle more.

His cheeks are flushed when he sits back down. "I do have an original song I've been working on. Would you like to hear it?"

They convince him with applause this time. I notice the barista perched on the bar; nobody has stirred to buy drinks or order muffins this whole time. Shane's captivated the whole room, and I 100 percent understand why. I can't look away either. So naturally, they applaud to encourage him, and he launches into something new.

"Monday, midnight / People say it'll be all right / I see the tunnel / But there's no light."

It's a simple melody, but haunting. The people around me seem to be barely breathing. *"Life is bitter, bittersweet / It all changed in a heartbeat / Too little, too late / Only my heart to break / I close my eyes and / I fade away / fade away."*

I listen as he sings on, pouring his heart into this song. There's so much raw sorrow in his voice that I could cry listening to him, and I already fought it down once. His music is a direct line to emotions I've pretended I don't feel anymore. I'm afraid to be sad or angry, afraid Shadow Sage will slip her chain and I'll find myself in the dark place again. I can't afford that when I've fought so hard to stay in the light. His voice scours me raw; he's relentless.

"Sunday, sunny day / Wish the world would go away / Dreams cost too much / And I can't pay." From there, he shifts smoothly into the chorus. *"Life is bitter, bittersweet . . ."*

I close my eyes.

His voice deepens on this verse. *"Wednesday, gray dawn / All night, I left the music on. / The silence is too loud / Without your song."*

This must be about his mother. So many questions occur to me then, and they drive away my own pain. Shane has that power over me, and I'm grateful for it. The chorus flows over me. *"Life is bitter, bittersweet.*" I hate that he's hurting. I mean, I knew it, but the lyrics drive the point home. He must've felt so helpless, unable to do anything to make his mom get better, and yet he never ran like his dad. That takes a special sort of strength.

Shane takes a breath, then sings the last verse, soft and low. "*Friday, evening, / Is when I stopped believing. / Wanna find my smile again / But I can't stop grieving.*"

The final refrain flows in his soulful baritone, only he changes it up on the last few lines. "*I close my eyes and / I fade away / Don't let me / . . . fade away.*"

I can be forgiven for hoping that he's singing that last part to me. I'm aching to console him. He comes off his stool and surprises me by striding directly toward me. When he pulls me up into his arms for a public kiss, it's the best moment of my life.

CHAPTER EIGHTEEN

THERE ARE TWENTY-FIVE PEOPLE IN THE COFFEE SHOP; it's not exactly a huge audience, but from the sound of their clapping, you'd think there were a hundred people in here. This startles Shane into breaking the kiss. I swear he forgot there were other people around us, and my heart soars. *He* was *singing just for me.* A few of them even push to their feet. At first I think it's a standing ovation, but instead they're moving forward with bills crumpled in their hands.

"Not that this isn't romantic . . . but where's your tip jar?" a woman asks.

Shane pulls back, sheepish. He glances around with a blank look, and I quickly grab an oversize coffee mug from the shelf, then pass it around. If I know this boy at all, he's frozen. Before, he was caught up in the moment, but deep down, he's pretty shy. He needs the money, so I'll help him collect it. I don't mind; it's always easier to be strong for someone else.

"You're really good," the barista tells him. "If you want, I'll talk to Barbara about giving you a permanent spot in the showcase."

"Not mine, I hope," Jace mumbles.

But the complaint has no teeth. The guy hasn't even asked for his guitar back.

Shane hands the instrument over. "Thanks, man."

"No prob. You're really good, dude." Jace gives the compliment easily, which makes me like him. "We should get together and play sometime. What's your number?"

"Just leave a message for me here, okay?"

Shane doesn't have a phone, cell or otherwise. I know that about him, but Jace doesn't, and seems to think Shane's blowing him off. "Right. Whatever."

"I have to get home," I cut in.

"Right. Catch you later." Shane waves at the crowd in general and they give him another round of applause.

Quickly, I clean all the bills out of the mug we borrowed, set it on the shelf, and then lead the way out of the Coffee Shop. I hand him the money as we reach the sidewalk. He counts his haul carefully, smoothing out the crumpled ones and fives. Then he stares at me, astonished. "There's eighty-seven bucks here."

"Put it away," I advise.

He gets out his wallet like he's dreaming. Though I'm not trying to be nosy, I can see there's nothing in it.

"If you don't mind, I'd like to stop by the P&K before I head home. That's the opposite direction from your house."

I can see he's torn. He needs groceries, but he wants to walk me home, too. There's no easy way to do both.

"Go shopping," I tell him. "But be careful. It'll be really late before you—" Then it occurs to me. I know someone who has a car. "Hang on." Shane's frowning as I dial. "Conrad? What're you doing?"

"Watching TV with my mom," Conrad says.

"Listen, can you give Shane a ride home? It would help a lot."

He's so chill that he doesn't ask questions, and he won't wonder about where Shane lives. A lot of people live in trailers because they own land, but they can't afford to build just yet.

"Yeah, it's cool. Where?"

"Pick him up at the P&K in half an hour. Thanks, man. We owe you." It gives me a warm feeling to use the word *we* in that context.

But Shane's frowning at me when I disconnect. He crosses his arms, making it clear he's pissed. "I could've walked. It's fine."

So I try to explain. "This is what friends do, help each other."

"Conrad's not my friend. I barely know the guy."

"I've known him for a while. He has a good heart." It didn't even occur to me that Shane would get prickly over this. Who wants to walk five miles home in the dark while carrying grocery bags? I thought I made things better.

Apparently not.

"I told you before, I don't like it when you do shit like this. I can manage my own life, Sage. You may feel sorry for me, but I'm dealing. I got by *long* before I met you." A number of responses battle in my head, but before I can offer any of them, he spins and heads off, muttering over one shoulder, "I gotta go. Apparently I only have half an hour to get to the store and do my shopping."

My stomach feels sick. I considered only how much I worry about Shane, never once imagining how I might be making him feel. I'd hate it if anyone felt sorry for me. But I don't pity him; that's not it all, I just want to *help*. I've gotten good at fixing things over the past three years. It's an easy part of myself to offer, but he doesn't want that from me.

After today, he might not want anything at all.

For a few seconds, I stand there, staring upward. It's a clear night, a blue velvet gown of a sky dressed in diamond stars, but I feel like such an idiot that I can't appreciate any of it. I do my best to shake it off, then I trudge home. For a day that started out awesome, this one went to hell pretty fast. I'm happy Aunt Gabby is on the phone with Joe when I get back. That way, I can disappear into my room. I love her but she's all about talking about my emotions, and sometimes I can't manage it. My feelings are awful and messy and it seems best, today, to ball them up and pretend they don't exist, even though I can feel them chewing at me from the inside.

I don't cry myself to sleep.

In fact, I don't sleep. Much.

The next morning, I look like hell. There isn't enough concealer to cover the crappy night I had. Over breakfast, Gabby takes one look at me and asks, "Did you have bad dreams? Your mom?"

"No," I manage to say. "Just a rough night."

I used to struggle with insomnia, so she's not surprised. She just nods and kisses my cheek. "Let me know if I can do anything."

By that I hope she means some herbal tea, not more counseling or actual meds. While sleeping pills knock me out, they also leave me feeling thick and disconnected. I hate taking them, so I was glad when my aunt let me stop. When I first came to stay with her, she hovered. She fussed. She acted like I was delicate machinery about to break down. And this is exactly how I make Shane feel, like I see him as a project or a problem to solve instead of a person—and that's so far from the truth. Right now I feel miserable and helpless, a delightful combination on Monday morning. Though I haven't known Shane as long as Ryan, this is ten times worse than our faux breakup.

Just then, my phone pings. A glance tells me it's from Ryan. *Speak of the devil.* I have to work this afternoon, so I don't have time to get into whatever he has in mind—but he isn't asking me to get together. Instead he just says, **I get it, ok? I'm sorry about everything.**

I have no idea what he gets. No time to think about it. I'm already late so I grab a protein bar to eat in my first class and throw together some kind of a lunch. I don't bring enough for everyone or even Shane. The way I feel today, I may go sit behind the school with the burners and inhale enough secondhand smoke to get a buzz on. My ride to school seems longer than usual, and it's a cold, gray day. Most of the crimson and gold leaves seem to have fallen, leaving skeletal limbs on the dark boughs of the trees. I have no idea how all the color could've drained away overnight, but I suspect the answer has to do with Shane. Deep down, I realize I'm being dramatic; there are still trees dressed in gorgeous autumnal hues. I'm just choosing to focus on the bleak, barren ones instead.

It's that kind of day.

Hurriedly I chain my bike up outside and run to my locker, where I should run into Shane. Only he's not there. I guess he came and went early to avoid the awkward moment. I should be grateful but my backpack still feels like it weighs forty extra pounds. Lila nudges me as I go by.

"What's the matter? You look like shit." Today, she's wearing a short black skirt, white-and-black-striped tights, black combat boots, and a corset sweater thing in scarlet. She's way too stylish and dramatic for this school. I wonder how long her hair will be red.

"Thanks," I mumble.

Her expression softens. "See you at lunch."

"Yep."

Somehow Shane manages to dodge me the rest of the day. I never see him at our locker, though his stuff comes and goes, which makes me feel marginally better. Each time I open it, I expect to find all of his things gone, which is so stupid. What does it matter if he takes his junk for good? It's a locker, not our family home. I sleepwalk through my classes.

Now he's sitting one row over in math, but he hasn't looked at me. I might as well not be in the room. Shane's back to silent, invisible mode, not even making eye contact. But I do get a happy surprise when I take a surprise math quiz and I know a good portion of the answers.

Today I avoid the cafeteria. I pick a random locker and leave a generic message on it. This is the first time I've phoned it in like this. After grabbing my lunch bag, I head out back. The halls are grungier back toward the shop departments, and the alarm doesn't sound when I slip outside. A few guys eye me but nobody says anything. This isn't a group known for talking. Instead they silently pass around a hand-rolled MJ while a kid in a beanie lazily stands watch. I guess somebody would eat the thing if teachers ever came back here.

I park it nearby and pretend to eat my lunch. It's cold as hell and I'm not hungry. I'm counting heartbeats like I did in therapy, as it's supposed to help me stay calm. Right now I want nothing more than to cry or scream, but that would alarm my new not-friends. I'm silent, like they are. Now and then, one of them tells an unfunny joke, and the rest laugh. I wait out the break while my hands and feet go numb. This day is endless.

Ryan looks better in chemistry, however, like he got a good night's sleep and perversely, this upsets me. Since he claims to be in love with me, our situation should bother him for more than a week. *Asshole,* I think. But he doesn't notice. He smiles at me.

"Hey," he says, like nothing's changed.

Everything has.

But I get to work. There are chemicals to mix in careful ratio, and Mr. Oscar seems delighted when I get the liquid to smoke and change colors, as intended. I'm supposed to learn something about bases and alkalis, I think, but it's beyond me. I can't believe I have to work today.

"Do you want to—" Ryan starts, but I'm already gone.

Shane's nowhere to be found, and that hurts because I've gotten used to him showing up at most of my classes. I started counting on him . . . and I feel stupid because I should know better. I can't even be mad at him because this is my fault. He told me before how much he hated it when I fix things for him, like he can't do it himself, but I went ahead and did it again, so I can only blame myself that he's bailed. Miserable, I put my assignments in my backpack and then head for the bike rack. I have a four-hour shift waiting for me, then homework.

Shane's working at the P&K today, so I could swing by there if I wanted to stalk him, but I've already been there, done that. Instead I head to the Curly Q way early and start sweeping up the hair.

Mildred glares at me. "You know I'm not paying you extra."

"It's fine. "

She seems to sense it's been a terrible day because she mutters, "Well, maybe this once. Clock in for three p.m. I can afford an hour since you're here anyway."

Eight dollars may not seem like a big deal, but my boss is pretty cheap. I must look worse than I imagined. Grace has a customer so she can't do more than wave for the first hour; in the meantime, I tidy up the salon and examine the appointment book to get an idea of what the night will be like. Slow, it seems. There are two cuts on the schedule, one highlight, and that's all. If there are no walk-ins, I'll end up playing practice doll before the shift's over.

The evening goes according to my predictions. Mildred leaves around six . . . and by seven, Grace has me in the chair. This is why I have twenty tiny braids in my hair, the other half loose, when the bell jingles. I glance up because it's my job to greet customers . . . only this time, I freeze. Because it's Shane.

I have a thousand questions. *Isn't he supposed to be at work now?*

"I'm on my lunch break." He's a mind reader or something.

"Do you want a haircut?" That should go on record as the stupidest thing anyone's ever said.

Of course he doesn't. At least, I hope not. I love his shaggy curls. My fingers itch to touch them, but I'm pretty sure that's not allowed when a couple is fighting. Are we fighting? *Are* we a couple? Nobody ever told me the rules; it's still kind of undefined. I've seen happy pairs holding hands in the halls at school, sneaking long, greedy kisses when they think the teachers aren't watching, and they make it look so easy.

He shakes his head. "But I know I can't be here if I'm not paying."

"Mildred would be pissed," Grace agrees.

I stare up at the security camera blinking red above the front door. The old lady had it installed after other businesses in the area got burglarized, and now she uses it to spy on her employees. Which means she'll definitely say something if I stand here talking to Shane, and he purchases no products or services.

"So I was hoping for a shampoo."

"Seriously?" That's the only service I'm allowed by law to provide, apart from fetching water and magazines.

Grace is wearing the biggest, dumbest grin ever. "Don't mind me. I'm gonna put in my earbuds."

"How much do I charge?" There's no fee schedule for just a shampoo. Usually it comes with a trim or a blow out.

"Use the coupon for first-time clients. They're in the top right drawer."

This flyer is expired, plus it's good for shampoo with haircut, but I don't protest. I have no idea how to act right now.

CHAPTER NINETEEN

"COME ON BACK," I MANAGE TO SAY.

Grace and I know this is mostly to get out of sight of the cameras, so Mildred can't bitch about me talking to my boyfriend while I'm on the clock. Apparently Shane doesn't. To my surprise, he sits in the faux-leather reclining chair, like he really expects me to wash his hair. Does it make me weird that I want to?

Covering my nerves, I start the water, testing it on myself before I pull out the sprayer. "Let me know if it's too hot."

"It's fine."

His blue, blue eyes are closed, lashes smudgy fans against the pallor of his skin. He hasn't shaved, so I can see the dark bristles on his jaw, and the delicate skin beneath his eyes seems bruised, as if he didn't sleep last night, either. Suddenly my chest hurts . . . in a good way.

In silence, I spray the water through his hair, then get the shampoo formulated for curls. Most salons use fancy products, but like I said, Mildred's cheap, so this is a generic jumbo container from the beauty supply shop, and it has a faint lemon scent. His chest moves in a sigh when I work the shampoo from scalp to ends and back again. I create lather, scrub gently, and then, like I do for most clients—unless they're in a hurry—I massage his scalp.

His eyes fluttered open then, and his lips part. A faint flush tinges his cheekbones, and he's looking up at me. I've never seen a stare like this. It's deep, hungry, and it makes my toes curl.

"Rinse," he says softly.

I do.

Before I can get a towel from the shelf above, he's out of the chair, and I'm against his chest. Water sprinkles down on me, but I don't care. I put my arms around his waist, surprised by the urgency of his hold.

"You're the only person in the world who gives a shit about me," he whispers. "I can't believe I got pissed at you for showing it."

"It was my fault. I didn't listen . . . and I don't blame you. I shouldn't have done it without asking."

"Maybe not . . . but I was an asshole."

I shrug. "You're entitled."

"Not to you, Sage. I want to be the one person who never lets you down."

I exhale a shaky breath. "This was horrible," I admit quietly.

And a little scary. I didn't realize how fast—maybe *too* fast—I'd come to trust him. For him to vanish, it felt like the rug was yanked out from under me. Possibly I should pull back now, saying smart, cautious things about how we might need each other too much and that's not healthy. But that's the therapist talking in my head, not me. I hope. I only know that we've made an actual connection, and it will take more than this to make me give it up.

"For me too. Nothing even felt real without you."

Wow. It's quite a revelation to discover that I'm as important to him as he's become to me. This is like being poised on a preci-pice, not knowing whether you'll fall or fly. But I'm leaning into the wind, enjoying the freedom. I wish this moment could last forever.

"I sat outside with the burners," I confess.

Shane smiles wryly. "Lila was worried about you at lunch. She was eyeing me like she thought I killed you and stashed your body."

"You sat at our usual table?" That surprises me. I figured he'd be hiding somewhere. Before we started talking, he kept so much to himself.

He nods. "I was hoping you'd be there."

"I was afraid you wouldn't." I pause, rubbing my cheek against his chest. Even in his P&K uniform, he's hot. "Maybe we should talk about how to keep this from happening again. I care obvi-ously . . . and it bothers me to think of you walking five miles in the dark. That's not crazy, right?"

"No. But . . . I'm not big on having my choices taken away."

Yeah, he wouldn't be. So many things have been beyond his control.

"So if I ask first, that would be better?"

"Yeah." Shane glances at the cat-shaped clock on the wall, the kind with the google eyes and a pendulum for the tail. "Crap, gotta go. I'll have to run to make it back before my break ends."

"Wait!" Quickly, I pat his hair dry and then crinkle my fingers through it with some product designed to enhance soft curls.

He ducks for a quick kiss and then he's gone in a jangle of the front door. Grace comes back to the shampoo station, grinning like mad. "He's *cute*." She stretches the word into twelve syllables. "How long's that been going on?"

"A few weeks?"

For me, honestly, it began the minute he walked into my math class, but I couldn't tap his shoulder and say, *Hi, I'm yours, take me home*. Surprising as it may sound, the crazy approach makes some dudes nervous. So I'm trying to save my insanity, dole it out in trickles, so he doesn't run screaming. He still might when he figures me out, but I'll have some sweet memories by then.

Like him saying, *I want to be the one person who never lets you down.*

The bizarre part is that *I* would like to believe in him. He's that mythical being, rare as a unicorn. He's the one I can trust, right, universe? *I've been waiting a long time for you, Shane Cavendish. You have no idea.*

"Tell me everything," Grace demands.

She's my favorite of the stylists, a young twenty-eight who didn't know what she wanted to be when she grew up . . . and still doesn't. Grace fell into beauty school because she had a coupon. As it turned out, she was pretty good, but she still doesn't see this as her life's work. She's always looking for the handsome prince who'll take her away from all this. But there aren't many around here.

My plan is to leave town in two years. After graduation, I picture myself going to Unity College in Maine, and after that? I have no idea. Wherever I can find work, I guess. The future sometimes looms like a monster, a horrible scary one with teeth and claws. It's hard to plan your life when all the news talks about is how screwed up the world's become.

I tell Grace a little about Shane as we lock up. She beams at me. "I envy you, Sage. First love is the best. He's the one you'll compare everyone else to hereafter."

Her assumption that we'll break up takes the shine off my joy. I don't say anything because Grace treats me like an adult, mostly, and she'd be upset if she knew how much reality bums me out. I mean, she's right. Romance usually doesn't last at sixteen, but you don't want to *think* about it. You just want to feel.

"Great," I mumble. "Night, Grace."

I unfasten my bike chain while she locks up. Then I go about my nightly reflective tape ritual. So embarrassing. She laughs at me, shaking her head as she walks to her car. The streetlights are bright here, but once I leave the small downtown area, it gets dark fast.

I'm pedaling slowly toward home when I hear a car coming. Since I'm on the sidewalk, it shouldn't be a problem, but the screech of tires scares me. I throw a look over my shoulder and find a black truck about to eat me. I wobble sideways and land hard on my hands and knees. Its tires hit the curb, bouncing toward me. Scrambling backward, I come against the fence that keeps people from screwing around in the auto body parking lot.

The headlights switch to high beam, practically blinding me. I clench my phone, already finding 911 with my fingertips. Then Dylan climbs out of the cab, propping his arms on top of the door. "Not such a scary bitch now, are you?"

His stillness is the only reason I don't complete the call. "Isn't it exhausting?"

"What?"

"Being such an asshole all the time. Don't you occasionally want the day off?"

"You don't know anything about me," he snaps.

"I know there's something really wrong with you."

He growls and comes around the door, but when I raise my phone, he stops. "You pretend to be so nice, but deep down, you're as bad as everyone else."

"I'm nice to those who deserve it," I correct.

"And you think I'm not?"

"No," I say. "You made life hell for a couple of people who are important to me."

Dylan clenches a fist. "Lila's using you, she's tired of her old crew. That's what she does, constantly reinvents herself because if she didn't, she'd have to take a long look in the mirror."

"Says the guy who lied when he told the whole school he popped her cherry."

"Whatever. You'll get a taste of her poison sooner or later."

"What do you want, Dylan?"

He bites his lip. His followers would lose all respect if they could see how uncertain he looks at this moment. "I was wondering . . . how do you know about . . . them?"

No question that he means his mom and the principal. "I saw them kissing in his office."

"Goddammit. I warned her. I told her to be careful." He runs a harried hand over his short hair. "Do you have any idea how tired I am of dealing with this shit?"

"No." I consider saying *I don't care, either* but maybe it will help me understand why he's such a dick to everyone if I listen.

"Since I was thirteen, I've been hearing guys talk about what a MILF my mom is. I have to pretend it doesn't bother me or they'd just do it even more."

"So that's why you pick on people at school? You're deflecting."

Dylan makes a derisive sound. "You sound like a shrink."

"That doesn't mean I'm wrong."

If he acts the way he does out of some misguided idea that he's protecting his mother, then I can't hate him entirely. Dylan,

Shane, and I are tied together through a bizarre trifecta of the maternal spectrum. This jackhole won't thank me for that insight, however. And I still don't know what he wants, so I fold my arms expectantly.

"I'm giving you a chance to back off. Bad things happen to people who threaten my mom."

"Excuse me?" Both my brows go up. "I haven't done anything. And I won't, as long as you leave us alone. That was the deal. It hasn't changed."

"I'm just supposed to trust you? I don't think so."

"Even if I say, Okay, I promise I won't tell, even if you go back to picking on my friends, how does that change anything, since you *don't* trust me? Did you think this conversation through at all?"

A look of dismay flickers across his handsome face. I mean, I don't want to date him but he's attractive, no denying that. "I'm not stupid," he snaps.

You could've fooled me.

"But my mom is," he goes on quietly. "She trusts people . . . sees the best in them. So when that asshole Warick tells her it's just a matter of time until he leaves his wife—"

"It means it's never gonna happen," I finish.

"Yeah. And it seems like I've spent my whole life protecting her, trying to keep her from making another stupid move, including sleeping with my friends."

Wow, why the hell is he telling me this?

"They'd get her drunk, nail her, and then give me shit about it for the rest of my life. Which is why I have to be the baddest, scariest asshole at school. These guys have to know I will not hesitate to pull the trigger if they cross me."

Dammit. I finally see his point.

"And if you back off Shane and Lila after our private convo, they'll see it as weakness."

He nods. "Blood in the water. So we can go down this road, but I guarantee I've got more practice being bad."

"You might be surprised."

"I doubt it. What's it gonna be, Princess? Do we call a truce, you forget what you know and things go back to normal, or do I start digging for *your* secrets?"

My blood chills. Though I'm not sure, my case file *should* be confidential. Since everything happened when I was so young, the records are sealed and they'll be expunged when I turn eighteen. I'm terrified, but I can't reveal my vulnerability to Dylan. Right now, he's just guessing that I have something to hide. I shouldn't confirm it.

Silently, I shake my head.

"Bad move," he says softly. "I'll do whatever it takes to protect my mom."

Ignoring him, I pull my bike off the ground and ride away, half expecting him to come after me with his truck. But he doesn't. If nothing else, I've learned the key to Dylan Smith tonight. He's not a bully for the fun of it, and I don't think he's a sociopath, either. He's just driven by the desire to defend his mother. I'd almost feel sorry for him, except for the dread churning in my gut.

He's not playing. He'll search for anything he can use to discredit me. Logic dictates I should wreck him, shoot first, so to speak. If the whole school's talking about what a slut his mom is, they won't listen when he shit-talks me later. But . . . I don't know if I can.

CHAPTER TWENTY

THE NEXT DAY, I EXPECT THERE TO BE IMMEDIATE FALLOUT, where Dylan challenges my resolve by going back to his old habits, but instead we maintain a cautious truce. This can't last, however. Once he has some bullets for his figurative gun, I'm going down. It's only a matter of time before the peace I've won for Shane and Lila runs out. So now I have to decide what kind of person I am—the good girl I've been pretending to be or Shadow Sage, bad enough to ruin someone else's life. The idea horrifies me, but I'm nearly frozen over the idea of everyone learning my secrets. *Rock and a hard place, devil and the deep blue sea.* At this point, my two choices seem to be bad and worse.

At least Shane's leveled up socially. One of the girls from the Coffee Shop recorded a few songs on her phone and posted them on YouTube, then she forwarded the link to everyone she knows on Facebook. He has almost two thousand views on his Good Charlotte cover already, and today, people know his name as he walks me to my next class. They chin-lift at him, call his name, and say "sup" when I can tell he has no idea who they are.

"This is so weird," he says, shaking his head.

I shrug. "It's a small school."

"Better than getting shoved around on a daily basis," he decides.

With a quick kiss, he darts off to his next class since we only have math together. He has to work tonight, and I don't, so this will give me a chance to catch up on homework. So I think, until I find Lila waiting at my locker after school. Today she's a goddess in black; nobody should make leggings, boots, and a belted sweater look that good.

"You ditched me at lunch yesterday."

"It was just a bad day."

"I ended up sitting with Shane, your freshmen, and those random sophomores."

"Sorry. Want to hang out today?"

"I'm pissed at you."

"So that's a no?"

Her scowl eases up. "Just don't do it again. I want to hear about it if you're having a shitty day or fighting with Shane."

Heat creeps into my cheeks. I'd like to say that's a lucky guess on her part, but I've made no secret that I think he's awesome. So I just nod. "Come over. My aunt's making soup."

"You think it's that easy?"

I grin. "I hope so. I'm not in the mood for drama . . . and besides, remember how happy it makes your mom when you hang out with me."

"That's true. She gives me forty-six percent less shit these days."

"You did the math?"

"Obviously. Let's go."

She rides on the back of my bike again, and I pedal over to my place. If we keep doing this, I'll lose weight, hopefully in my butt. I don't have the chest to spare. We hang out in the living room because my aunt isn't home yet. We'll probably migrate once she gets back.

"I'm trying to decide why you live with Gabby," Lila says.

It's not what I expected to hear. "My parents aren't around anymore."

"Like . . ." I can see her trying to find a tactful word. "Passed on?"

I nod, grateful that she's too uncomfortable to pursue this line of questioning. She's curious if it's a recent loss, but afraid of making me feel shitty. Good thing she's a nice person. Otherwise, she'd definitely be digging to find out why I'm an orphan. God, that's such a stupid word. It conjures visions of pasty-faced children in Victorian clothes with tin cups, dining on gruel. The reality is depressing in a different way.

"So what do you wanna do?" she asks, changing the subject.

"Homework, if you can talk and write at the same time."

"I can manage. Wait, let me call my mom. She likes the new, improved responsible me."

While she dials, I make popcorn. I hear snatches of conversation over the *ping* of hot kernels hitting the lid of the pot, and Lila sounds slightly annoyed. There's a lot of sighing from her end, anyway.

"Everything good at home?" I ask, coming back to the living room.

"Yep. Speaking of which . . ." She sighs. "Would you mind coming over to prove you exist? I swear my mom is starting to think

I've hired someone to play my friend on the phone. Plus, I need to repay the times I've come to your place. My mom's cooking isn't as healthy as your aunt's, though. Butter is her best friend."

I laugh. "Sure, when?"

"Tomorrow night, after Green World."

"Are you sticking with it?" I'm doubtful, even though the meetings have gotten bigger and more productive lately.

This week, we're planning a recycling drive. We still need to agree on a drop-off point . . . and convince the school to let us include the event in the morning announcements. I don't know how many people will bother, but I intend to talk to my social studies teacher about offering extra credit if they do. The class is supposed to teach us to be responsible, right?

"It's better than spirit squad. And I need a few meaningful activities on my college apps or my parents will never shut up."

I open my backpack and dig out my math notebook; it seems best to start with the worst of my assignments. "Well, I know it's not most people's idea of a good time. But it's more entertaining when you're around."

"Everything is." Lila tosses her hair like the especially vapid girls do when they're trying to attract some guy's attention.

Which reminds me.

"Are you ever going to tell me exactly what happened with Dylan?" It's a non sequitur, but anything I can learn about him might help me later.

She frowns, chewing on her pencil so that she leaves neat rows of teeth marks in the yellow paint. By the look of the wood, this isn't the first time. "That's ancient history. Why?"

"He hassled me after work last night." I figure it's safe to tell her that much. "I was just wondering how bad is he really?"

How seriously should I take his threats?

"That asshole," she snarls. "Did he scare you?"

"He tried to."

"If he's screwing with you, then I guess I owe you the full story. But I expect some Shane gossip afterward to wash the taste out of my mouth."

"Deal."

"Dylan and I got together freshman year. He wasn't as bad then." Here, her gaze softens, like she has some good memories. "He was . . . sweet. I know it's hard to imagine now."

I barely remember anyone but Ryan from that period. Back then I shadowed him so hard that it's a wonder we didn't fuse together. Eighth grade had been a battle of epic proportions and my freshman year I was struggling to find a balance. Mostly, I went to school, did my homework, and tried *really* hard to be perfect, so Aunt Gabby wouldn't dump me back in state care. I'm still doing that, to be honest. Sometimes it's hard to feel safe.

"He wasn't on my radar," I admit.

"Something happened between our freshman and sophomore years. I have no idea what . . . he wouldn't say. But he changed. Suddenly he wanted to know where I was every minute. He tried to tell me who I could talk to, how I was allowed to dress . . ." Lila shakes her head and sighs.

Given what I know about Dylan's relationship with his mom, I suspect this has something to do with her. "That's bizarre."

"Right? But it gets weirder."

"I'm listening."

"We'd been dating for nine months or so . . . and I wanted to sleep with him. I was stupid. I thought it might reassure him that I loved him."

At this, my brows shoot up, because I thought they broke up because he told everyone they did it when they really didn't. "Not what I was expecting."

"I guess not. So one night, we had his place to ourselves. His mom was out with her flavor of the month. We started messing around, but when I touched him through his jeans, he pulled away and started crying."

"Holy shit."

"I hugged him and said it was no big deal. But I could tell something was bothering him, like, a lot. He basically kicked me out. And the next day, he was claiming we hooked up."

Now I understand why Dylan hates Lila. She witnessed a weak moment, so he had to ruin her at school, so nobody would believe her if she told anyone the truth. In other words, he shot first. I'm willing to bet something happened that summer, end of innocence, or some shit like that. *Too bad.* I might have liked the sweet Dylan that Lila dated two years ago, but he's gone and I'm left to square off against the asshole who's taken his place.

"And he was mean about it," I guess.

She nods without looking at me. "I never told anyone what really happened—like they'd *believe* me. In the official record, he gets to be a player who popped my cherry while I'm the slut who gave it up, then went batshit and broke up with him because I didn't want everyone to know."

"You loved him."

"Yeah. Shows what poor judgment I have. Now you owe me something good. Spill."

So I tell her about Shane and the Coffee Shop, how he seemed like he was singing just to me. Next I mention that he spent the night here, and by this point, she's bouncing. "Christ, Sage. I never would've guessed. You look so innocent. But you're sneaky!"

"Who's sneaky?" my aunt asks, coming in the front door.

"Uh," I say.

But Lila covers smooth as silk. "She's got the smartest plan to get people to bring in their old newspapers and magazines. Extra credit! Provided we can get the teacher to agree."

"That *is* sneaky." But from Aunt Gabby's tone, she approves, so I'm clear. "Are you staying for dinner, Lila?"

"If you don't mind. We'll feed Sage tomorrow night."

"Sounds good. Just let me change and then I'll dish up the soup."

"I can do it," I offer, dropping my math notebook.

"Thanks." Aunt Gabby heads down the hall to her bedroom.

I jump up and hurry to the kitchen and get three bowls. Lila follows, looking bemused. "She doesn't seem like the type to beat you if you aren't super efficient, super helpful, all the time."

There are so many things I could say, but I don't offer anything honest. I hate myself for it, too. "Isn't this exactly how you pictured the Post-it Princess acting at home?"

"Yeah. But now I'm starting to wonder if that's the real you."

Lucky for me, my aunt comes in before Lila can say more or I'm forced to acknowledge or deny her insight. Dinner passes quietly, and half an hour later, Lila's mom comes to pick her up. I think she just wants to get a look at Aunt Gabby and me, so we come to the front door to wave as she backs out of the drive.

"I'm glad you're having people over and making friends other than Ryan. Lila seems nice."

"She is," I agree.

"What's going on with Ryan, by the way? He didn't seem to be brokenhearted when he was here on Sunday."

I shrug. "You're asking the wrong person. I don't know if he's moved on, or if he's covering his feels better."

"Talk to him," Aunt Gabby advises.

"I'll text him now."

After washing the dinner dishes, I carry my backpack to my room and close the door. My aunt respects my privacy; she doesn't rummage in my stuff, but a closed door is comforting. It says, *This is my space, and you can't come in unless I let you.* I also know how fragile that barrier can be.

I get out my phone and send, **im ready to talk.**

A few minutes later, he replies. **We ok?**

Yep. I forgive you.

I don't know if that's enough to patch the rips in our friendship but it feels like a beginning. That night, I fall asleep feeling pretty good, and there are no bad dreams.

CHAPTER TWENTY-ONE

DINNER WITH LILA'S FAMILY GOES WELL, THOUGH I'VE never seen so many chicken-fried foods in my life. Mrs. Tremaine seems to think that if she fries it enough, it's not meat anymore. But the mashed potatoes are delicious and I rearrange the beef on my plate enough to make it look like I'm enjoying it. If Lila told her I'm a vegetarian, she doesn't care, and that's a Midwestern attitude. People seem to think if they offer meat often enough, you'll be seduced by your salivary glands or something.

"So, Sage," Mr. Tremaine asks. "What does your future look like? It's never too soon to start planning." He aims a pointed look at Lila, who sighs.

"There's a college in Maine that looks right for me."

"What do you plan to study?" Mrs. Tremaine asks.

"Adventure-based education."

I can see they have no idea what I'm talking about, so I try to explain, and now Mr. Tremaine is frowning. "That sounds like you want to be a camp counselor."

"*Dad*," Lila protests.

"It's okay." For the rest of the meal, I clarify the difference—and about how we can change the world if people are taught young about conservation, green practices, and natural resources when they're young.

Mr. Tremaine gives a grudging nod. "That's true. If there had been a program like that at school when we were growing up, it wouldn't have taken us so long to start recycling."

"Exactly."

When we ask to be excused and I follow Lila to her room, she's looking at me like I'm magical. "I've never gotten my dad to see my point of view on *anything*."

"Did you really try, or did you stomp off when he failed to get it the first time?"

"Shut up," she mutters.

We work on homework—and gossip—until eight, then I cover myself in reflective tape. She shakes her head at me. "There's no way I'd be seen like that, dude. I'd just get in a car even if it violated all my principles."

I ignore that. "Night. Thanks for having me over."

"You already said nice things to my parents. It's cool."

She stands in the doorway, watching until I turn the corner. It's not a long way from her house, but I'm nervous, mostly because I'm keeping an eye out for Dylan's truck. When I ride onto our gravel drive, my heart is racing. I hate that I've let him make me feel this way; I remember what it's like to live with fear constantly gnawing at you, and I refuse to go back. After stowing my bike in the shed, I slide in the back door. Thoughtfully, my aunt has left a snack on a plate for me.

I carry it into the living room, where she's watching a movie on DVD. "Have fun?"

"Yeah, it was fine. Lila's mom doesn't cook as well as you, though."

Aunt Gabby grins. "Flattery will get you everywhere."

"How are things going with Joe?"

"Really well," she answers, both surprised and cautious. "He's a great guy. Funny. Quirky."

"Quirky how?"

"Well . . . he's a *huge Star Trek* fan. Not the original, *The Next Generation*. Apparently he has a Star Fleet uniform that he wears to sci-fi conventions."

"Really?" I have no idea why, but I'm startled to learn this. Joe is a fairly big guy, good build, and he looks somewhat athletic. Plus, he drives a silver Ford. In other words, he's a pretty standard manly man, and I'm delighted to find out he's a secret geek.

"Yep. I told him I'll go to Indy with him this summer for GenCon."

Whoa. If she's willing to make plans ten months out, things must be going extremely well. "I haven't talked to him that much, but I like him."

"He holds up to closer scrutiny," she says, then she laughs, because she seems to realize how suggestive that sounds.

We talk a little more about Joe, then she asks, "How're you doing with Shane?"

"Good. We've had a few hiccups, but nothing serious."

"I'd be surprised if you didn't." There's no way to be sure what she means, whether she's talking about my past or the fact that I haven't dated much.

I lean toward the latter because Aunt Gabby tends not to rock the boat, where my dark side is concerned. She figures if the therapist said I had talked it all out, then it's counterproductive to dredge it up again. I'm so grateful for that. It doesn't help to have it on my mind constantly. I'm coping. Time is supposed to make things easier, so I just need to breathe and wait.

"He's wonderful," I say softly.

That word doesn't begin to encompass him. I eat the cheese, crackers, and fruit while she tells me about the weekend Joe has planned. "He wants to take me to Chicago, get tickets for the theater, but I'm not sure—"

"If you should leave me for that long?" I can practically read her mind.

"Yeah," she admits.

"I can probably stay one night with Lila if that would make you feel better. And you'll be back on Sunday, right?" I can't imagine that she's considering a long holiday. My aunt hasn't taken a vacation as long as I've lived with her.

"That sounds good." From her expression, she's relieved. She's apparently okay with letting me stay one night alone, but two makes her feel neglectful, I guess.

"He's buttering you up so you'll be willing to go to sci-fi conventions, huh?"

Aunt Gabby smirks. "That's a possibility."

"Heh. I'll talk to Lila. When are you going?"

"In a month or so, the weekend before Thanksgiving."

Which means it's almost Halloween. The warm weather won't last too much longer; it's weird, some years, the trick-or-treaters need to bundle up over their costumes, and other times, it's so warm, it almost feels like summer. I wonder how it'll be this time. Not that I go out—I generally stay home and give out candy. I tease Aunt Gabby about giving away that sugary junk, but she just grins and says she doesn't want her house egged or her trees TP'd.

The rest of the week, school is quiet. If I was skittish, I'd say too much so. Because I notice Dylan watching me, but he doesn't make a move. I go about my business: planning the recycling drive, working, seeing Shane, doing homework. And I leave cheerful Post-its on people's lockers, like usual. I'm walking with a little more swagger these days instead of rushing around with my head down. Maybe it's my new attitude that results in so many people talking to me between class. Whatever the reason, I like the change.

Friday morning, Shane's escorting me to my first class. "You wanna do something tonight?"

Duh.

"Yeah. Our choices are limited, though."

"I'd kinda like to hang out at your place if that's cool."

"Sure. If you want, come over after school." That will save him a ten-mile round trip.

"I'll meet you at our locker, then." He drops me off at my classroom with a kiss on the forehead. A teacher catches it, but since it isn't mouth-to-mouth contact, she contents herself with a frown.

Lunch is weird. Ryan pulls up a chair, joining us at the new integrated table. Things are a little crowded, but people are talking a lot about the recycling drive, so it's not awkward. Gwen has talked her dad into sponsoring the operation, so he's permitting people to drop off stuff at his hardware store, and she's even gotten him to rent some proper containers.

"We'll need people to ferry stuff over from the school," Tara is saying.

Kenny immediately volunteers his mom's minivan to earn a

smile from Tara. Then he starts texting, which makes me think that his mom knows nothing about this. I stifle a smirk.

"So what're you doing tonight?" Lila asks, as the others discuss Green World stuff.

"Hanging out with Shane."

"Oh."

I swear she looks disappointed. Now I'm torn. I don't want to be one of those girls who gets a boyfriend and stops hanging out with her friends. Hoping Shane will understand, I say, "Do you want to come over? We're probably going to watch a movie."

She arches a brow at me. "Sounds awesome. I love preventing people from making out."

Before I can think better of the impulse, I nudge Ryan with an elbow. "Wanna do movie night? Shane and Lila are coming."

"Usual time?"

I nod. Only then do I look at Shane, as our date has doubled. "Hope this is okay," I whisper.

"Too late to be asking now." But he doesn't *look* mad.

I realize I've done it again, made plans without asking him. I'm just not used to being half of anything. When I spent all my time with Ryan, we were a closed circle that didn't let anyone else in.

"I'll make it up to you." I whisper the promise. Both his brows go up, then my face heats like a radiator. "I mean. Uhm. We can do something, just us, before you go to work on Saturday? I can make a picnic if the weather's nice, and we can eat in the park."

"Okay. I'll bring my work clothes and change at the store."

Soon, lunch is over, and I get through the day. After classes end, Shane meets me at our locker, as promised. It occurs to me that we have a few hours before the others arrive. This can be a mini-date. Since we're not in a hurry, I push my bike and Shane walks alongside me.

I'm about to jokingly suggest he needs some way to keep up with me when I spot a yard sale. There's an older woman puttering among the tables, and I can't resist. It's not that I love rummaging through other people's junk, but sometimes I can find cool stuff that doesn't cost a ton. Aunt Gabby appreciates it when I do my own clothes shopping.

"Do you mind?" I ask.

"Go for it."

While I'm poking through piles of T-shirts, Shane wanders toward the garage. In fact, this is more of an everything-must-go sale, since it's lined up on the lawn, up the driveway, and beyond. I find a couple of vintage T-shirts, priced cheap, along with various tank tops. This stuff looks like it's from the eighties, but it'll work now. Off the shoulder tops are coming back.

He comes out looking purposeful, heading for the old woman. "How much for the bike?"

"That belonged to my grandson," she tells him. "He's thirty-one now. I can't even remember what we paid for it, but I'll let you have it for twenty-five dollars."

Shane's about to accept her offer. I can see him reaching for his wallet, but I know he only had eighty-seven from the Coffee Shop on Sunday, he's bought some groceries, and I don't know if he's gotten paid from the P&K yet. I can't resist haggling.

So I carry my purchases over and point out, "The tires need to be inflated and repaired and there's some rust on the chain." Not enough to make the bike unusable, but it's worth noting. "Fifteen."

"I could get far more for it on the Internet," she says, frowning.

"And you'd have to list it on an auction site, give them part of your proceeds, and then figure out how to ship it. It would be simpler to make us a deal."

"Twenty," she counters.

I nod at Shane, who's already got a crumpled bill in his hand. He says, "I'll take it."

"Excellent. I hope you enjoy it. Did you find some things?" she asks me.

I nod. The prices on the clothes are so low that I don't feel right about bargaining. I mean, I'm getting five tops for less than three dollars. "Here you go."

She hands me fifty cents and then hurries away to scold a kid who's about to break a cookie jar because his mother is absorbed in a fringed lampshade. I stuff my purchases into my backpack and then kneel to examine his bike. It needs some fixing up, but the repairs are mostly cosmetic.

"I got a bargain, huh?" Shane's smiling, so I guess he doesn't mind that I haggled for him.

"Definitely. You can ride it now, if you want. And I can help you fix it up. We have bike stuff left in my shed from when we restored mine."

"You and your aunt worked on your bike?" He seems impressed.

"Yeah. I mean, it wasn't a big deal. Come on, let's see how well yours works."

He nods, swinging onto the bike. It's ridiculously fun riding with Shane to my house. I'm used to being the lone geek pedaling away, long after the weather turns. With him behind me, this feels like an adventure, and I take pleasure in the sun shining down and the wind in my face. As I zoom down the hill, I throw up both hands, showing off a little. I can't count all the times I fell over before I perfected that trick. I've never had anyone to show before now.

When we stop in my driveway, I'm laughing so hard, and Shane pulls me off the seat into his arms. "That was crazy."

"But cool?"

"I should say it was just crazy. But . . . yeah. Sometimes you strike me as fearless, the way you do whatever the hell you want, and it doesn't seem to bother you what anyone thinks."

"I care what you think," I say softly.

"From where I'm standing, it's all good," he answers.

Then he kisses me. *Mmm*. Shane tastes like mint, and his lips are magical. If our neighbor hadn't come out of her front door and stood there clearing her throat like she was choking on a corncob, we might've gone on all afternoon.

"Hey, Mrs. Darnell. How are you?"

She's muttering something about *in her day* when I pull Shane around the side of the house. "I guarantee she'll mention this to my aunt."

"Will she mind?"

"Nah. I'm sure she'll figure it's better that we do it where we can be interrupted. So this is the bike-parking shed."

While I'm in there, I take stock of the parts. We'll need to buy a few things from the hardware store, but I have oil. The paint could use touching up, but that's wholly cosmetic. My primary concern should be the tires and the chain. I'm mumbling this out loud, as I take inventory, then I give him a short lecture on proper bicycle maintenance. Belatedly, I realize this probably isn't normal girlfriend behavior. Shane's looking really bemused. I stash both our bikes, then close the door behind me.

"What time are Ryan and Lila coming over?" he asks, following me into the house.

"Around seven thirty." I check the time on my phone. "We have almost four hours. Do you want something to eat?"

"You really have no idea, do you?" His voice holds a wondering note.

I'm wary. "Of what?"

"How incredible you are."

Um. Apparently he likes that I can take care of my sporting equipment? I choke the instinctive protest because I hear Aunt Gabby chiding me: *When someone gives you a compliment, you simply say thank you, even if you don't feel you deserve it.* So I murmur an awkward "thanks."

"No, I don't want anything to eat."

"Then what do you—" The question's cut off by his mouth.

Wow. Me. That's what he wants.

My back hits the refrigerator door as Shane kisses the hell out of me. I wrap my arms around his neck because I can't get close enough to him. Countless seconds later, he breaks away, breathless. "I'll die if we do that for four hours."

"It might be worth it," I whisper.

His fingers cling to mine as he tugs me toward the living room. Shane flashes the smile that squeezes my heart: equal parts shyness, innocence, and yearning. God, I'm so into him; it's a physical pain that won't go away. He pulls me down onto the couch and we make out for like an hour. It might've gone further if my aunt hadn't come home early to get ready for her date with Joe.

We spring apart as she unlocks the front door, and I hope I don't look as guilty as I feel.

CHAPTER
TWENTY-TWO

"WHAT'RE YOU TWO UP TO TONIGHT?" SHE ASKS.

I suspect she knows what we *were* doing, and I grin really big, trying to look innocent. "Watching a movie with Ryan and Lila. They'll be over later."

"That's reassuring. I'll be home by midnight. Do you want me to cook before I go out?"

I shake my head. "I can make grilled cheese or pasta."

Lila and Ryan will probably eat at home, so popcorn will do for them. I glance at Shane. "Should we make something now?" It's almost five. Depending on what we fix, it might be almost six by the time we finish.

"Yeah," he mutters.

I can tell he's uncomfortable that my aunt almost caught him on top of me, and for some reason, I want to laugh. We make spaghetti with a creamy tomato sauce; I puree some soft tofu to add protein. Along with a green salad, this is a decent meal.

"I need to cook for you sometime," Shane says, as we sit down.

"What's your specialty?"

"Slow-cooker pulled pork, but I guess that's out. I can also make decent vegetable soup."

"Nom. I'll bring fresh bread."

"Do you use a machine?"

I shake my head. "My aunt believes in old-fashioned kneading. Good upper-body workout." Then I pretend to flex, which is obviously absurd, and Shane smiles.

God, I'd do anything to make him laugh. When I'm being silly, some of his shadows seem to melt away, and *this* is how he should be, full of sunshine and laughter. The somber darkness I sometimes glimpse in him isn't natural. Yet I recognize it, and I wonder if that's what pulls us together. I remember Ryan mentioning Shane's "thick file" when he started at our school, but I'm in no position to judge, no matter what he's done. The important thing is who he is now.

I can hear my aunt moving around, getting ready for her date. She comes out once to ask my opinion on her outfit, and I give her two thumbs-up on a red dress with silver accessories, then she hurries off to do hair and makeup.

Shane appears baffled. "I had no idea it was such a thing for a girl to get ready. Do you . . . ?" He cuts the question, seeming to decide he shouldn't ask me.

But I can finish it. Do I flutter for him the way my aunt does for Joe? "Yeah. Sometimes I can't decide what shirt to wear or if I should go with or without lip gloss."

"I don't care about fashion," he answers. "I'd take you with no shirt at all. Uhm. I mean." Then he's as red as the tomato sauce.

I laugh. "My aunt's in the next room!"

Groaning, he buries his head in his hands. "Hopefully that's the stupidest thing I'll say tonight. It should be noted that I don't like lip gloss."

By the time we tidy up the kitchen, Joe has arrived and my aunt goes off with him, somehow managing not to say anything embarrassing before she does. I love her even more for that. Ryan and Lila arrive shortly thereafter, then there's more laughter, a stupid comedy that I've seen four times, so it doesn't matter if I sneak looks at Shane the whole night. We eat popcorn and throw it at each other, and by the time my aunt gets home, it's just the two of us again.

"Looks like you had fun," she comments, counting the cups mentally.

I can see that she's relieved that we spent the evening as a group. Now she doesn't have to worry that I'm pregnant; it'll be a while before she has to deal with that concern. Shane tries to duck out the back without a lot of fuss, but there's no way my aunt's letting that happen.

"Reflective tape," she tells him sternly. "Or I'm driving you home myself."

Shane shoots me a horrified look. Yeah, if she sees where he lives, she'll ask to meet his parents . . . and since they're not around, she'll call social services. Then he'll end up in foster care, and I know that's not what he wants. But if I'm being honest, this is a selfish move because I can't stand the thought of him going away. Even if it would be better for him.

I know that makes me a horrible person.

"I'll get the tape," I say. "Shane's got a bike in the shed. You'll be careful, right?"

Relieved, he nods and he doesn't protest when I stripe his arms and legs and one down his back for good measure. "See you tomorrow."

He kisses me quickly, then he's gone. I watch out the window until he's out of sight, then I turn to find my aunt studying me. "You're in love."

"Shut up, so are you."

Her cheeks pinken. "Maybe."

"It's a good year for us, huh?"

"Possibly the best yet," she admits.

SATURDAY, I PACK A PICNIC, WHICH WE EAT IN THE PARK. Afterward, Shane sings to me; he's brought his guitar this time, and I fool around, recording him on my phone. I tell him it's because I want to sell the video when he's famous, but the truth is, I just want to watch it when I'm not with him. How lame am I? Afterward, we stop in at the Coffee Shop, and the barista asks if Shane's interested in doing a regular Sunday performance, once a month. He's excited, so he's in a fantastic mood by the time he has to go to work.

That weekend sets the tone for the next few. Shane and I hang out in between work, school, and homework, but often we drag Ryan and Lila along with us, as they get along better than expected. The recycling drive goes well, though it doesn't set any records. I'm pleased that my social studies teacher approves the extra credit scheme.

Halloween rolls around, but I don't hit the party out at the Barn. Instead, I have friends over, the first time it's been more than Ryan and me; we used to do a scary movie marathon. He seems a little sad, but resigned, I guess, that things have changed for good.

And I think it's a positive change. The house is noisy with the freshmen and sophomores, Ryan and Lila, me, Shane, and even Conrad and Gwen make an appearance. Mostly the night involves eating candy, giving sweets to little people, and watching horror movies. My aunt is smart enough to hole up in her room and just ride it out. The next day, I learn that the cops raided the Barn and all minors who were present and drinking have community service . . . except the football team. Funny how that works out.

At school, I watch Dylan and he observes me with cold determination, but he hasn't been able to find anything out about me; his silence can't mean anything else. *Excellent.* I'm relieved that my case files are actually confidential. I hesitate to say so, but things might be okay. Life is good. It's odd to think that, but with Shane's arms around me, his chin on my shoulder, it's hard to feel otherwise. People know his name from his gig at the Coffee Shop, and music geeks are constantly coming up to him, trying to get him to join a garage band.

In fact, we have three grungy guys in front of us now. They're trying to talk him into it. "Come on, dude. Your guitar work is awesome, but I play bass, and Andrew is pretty good on the drums."

"What does the quiet guy do?"

The first dude grins. "He brings beer."

Yep, they sound like committed artists. I look at Shane, curious if he's interested.

Who says, "Thanks, but I don't have time."

I've learned my lesson, though. No matter how awesome a musician I think he is, I don't try to talk him into joining them. Shane knows his own needs best. He smiles at me as we walk away from the wannabe–rock stars.

That night, I get a surprise—an unknown number texts me: **hey, princess. :)**

Shane's the only one who calls me that in a sweet way. But I check just to be sure. **Shane? You got a phone?**

Yep.

Maybe I'm too suspicious but this could be Dylan, trying to trick me. I don't know how he'd get my number, but he could've bribed one of the freshmen or sophomores who have it. They haven't been friends long enough for me to be sure they'd side with me.

So I type, **what question did you ask me in detention? Explain to me why this was worth a tardy.**

Good. He's talking about the Post-it I left for him. While Dylan could know about that, I don't see how he could answer what Shane said to me. Then I get another text: **Right answer? They sell cheap prepaid ones at the P&K. Figured it was time.**

Me: **Yep. You should leave your number for Jace at the Coffee Shop. If you wanna play w/ him.**

Shane: **Not really. I don't play well with others.**

Me: **You play with me fine.** It's only after I hit send that I realize how that sounds. Oh, crap. There's no way he'll let that go.

Shane: **. . . are we sexting?**

Me: **OMG. I'm leaving now.**

Shane: **Night, princess.**

The next day, he smirks at me, waggling his phone, like there's something really dirty on it. The blush nearly sets my face on fire. On the plus side, his new phone means I get the sweetest messages at random points in the day . . . and sometimes when he's on break at work, too. He starts leaving Post-its on our locker, too—nothing embarrassing, little things I did that make him happy. Shane takes some shit for it, but I bet other girls wish their boyfriends were more like him. Mind you, I don't stop leaving compliments for people having a crappy day, but not gonna lie, it's easier to see the bright side with Shane shining just for me.

I have never, ever been this happy. I'm terrified. I'm on fire with joy. I'm . . . alive, for what feels like the first time, ever. I'm not pretending anymore, hoping nobody notices that I'm the freak who doesn't fit, who has darkness graven down to the bone.

A week before my aunt's big holiday in Chicago, as promised, I talk to Lila about sleeping over. She cocks her head. "Seriously? Your aunt is going away for the weekend and you want to waste one of those nights at my place?"

"*Want* is a strong word," I mumble. "But it's one of the conditions to my getting even one night on my own."

"She's protective of you, huh?"

"Do *your* parents leave you home alone that long?"

"Ha, never. Maybe not even when I'm thirty. But they don't *trust* me. It seems like you and your aunt get along pretty well. And you're not the type to throw a wild party the minute she leaves."

Lila doesn't have all the facts. The reason my aunt doesn't want to leave me alone so long has nothing to do with rapport or trust. But I don't go into that.

"Will your parents mind?"

She shakes her head. "Not at all, they love you. My dad thinks it's awesome that you have a plan, even if it's a hippie goal. Which night were you thinking?"

"Saturday."

Shane works that night, so we'll have more time together if he sleeps over on Friday, like he did before. And though I'm not positive, I might be ready to do more than kiss. How much more, I'm not sure, but I'm scared and excited, my heart trembling like a butterfly at the idea. I remember how it felt to curl up in his arms.

Finally the week I've been looking forward to arrives, when my aunt's going away with Joe. School and work seem like distractions from my ultimate goal: Friday night. Shane will arrive at my house at eight, and he's bringing clothes for work the next day. As I ride my bike home that afternoon, I've got a hundred questions swirling in my head: what I should wear, if we should cook or order from Pizza the Action, but pizza isn't very romantic. It's chill, for when you're hanging out with a bunch of people, but you'd never be, like, *Please, baby, take me out for a slice.*

But when I get home, things are *so* not okay. My aunt is home from work early, which almost never happens. This makes me think she's sick, and her depressed expression reinforces that impression. "What's wrong?" I ask.

"Joe's got strep," she answers.

"Oh, shit."

So obviously, the weekend she—and I—have been looking forward to isn't going to happen. No trip to Chicago, no swanky hotel, no theater tickets, no champagne, and for me—worst of all—no overnight with Shane. This isn't Joe's fault, but I'm totally frustrated. Instead of a romantic weekend where I kinda planned to fool around with Shane, I get to cheer my aunt up.

"I need to call Lila and cancel our sleepover."

"No, you don't have to do that," she protests.

"I want to. You shouldn't sit around by yourself, feeling crappy. You need chocolate therapy and a bunch of girl movies. Strep is contagious, right? So you can't even *see* Joe."

"Don't remind me." She brightens. "Hey, maybe Lila wants to come over here instead?"

"I'll ask. Let me drop my stuff in my room, change clothes, and call her."

"No problem. Julia Stiles and Heath Ledger aren't going anywhere."

For the first time, I notice she's watching *10 Things I Hate About You*, for probably the hundredth time; it's her self-comfort I'm-so-depressed-I hate-my-life movie. Mine is currently *Pitch Perfect*. But I like this one, too.

I rush to my room, close the door behind me, then text Shane.
Abort, abort! My aunt's staying here this weekend.

Shane: **Shit.**

Me: **I know, right?**

Shane: **Do you still want me to come over?**

Me: **No. She needs me to hang out with her this weekend. I'm sorry.**

Shane: **It's cool. Maybe I'll call Jace.**

Me: **You got his number? I thought you don't play well with others.**

Shane: **I'm trying.**

This is where I wish I was brave enough to key *I love you*. But I'd never send it before saying it in person. I should tell him . . . at the right moment. And it's too soon. How long have we actually been together? Maybe two months. That's *definitely* too fast. I'll scare him.

Me: **See you Monday. Miss you.**

Shane: **You too, Princess.**

Then I actually call Lila, so she knows it's important. She picks up on the third ring. "This is retro. Why didn't you text me?"

"Change of plans. You want to spend the weekend with us instead?"

"Oh, snap. What happened?"

I explain about Joe, strep, and how my aunt now has epic sad-face. "So now we're gonna watch movies endlessly and eat chocolate. I can't promise my aunt will shower. Hopefully by Sunday."

"God, what would she do if he broke up with her?"

"I have *no* idea."

And it kind of scares me because Aunt Gabby is my rock. Joe might have the power to break her heart, which makes me want to ride my bike across town and stand under his window yelling at him, even if he's sick. I restrain the impulse like I always do.

But I have to defend her. My aunt isn't the type to lose it over a guy. "She hasn't taken a vacation in years. She's just disappointed."

"Yeah, I'd be bummed, too, especially if I bought new clothes to wear."

"She did."

"Then I get it. Hang on, let me ask my mom."

I hear snippets of their conversation, then Lila comes back. "She wants to talk to your aunt to make sure it's okay with her, and that the whole weekend isn't too long."

"And make sure we'll be adequately supervised," I guess.

"You know my mother so well."

Moving down the hall as we talk, I gesture for my aunt to pause the movie. "Mrs. Tremaine wants to speak with you."

"Oh. No problem." I hand her the phone. "Yes? Okay, Lila." Then a few seconds later, "Yes, this is Gabby. No, it's no trouble at all. In fact, it was my idea. We'd love to have Lila over for a girls' weekend. She's so much fun, so great to be around." Then she pauses, listening. "All right, drop her off around seven. Sounds fine. I can bring her home on Sunday. All handled," she adds, returning my cell.

"You *are* a joy," I tell Lila when she comes back.

"My mom thinks there's an alien running my body now. The sad part is, I think she likes the parasite better than the old me."

"You're still you. See you later."

I disconnect, put away my school stuff, and change clothes. Then I join my aunt for an orgy of sweets and feel-good movies. It turns out to be a really fun weekend, even more so after Lila arrives. By the time she leaves on Sunday, my aunt is in a better mood, and I'm not totally sorry things worked out like this. I mean, I wanted Shane here. But girl time was fun, too.

CHAPTER
TWENTY-THREE

WHEN I HEAD TO SCHOOL ON MONDAY, IT'S A SHORT week, only three days, since Thursday is Thanksgiving. I'm looking forward to the break. Green World is canceled for the holiday, and I don't have to work on Thursday, obviously. Shane has the day off, too, but I haven't invited him over yet. I should clear it at home first. So Monday night, after my shift at the Curly Q, I bring it up with Aunt Gabby. "I was wondering, is it okay if Shane spends Thanksgiving with us?"

"What about his family?"

"It's just his dad . . . and he's a truck driver. He can't get time off, and they've scheduled him for a long haul this time."

"That sucks." I nod, hoping she doesn't ask anything else about Shane's father. "No grandparents nearby?"

I shake my head, though Shane hasn't mentioned them. Maybe they've passed away? "We can't leave him alone for the holidays."

"I don't mind, if he's okay sleeping on the couch."

So instead of a two-day weekend with Shane, unsupervised,

I'm getting four days with my aunt in the house. I'll take it. Impulsively I hug her. "You're the best."

"So you occasionally tell me," she mumbles, smiling.

"Is Joe coming over?"

"Not this year. He's driving to Missouri to see his folks . . . if he feels up to it."

"Yeah, the demon strep. How's he doing?"

"I haven't seen him all week. He was off work for four days."

"Well, I hope he feels better and has a good holiday."

After eating a quick dinner, I head to my room, happy with how this worked out. Tuesday morning, I pounce on Shane at our locker.

He hugs me, looking startled. "Good news?"

"You're coming home with me Wednesday. It's cool with my aunt if you stay until Sunday."

His eyes widen. "You didn't—"

"I explained that your dad got stuck with an unexpected job and you're at loose ends for Thanksgiving." With my eyes, I warn him not to say anything else. If Dylan can't make trouble for me, he might go after Shane. And he *does* have a secret he's keeping.

I glance around, and sure enough, a member of Dylan's crew is leaning against the lockers nearby. It's not like I haven't noticed his people watching me, but I spend all my time being good. They won't catch me doing anything he can use.

He nods. "Should I bring anything?"

"Nah, we'll handle it. Hope you like Tofurky."

"I can honestly say I have no idea."

"Don't worry, there will be plenty of other trimmings. Cornbread dressing, sweet potato casserole, green beans and mushrooms, fruit salad, fresh yeast rolls, pumpkin pie, and homemade vanilla bean ice cream."

"Wow. Sounds like you guys go all out. I . . . haven't had that in a while."

"Before I came to live with my aunt, me either." That's more than I usually tell anyone about my time with my bio-mom, but I want Shane to know I understand, at least somewhat.

"Thanks, Sage. This will be awesome."

People push past us, reminding me I need to get to class. There's still Tuesday and Wednesday before the fun begins. I'm nervous thinking about having him at my house—what if I do something embarrassing or he catches me going into the bathroom with bed head and morning breath—but I'm excited, too. Shane squeezes me before letting go, just as the bell rings, and we run in opposite directions. I slide into my chair just in time.

I wish I could say the time races like white-water rapids, but it's more like honey in cold weather. But the clock hands can't actually run backward, so eventually, it's Wednesday afternoon. Shane and I head out to the bike rack, but I draw up short.

The tires on my bike have been slashed. I get the message loud and clear. If Dylan can't ruin me socially, he can hurt me in other ways. There are no security cameras, so it would be my word against his, and he occupies a higher social echelon. Plus, Principal Warick's banging his mom, so he has reason to keep Dylan happy. That means he's practically untouchable.

"Well, that was a dick move right before Thanksgiving. It'll be days before you can get that fixed."

"Yeah," I say quietly.

I'm sure that was the point—to make me feel helpless and

crippled. And it upsets me because it works. I would *love* to let Shadow Sage answer this challenge. I could escalate so fast, it would make Dylan's head spin. I imagine slipping a cotton cord into his gas tank, then lighting it up. The flame would burn inward, like a fuse, until it caught the fuel inside. That would make a really satisfying explosion. I'm enjoying the thought when Shane's hand wraps around mine.

"Don't just leave it here. Some asshole might make it worse over the weekend."

His touch recalls me to the person I've chosen to be. So instead of doing something horrible, I unlock my bike and push it home on the shredded tires. A quick check in the shed tells me that I don't have the supplies to fix this myself. I'll have to take it to the repair shop, and it'll take a chunk out of my college fund.

Shane grabs the basket and starts attaching it to his bike, distracting me from thoughts of revenge. "What're you doing?"

"I'll handle the shopping. It's the least I can do."

Since I'm barely keeping my shit together, I don't argue. I dart inside to get the grocery money from the coffee can in the cupboard, then I hand over the list and he's off. Long after he's gone, I sit in the shed, staring at my shredded tires. It's just a bike, right? It's not like Dylan hurt me. A little voice whispers, *You don't have to blow up his truck. You could hit him in a quieter, deeper way.* Right now, I'm restraining the urge, but only just. It takes all my self-control to bury the desire to wreck him and pin on a smile by the time Shane gets back.

LATE THURSDAY, AFTER MY AUNT HAS RETIRED IN A FOOD coma, Shane and I are curled up together on the couch. He's got an

223

arm around my shoulders and I'm leaning against his chest. I'm sleepy, but not tired, and I'm 100 percent reluctant to end what has been the most perfect Thanksgiving ever. I've buried my anger beneath food and the sweetness of spending time with my favorite people.

Lazily I flip through the brand-new memories: Shane helping us cook, him scarfing down our traditional feast, and then us breaking out the artificial tree. It's kind of ridiculous but Aunt Gabby always puts up our god-awful white Christmas tree after we eat Thanksgiving dinner. Now it's twinkling behind us, throwing interesting shadows on the walls. We could be watching a movie, but I turned on the radio instead.

"This was . . . a phenomenal day," he whispers.

It's raining now, just a gentle patter, and I bet it's chilly outside, but snuggled up against Shane, I can't imagine ever being cold. "I'm glad you had fun. I know our traditions are a little weird. My aunt doesn't believe in killing trees, so we've had this kitschy fake one forever. It grows on you."

"No, I liked it. All of it. But especially this part." He pulls me a little closer, so he can kiss my temple, and the tenderness of the gesture curls my toes.

"Me too," I admit.

"So, I was wondering . . . are we official?"

"Are you asking if I'm your girlfriend?" Though I'm trying to be cool, inwardly I'm screaming my head off.

"Yeah. I mean, you had that problem with Ryan, where you were always together, and people thought you were a couple but you really weren't. And people have been asking me, and I wasn't sure, and I didn't want to do to you what he did, so I thought—"

"We're official." I put him out of his misery, though I've never seen Shane ramble so much. It's tempting to let him continue. "And it was never like this with Ryan. We never kissed."

"Good," he whispers, surprising me. "I wish I could have all your firsts, because you're getting all of mine."

Instead of saying something profound, I make a weird noise because I literally have no words. *I am awesome at romance. Two points.* He doesn't seem to mind, though. When he kisses me, I forget why I needed to talk or what I meant to say.

Half an hour later, I reluctantly make up the sofa for Shane and head for my room. It's hard to leave him, but I'd die of humiliation if my aunt came out to use the bathroom and caught us rolling around. So I savor a final good-night kiss and go to bed on my own. I'm not expecting any problems—this was such a good day, but for the first time in weeks, I have the Dream. I wake with a scream strangling in my throat, sweat pooled on my back, and the sense that the scene has changed. My bio-mom was there, like always, and I'm left shivering, hands tucked inside my sleeves. With my fingertips, I count, inspecting the scars that won't go away. When I first moved in, my aunt bought vanishing creams, but . . . they didn't help. Anyway, the worst marks are those that *don't* show up on my skin.

For some reason, Dylan Smith has become one of the demons in my head, too. Maybe because he got away with slashing my tires, it's like he has power over me now. I know from experience that I can't go back to sleep, however, so I get a book and I'm curled up on my daybed, reading, when someone knocks on the door. The clock tells me it's 5:22, not a normal time for anyone else to be awake. My aunt won't stir for three more hours since the shop opens at ten; and she's not looking forward to Black Friday, the only day of the year when they're open until eight at night.

"Come in," I call softly.

I'm not surprised to see Shane standing there, his hair adorably tousled. Overnight, he's grown some scruff, and in this light, it has a hint of ginger. Somehow this makes him even cuter. "You okay?"

"Why wouldn't I be?" Parrying one question with another is a standard defensive strategy, and I instantly regret it. But I'm so scared of what he'll think of me when I crack the fragile, painted eggshell I show the world and expose the gooey mess within.

"Well, I saw your light, and it's pretty early. We were up late."

It's true; I'm running on five hours of sleep. "You can come in if you want."

Shane steps into my room, but leaves the door open, so we don't get accused of dirty deeds, if my aunt wakes up unexpectedly. His blue gaze flicks around, taking in the pictures I've cut from magazines and framed, the tangle of beads and Christmas lights that I've draped around my mirror. This room is cheerful, but I wonder what he thinks of it the second time. The throw pillows are piled on the floor beside the bed, so he steps over them in coming closer.

Shane perches on the edge of the bed, studying me with a faint frown. "You know me better than I do you. And I feel like an asshole for just realizing it."

My chest hurts. I rub it, trying to reduce the tight sensation. Too sharply, I remember the group home and the way one of the workers had to restrain me. See, they're trained on how to hold an out-of-control kid. I can still feel Mr. Rennick's arms around me, hard and impersonal, to keep me from hurting anyone, myself included. I remember the crunch that came before, when I hit the girl I caught going through my things, crimson spattering from her nose. I remember the burn of the knuckles I scraped on her teeth and the raw feel of my throat from constant screaming. Rage has a scent, bitter and metallic.

"What would you like to know?" The question tastes like blood because I don't know if I can be honest with him. But I'll try. That's how much I trust Shane.

"I know your dad died when you were seven . . . and you lived in a bad part of Chicago when you were with your mom." He pauses as if to think. "Then you came to live with your aunt when your mom took off?"

No, he's skipped a whole section in my life, one I prefer to pretend never happened. "There was some time in government housing between the two. Gabby is my dad's half sister, and it took time for social workers or whoever to make the connection."

Please let that be enough for now. Please.

"How long?" he asks.

This much, I can manage. It's like tiptoeing around the edges of a chasm. If I fall in, I'll lose the person I've built in the last three years. She might have started as a persona I created so Aunt Gabby wouldn't send me away, but little by little, I feel like this Sage could be real. I want to live *her* life, not the one I left behind. People can do that, right? Make up their minds to change and be better. It's possible. *Please, let it be.*

"Until I was thirteen." That's not strictly true. I can't give him the timeline without telling him everything, though, and I'm not ready to do that. I want to live in this dream a little longer.

"So, like, foster homes or what?"

"And a group home, when the foster home didn't work out." I don't explain why.

And he must sense my reticence because he doesn't ask. "That's exactly what I'm trying to avoid. I guess you understand how come."

"Yeah," I say softly, gratefully. "I get it. And I'll help you anyway I can."

"I know you will, Princess."

I used to make fun of girls who let guys give them quasi-adorable pet names, but I don't say a word. It makes me happy that he's reclaimed one that used to bother me. I melt a little, and Shane reaches for me. His arms feel warm and strong, his hands splaying over my back. He holds me for a while, then he says, "This might seem weird at this hour, but I need to borrow your laptop."

"Not a problem." I get it for him and hand it over. "Everything okay?"

"Yeah. I've been thinking about this for a while. And I need to apologize to Mike, the guy I stayed with in Michigan City. He was nothing but nice to me, and I was an asshole."

"Your mom's friend. But why are you sending this at five in the morning?"

Shane taps my nose gently. "No 'net at home, remember? I'll have to make a special stop at the library if I don't do it now, while it's on my mind."

"That makes sense."

He nods, logging in to Gmail. I realize I don't have his email address, so I peek at it, memorizing music4life, along with four numbers. At first I think, it's a PIN, then I decide that's probably the year he was born. After I do the math, I realize it's too long ago.

"What's 1994?"

Shane lifts his shoulder in a sheepish shrug. "The year Kurt Cobain died. I used to be really into Nirvana, I opened this account when I was younger."

"Mine's Ecogrrl60167," I mumble. "So I can't talk."

"Isn't that the zip code here?"

"Yep. I'm creative that way."

"I don't know if he'll care, but I feel like a dick for what I put him through. None of it was his fault. I just . . . went nuclear or something."

"You were in shock." I don't know if that's the right word for what he went through. He spent years watching his mom die, taking care of her, but not knowing when it would end. Then . . . it did. It would be hard to deal with that.

Shane hesitates, pausing between words, deleting and erasing, and I glance away from the laptop, not wanting him to think I'm reading over his shoulder. A few minutes later, he sighs and says, "There, sent. An e-mail's not enough, considering all the nights cops dragged him out of bed because of me."

"You're different now. People can change." Now I'm telling Shane what I want so desperately to be true. Maybe if I say it often enough, we'll both believe it.

"I hope so."

It's almost six by this point, so I suggest, "Let's fix breakfast."

I make drop biscuits while Shane scrambles some eggs. My aunt comes out of her room just before seven, sniffing sleepily. "Something smells good."

Shane tells her, "We wanted to surprise you, after all the cooking you did yesterday."

Her smile is warm and open. Yep, she likes him. "That's so sweet."

After breakfast, my aunt rushes around getting ready. The fact that she doesn't mind showing Shane how disorganized she can be strikes me as endearing, like she already sees him as family. I clean the kitchen while he showers, then as he works on a new song, strumming his guitar and then making notes on the hand-drawn sheet music, I head for my turn in the bathroom. This melody sounds a little more upbeat, less brokenhearted, and I'm humming the only line I heard as I step into the shower.

You're the one who makes me whole.

I wonder what he'll rhyme with that. Soul, maybe.

Later, Shane and I go for a walk, drop my bike off to be repaired, eat lunch at the Coffee Shop, then get home in time to meet Ryan and Lila for a movie at the Capitol. We wait in line together, and for the first time, I feel like all the pieces fit. Ryan and Lila aren't a couple, but they seem to like hanging out. In fact, I'd swear she's flirting with him tonight. To me, he seems the same as usual; he's wearing skinny jeans that make his legs look ten miles long, a button up over a weird graphic tee, plus his hipster glasses. His black hair is the usual riot of cowlicks and chaos.

"What's the deal?" I whisper, nudging her.

Lila has just flipped her hair. And I don't think she did it ironically. To my astonishment, color touches her pale cheeks. "What? He's cute. You don't mind, right?"

"No." And I truly don't.

Ryan's my friend. He always has been. And, yes, he screwed things up, but I'm glad I listened to my aunt when she advised me not to let the silence run too long. I will always love his stories. Right now, he's telling a convoluted one about his mom, a squirrel, and a bird feeder. This shouldn't be hilarious, but somehow it is. I'm overwhelmed by the urge to hug them all, because they're here, and I have *friends,* and considering what my life was like three years ago, this seems flipping miraculous.

Ryan finishes the story, and we're all cracking up, but I have this pinch in my heart, like moments this beautiful just can't last.

"You okay, Sage?" Shane asks, as we step up to the ticket counter.

For him, I muster a smile and put aside my dark thoughts. "I'm perfect."

CHAPTER TWENTY-FOUR

IN EARLY DECEMBER, THE FIRST SNOW FALLS, AND IT'S cold enough to stick around. I don't even mind, though the ice makes biking tough. There's nothing more depressing than dead grass and bare, wet trees in winter. Snow covers all the bad stuff, making the world fresh and clean.

A while ago, using my awesome Google-fu, I tracked down the guy who owns the land we cleared in the fall. He's in a nursing home, which is why he hasn't done anything with the property. When he dies, his grandchildren will inherit, but until then, he signs a paper granting us permission to plant a garden for the beautification of the town. I'm exuberant when I come out of the old folks home and swing onto my bike. Green World will be pleased at our next meeting.

Sure enough, on Wednesday, Gwen nominates me as MVP, though that's not something we've ever done before. She also takes charge from there. "We'll need donations from various merchants, so we're ready in the spring. We'll need seeds and seedlings, fertilizer, topsoil . . ."

Briskly, she divides up the responsibilities between us, and we're left with the joyous prospect of begging for handouts at the holidays. I feel like I need to point that out. "Christmas is in a couple of weeks, and the stores will be really busy. Doesn't it make sense to wait until after the holiday rush?"

"Yeah," Ryan says. "I say we start this in January."

Conrad surprises me by siding with us. "Agreed. We can't even start working on the garden until spring. If we plant too soon, frost will kill everything."

"Then what do you propose we do in December?" Gwen wants to know.

"Canned food drive," Tara suggests. The sophomores, who are usually quiet at these meetings, nod in agreement. Thus encouraged, she continues, "I know it's not exactly green, but it's right to help others at the holidays, you know?"

"Seconded," Kenny says.

We vote and in the end, most of us are on board with the canned food drive. Since the recycling effort went well, we have the process in place already. I just need to find a teacher willing to sponsor this one and grant extra credit.

I do the cleanup, like usual, and this time, Shane, Ryan, and Lila all stay to help; it goes much faster. The librarian isn't even turning off the lights when we head downstairs. I wave to Miss Martha, who smiles at me. This makes me wonder if she felt sorry for me before, forever alone and stuck with the janitorial work. Ryan detours to the bathroom.

"Who do you think?" I ask Shane and Lila as we step outside.

"About what teacher might go for the project?" he asks.

"The home ec lady," Lila jokes.

"So few people take that class . . . I don't think that would help much."

"Probably not," Shane says.

Ryan catches up with us at a run. "You guys want to come to my place for a while?"

I check the time and shake my head. "By the time I get home, it'll be late. Thanks, though."

"I'll come," Lila says. "If you can give me a ride home."

"Not a problem. My car's this way."

Ryan and Lila wave as they stroll toward the parking lot; his parents bought him a car in payment for his good grades. I mean, it's not that I *want* a car, unless it's an electric one, but if I did, I'd have to save every penny for a year. Shane brushes the hair away from my face, tugging on my knit hat. "I should get moving, too. At this rate, it'll be past nine when I get home."

In answer, I raise up on tiptoe for a kiss. His arms go around me, and he holds me as if it's hard for him to let me go. He's warm against the night chill; for a few seconds, I relax in his arms, relishing Shane's familiar scent. I give him another kiss, then step back. He grimaces, but we put on the stupid reflective tape together.

"When we met a few months ago, I never would've believed you'd get me doing this, too."

"You probably thought I was a total weirdo."

He thinks about that. "No. Just . . . cautious, I guess. And I had no reason to be."

"You do now. So be careful."

"I will," he promises.

The canned food drive goes surprisingly well. People at school are actually taking notice of Green World, and we acquire a few new members. I'm not sure if the interest will last into the new year, but it's helping now. We wind up collecting nearly a thousand cans for a local aid program, and Principal Warick commends us at an assembly, where Gwen gives a speech and accepts the certificate on behalf of the whole club.

But a week later, the universe slams on the brakes. Apparently we're spending winter break with Gabby's aunt Helen. It's a five-hour trip, and I'm not technically related to this old woman since she's connected to my aunt's mom. I protest at first, until Aunt Gabby gives me a reproachful look.

"She's been asking us to visit for two years, and I've been putting her off . . ." She doesn't say it, but I hear it. *Because of you.* "Anyway, this year, I don't want her to be alone on Christmas, Sage. It could be her last."

But what about Shane, I want to say, but my aunt doesn't know his circumstances; she doesn't realize that his dad hasn't been to the trailer since he bought it. She can't know. Which means there's no point in arguing. As far as she's concerned, he'll be spending the holidays with his dad. And he would be, if his father wasn't such a coward. Besides, Shane's loneliness isn't more pressing than Aunt Helen's. I resign myself to the inevitable.

"When are we leaving?" I ask.

"You get out of school on the twenty-second?"

"I think so."

"Then we'll head out the twenty-third."

"When are we coming back?"

"January second. It will be safer to avoid the New Year's traffic."

Though I don't say anything, I'm quietly crushed. I've always wanted to kiss somebody on New Year's Eve, and this time, I want to start the New Year with Shane. But there's one more tactic I can try.

"Won't you miss Joe?" I ask her.

She sighs. "Of course. But I haven't seen Aunt Helen in years. Hopefully he'll be around for a while. She may not be."

There's that old superstition about whatever you're doing on New Year's Day, that's how it'll be all year. So people try to avoid conflict and spend time with their loved ones. In my case, it looks like I'll be sad, lonely, and wishing I was somewhere else.

I'm not looking forward to this trip, but when the time comes, I pack my bag and trudge out of the house with my aunt. She pauses at her car with a faint sigh.

"It'd be a lot easier if you would road trip," she tells me with a flicker of impatience.

I brighten immediately. "I'm happy to stay home."

"I don't care if it's more work, that's not happening."

I sigh and follow her down the driveway. Greyhound stops at the gas station, and from there, we ride to the train station an hour away. I don't object to public transportation since the system moves a lot of people; it's less wasteful. My idiosyncrasies stretch a five-hour trip to eight, by the time you factor our trip on the local bus that carries us relatively near Great Aunt Helen's apartment. Gabby is rumpled and grouchy when we arrive.

I wish I could say the holidays are awesome and that Great Aunt Helen's delightful, but in truth, she's old and irascible, and she has too many cats. There's a lumpy sofa with my name on it, and I live for texts from Shane, and What'sApp messages from Lila and Ryan. I'm reading one now, three days after Christmas, and trying not to laugh.

Lila: **did she ask you to rub peppermint lotion on her feet yet?**

Ryan: **please tell me she knitted you something**

Lila: **was there a cheese log? Please let there be cheese log!**

Despite my bad mood, I'm smiling when I curl up on the couch much later. It's so lame, but I actually go to bed with my phone, just in case Shane sends me something when he gets off work; he's pulling overtime during the break, giving other stockers a chance to be with their families. I hate that he spent Christmas alone. What was it like? Did he make some real food or just open a can of soup?

Sure enough, my phone vibrates just past midnight. **You up?**

I text back, **Waiting for you. How was work?**

Sucked. Miss you.

Me too. I wish I could hear his voice, but then I might wake up the aunts. Or Great Aunt Helen might yell at me for being a rowdy miscreant; she's always saying that about her upstairs neighbors, and that's an ordeal best avoided. So texting it is.

Seems like you've been gone longer than 5 days.

Tell me about it. There's nothing to do and I haven't seen anyone younger than 65, besides my aunt Gabby, since we got here.

Only 5 more days. We're halfway there.

It makes me absurdly happy to know he's counting the days, too. **Yep.**

He texts a little longer, telling me about this guy who came in with nine dollars in his pocket and then he had to put stuff back, which mean Shane had to restock it all. He was apparently an old man, who thought his money should go further than that, so he insisted they call the manager. I decide working at the Curly Q isn't so bad.

How's the song coming? I type. He's been working on a new one since Thanksgiving but he won't play it for me yet. I've only caught strains and snippets.

Almost done. Trying to have it ready by Valentine's Day.

God, I hope that means he's writing it for me. **Sweet. Bed now. Talk tomorrow?**

Definitely. Dream of me.

This is possibly the most romantic text ever. I push out a happy breath and fight the urge to hug my phone. If I was watching my own behavior, I'd probably find it ridiculous. But when I fall asleep, I *do* dream of Shane, and he keeps the monsters away.

Before we leave, I go shopping. It's cheating to buy Shane's present after the holidays, but this isn't a marked-down item. The one benefit to Aunt Helen's apartment is that she lives a lot closer to shopping. Though this isn't a city by New York standards, compared to Farmburg, it's a bustling metropolis. And it doesn't take me long to find the perfect gift for Shane. Well, it's a complement, actually, to something I already have.

By the time the visit ends, I don't hate Great Aunt Helen, but I'm tired of her cats and relieved to head home. We pack our things, say good-bye, and take the bus to the train station. It's a lengthy trip, which ends in us walking almost two miles from the bus stop to our house. Joe offered to pick us up, but Gabby knows I won't go.

"Sometimes your principles are a pain in my ass," she mutters.

That's annoying. She can go with Joe; it's not like I mind. "Call your boyfriend. I can go home alone."

"It's fine." But her tone says maybe it's not.

And I'm afraid of making her mad, but I'm also unwilling to change. This is one thing I *can* control. So I'm scared and trying not to get upset, as we drag our suitcases up the sidewalk. "You should get a ride. Seriously, it's not a big deal."

"If it wasn't, we wouldn't both be walking." She sounds a little snappish, tired from traveling, probably, and so am I.

Hunching my shoulders, I get my phone out.

Aunt Gabby makes an effort to smooth things over. "Texting Shane?"

"And Lila and Ryan," I mumble, though I was, in fact, telling Shane I'm home.

"Is he working tonight?"

"Yeah. I probably won't get to see him until tomorrow."

"I admit, I was a little worried about how fast you two got together, but you handled the separation well."

My prior irritation flares stronger. "Is that why we left?" I demand.

Does she think that I can't function without Shane? I miss him. I might even . . . Do I *love* him? I have no idea. There's no precedent. But . . . he matters a lot.

"No, it was so my aunt wouldn't be alone. She can't travel anymore, and she's lonely."

"Your good deed just happened to test how well I cope?" I'm tempted to get mad, but I back off the feeling. I can't get angry. It's Hulk-ish, and bad things happen when I do. So I wrestle the feeling into submission and summon a teasing smile. "Anyway, she seemed to enjoy having us."

"Definitely. And she loves meat, so it was a sacrifice for her to agree to a meal without it on Christmas Day."

The first thing I do when we get home is get on the Internet. I didn't bring my laptop with me, so I haven't checked e-mail and Facebook for a while, and I'm behind on my YouTube channels and Web comics. This is why I don't miss cable TV. We had it at the group home, where I had no computer and no privacy, but I much prefer controlling what I watch and read. Since my friends talk to me on my phone, I don't really have any e-mail but I catch up their status updates. Ryan in particular is great about posting funny, stupid things. I take a picture of myself making a weird face and then just type **cheese log,** and tag Lila with it.

Shane texts me late. **Sorry I couldn't come over tonight. Done with overtime now. Have tomorrow off.**

What time can you be here? I send back. It will be Sunday, which means school starts the next day. I feel like a miser, hoarding this one final day of winter break. The snow is thick on the ground, so it'll be hard for him to get here—they don't always plow out where he lives—but he must think I'm worth it.

Ten too early?

Nope. My dominant feeling is yay! Though I'm not sure if that qualifies as an actual emotion. So I'll call it excitement. The prospect of seeing Shane is more thrilling than Christmas, even though I got a few cute shirts and a new pair of jeans, as well as a gift certificate for an online bookstore. I guess that means he's better than all presents combined.

And he's writing me a song.

I'm up by eight and in the shower, which is extreme. Usually I stay in bed, read, or watch something on my laptop. Not today. I waffle over what to wear, going back and forth between a couple of outfits, then I remember what Shane said about taking me with no top on, and that makes me laugh. Then I put on jeans, a camisole, and a white hoodie with silver writing. I leave my hair to dry naturally while I have breakfast, then I put on a little makeup, omitting the lip gloss.

Shane's fifteen minutes early, but I'm smiling as I throw open the door. He hugs me hard, drops a kiss on my mouth, then we step into the house. My aunt's still asleep. He's got his backpack, and I peer at it. Surely we're not spending the day on homework. I had plenty of that while I was gone.

"I brought your present," he explains. "Since we weren't together on Christmas."

Oh, wow. I've never gotten anything from a guy, unless you count the valentine I got in second grade. "Yours is in my room. I'll be right back."

He looks surprised, like I'd fail to get him a gift. I bring the wrapped package out and we swap them. "You first."

Shane seems like he might argue, but in the end, he tears open the paper. It's two things, actually: my iPod, loaded with songs that I think he'll like . . . and a package of printed sheet music, so he doesn't have to draw his own. "Whoa. This is too much."

"It isn't if you like it." I can listen to music on the radio and online. He doesn't have either option at the trailer.

He kisses me sweetly, until I forget I'm supposed to open my present, too. "Your turn."

I feel like a little kid as I pull off the wrapping paper to reveal a little white box. When I removed the top, there's a delicate silver chain with a finely made musical note for the pendant. I think that's the eighth note, the one with the single flag, and I totally get this present. It's as if he's giving me part of him to keep with me always.

"Do you like it?"

"It's beautiful," I whisper. "Put it on me?"

The odds are excellent that I'm never taking this necklace off.

CHAPTER
TWENTY-FIVE

JANUARY IS USUALLY A BLAH MONTH, BUT THIS YEAR IT'S kind of magical. Shane and I have become a couple that people pay attention to. They yell, "Sup, Shage," when we walk past; we're a smush name now. Most days this strikes me as a good thing. I'm not sure why, but they're not calling me Princess anymore, though I'm still writing pink Post-its in purple glitter pen, and I *love* that Shane's not embarrassed by this. Sometimes he even points people out to me who could use some cheering up, a long way from the boy who wouldn't look anyone in the eye at the beginning of the year.

I manage to bring my grade up to a B– in geometry and my aunt is delighted. She cooks Shane and me a special Italian feast to celebrate. If I read her right, she likes him a lot and no longer worries that we're too attached. But I make sure we spend an equal amount of our time with Ryan and Lila, so they don't feel left out. It's cool that we've all gotten to be friends, and I'm not the only glue holding our group together.

• • •

AT THE END OF JANUARY, WE ALL EAT LUNCH AT MEL'S house because she's been bothering her mom to have us over. In other words, I have a social life. It's *so* weird.

We cruise toward Valentine's Day, and I've almost forgotten that Dylan Smith exists. Until he reminds me. He must think he's safe—that I probably won't repeat what I know about his mom— and I catch him hassling Shane. It's early, before most other students are around. Dylan and his crew have Shane hemmed in outside. Shane looks like he wants to start swinging, but there are too many, and I can see him reminding himself, *No more trouble*. His fists uncurl.

That's more than I can take. I overlooked the thing with my bike, but this? No. I quietly go and get Mr. Johannes. "Some guys are bothering Shane outside. Do you mind? It's really unfair, six on one."

"No problem. I think I left something in my car anyway." He winks.

From my vantage, I glimpse how the jocks spring away when Mr. Johannes steps outside, giving Shane the chance to slip into the building. When he sees me, he says, "You sent him?"

"Is that okay?"

"Yeah. Better than a punch in the face. I don't know what that guy's damage is."

I do. But this is a battle between Dylan and me. He might have lost interest in Shane if I hadn't stood up for Lila. So I intend to enlist her aid in teaching the asshole a lesson. At our lockers, after Shane heads to his first class, I tell her what went down.

She's scowling. "What is his *problem*?"

"You know one of them."

That's mean, I tell myself.

But Shadow Sage is stirring in her shallow grave, raking the earth and whispering in my ear. Since I'm holding a figurative sword over Dylan's head, I have to decide what to do. I could retaliate for him picking on Shane, but I'm not ready to ruin so many other lives. Yet he shouldn't get away with *hurting* people. Someone needs to show him how it feels. Only I don't want to drag his mom into it, let alone the principal, his wife, and his kids.

Lila snickers. "I never knew you could be so bitchy."

"It's a closely guarded secret."

Then she sighs, watching Dylan and crew sweep past. "I wish we could bring him down a peg or two."

Tall and fit, dressed in jeans and letterman jackets, the jocks are untouchable because being good at sports makes them the next thing to royalty at this school. None of them got punished for underage drinking out the Barn, unlike the rest of the student body. I hate that they get away with everything. In particular, there are *no* consequences for Dylan. He flattens people like a steamroller but nobody ever brings the fight to him.

"Give him a taste of his own medicine, you mean?" An idea takes shape, though it's absolutely the inverse of being the Post-it Princess.

"I wouldn't say no," she whispers.

Her eyes are deep and hurt; she's still not over the way Dylan trashed her reputation. Once people think you sleep around, it doesn't much matter if you do or not. So I let the idea develop fully before speaking. It's deliciously awful, and I put away my misgivings. He's earned this. And if we're careful, we can get away with it.

"Do you know where the spirit squad stores their supplies?" I ask.

Lila nods. "Why?"

I tell her. And her smile is both wicked and luminous.

After school, we raid the closet and take poster board, balloons, and streamers. Since the girls sometimes decorate players' vehicles, at first glance, nobody will realize there's anything wrong with Dylan's truck. But wait until they read the messages. Giggling like mad, we sneak into an unlocked classroom after school and get to work. We have to be fast since the team's at practice now.

Lila scrawls half the messages and I cover the rest. Most of them are childish, taunts about his habits and personal hygiene. *I'm a nose picker. I eat them, too. I wet the bed until I was 12. My favorite porno mag is* Grannies Gone Wild. *I'm afraid I will die a virgin.* But I save the best for last, writing in huge block letters: I CRY WHEN GIRLS TOUCH MY WIENER.

Since we don't care about neatness, it doesn't take long to finish up. In stealth mode, we creep out to the parking lot, which is deserted at this hour. The teachers are gone except for those who sponsor afternoon activities. Students in clubs haven't come out yet; the rest are on the way home. *I forgot how good it feels to be bad.* This is a rush, but I remind myself *why* we're doing this. The justification definitely matters.

Lila and I keep watch while duct-taping the signs, balloons, and streamers all over Dylan's black truck. I cross my fingers that someone sees it before he and his buddies arrive. But still, just humiliating him in front of his teammates is better than nothing, more of a comeuppance than he usually gets. One of his asshole friends drove Jon Summers to his death. Dylan didn't lead that witch hunt, but he didn't stop it, either.

"We should get out of here," Lila says.

"Agreed."

We take off before anyone spots us and I'm on pins and needles all night, wondering about that asshole's reaction to our prank.

The next morning, I'm locking my bike up when Dylan's truck screeches into the lot. The evidence is gone, but people are still laughing like crazy when he parks.

One kid yells, "Maybe you'd like wiener touching better from a dude, bro!"

I glance over, and he's waving his phone. Even at this distance, I glimpse a photo of our handiwork. A few seconds later, my phone pings, as Kimmy's forwarded the picture. I guess that means everyone knows, because I hear text tones all around me, and the laughter gets louder. To make matters worse, Dylan's given his mom a ride to school; she looks so confused and upset, especially when she hears what the guy said. She touches Dylan's arm and he shrugs her off, looking mad as hell. Since Shadow Sage was running the show, I didn't think about how he'd feel about his mother's reaction. I've given him the shittiest Valentine's Day ever, and . . . I feel crappy.

Yeah, there's always fallout to being bad. Always.

He comes over to me, smiling, but the expression doesn't reach his eyes. "I know you did this. And I'm going to make you sorry you were ever born."

I meet his gaze, trying to seem calm. "Good luck with that."

Inside school, I see flyers posted all over for the rose sale the student council sponsors to help fund the prom. I'm not part of that committee, and I figure Shane won't be interested in a school dance. He does romance in a different way; I touch the eighth note at my throat.

Later, the delivery people delight in interrupting class, and Mr. Mackiewicz is particularly perturbed by the delay. But since they have permission to do this, he can't complain. He harrumphs and stomps to his desk while they circulate, handing out roses. I can see which people expect to get one by the way they watch. Others pretend to work on their geometry, and I'm one of the latter, until the guy taps me on the shoulder.

"For you." He hands it over with a flourish.

"Thanks." I glance over at Shane, who's watching me with a faint smile.

The sun's shining through the window, brightening the classroom. Everything seems more vivid. All around me, girls are smiling like goofballs because they got a red rose. A few of them have no idea who it's from and they're whispering with their friends, trying to figure it out. Mine has a card attached. I smile as I fold it open and read: *You're the one who makes me whole.* I recognize that as a line from the song he's been working on.

Mackiewicz puts us back to work as soon as the roses are handed out, so I don't have a chance to talk to Shane until after class. "Thanks. But you didn't have to."

"I wanted to."

At lunch, I learn that Lila got a rose from a secret admirer, and Kenny sent one to Tara, who apparently isn't sitting with us anymore. I guess she finally realized how much he likes her and took steps to make her disinterest clear. It sucks to have your dreams crushed on Valentine's Day; even his Mario hat looks sad.

In the afternoon, teachers have a hard time getting us to focus, so we mostly watch videos. Then they show they have souls by choosing not to give us homework. I cheer along with everyone else, then go meet Shane, who's already at our locker, waiting.

"I'm cooking for you. I switched my shift so we could be together tonight. Are you up to a ride out to my place?"

"Really?"

He nods. "I hope so. Everything's set up."

"Absolutely. Let me text my aunt." I'm sure she's going out with Joe anyway.

They've been seeing a lot of each other, like her trip to see Aunt Helen made him realize how much he missed her. That could have been part of her strategy, actually. My aunt is smart. Gabby replies quickly that it's fine; she's going to Rudolfo's with Joe.

"Called it," I say, climbing on my bike.

The trip to his house doesn't let us talk much, and Shane rides faster than I do. I'm a little out of breath when we turn down the weed-choked drive. I'm surprised all over again. I haven't been out here since I brought him soup and his homework assignments, thinking he was sick. He prefers for us to spend time at my place or somewhere else in town. Honestly, I don't blame him. This trailer's a reminder of how poorly his dad's doing at taking care of him. Shane would argue that his father was relieved of that responsibility when he walked out on them years ago.

I disagree.

It feels good to get out of the wind when we head into the trailer. He's fixed it up quite a bit—*oh*. Shane flips a switch, so that the whole room glows with white twinkle lights, and he's woven white silk flowers along the wiring, turning this into a magical bower. It looks like springtime and love in here. *Just . . . wow.*

"This is great," I whisper.

"Yeah?"

"I love it."

"There's more." He indicates the slow cooker with a flourish.

From the warm, inviting smell, I can tell he's made the veggie soup he promised me. "I know it's not romantic, but I can't do champagne and chocolate-dipped strawberries."

"It's perfect."

"The soup won't be done for a while. But I made some other stuff."

Wow, what time did he get up this morning? The other stuff turns out to be a cheese and fruit plate, simple but I can see how much time he devoted to this. We sit down on his old couch and dig in. Shane's telling me about a music college that he heard about, and I can hardly keep from asking how far it is from Maine. I hate that this won't last forever.

But nothing does, right? I should just be happy now.

Shane breaks off what he's saying with a faint frown. "You okay?"

"Of course. Why?"

"You looked really sad there for a minute." He glances around the trailer, hardly recognizable the way he's decorated it, like the setting is the reason I'm unhappy. "I'm sorry I couldn't do more, but—"

"No," I cut in. "This is perfect. I was just thinking about college . . . and how we might not end up at the same one. So if I'm sad, it's at the thought of saying good-bye to you."

"Oh." His expression softens and he cups my cheek in his palm, feathering long fingers down my jaw. "I can't promise we'll always be together like this, and long-distance relationships suck. But I'll always want you in my life. So . . . if it doesn't work out at university, I'll be texting you and sending stupid e-mails. I'm sure I'll have a laptop by then, and we can Skype."

"That helps."

"Hey, let's not talk about breaking up on Valentine's Day. That's a long way off. Who knows what will happen between now and then?"

"You make a good point." Making an effort not to be too dark today, of all days, I say, "So I've been wondering . . . you don't have much stuff. What happened to it?"

Most people have a few toys, but when we met he didn't have an iPod or a phone, no laptop, and he only has the iPad because of school. But he has no Wi-Fi out here to check his e-mail on.

He shrugs, like it's not a big deal. "Everything I had before my mom got sick, we pawned to pay off her medical bills. Dying is expensive."

Damn. This is my second conversational gambit that has turned down a depressing path. Maybe I can change that. "What was your favorite thing about her?"

"Her hugs," he says right away. "You know how, after a while, some people will pat you a couple of times to let you know they've got better things to do? She never did. She'd just stand there hugging, like there was nothing more important in the world."

"I bet she didn't think there was." I wish I'd met Shane's mom.

"I miss her," he confesses in a raw voice.

I can't fix this; only time can. But I wrap my arms around him anyway, trying to live up to world-class hugging. He whispers into my neck, "You know when you held me before, that first trip out here, it was first time anybody did since she died?"

"I had no idea."

"Everyone was afraid to get near me, afraid of setting me off. And then you just showed up with soup and started hugging me. Is it weird that I thought maybe my mom sent you?"

I smile at him. "I hope that's true."

"Sometimes when I'm feeling guilty that I'm happy, I imagine her telling me that it's okay . . . I'm allowed to have a life even if she doesn't anymore."

"That's how I feel about my dad. Sometimes I'll go weeks without thinking about him at all . . . and then I'm, like, this is the guy who pushed you on the swings for two solid hours."

"It's such a relief to talk about her. Most people can't handle this. They get weird and they don't know what to say." He pauses. "I have some pictures, if you want to see them."

"I'd like that."

Shane gets out a packet of photos, and then his life is arrayed in front of me. Though the point is for me to see his mother, I also meet little Shane with his missing teeth, on the rocking horse, with no shirt on, and one with him holding what I imagine is his first guitar. He's smiling as he pages through, telling me about what life was like before.

Before. It's kind of a magical word. Warmth swells up inside me. I've never felt this close to anyone in my life.

After that, we eat vegetable soup, which is delicious. Then we curl up with my old iPod, his now. He doesn't have a dock, so we share the earbuds, listening to a playlist Shane has created especially for this occasion. It's past nine by this point, and I'm wondering if he ever plans to play me the song he claimed to be working on when he pushes to his feet and heads down the hall to his room. *Am I supposed to follow?*

No. He's coming back.

Ah, he's got his guitar, wearing his shy-delightful smile. By the twinkle lights, he looks so beautiful that it hurts me to see him, and I think in wonderment, *He's mine.*

Shane settles beside me. "I wrote this for you, Sage. I hope you like it."

And I'm too breathless to respond as he starts to play.

"*Rock bottom, left for dead, / Furies screaming in my head— / I was off the rails, way off track / Somehow you brought me back.*"

This song is soft and slow, his voice deepening, lending the lyrics greater intimacy. He gazes at me as he sings, and I melt. My hands are folded in my lap, and I restrain the urge to throw myself at him. My body isn't big enough to hold this feeling. *God, he wrote me a song.*

Shane launches into the second verse, cradling the guitar tenderly. "*You're the one who makes me whole / When I'm broken in my soul / The queen of bright and shiny things, / Not designer clothes or diamond rings.*"

I push out a shaky breath, listening.

"*So you're the calm and I'm the storm; / I'd sell my soul to keep you warm. / You're the angel in my bed; / You're all the words I never said.*"

My cheeks heat when he says I'm the angel in his bed. Technically, he was in mine, but I'm thinking that will change tonight. But words, which ones? The big three? I can't stand this. It's too beautiful and personal. I ache all over.

"*Princess, let me fight for you / I'll go to war if you want me to / But I'd rather take you home tonight / Hold you close and treat you right.*"

I remember the way his fist balled up when Dylan was giving me shit. Shane really *would* fight for me, I suspect, but it's enough that he wants to. Because of him, I don't hate that nickname anymore; I used to hear "princess" and flinch, but now it makes me smile.

His voice drops, so intense and heartfelt, and his eyes blaze blue fire as he plays. *"Other men could give you more / But none of them could love you more / They can keep the world if I've got you / I'm forever yours, forever true."*

Did he just say he loves me? I'm pretty sure he did. For a few seconds, I'm so overwhelmed that I can't speak, let alone move.

"Well?" he prompts, looking worried.

"It was the most beautiful thing I've ever heard. I can't believe you wrote that for me."

"I'd do anything for you," he says softly. "That was just a song."

"*That* was the best present anyone's ever given me." Sliding off the sofa, I take his hand. "Wanna show me your room?"

Shane's off the couch like a shot. "It's not decorated like the rest."

"Doesn't matter. I just want to be close to you."

The twinkle lights from the other room cast enough of a glow for his room to seem less stark. His bed's right there, so there's no doubt why I wanted to see the room. Otherwise, there's not much scenery.

Shane comes up behind me and I spin, leaning toward him. He meets me halfway with a kiss so sweet that the top of my head tingles. One-armed, he puts his guitar down and then draws me up against him. His hands drop to my hips, the boldest he's been in touching me.

Tonight, he can have everything.

I wrap my arms around his neck, and the world disappears. The next thing I know, we're a tangle of arms and legs, lips touching again and again. He runs his palm over my hip, stealing under my shirt to graze my bare belly. My whole body reacts.

"Do you want—"

"Yes." I answer before he finishes the question.

And then we're both in a hurry, though I keep my top on. Shane scrambles for a condom, and I don't care why he has them. I'm just glad he does. He's so close. We're both trembling. He kisses me as it happens, and I know this changes everything. I don't care. For these moments, he's part of me. I'm part of him. It's quick and strange and deep, like diving from a high board. I come up for air, gasping, holding on to him as he shakes.

Afterward, he holds me. I stroke through his hair. "Tell the truth, did you plan this?"

"What do you think?"

"You had protection."

"Would you believe I was a Boy Scout and my motto is Be Prepared?"

"Unlikely." I use his word. Our word.

"Then, no, I didn't plan it, but let's say I hoped." His smile is too beautiful for this world, and I am dying of love.

CHAPTER
TWENTY-SIX

I GO TO SCHOOL THE NEXT DAY . . . AND EVERYTHING IS
different. People are whispering, staring at me. I check my clothes
to make sure nothing's unzipped or tucked in where it shouldn't
be. No, no wardrobe malfunctions. No TP clinging to the back of
my shoe. It's weird, and I don't spot Shane at our locker. God, I
hope he's okay. Maybe something happened to him last night after
I left, and that's why everyone is talking. They just don't know
how to break the bad news to me.

Shit. I'm about to panic when I get swept into the pre-bell rush.
Somehow I end up in my first class, but nobody will make eye contact. Whatever it is, this is bad. I can't hear the teacher. I can barely
keep from screaming. I look for him in the hall between classes,
but I don't see him. My stomach doesn't settle until Shane sprints
into geometry, a few periods later.

He smiles at me and whispers, "I overslept."

Some of the sour feel eases from my stomach. At least whatever's going on, Shane is all right. The strange behavior from the
rest of the school continues until lunch, however. People aren't

greeting me like they did, no friendly smiles or fist bumps, no "sup, Shage" when I'm walking with Shane. In fact, one guy mutters to him, "Wow, you're brave, dude."

This can't be what I'm afraid it is. It *can't*. Then Dylan strolls by, smiling. He makes eye contact and his expression ripens into a grin. He aims a finger gun at me and pulls the trigger.

Worried, when I reach our table, I ask Lila, "What's going on? Have you heard?"

She shakes her head. "They aren't talking to me. People know I will cut a bitch if they start something with you."

Today, our crew is sparse, just me, Ryan, Lila, and Shane. I spot the others scattered among other tables. Whatever it is, I guess they heard . . . and they're gone. I try not to mind; I mean, they're freshmen and sophomores. They can't afford any social errors.

After lunch, I'm at my locker with Lila. It becomes crystal clear when a guy I don't know steps up to me, ignoring his friends' nervous laughter. "So . . . is it true?"

"What?" I fold my arms, pretending to be bored, when it feels like I might hurl. I have an inkling where this conversation is going, based on Dylan's clue.

"That you killed your mom."

My breath goes in a rush, and I literally see sparks, so Lila has to catch me. She helps me lean against the lockers, then she takes a step forward. "You will step off *right now,* unless you want to eat your nutsack."

When the kid doesn't move, she lunges at him and he flinches backward. It's enough for her to clear a path with an arm around me. I barely make it to the bathroom before I'm puking up the lunch I packed. Then I sit down on the toilet, not crying, but shaking. I can't stop.

He did it. That's the thought looping in my head. *Dylan promised he'd dig until he found something to wreck me with . . . and he did it. I even riled him up two days ago, gave him a reason to keep hate alive. I shouldn't have let Shadow Sage off her chain.*

There's always a price.

"Sage? You okay?" I hear worry in Lila's voice. She must be wondering what the hell is wrong with me.

I burst out in near-hysterical laughter. "No. Not even close. I can't go to class. Please get me out of here."

To my relief, she doesn't argue. "Let me check the hall." A few seconds later I hear her come back. "It's clear for now. We'll go out the back and circle around for your bike."

"Sounds like you've cut before."

"Trust me, I'm a pro. I'll take you home."

And she isn't lying. She knows exactly how to slip out of school and get us off property before anyone notices. Pretty soon she's pedaling my bike and I'm on the seat, which is good because I'd probably end up in a ditch. I can't go back to school now. I can't. I'd rather live in the group home again than face another day of this.

Once we get to my house, Lila makes tea, looking worried. "Should I call your aunt?"

"No, she'll find out when she gets home. That's soon enough to ruin her day."

"So . . . what's the deal? Obviously *something* happened with your mom or you would've told him to screw off. But why would some random dude know that about you?"

Since I don't feel like spilling my guts, I tell her the truth— about Dylan and the private war we've been waging, which I escalated yesterday, and he shot back. This is a hot button for Lila, and she'll forget about my past, at least for now. As expected, when she learns how he threatened to dig into my life and find something shitty to spread around, she starts pacing, ranting with more four-letter words than I've heard before in one breath.

"That son of a bitch," she fumes. "If he thinks he can get away with this, oh, *hell* no."

Well, he *did* warn me. I have no idea how he found out, but he won, fair and square. And he told me this was the way it would go down. I just . . . got cocky. I hoped that if we shamed him bad enough that he'd slink away, but that's not how he rolls. He's been the alpha dog for too long.

Eventually, she settles down long enough to ask, "Does Shane know what's going on?"

"I should text him."

For a few seconds, I just stare my phone. Then I type, **went home early. Skipping Green World. TTYL.**

"Do you have to work tonight?" Lila asks.

"No, that's only on Monday and Thursday."

Despite her trying to cheer me up, it's just not happening. I brush my teeth and get in bed, pulling the covers over my head. In the end, Lila stays until Shane shows up, just past three. She's eager to go out and implement some revenge scheme against Dylan, and I don't have the energy to tell her it's a bad idea. A part of me even admires how much he loves his mother. He ruined me, as promised, to make sure I can't say anything about her and the principal. Who would listen now?

I'm feeling like crap when I hear Shane's footsteps coming down the hall. "Sage? What the hell? There's some crazy shit about your mom going around at school. Why'd you take off?"

I can't look at him when I say this. I just can't. "Because it's true."

If he had any common sense, this would be the last I hear from him, and what *perfect* timing for Dylan's payback; I sleep with Shane, then he breaks up with me.

Right now, given what he's probably heard, he should be walking. Instead, Shane sits down on the edge of the bed. "I'm supposed to believe that? You don't even eat meat." Gently, he draws the covers off and pulls me into his arms. "Talk to me. I'm not leaving until you do."

Some shrinks say that it's best to share your trauma. You become less sensitized to it. And I've done all kinds of therapy: group, personal, specialized, hourly, artistic, musical. Some of those programs even felt experimental; they were supposed to fix me. But none of the awful shit I had to do in order to be released into Aunt Gabby's care horrified me half as much as the idea of telling Shane the truth.

But I have to. I owe him that much. He needs to know what I used to be. That way, he'll understand why he needs to bail.

"I told you part of my story . . . but not the really bad stuff."

"Okay." It's an encouraging word. I hate it.

Yesterday was perfect; yesterday was before. This is why *before* is a magical word.

I take a deep breath to offset the ache in my chest. "Things were fine with my dad. He died when I was seven. I spent a year in foster care, and that sucked, but I don't have any horror stories. Just . . . I never felt at home, I guess."

"I get it."

No, you really don't, I want to scream, but I'm not allowed to be angry. Anger is flames, showering sparks and death. And besides, I'm not even mad at him. I just want to burn the world down right now. And that's the impulse I'm hiding from. Because at this moment, I can imagine Dylan Smith's house on fire—and it makes me feel *better*.

"When I was eight, they found my bio-mom. She was clean, then. But it didn't last long."

Time for some show-and-tell. I sit up, pull off my hoodie, and show him my bare arms. There's a reason I always have on a sweater or a jacket. Years later, I'm still marked with cigarette burns, the scars lined up in neat rows. They were punishments for when I didn't do what my mom expected or sometimes even when I did. There was no pleasing her. She hated me, I think. I don't understand why she took me in when the social worker contacted her. Guilt maybe, or possibly the welfare money. I'll never know, now.

Shane takes my hands in his and runs his long fingers over the marks. I shiver; it's been such a long time since anyone touched me here. Even last night, I didn't strip down with him. I let him think it was because I'm shy, but that wasn't the reason. I've always had darkness to hide.

"Why didn't you tell me?" he asks.

The question's like a blade between my ribs. "It's not exactly cafeteria chat."

"We've had plenty of time alone, Sage."

"Yeah, but I didn't want to ruin it."

"Ruin it how?"

"With this." I bend my head, staring at my scars. "This happened when she was sober. Once she got back on junk, she stopped caring where I was . . . or who was in the house with us." I'm relating this in a monotone because it's just so ugly that I can't think of an emotional tone that seems right.

This is me. This is where I'm from.

"Oh my God," he whispers.

"I was eleven when I broke. Three years of this shit. We were renting this hellhole . . . and she couldn't come up with the money. So she gets this idea—" I break off. *Wow, this is harder than I expected. And I knew it would suck.* "To use me. To pay. So she invites the landlord over."

"Jesus Christ."

"They drank a lot that night. And passed out before he could . . . you know. Then I set fire to the place. And I went outside."

The memory surges to the front of my brain, how calm I felt, sitting on the curb across the street. It was summertime, and I was in my pajamas, too small since my mother hadn't bought me any clothes in a couple of years. They had SpongeBob on them—funny I remember that. I watched the house burn for twenty minutes before a crackhead neighbor called the fire department.

The police found me, an hour later. At first they dubbed me a survivor, until I admitted to setting the fire. Stupid kid; I should've lied. After that, the nightmare didn't end for years. They catalogued abuse: scars and malnutrition and had a doctor examine me down below. No sign of sexual assault. Then they put me where you stick broken people, ones who can't be trusted around normal ones. I tell Shane all of that; there's no point in hiding it now.

"I was in the group home for two years, where I went to a special school. They found Aunt Gabby when I was twelve, but I wasn't released until I was thirteen. Then I had more counseling and medication . . . she took me home with her and I started junior high here."

Why isn't he talking? I risk a look at Shane's face and he's blank, like he can't process it all. *Welcome to my world.* I try to pull back then, but he doesn't let go. His hands move over mine in gentle motions, as if I'm a song he can't remember how to play.

"Look, you were a kid," he finally says. "Is burning down your house the best defensive strategy? No, but what options did you have? That asshole was going to . . ." Yeah, he can't even say it. That's how ugly the truth is.

But I get to live with knowing that's how much my mom valued me. First, she left me, then she hurt me, then she was going to use me as currency. To her, I was nothing, and she got me to the point where I didn't care what happened to me, as long as she was gone, too. The rage washes over me all over again. And now everyone at school knows. Somehow.

Dylan Smith.

Everything I've built over the last three years is gone. Now I'm back to being a freak show. I can expect more whispers, more people rushing to avoid me, refusing to make eye contact. All the projects I've planned, including the town garden, will probably fail. Who wants to help a crazy girl?

"Sage, look at me." I do, mostly because his fingers are on my chin.

I feel numb. I should cry. I can't. My whole body's iced over.

"It's gonna be okay. People talk shit, then they get bored. Something stupid will happen and they'll forget."

The numbness gives way to pain and shame, oceans of it. I might cry after all. Determined to avoid that, I bite my lip. I close my eyes.

"You really think so? I guess you've never lived in a town this small before." To shock him, make him realize how insurmountable this is, I add, "They told me she died of smoke inhalation. It's supposed to be fast."

"What about the asshole?"

"He stumbled out the back. Some burns, but he lived."

"But he didn't try to help your mom?"

"He was drunk. I doubt it even occurred to him." I pull away from him, then. "You should go. Don't you have to work?" He's already late.

"I'll call in," Shane offers.

"No, don't. You still need the money. My shitty past doesn't change your shitty present."

"But it's not," he tells me. "And you're the reason why. Promise me you'll be at school tomorrow. The longer you hide, the worse it'll be. Remember, you're the one who says life doesn't get better if you look away."

"That is so *unfair,* using my own words against me."

"Promise, Sage."

"I'll talk to my aunt," I mumble. "If she agrees with you, then I'll go."

"Okay." He pushes off the bed, then leans down to kiss me good-bye.

I can't believe he still wants to. He knows *everything* about me now, that I've done the worst possible thing a human can do, and he's still my boyfriend? Is he nuts? But maybe I've tapped into the gallant part of him that couldn't leave his mother alone, no matter what it cost. "I don't understand why you're not already walking."

"You don't know everything about me," he says quietly. "You think you're the only one who glossed over stuff you didn't want to think about? But I'll tell you more tomorrow. If you're brave enough to show up."

Somehow, he's done the impossible. I'm actually smiling. Maybe I'll live through this after all, as long as Ryan, Lila, and Shane stand by me. That's how true friends respond to trouble, I guess. They rally around you and keep the vultures away.

"We'll see," I mutter.

"I'll call you on my break, okay?"

"If you want."

It's because of Shane that I'm not a total basket case when my aunt gets home. I don't try to sugarcoat it; I tell her that I cut school . . . and why. She pales, reaching out to hold the wall for a few seconds, and then she hugs me.

"Oh, honey, I'm so sorry. People can be such shitheads." Since my aunt almost never cusses, this makes me laugh. "You seem to be handling it, though?" It's a question. I'm sure she has my former therapist standing by on speed dial, ready with prescriptions and to resume our weekly sessions.

"I'm upset that they know. But . . . I can deal, I think. It can't be worse than what I've already gone through, right?"

Aunt Gabby hugs me tighter. "I'm sorry, baby. Do you have any clue how the story got out?"

There's no way I'm telling her; I'd have to confess my part in escalating the drama, and I can't stand her disappointed face. Plus, what does it matter? It's not like the school will do anything to Dylan for telling the truth about me. Football players get away with much worse on a regular basis. So I just shake my head. "It's just one of those things."

"You'll be okay," she promises me. "And if school is really bad, we can look into online classes."

I love how she doesn't promise the impossible. She doesn't claim she'll sell the house and move or transfer me to a different school. The options she offers are the ones we can manage. It's depressing to think of taking all my classes online, but I know people with emotional problems do that sometimes. I'm sure my friends would still come see me. Right? Anyway, we're not there yet.

"Shane says I should go tomorrow, show them I don't care. What do you think?"

My aunt nods. "Absolutely. If you can manage it, that would be best. If anyone gives you a hard time, contact one of your teachers . . . or the counselor. I'm sure if you explain your circumstances—"

"I can tough it out."

The surprise was awful, earlier today. I got comfortable. If I'm watching for the punches, then they can't knock me out. I tell myself I'm past the worst. I'll hang out with the friends I have left and ignore the people who give me shit. Maybe I can acquire a reputation as a badass, and then they'll be scared to mess with me.

My aunt throws healthy cooking out the window and we have giant ice cream sundaes with homemade hot fudge for dinner. "I'm not advocating this as a replacement for better coping mechanisms," she tells me, gesturing with a spoon. "But tonight calls for special measures."

"No argument from me."

A few minutes later, I hear my aunt on the phone with Joe. "No, this isn't the right time. I'll tell her later. And I have to cancel tonight. I'll tell you more tomorrow. Sage needs me."

I'd be lying if I said that wasn't true. I'm coping, but it's a thin veneer. I waver between fury and sadness, then I get distracted and it settles down for a while. Half an hour into my favorite movie— *Pitch Perfect*—Ryan messages me. **U ok?**

I'm glad he's checking it. Lila probably told him some of what I said this afternoon since I didn't say it was top secret. Likely, she's also still working on the best and most evil way to get revenge on Dylan. It won't change anything, though.

Me: **Watching Pitch Perfect.**

Ryan: **Again?**

Me: **Shut up.**

Ryan: **Can I do anything? Beat someone up for u?**

This is especially hilarious because Ryan is the last person in the world who could pull that off. He would probably hit himself in the face and pass out. I smile as he intended.

Me: **Nah. Just be there tomorrow?**

It's a short version of what I'm actually asking.

Ryan: **Try and stop me.**

Me: **Thanks. You're awesome.**

Ryan: **so im told by legions of screaming fans.**

Me: **Whatever. Movie. TTYL.**

By the time Shane calls, I'm ready to face the assholes at school. I've done my time, so to speak, and the court decided, in conjunction with my therapist, that it was safe for me to leave the group home. Therefore, I can handle anything. Even this.

Right?

Right.

CHAPTER TWENTY-SEVEN

THE NEXT DAY, SHANE'S WAITING FOR ME AT THE BIKE rack when I arrive.

Bravado has carried me this far, but I'm shaking. I remember all the unfriendly eyes, the people who can't understand, the ones who judge, and those who might even be scared of me. Deliberately he laces our fingers together, a show of solidarity.

"You sure this is a good idea?"

He nods. "I have some experience with this. It's best to get it over with."

I'm distracted by the reference to his secrets. While I'm considering what they could be, he opens the front door and we step inside. It's like yesterday, only worse, because it feels like everyone is staring. I put on a smile, but it must not look normal because people quickly look away. They're giving Shane and me a wide berth in the halls. He goes with me to our locker; Lila's waiting nearby.

"You look better," she says, linking arms with me.

I appreciate it so much that I feel like hugging her, so I do. She looks a little surprised, but she doesn't pull away. She falls in on my left, Shane on my right, and the two of them escort me to my first class, and though I always thought of him as gentle, he's got a hard edge today, a set to his jaw that dares anyone to say a word. They drop me off and run to make their classes before the last bell.

Nobody talks to me, but I can deal with isolation. I pay attention to my teachers, though I'm not delighted when Mr. Mackiewicz asks me to stay after. *I don't need this today. I'm doing better.* But I present myself before his desk as the other students file out. Shane glances at me, but I wave him on.

"Miss Czinski, I just wanted to let you know that I've registered your extra effort this semester. Did you find a tutor?"

"Yeah."

"It's certainly reflected in your work. You've shown the most improvement of anyone in class, and I wanted to say good job."

Wow, really?

"Thanks," I manage to say, surprised.

"That's all. Enjoy your lunch."

That's the least painful conversation I've ever had with Mackiewicz. I'm actually feeling . . . not horrible when I step out into the hall. Most people have already headed to the cafeteria—or wherever they eat—so it's just Shane waiting for me. He raises a brow in question.

"Everything all right?"

"Yeah, he just wanted to praise me, if you can believe it. Thanks to you, I'm most improved in geometry."

"Secret one: I've taken geometry before. I should be a senior this year." He lifts a shoulder in a shrug. "I missed more school than I should, taking care of my mom."

"So you're seventeen?"

"Eighteen in July."

Whoa, so he'll be within a few months of nineteen by the time he finishes school. I'm impressed that he hasn't just said screw it and gotten his GED. He's had more reason than most to quit. I take heart in his determination. If he didn't give up, I won't either.

But just as I think that, I glance down the hall because there's a bunch of people milling around my locker. They give way as I approach, and what I see freezes my heart in my chest. *So that's how he knew.* My case files were confidential, so he went looking through old newspapers. And sure enough, he struck gold. For a few seconds I can't get my breath. There's a pink Post-it note, just like the ones I use, and the two words are written in purple glitter pen, just like mine. But I'd never write PSYCHO KILLER and stick it on someone's locker. Taped beneath, there's a copy of the news article, covering the fire. The headline reads, CHILD STARTS HOUSE FIRE, 1 FATALITY.

I feel sick again.

Shane grabs the papers, tears them down, and crumples them in his fist. "Who posted this?"

Silence.

So he grabs the nearest guy by the shirt, shakes him hard, then slams him against the locker. "Tell me, or I assume *you* did it and beat the shit out of you."

"It-it was Dylan and his crew," the freshman gasps.

Someone else says, "Yeah, they just ran by, laughing their asses off."

Shane lets go of the kid and takes off running. During lunch, Dylan and his cronies can usually be found in the gym, shooting hoops. Alarmed, I race after him. For me, yesterday was the worst; now I'm braced and I can take whatever they throw at me.

I call, "Shane, wait! It's okay. I don't care."

But he's beyond earshot or just not listening. He bangs through the double doors, so hard that one of them hits the wall. Dylan's on the other side of the court, going up for a layup. Shane charges at him. No conversation, no accusations. And he takes him down in one hit. For a few seconds, I'm frozen. Rage fuels his strikes, and he slams him once, twice, three times in the face. I'm positive Dylan's never been in a fight like this. He covers his face with his hands and rolls to his side, but Shane doesn't let up.

"Think you can do whatever you want, you little bitch?" Another blow. "Fight me, asshole. Show your friends how tough you are." Shane pummels him again. "No? You sure?"

It takes four of Dylan's buddies to drag him off, and Shane punches two of them before the PE teacher intervenes. He drags Shane out of range and somebody runs for the nurse, because Dylan looks seriously messed up.

He spits a mouthful of blood and says, "Somebody call the cops. I'm pressing charges."

His friend gets out his phone and dials before the teachers can decide how to handle things. *Oh my God, no. I forgot. I forgot what he told me about needing to lay low—that if he gets in trouble again, he's going to juvie until he's eighteen.*

A huge crowd gathers while the teachers confer. They try to shoo us away, but nobody's budging. Dylan's mom comes from the office and puts an arm around him; she glares at Shane, who's still being restrained by the gym teacher. Eventually the cops show up and they talk quietly with the principal. I wrap my arms around myself because I can't stop shaking.

This is because of me.

I try to explain that it's not Shane's fault, but Mr. Oscar pulls me away. "This doesn't concern you, Sage. You should go to class."

Yeah, that'll happen when half the school's in the gym or just outside, rubbernecking. My gaze meets Shane's, but he's wearing that empty expression, and I can't tell what he's thinking. I feel like I've ruined his life when I only wanted to make things better for him. His beautiful musician's hands are spattered with blood.

"What happened?" Lila asks. I didn't even notice her arrival.

In a monotone, I tell her.

"Holy shit. I mean, Dylan totally had it coming, but this is bad for Shane."

"I know," I choke out.

I'm still watching when the cops cuff Shane's hands behind his back. It feels like the whole world slows down as he passes me. His eyes meet mine, and he's trying to tell me something, but I don't know what. He mouths the word *sorry,* and then life snaps back to normal speed when they take him away. I run all the way to the front of the school, keeping far enough back that the cops shouldn't complain. As I push through the doors, I see them shove Shane into the back of the car. He turns his face away.

Rage boils up inside me then. This is bullshit. After what Dylan's done, he gets to be the victim? I could do *horrible* things to him. For a few seconds, I let myself picture them. Then I wrestle the anger into submission. I've come too far to fall into the hole and let Shadow Sage out again. I don't want to be a bad person; I don't *want* these pictures in my head. What Lila and I did with the truck, that was as far as I can go.

"Maybe it'll be okay," Ryan says, coming up beside me. "The police will call his parents and they'll work something out. Community service, maybe."

There are no parents to answer. I imagine Shane sitting in lockup, waiting for them to realize nobody will ever come for him.

And my heart's a white ball of fire in my chest. He threw away his second chance for me, and I'm not worth it. I dissolve in Ryan's arms, crying for Shane like I never could for myself.

"Hey, we'll figure something out," he says, stroking my back.

"It's not fixable. He's gone."

"That's not like you."

"And you don't know the whole story." With a shuddering breath, I pull back, unwilling to tell Ryan that Shane's mom passed away and that his dad's abandoned him.

Eventually, the school staff herds us back to class, though we've missed the whole period after lunch. It's bittersweet but Shane accomplished what he intended. People aren't looking at me anymore. I'm pretty sure they've forgotten the reason he pounded the shit out of Dylan. Now Shane getting arrested is all anyone can talk about. And I wish it wasn't true.

I'm a zombie in my afternoon classes. For the first time in two years, I leave without putting a Post-it on somebody's locker. I refuse to believe anyone at JFK's having a worse day than me anyway.

Shane is.

I call in sick at work and pedal straight to my aunt's shop. There are a couple of women looking at hand-poured candles, but Aunt Gabby seems pleased to see me as I don't stop by very often, then she gets a good look at my face.

"I'll be right back," she tells the customers, then she takes me in back. "What happened?"

I tell her in a single breath, so fast that some of the words come out on top of each other. Then I finish, "Is there anything we can do? It wasn't his fault."

My aunt sighs. "Oh, honey. While I agree that kid had it

coming, the courts won't see it that way. And Shane made the choice to resolve the problem with violence."

"But we have to try. Please."

"His dad will handle it."

"No, he won't," I say furiously. There's no point in keeping the secret anymore, so I tell her that, too. My voice sounds bitter and angry, as I explain what an asshole Shane's dad is.

"So he's been living on his own since he got here?" she asks, incredulous.

"Basically. Which means he's on his own. Can we *please* try?"

Pushing out a breath, Aunt Gabby nods. "I'll call the station and see what I can find out. But, Sage, it wasn't okay to keep this quiet for him. He would've been better off with people who would take care of him."

"That's not what he wanted," I say stubbornly. "You don't know everything."

"Then maybe you should tell me." She's frowning over all the stuff I've kept from her.

Before I can, however, the ladies in front call out, "We're ready, Gabby!"

"Be right there." She points at a stool. "Sit. I'll be back. This conversation isn't over."

Because I'm too tired to do otherwise, I plop down and wait for my aunt. The back room of the shop is delightful chaos with sweet-smelling candles in the process of being packaged up, shimmering crystals with purported healing properties, silk flowers, and bundles of dried herbs. I can see why my aunt enjoys working here.

Soon, she returns, folding her arms to show me she's not happy. "So . . . spill."

I explain about Shane's mom and how he spent years looking after her. "He doesn't feel like a kid anymore, and he hated the idea of being stuck with strangers. After everything he's been through, was it really so wrong for him to want some peace?"

"That poor boy," she says softly. "I don't know what kind of record he brought with him from Michigan City, but I'll call the station right now."

CHAPTER
TWENTY-EIGHT

HALF AN HOUR LATER, MY AUNT SIGHS, HER SHOULDERS rounded in disappointment. I already know she has bad news. "I tried, Sage. But I'm not his guardian, and apparently, he has a list of offenses."

"Did they tell you what?"

"He wasn't supposed to, but I've known Officer Delaney since grade school. Breaking and entering, theft, damage to private property, vandalism, possession of an illegal substance, and there would've been an assault if the other kid had pressed charges."

That's no worse than I expected. He did tell me he was out of control when he lived with Mike, his mother's friend. Since his mom had just died, I can understand why he lost it. I suspect he thought it didn't matter what he did. Who would care? I wish he had gotten to tell me about this stuff himself, but maybe he's like me, thinking I wouldn't want to be with him if I knew exactly who he is. Or more accurately, who he was.

I sigh audibly. "Dylan's not the type to let this go."

"Then . . . I'm sorry, honey." She sounds genuinely regretful that she can't fix it.

This is a lesson, huh? Some actions have consequences that can't be waved away. Guilt squats in the pit of my stomach. If I hadn't tried to fix everything for Shane and Lila, it would've been fine. I started this by challenging Dylan. And now things are just so screwed up.

"Is there anything I can do to help while I'm here?"

"If you don't mind. You can wrap those crystals in tissue paper, then pack them in the boxes with the biodegradable peanuts."

It's mindless work, but Aunt Gabby and I parcel up like thirty Internet orders by the time the shop closes. As she locks the front door, I say, "I'm heading home if that's okay."

"Why don't you wait for me? It's been a rough couple of days."

"Yeah, it has, but . . . don't put me on lockdown. I'm coping. Trust me, okay?"

She stares at me for a long moment before offering a reluctant nod. "Fine. But be careful. I just have to balance the cash, then I'll be there."

I nod, slipping out the back. A few minutes later, my legs pump mechanically, making the wheels of the bike turn. It's good I could find our house in my sleep because my brain is mostly turned off. I can't believe Shane's gone. He won't be at school tomorrow, or on Monday. The worst part is, I can't even imagine what it will be like for him. I've never been to juvie, so I picture it like prison for young people with bars on the windows or maybe even cells for them to sleep in.

The group home was a cluster of brick cottages. Each one housed ten boys or girls, and I shared a room. Our bathroom time was tightly scheduled and supervised. During the week, we ate in a big hall together, but on weekends, the workers cooked for us in the cottages. Depending on who was on duty, this could be better or worse than institutional food.

Shane's probably still in lockup, though. How long will they keep him there while they try to get in touch with his dad? Before I know it, I'm outside our house. Part of me wants to keep riding, keep the wheels moving until I'm lost. I don't deserve to sleep in a warm bed tonight. Though I didn't ask Shane to do that, he decimated Dylan because of me. It kills me that he could shake off their shit all day, but he lost his mind over me.

It hurts to breathe.

For a few seconds, I consider asking my aunt to call in a refill for my prescription. I had no problems with unruly emotions then . . . mostly because I didn't feel anything at all. But that seems cheap, like I don't care enough about Shane to feel this way for him, after what he did for me. Nobody's ever fought for me before. Aunt Gabby can say what she wants about violence not solving problems, but a tiny part of me is elated. Not that he's gone, never that. But that he cared enough to do it.

So I go inside, determined to cope without chemical aids. Over dinner later, I ask my aunt to find out what she can about juvie rules, if Shane can have visitors, if so, when. I don't even know where the nearest juvenile detention facility is.

"It's about an hour away," she tells me. "I could drive you."

Silently I shake my head. If my first trip in a car is to see Shane while he's locked up, it'll just be another awful association. The boycott stands.

I tilt my head, considering. That's sixty miles or so. It'll take at least five hours to ride that far. And then there's the return trip.

But I'll totally do it. I can start at daylight, get there in time for a visit, then make the return trip before it's too late.

"I'll make some more calls tomorrow, see what I can find out," my aunt promises.

"Thanks."

I don't sleep much that night. Ryan and Lila both text me, but Shane's number is silent. They've probably confiscated his phone. I can't help being glad that his guitar is at the trailer, where nobody can take it. I don't reply to my friends, mostly because I don't know what to say. Maybe I'll have some idea in the morning.

School is quiet the next day, like everyone's trying to pretend things are okay. I'm back to being invisible. Nobody calls me princess, but they aren't shying away, either. I'm tempted to give up on the Post-its, but then I remember Shane said he liked that about me—that I care if somebody's having a bad day. I notice the jocks knocking the books out of this freshman's hands, casually, not intentionally, so even though my heart's not in it, I write a note and stick it on a her locker. *You have a nice smile.* True, as her braces came off recently, and it seems to cheer her up.

Ryan and Lila stay close, as if I might flip out without their supervision. That almost makes me laugh. Almost. I listen to them talk at lunch, the words washing over me. I'm a rock in the river; it will take years but the current might wear me smooth someday.

"Okay, I'm just gonna come out with it," Lila finally says. "Shane's gone and it sucks, but he wouldn't approve of the android version of you."

Ryan frowns. "Leave her alone, Tremaine. It's only been a day. She's probably still in shock."

I get up and leave when they start arguing. I finish the lunch hour in the girls' bathroom, and I only come out after the warning bell. I don't care if I'm late to class, but I manage to slip in as the last one rings. I sit down and look out the window. The snow is melting, leaving a gray and slushy mess in the parking lot. Beyond, the fields are bleak.

When I get to my locker after school, I stop, staring at it in astonishment. The entire surface is covered in Post-it notes. They're lined up neatly in a rainbow of hues and ink colors, different handwritings that tell me this show of support comes from a vast array of people. I read them with dawning wonder, and the ice cracks a fraction in my heart.

You made me not want to kill myself.

I took a college art class because of you.

Your kindness gave me hope.

I thought I was invisible until you saw me.

You reminded me that I matter.

I'm not scared anymore.

You proved one person can make a difference.

I'm happier since you moved here.

As I read them all, I'm on the verge of tears. Some of the messages are so personal that I can't believe someone had the nerve to write it and post it on my locker. I wonder who started it and how it became an outpouring. My locker looks like every person I've ever tried to cheer up has now done the same for me. The final message is the one that truly brightens my mood.

Have faith, Shane will come back.

"I hope so," I whisper.

It takes me a while to remove all the messages, mostly because I'm afraid people will steal them. I stick them inside my locker instead, on top of the pictures I've posted. They fill the inside of the doors and the back of my locker, along the sides. The one about Shane, I keep with me, and I stick it next to the Post-it he wrote, so now my binder says, *You are the silver lining,* and *Have faith, Shane will come back.*

I'm feeling slightly better, so I go to the Coffee Shop because someone needs to tell them that Shane won't be showing up for his Sunday showcase in the foreseeable future. The barista actually seems sad to hear it. "I hope everything's okay?"

I don't answer her because it's not, but I don't want to go into it. I order a chai latte, realizing that I never bought Shane his hot chocolate, and it's all I can do not to burst into tears. Taking my drink, I head to the Curly Q to offer help for a couple of hours since I missed my shift on Thursday. My boss accepts with the usual amount of complaining. Because Grace is busy and Mildred is cranky, neither of them notice my mood. For my usual four hours, I sweep up hair, shampoo a few clients, make appointments, and handle the register.

On automatic, I put on my reflective tape and pedal home. By seven, Aunt Gabby's waiting with seitan tacos. I pick at them as she says, "I have good news and bad news."

"Bad first. Get it over with."

"Shane's been sent to Ingram, as we expected. They permit only parental visitation."

I mutter a bad word and she doesn't chide me. "So I can't see him."

"I'm afraid not."

"What's the good news?"

"He can receive unlimited letters. I got the address for you."

"Wow. That's old-school. No Internet?"

"From what I've gathered, no. But it gets a little better. Once a week—on Saturdays—he's allowed to make one collect call."

I'm not even sure if Shane has our home number. He has my cell, but I don't know if he memorized it, and I have no idea if you can accept collect calls on a cell phone. I suspect not. While I'm thinking of the logistical problems, my aunt hands me a packet of fine stationery, a gel pen, a Post-it with an address on it, and a pack of stamps.

"This will get you started."

"I'm surprised you're not telling me I'm better off without him . . . that he's trouble."

"Everyone deserves a second chance," my aunt says softly.

"Thank you."

"Anytime. Let me do the dishes tonight. You write to Shane."

My instinctive reaction is to refuse; I always clean up. But . . . I want to do this more than I want to be perfect. So I take a deep breath and nod. Oddly, my neck and shoulders feel a little looser as I take everything to my room and shut the door. I don't think I've ever written anyone a letter on actual paper before. I put the date and the time at the top; that might be more journal etiquette than proper letter writing, but Shane won't care.

Shane,

I wish you hadn't done that. Dylan Smith isn't worth your future. It meant more to have you next to me. I felt like I could handle anything then. I really miss you. I have no idea what it's like for you there. Tell me?

The words come easier after that, and pretty soon I've filled a page. Before I can think better of it, I fold the paper and put it in the envelope, then lick the stamp. *Gross. I'll mail this tomorrow.*

This sucks in an understated way; I'm acutely conscious of the hole in my life. It's not that I can't function without him like my aunt feared, but life has gone monochrome. Shane painted my world in the brightest hues with his smile and his music. Now it's dull and dark, the worst part of winter without the promise of spring.

Later, Lila and Ryan drag me to a movie, but it's the opposite of fun.

So, on Saturday, I decide it's time to take action. I'm sick of feeling sad. I leave a note for my aunt, who's at the shop, then I ride out to the trailer to check on things. Forty-five minutes later, I push the door open. Shane's left it unlocked, like he'll be right back. The lights from Valentine's Day are still hanging everywhere, the white flowers, too. He didn't have time to take them down.

I can't stand this. I can't.

It smells musty in here after a few days of vacancy. The food in the small fridge will go bad if I don't clean it out, so I bag that up, feeling awful and guilty. Wandering the trailer, I end up in Shane's bedroom. His guitar is propped against the wall by the bed, and books are scattered on the floor. This is a tiny room with the bed built into the wall. I didn't register much the other night; I saw only him. I lie down on his bed and pull his pillow to my chest, breathing him in. This is what home smells like.

He's pinned a few pictures on the wall, including one of me. My chest tightens until I can hardly breathe, so I squeeze my eyes shut. I fall asleep in his bed, and half an hour later, I wake up feeling better, more centered. So I head back into the front room, where I poke around, unsure of what I'm looking for. I open the packet of photos he showed me and find some new ones. This is all

Shane has left of his old life. A few minutes later, I find an old picture of his mom and dad, dated 1989. They look so young. On the back, it reads: *Jude and Henry, together forever.* But life tears people apart, breaks them down. Young, pretty Jude got cancer and Henry ran away. In my head, I hear the chorus of Shane's song: *Life is bitter, bittersweet . . .*

Then I find it—the postcard tacked to the wall. On the front is a photo of some diner, nothing special. Pulling it down, I flip it over and read: G*lad things are going well at your new school. If you have an emergency, this is where you can reach me.* There's a phone number, but no address. The card is signed, *Dad.*

Asshole.

But now I have a plan.

Once I check to make sure I didn't leave anything plugged in or turned on, I grab his guitar and iPod for safekeeping, get back on my bike, and race home. This time the trip takes me less than half an hour, though I'm sweaty and panting when I run into the house. After putting Shane's stuff in my closet, I head straight for my computer, fingers crossed that the reverse lookup will work. A few seconds later, I have an address. I input that into Google maps, which tells me it's fifty miles away. I switch to street view and zoom in, until I can tell it's a crappy motel. *Well, Shane did tell me his dad usually just crashes at truck stops when he's not driving. So I guess he has a room here.*

I dial the number on my cell and a male voice answers on the fourth ring, sounding groggy. "Hello?"

He's there. Shocked, I put down the phone. I could call back, beg for his help, but it's too easy to turn somebody down and hang up. In an instant, I make up my mind, grab the old note I left my aunt, and write a new one. Because I'm not trying to worry her,

I'm specific, leaving both the name of the place, the address, and the phone number. Then I wrap up by promising to be back as soon as possible. It's past noon already, so it might be midnight by the time I get home. She'll be furious, as I've never gone for such a long ride before, but I don't care.

I can't breathe until I talk to Henry Cavendish.

CHAPTER TWENTY-NINE

IT'S COLD AS HELL OUT HERE.

That's actually a plus because I'm not as sweaty as I would ordinarily be when I ride into the motel parking lot, five and a half hours later. The place is L-shaped with the office situated at the center, upstairs and downstairs running on either side. At some point, it was probably blue, but most of the paint has peeled away, leaving gray concrete blocks. The drive is gravel, making it precarious for me to ride farther, so I get down and walk my bike.

It's almost six, and it's starting to get dark. Overhead, I can't even glimpse the stars through the heavy cloud cover. The day has been gray, so the night probably will be as well. I rub my hands together while I consider my next move. I don't have Cavendish's room number, but it seems like I read a book where the room number is the last three digits of the phone number. I check that, and there *is* a 243 upstairs. I'll risk it.

I lock my bike to the pole supporting the seedy MOTOR LODGE sign, then I head up the external stairs. My knees feel like jelly, but I push on. I tell myself it's because I'm not used to riding so far, not because I'm nervous about confronting Shane's dad. I don't care if this seems like too much to other people; I'll do anything to help Shane, anything at all.

Steeling myself, I bang on the door. At first I think he's gone out because there's no response, then I hear movement, shuffling toward me. He's a tall, gaunt man with thinning gray hair and glasses, and he looks nothing like the handsome, hopeful young man in the picture with Jude. I'm not sure what I expected, but he doesn't look like a degenerate asshole. Mostly he looks tired, squinting at me in the twilight. Behind him, there's a TV playing, the sound muted, and the pictures cast flickering shadows in the dark room.

"Can I help you?" he asks.

I have to be sure, before I go into this. "Are you Henry Cavendish?"

His expression becomes wary. "Who's asking?"

"I'm Sage Czinski. I go to school with your son."

He actually takes a step back, like he's about to slam the door in my face, and the old rage ignites. I stick my foot over the jamb, keeping him from a full retreat. "You've done enough running for one lifetime. He already told me what a worthless asshole you were, but I'm hoping he was wrong. See, Shane's in trouble, and he needs your help."

"Shane prefers that I don't interfere—"

"Bullshit. He ended up in Ingram, defending *me*. And he needs you to be there for him for once in his life. He'll have a court date and he needs an attorney. How long do you plan to pretend he's not your responsibility? He's *your son*."

"You've said enough. You need to go."

"So you're going to act like this isn't happening? Let him rot." I shake my head, so disgusted that I don't even have the words.

I want to scream; I want to punch him. I'd love to kick him as hard as I can, right in the nuts, and it's a hot, glorious feeling. I haven't let myself get angry in so long because I was afraid of what would happen, what I might do. But I'm standing here, furious as hell, and if rage was deadly, Cavendish would be dying at my feet. But it's not; it's just an emotion like any other, and I can be mad when the situation calls for it. I can *feel* this and not lose my shit; I'm damaged but not a monster. I didn't murder my mother; I was just a terrified kid.

To prove it, I take a step back. "You really are worthless."

Then I wheel and run down the steps. After dark, this place is spooky as hell, so I hurry through the gravel parking lot to the crappy restaurant that's attached to the motel. I have enough money for a side salad and some fries, so I eat those while inwardly bolstering myself for the long ride back. I feel like such an idiot. Deep down, I hoped my begging for Shane would mean something, but his dad really has cut him loose.

Thanks for taking care of your mother, son. Good luck with life.

The waitress has been watching me for five minutes, looking like she might call somebody, so I pull it together and head into the bathroom to wash my face. I slip out the back when she's not looking and get my bike. At least it's still where I left it. No surprise, it's not worth much to anyone but me.

It's scary dark. I put on my reflective tape, hoping I'm not about to become a life lesson. Since I got myself into this mess, there's nothing for me to do but go home. Shortly after I set out, my cell phone rings. A glance tells me it's Aunt Gabby, and I don't want to listen to a lecture while I'm trying to keep from being run over by semis, so I let it go to voice mail. Then I text her, *I'm fine. Home late.*

Hopefully that will keep her from losing her mind. After this, she'll probably send me back to the group home, something I've tried so hard to avoid by being the best possible kid in the whole world. But now I just don't care anymore.

My bike wobbles as cars zoom past me. I hope that nobody stops. And they don't. People don't care as much as they used to, or maybe they're scared. I might be a lunatic or a lure, so when they pause to rescue a girl alone at night, six armed men will burst out of the bushes and mug them. Whatever. I wouldn't get in a car unless they sedated me anyway. My principles feel like all I've got left.

Four hours later, I've never been in so much pain. My thighs burn, my arms ache, my back, too. Hell, even my ass hurts. It's close to midnight now. I've got twelve messages and twenty texts from Aunt Gabby. I answer periodically so she knows I'm not dead in a ditch. That's all I can manage at the moment, as the drainage area beside the road is starting to look inviting.

Eventually, I pass a green sign that tells me I'm ten miles from town. That's an hour if I can pick up the pace. I'll be home by 1:00 a.m. *Jesus.* I'm so cold I can't feel my fingers anymore; it's like they're frozen to the handlebars. Seems like it's almost chilly enough to snow, but lucky me, I get rain instead. The clouds open up as I pedal on, leaving me soaked and shivering.

I can't do this. I can't.

But somehow, pressing on has become the only thing in the world that matters anymore, like I'll be giving up on myself *and* Shane if I stop moving. So I move my numb feet on the pedals, round and round. I haven't seen any cars for a while, so I'm startled when a truck swerves off the road and stops on the shoulder in front of me. The rain pounds the pavement, glimmering red in the taillights.

If this is Dylan, I think I have to kill him. As I consider whether I can strangle him with my bike lock, my aunt jumps out of the passenger seat. *I realize this one is silver, not black. Right. This is Joe's truck.*

I can hardly process what Gabby's saying, my mind is working so slow. She's yelling at me and hugging me, and saying stuff like *Do you know how long we looked for you? We've been driving up and down between here and the motel all night.*

I just stare at her and she sighs. "Get in the truck, Sage."

She's soaking wet too now. My teeth are chattering with cold. Joe swings down from the driver's seat and I back up. If she lets him manhandle me, if he puts me bodily in the cab, I will never forgive either of them. This is the only choice I have left, and I'll break into a million pieces if they take it away from me. I don't care that it's stupid. I started this journey for Shane, my way, and I'll finish it for him, even if they think I'm insane.

"What do you want to do?" Joe asks my aunt.

"Get my bike out of the back."

What? She's gonna ride with me? No.

"You can go home. I'm okay." I'm not. I'm freezing and drowning and sadder than I've ever been in my life, because my mom didn't care, and Shane's dad doesn't, and I'm hurting Gabby, the only person who's cared about me in years.

Aunt Gabby grabs my shoulders as Joe lifts her bike from the back of his truck. "I don't know how much you're hearing right now, but understand this: I *love* you. And I will never, ever leave you. No matter what you do or where you go, I'm there for you. If you need to ride a bike home in the pouring rain, I'll be right behind you." Then she's hugging me so hard that it hurts.

But it's a good hurt because when did anyone ever say that to me? *I'll never, ever leave you.* The sob explodes out of me and I grab on to her, my feet slipping on the wet asphalt until we reel against Joe's truck. I'm sure he thinks we're both crazy, but it doesn't matter. Aunt Gabby runs her hands through my sodden hair, and I cling. I cling.

"I never knew about you, Sage. I wish I had, but I didn't grow up with your father. By the time the state told me about you, you had already been through so much. I've tried so hard to show you—"

"I was always afraid you took me in because you felt sorry for me. And that if I did anything wrong, you'd get fed up and send me back."

"Forget that shit," she snaps. "You're my daughter in all ways but biology, and I will never give you up . . . or give up *on* you. Now . . . are you ready to go home?"

I swipe rain and tears out of my eyes, then step back and swing onto my bike. Gabby tells Joe, "Meet us at the house, okay? Run a hot bath and make some tea."

"You got it," he replies.

I kind of love him right then because most men would try to assert their will, convince me how stupid I'm being. And I know that I am. I know. But the heart isn't logical. You can't force it to make sense all the time. Sometimes only the dumbest thing in the world can give you any peace.

He kisses Gabby and climbs back into the truck. Then I push off on the wet road and pedal hard into the wind. That rush propels me to the top of a small rise, and when I sail down it, I lift my palms to the night sky, remembering that Shane thought I was fearless, instead of a girl governed by silent dread.

"Be careful," my aunt shouts.

I put my icy hands back on the handlebars. There's eight miles to go. And like she promised, Aunt Gabby is behind me every step of the way.

CHAPTER THIRTY

JOE IS WAITING FOR US WITH HOT TEA, SOFT BLANKETS, and a tub full of warm water. He doesn't yell at me. He just says, "I'd appreciate it if you wouldn't worry your aunt like that again."

"I'll try not to," I say.

I take my mug to the bathroom, undress, and climb into the water. For what seems like an hour, I soak, then I remember that Gabby is cold, too. But when I hurry out, wrapped in my robe, I find that she's already changed clothes.

"We need to talk," she says.

"I know." I sit down on the sofa.

There's no avoiding this lecture. I deserve it. So I listen to everything she says about how scared they were, how she never wants to feel that way again. And she ends with, "You know, I always wanted kids. But I didn't have any with my ex, so I thought it was too late. Then I found out about you, and it's the best of both worlds. I get to watch you turn into a wonderful woman, and I'll get all of the grandchildren, none of the potty training."

This surprises a watery laugh out of me. "Don't count on them too soon."

"Ten to fifteen years?" she suggests.

"Sounds about right."

Then my aunt sobers. "Obviously, you're grounded. Two weeks, nothing but school and work."

"What about Green World?"

"I can't say no to community service. But no sleepovers, no visitors, no movies out, no hanging in the square, and I want your phone."

Jesus. She's really mad. But I don't argue; I just hand over my cell. "I'm sorry."

"Did it help? Did Shane's dad listen?"

I sigh. "Doubt it."

Joe comes out of the kitchen and sits down next to my aunt. Around me, he's pretty quiet, letting her do most of the talking. I appreciate that because I wouldn't be amused if he suddenly started acting like my dad. "I think it's time, Gabby."

"Tonight? Really?"

"She's stronger than you give her credit for," he says. "The girl rode a hundred miles today. She can handle it."

It's true; I did. I can barely walk, barely sit, actually. The cushions help. "Whatever it is, just tell me. I heard you talking on the phone before, anyway."

"Okay." My aunt gets up and goes to her room. When she comes back, she's wearing a diamond ring on her left hand. "Joe proposed."

"Congratulations." Yeah, I was scared he might ruin my life before, but it's already screwed up and he hasn't made it worse tonight. "When?"

294

"We were thinking after you graduate. You're okay with this?" she asks.

"Of course. You deserve to be happy. Both of you," I add, including Joe in my smile. "I'd be more enthusiastic, but I'm really tired."

"I know you are, baby. Get some sleep. Things will look better in the morning."

Gratefully, I say good night to both of them, after thanking Joe for the tea and the bath, then I stumble to my room and pass out. I dream of cold instead of fire and I wake with my fists balled up so tight that my hands hurt.

THE NEXT TWO WEEKS ARE BORING AND LONELY, BUT I survive them. I don't write again; I'm waiting for Shane to reply. That's how snail mail works, right? Ryan and Lila talk to me on Facebook, at least. At last, my punishment ends, and we're into March when I get the first letter from Shane. I wasn't sure if he'd be allowed to write back. I'm glad that he is. I open the letter with trembling fingers.

Sage,

I don't know what to say. Obviously I messed up. He was hurting you and I couldn't let him get away with it. People like him have everything, and we're just supposed to let them do whatever they want? I probably should be sorry, and I am a little sometimes, but only because I'm locked up away from you. I'll never be sorry for kicking Dylan Smith's ass. He had it coming.

That part makes me laugh. I read on.

I'm waiting for my court appearance. If my dad had come for me, they might've released me into his custody. With my record, though, it's hard to be sure. I'm sorry I never told you. I mean, I hinted, but that's not the same. In the end, you were so honest, even though it was hard.

It sucks here. I don't know what else to tell you. Part of me can't believe I'm here when I was so sure I could handle myself. But like I said before, I never expected you.

I miss you, too. Don't know when I'm getting out and I refuse to write something stupid like wait for me, *but I can't help hoping you will, even though I flushed my last chance. Write back, okay?*

Love, Shane.

I fold the plain notebook paper and slip it back into the envelope, then it goes into my underwear drawer. Things have gotten better with Gabby. Now that I know even my worst behavior won't scare my aunt away, I feel safer, more at home. I still pitch in around the house, because I love her and want to help, not because I'm afraid if I slip an inch, I'll be out the door.

Friday night, later that week, I'm sitting in my room, aching for the sound of Shane's voice. Then I remember—I recorded him on my phone. I pull up the video and tap the screen to play. His music fills the room, making me feel closer to him. The idea bulb flickers over my head. This isn't great quality, but it's not like I have anything else to do tonight. So I connect my phone to my laptop and import the file. I've done video projects for school before, so I know a little bit about this sort of thing. I can do basic cuts and edits and pretty soon I've assembled a decent music video from the raw stuff.

I play it a couple times, then I upload the file to YouTube. After a few seconds of thought, I type into the description: **This is my boyfriend, Shane. He's incredibly talented. And right now, he's in trouble for standing up for me. If you knew the whole story,**

you wouldn't blame him. If people watch this, they'll see his heart in his music . . . and they'll understand that he's not bad.

Then I record my own video, explaining the entire story. I make sure to mention that Shane got in no trouble at all before his mom died, so clearly these are extenuating circumstances. I don't omit anything; I put it all out there, including how I blackmailed Dylan with a secret about his mom, how my tires were slashed, how he started picking on Shane again, and I escalated the conflict, and how he retaliated by telling the whole school about my past. I end with, "If you're punishing people, you need to include Dylan Smith . . . and me. Because we started this, and Shane is paying for it."

This is the only move I can make because I can't let Shane suffer for something I dragged him into. He's only locked up because he cares about me. So whatever the consequences of telling the truth, I'm ready for them. Aunt Gabby has some contact information for the people handling Shane's case, so I dig those cards out of the file box. There's a public defender and a social worker. It won't hurt to send links to their e-mail. It might not help, but I can't rest until I put this right. Shane doesn't belong there. He won't go on a crime spree if they release him just like I won't burn anything down.

Like my aunt says, everyone deserves a second chance.

When I send out my e-mail, I also copy the principal and the office staff. Maybe it's petty of me, but I want Dylan's mom to know exactly what he's been doing. Possibly she won't care, or she'll even think it's sweet of him. From her perspective it is, but it's also mean and destructive.

Before I can reconsider, I hit send. Then I message Ryan. **Can** u get a couple of videos on the school blog and Facebook page for me?

Right away, he answers, **Absolutely. Send them to me?**

I forward the e-mail. This way, the school officials can't keep this quiet. People will be talking about it, at least. It's possible that they'll ignore everything I have to say. I'm still the crazy girl who burned a house down, once upon a time. But I refuse to let that moment define me. Aunt Gabby has been telling me for three years that I'll be okay, that I can do more, be more. And I believe her.

I don't have to scream to be heard. I just need to believe what I say matters.

Holy shit, Ryan sends back. **Coach will have a field day with this. He's all about ethics and honor. This is a serious violation of his moral code.**

I reply, **exactly.**

The rest of the weekend, I watch the hit counter go up slowly, each time the site updates. The video of Shane singing has more hits than the one of me explaining, but they're both climbing upward. I'm almost too nervous to go to school, but I opened this can of whoop-ass. Time to see how it smells.

As I walk to my locker, Alex of the awesome Chucks says to me, "It's so shitty, what Dylan Smith did to you. I hope they expel his ass."

"That should count as bullying or harassment or something," a girl adds.

I nod in acknowledgment, moving past them to where Lila's waiting. "You went for it, huh? I hear they called an emergency staff meeting this morning."

"Really?"

"Yeah. They're worried about enabling a 'toxic learning environment.' If your videos go viral, the school board will have a shit storm on their hands."

"I hope so."

Mid-morning, I'm called down to the principal's office over the intercom. The room is ominously silent as I gather my things and step out. I walk down the hall slowly, torn between dread and elation. *No matter what happens, they're paying attention.*

The main office is quiet, and I don't see Dylan's mom anywhere. Another secretary avoids my eyes as she pretends to photocopy something. I pull up short when I spot Dylan waiting just inside the doors, but I don't let him intimidate me. Instead I take in the fading bruises. Even weeks later, he's still green in places. I'm about to sit down next to him when Principal Warick clears his throat.

"Miss Czinski, I'll see you now."

Dylan makes a sound in his throat as I walk by, but I ignore him and follow Mr. Warick into his office. The room is filled with books and quasi-motivational posters. He has a laptop open on his desk, tilted so that I can see he's been looking at the videos I posted. I take a seat across from him, waiting for him to speak.

"It appears we have a situation. You allege that Dylan Smith followed you from work, threatened you, revealed certain painful secrets about your past in order to ruin your reputation and humiliate you in front of your peers."

"It's true. It happened."

"What possible reason could Dylan have for singling you out in such a way?"

"I threatened him first," I admit. "Because he was picking on my friends."

Now the principal looks slightly alarmed. "You mentioned that in your vlog, but you didn't say how."

Even now, I'm not willing to do what he did, at least not in a public forum. But this is a private conversation. So I say, "I saw you kissing his mother."

Make no mistake, Principal Warick is very married. He has two children in elementary school up the road. So there's a reason he looks ill.

But he still tries to bluff. "Perhaps you misinterpreted what you saw."

"Your hand on her ass, hers in your hair, and—"

"That's enough," he cuts in. "You realize these allegations could ruin my reputation."

I nod. "I wasn't going to say anything. But I needed Dylan to leave Shane and Lila alone. He said basically that he doesn't like to lose and I could expect him to do something horrible to make me sorry. And he did."

"Which led to the altercation with Mr. Cavendish."

"Someone wrote 'psycho killer' on my locker. Do you wonder why my boyfriend got mad?"

"In fact, I do not." Warick sighs heavily. "What is it that you're trying to achieve with these videos, Miss Czinski?"

"I just want people to know the truth, I guess. It's not fair that Shane's taking all the blame when Dylan and I did terrible things, too."

"So you own your part in the conflict?"

"Yeah. I guess you could even say I started it, although if Dylan would just stop harassing people, it wouldn't have been an issue."

"What do you mean by 'harassing'?"

"Pushing them, knocking their backpacks out of their hands, calling them names, starting rumors that aren't true." I could go on, but I don't. He already knows that Dylan followed me from work with the express purpose of scaring me.

"Do you have any witnesses?"

"Sure. I can think of two off the top of my head." I can count on Lila and Ryan to tell the truth. "Oh, and I asked Mr. Johannes to help once. He'll confirm what he saw."

"Then I'll open an investigation. If the situation turns out to be as you've described, then we'll deal with Mr. Smith accordingly."

I have no idea what that means so I just nod. Maybe I can't get Shane released, but I can make sure people know he had a reason for what he did. It's better than nothing.

"You've put me in a delicate situation," he says quietly.

"Because of what I know?" No point in pretending.

"Precisely. Can I count on your discretion?"

"If I was going to spread rumors, I'd have done it already. But Ms. Smith deserves better. Your wife and kids do, too." I startle myself by being bold. Apparently, the new Sage speaks her mind and she doesn't fear the shadows.

To my surprise, he flinches. He doesn't acknowledge what I said, but he opens the door, looking like he's got a heavy weight on his shoulders. I wouldn't want to be in his shoes. Since I know, he must be wondering if other people do, too. And if so, how long before this explodes in his face?

"I can't believe you pulled this shit," Dylan snarls at me. "You couldn't just admit that I beat you, huh? You had to go for round two. Well, guess what? I'm gonna—"

"Stop talking," Principal Warick cuts in. "And get in my office. Right now."

I get a pass from the secretary and head toward my next class, but before I get there, I hear the rapid click of high heels. Turning, I spot Ms. Smith coming toward me. She really is beautiful, tall and slim, with legs that go on forever in a black pencil skirt. She's wearing a simple white blouse that looks more expensive than it is, because of her elegant frame. Her long blond hair is caught in a tortoiseshell clasp, and she hardly looks *old* enough to be Dylan's mom. I understand all over again why he's worried about his friends trying to sleep with her and I'm sad that he needs to be.

The world is so screwed up.

CHAPTER THIRTY-ONE

"YOU'RE SAGE, RIGHT?" MS. SMITH ASKS.

I nod, wondering what she wants.

"I saw your videos. Your boyfriend's really good." She fumbles, twisting her fingers together. "The secret . . . the one about me . . . is it what I think it is?"

Oh, shit.

"Probably," I mumble. This is so awkward. I never wanted to hurt her. She seems like a sweet woman, if not the most discerning about men.

"And my son *really* did all those things to you? He followed you?" This is what's bothering her, I guess, not that her secret affair might get out. I like her better for it.

"Yeah. I'm sorry. I never intended to say anything. I just wanted Dylan to leave us alone."

"I know he can be protective of me, but I *swear* I had no idea." Ms. Smith bites into her lower lip, looking even younger. I feel like buying her ice cream. It must be hell to be her son. "What can I do to make this right?"

My answer doesn't require much thought. "You could drop the charges against Shane. Unless Dylan's eighteen, he can't pursue this without your backing. That would be a start."

"You can guarantee that Shane won't go after Dylan again? He shouldn't have done any of this, but he's my son, and I love him. I won't see him hurt."

"I promise. I'll make sure Shane knows it's a condition of the deal." It's not a legal solution, but if Ms. Smith drops the charges, Shane could come home, right? Excitement surges through me.

"All right," she says, her shoulders drooping. "I'll go down to the station tonight. Dylan won't like it, but I'm in no mood to care."

"Thank you," I say. "Dylan's lucky to have a mom like you."

"He doesn't think so."

There's not much I can say to that. So I give her a half smile. "Anyway . . . I should get going." My pass has a time written on it, and while I suspect teachers will cut me some slack, given the drama I've created with my videos, I can't push it too far.

"You seem like a nice girl. I'm sorry about all of this. Dylan should've known better than to dredge up the past. Lord knows I've made my share of mistakes."

I'm curious if she counts Principal Warick among them, but I only wave and hurry down to the hall to my classroom. Everyone looks up when I slip in, but the teacher doesn't pause. I'm grateful for that. Since it's chemistry, I join Ryan at our table, where the experiment's already underway.

"How did it go?" he asks.

"I'm not sure. But . . . I'm hopeful."

Three days later, Dylan is suspended from school for a week . . . and the most astonishing part? Mr. Warick is seen at a local hotel because he's apparently moved out of the family home. I feel bad for his wife and kids, but I guess it's better to have a clean break. But I'm not sure if *clean* is ever the right word for a situation like his.

I pester Aunt Gabby daily for updates on Shane's situation. And the day after Dylan returns to school, she comes home wearing a frown. My stomach clenches.

"What happened?"

"I talked to Shane's lawyer. Since Ms. Smith has dropped the charges, his offense no longer goes on his permanent record, and he can be released from Ingram."

"But that's *good* news, right?" I don't understand why she looks so sad.

"His dad still isn't around, Sage. Since he's not willing to assume custody, the state has to send him into foster care until he turns eighteen."

"That's only four months away," I protest, remembering he told me his birthday's in July.

"It doesn't change anything. Four months or four days, right now he's a minor, and he can't live on his own."

"He could get . . . what's it called . . . emancipated. Can't his lawyer help him with the papers?"

"I'll check into it," my aunt promises, "but legal petitions take time. It may end up being faster for him to wait until he ages out of the system."

"What does that even mean?"

"When he turns eighteen, the state will no longer assume responsibility for his care."

What the hell. This seems incredibly messed up. Now, he's facing the one situation he wanted to avoid—having to deal with a strange family. After taking care of his mom and managing his own life, he'll have to follow their rules. I hate that it's worked out this way; it seems so unfair. He deserves better.

"Where is he?" I demand.

"He's with a family two hours away."

Two hours by car, roughly 120 miles. There's just no *way* I can bike to see him. I'm still recovering from the trip I took to see his dad. I curl my hand into a fist, taking comfort in how my nails bite into my palms because I'm sad and angry at the same time. But for Shane? For a *happy* reunion? *Okay. Maybe I can ask Aunt Gabby to drive me.* I still don't approve of gas-guzzling vehicles, but Shane's worth an exception.

"Do you have his address?"

Aunt Gabby shakes her head. "The social worker wouldn't tell me since I'm not family."

"Did they give his phone back when they released him from juvie?"

"I imagine so."

Then why hasn't he called me? How long has he been out? But maybe his battery's dead—he probably didn't have a charger with him—or he might be out of minutes, since it was a prepaid phone. With some effort, I calm down. Honestly, I can't wait to get to my room, so I can try texting him. If he doesn't reply, it might not mean anything bad.

"Thanks," I say quietly. "It means a lot to me that you've been calling around."

"No problem. I like Shane, too. And I don't want you running off again."

A wry laugh escapes me. "I won't. My thighs were sore for a week."

"You had it coming."

"I know. I'll be in my room until dinner, okay?"

"Sure, honey."

Once I get in there, I shut the door behind me and lean on it for a few seconds, eyes closed. I wish I'd memorized every moment with him, so they'd be sharp as crystal instead of dream-fogged. Lonely, I pull out my phone and type:

You there?

No reply.

I fling myself on my bed and lie there on my face. Ten minutes later, my phone vibrates. I snatch it up and swipe the screen to unlock it. I don't recognize the number, but the message clues me in.

This is Cassie. I know it's short notice, but I wondered if you had time for coffee.

I text back, **sure. OMW.** It's better than sitting here, worrying about Shane. So I put my shoes on and call to my aunt, "I'm meeting a friend at the Coffee Shop. Is that all right?"

"Who?"

"Her name's Cassie."

She brightens at hearing a new name. "Okay. Be home before dark."

The days are a little longer as we roll toward spring, so I think I can manage. After putting on a jacket, I get my bike out of the shed and head into town. Cassie's already waiting when I arrive, but she stands up when she sees me. For a minute I think she's going to hug me like we're old friends instead two girls who were briefly infatuated with Ryan McKenna. He'd die if he saw us together.

"You look like you've lost weight," she says.

Do I? I have no idea. But I guess riding your bike a hundred miles in the cold burns a lot of calories. I decide to pretend it's a compliment. "Thanks. You look good, too."

She's got some highlights and new glasses, and she's wearing jeans and a cute sparkly top instead of her work uniform. "I got a coffee already. Hope you don't mind, but I could use an actual caffeine transfusion."

"Still working both jobs?"

"Yeah. I don't see an end to that for another two years."

"I admire your dedication."

She shrugs. "If you want something bad enough, you do what it takes to make it happen."

Her words take root inside me as I'm standing in line for my chai latte, but the problem is, I don't know what more I can do for Shane. I can't magically emancipate him or roll time forward so that he turns eighteen faster. What else can I do?

"You look thoughtful," Cassie says as I sit down across from her.

I don't know what comes over me then, but I dump the whole story in her lap. Her eyes widen as I unburden myself. Finally, I pause to draw breath and she holds up a hand. "So what's your ultimate goal here?"

"To bring Shane home."

"And you can only achieve that through emancipation or his father's cooperation, correct?"

"Sounds about right."

"So go after Cavendish again. I'm not suggesting you ride out to visit him," she adds hastily. "But call him. Call him every damned day until he can't take anymore. Pressure him into doing the right thing."

"You think that would work?"

Cassie shrugs. "It can't hurt. Isn't it better than sitting around for four months?"

"Yeah."

"This isn't how I imagined this conversation would go," she admits, taking a sip of her coffee. She drinks it black, no cream or sugar to dilute the caffeine.

"What did you picture?"

"I figured we'd talk about Ryan. This was better, I think."

"Did you want to ask about him?" I don't blame her if she still cares about him. They were together, so to speak, for a while. There are bound to be residual feelings. It's impossible to turn them off and on. All around me, I see relationships in stages of coming together and falling apart. Sometimes it feels like it's happening at the same time, like a cascade of fireworks that sets a house on fire.

"Maybe. Is he seeing anyone?"

I shake my head. "I'm not sure what's going on with him, romance-wise."

"It's immature, but I'm glad he hasn't moved on. I haven't. Not that I have time."

"I get it. You loved the guy you thought he was. And it's hard to let go."

"You're pretty wise," she says.

"I'm still figuring things out. For the first time, though, I think maybe I have a clue."

She laughs. "Just one?"

Before she leaves, we take a duck-face photo together with my camera and I promptly post it on my Facebook wall, along with a tag for Ryan. My caption reads, **Cassie and me, girl talk. Yep.**

Ryan responds immediately. **OMG. WTH! More acronyms!** Cassie's laughing so hard she can hardly stand to leave. Soon, she has to run because she hasn't had any sleep in two days. Time for me to imitate her determination.

Like Cassie advised, I call Mr. Cavendish daily. The first time, I'm polite. "Did you know Shane's out of juvie? He's in foster care now. But you could save him."

He hangs up on me.

Day after day, I'm relentless. He keeps slamming the phone down. Finally, I say, "Look, do the right thing. Shane gave his mother how many years? You can give him a few months."

In time, he stops answering his phone, so I leave messages with the front desk. I don't care how he feels about the office workers knowing his private business. Like Cassie said, you have to be willing to fight.

School is . . . normal, I guess. My geometry grades slip a little without Shane tutoring me, but Ryan and Lila take up the slack. We're like the Three Musketeers, but I miss the fourth side of our quadrangle. Shane still hasn't texted me.

And I haven't received any new mail from him, either. It's been a month since he left juvie.

Where the hell are you, Shane?

It seems like he could find *some* way to get in touch with me. I told him my e-mail when he was sending that message to Mike, his former guardian. If he remembers.

If he remembers *me*.

Pain overwhelms me. Maybe he just wants to forget everything. Start over. And it would be selfish of me to drag him back here, back to that crappy trailer, if he's happier where he is.

And I want Shane to be happy. I *do*.

I just thought he was happiest with me.

CHAPTER THIRTY-TWO

SO I'M PLANTING THE GARDEN WITHOUT SHANE.

It's a warm day. Sunny. Green World is hard at work. Both Lila and Ryan are here, our usual members, and even the four sophomores who deserted me. They've all apologized. Mel told me that she reported seeing Dylan bully people, so that's something. She's partially responsible for his social downfall, and it's scary how fast people turn when you're booted off the football team. Now Dylan Smith's a pretty face with no crew, and payback is a bitch.

So I'm absolutely stunned when he shows up here. Everyone freezes.

I've got my fingers in the dirt, planting the seeds according to Gwen's directions. I don't know that much about gardening, but I like how it looks already. This lot looks like somebody cares. *We* care. And I would've sworn Dylan Smith doesn't—about anything except his mom, that is—so nobody knows what to say.

I push to my feet. "What're you doing here?"

"Can we talk for a minute?"

"I guess." I move away far enough that the others can't over-hear, but they can still see us.

"It's weird that you said yes," he mutters. "Nobody else is talking to me."

There are two ways I can handle this. I can be bitter and say he deserves it, but that's not how Aunt Gabby has taught me to behave, even to my enemies. She's kind even to cranky old Mr. Addams, who's forever holding up the grocery lines. And *she's* the kind of woman I want to be. So I don't tell Dylan what an asshole he is. I figure he knows.

"What's this about?" I ask instead.

"My mom's got me in therapy. She's worried that I'll turn into a serial killer with mommy issues or something."

"I hope it helps," I say quietly.

"God, this is screwed up. You know so much about me, and we're not even friends." He goes on, "Anyway, that's why I'm here. I'm supposed to make things right, if I can. So I'm offering to help."

He wants to plant a seed? Okay.

"No problem." I point at the pile of supplies. "Conrad can get you started. He's kind of the site foreman."

"Really? That's it?"

The others are frozen, watching how this goes down. They seem to be letting me set the tone. And I've learned the most important thing from my aunt: Forgiveness is freedom.

"My personal feelings don't matter, dude. This is an important project. It's good for the town *and* the environment."

"Okay. Then I'll get to work."

With Dylan's help, Conrad creates stone paths between the seedlings and he's so zen about everything that I feel like I'd like to get to know him better. Dylan doesn't complain or slack; he's quiet and polite, speaking only when spoken to. I could feel sorry for him if he wasn't the reason I lost Shane.

Work takes all day but by the time we finish, there are three sections. Near the front, we've planted flowers and Gwen's dad has donated a simple wooden bench where people can sit and enjoy them. The back of the lot is divided into rows of vegetables, and we'll send what we grow to the aid center that received the canned goods from our food drive at Christmas. And to the left, there's a small herb patch. I can't wait to see these plants thrive and bloom.

After we finish, Gwen prevents us from running off. "This was our big project for the year . . . and it's finished now. I move we work out a care schedule for the garden and let that stand in lieu of regular meetings for the rest of the school year."

"Works for me," Kenny says.

"We need to weed, water, and fertilize regularly," Conrad adds.

In time, they come up with a fair division of labor, so nobody's working more than an hour a week, exactly the time we'd spend at the meeting, and the garden should be in great shape by the end of the summer.

"Wait," Tara says. "So we keep this up through the summer, too?"

Lila laughs. "The garden can't tend itself."

"If you go on vacation, call someone to cover for you. Don't let the garden die, okay?" Gwen looks particularly concerned with this point.

"We got it," Mel says.

The club starts to break up, but Gwen yells, "Not yet! I have something else to say."

"When don't you?" Kenny mumbles. Tara frowns at him, but

he's over his crush, and he ignores her. I'm glad he didn't quit the group since I think she's why he joined in the first place.

"I just want to tell you all that I think you did a great job on this project. As most of you know, I'm graduating, so I won't be around to lead next year. So I'm nominating Sage to take my place. All in favor?"

Unanimously, despite the crap that went down at school, despite my past and Shane going away. *They picked me.* This might not seem like a big deal to anyone else, but to me, they might as well have written me a Post-it and stuck it on my locker that reads: *Hey, we know who you are, and it's okay.* The feeling is like riding down a hill on my bike with my arms up. At this moment, I feel like I might be able to touch the sky.

"Thanks," I say softly. "I'll try to do a good job."

I have a future. I love Shane and I miss him. But I'm okay. I've lived through much worse than this. I came out broken, but Aunt Gabby helped me put the pieces back together. They say that a broken thing is never as strong again where it fractured, but I don't know if I believe that. In this moment, I feel *powerful.* I feel free.

After that, Ryan and Lila leave with me. I watch Dylan, watching Lila, and he doesn't realize that I am. There's so much naked longing in his look that I have to turn my head. He balls up a fist as Ryan opens the door for her, and then he strides away. My friends take Ryan's ride, so they get there faster, and when I pedal up, they're staring at the car parked in my driveway. It's an old beater, rusted, and there's a man sitting inside it.

"Do you know him?" Lila asks.

Ryan steps in front of us protectively. "Should I call the cops?"

My heart's beating so hard, I can barely hear them. "I'm pretty sure that's Shane's dad."

"Oh, holy shit." Lila's mouth is practically hanging open. "What're you gonna do?"

I've left my phone number and address with the front desk a hundred times. I just never thought I'd see Henry Cavendish again. Trembling, I crunch my way up the gravel drive to the driver's side door and tap on the window. He jumps. A picture tumbles from his hands. From that I know he's been out to the trailer because it's the one that reads *Jude and Henry, together forever* on the back.

For the first time, I imagine myself in his shoes. I've been with Shane for years, and then I learn he's dying. He's my whole world; I love him more than life itself. I mean, thinking about how I feel now . . . and I'm just not with him, but at least I know he's out there, somewhere. How would I react to a world without Shane? I like to think I'd be brave enough to stay with him until the end. But I don't know. I don't. There are no guarantees, and sometimes you don't know how you'll jump until your feet are in the fire. Now I see a weak and lonely man in Henry Cavendish, not an evil one. Sorrow has eroded him until there's only a dry channel left that once flowed with a river of love.

He climbs out of the car, moving like the Tin Man with rusted joints. "Stop calling me. Please."

"Never," I answer. "If you think asking me to go away will work when Shane needs me, then you don't know me very well."

"No, I mean . . . you don't need to. I'm not at the motel anymore." He digs into his pocket, producing the business card of the social worker Aunt Gabby has spoken to more than once. "I'm working on this. I'm trying to do the right thing."

This is the lesson I learned from Cassie. *Don't give up. Don't let people tell you no.* She looks so quiet and timid, but deep down, she's fierce. I understand why Ryan fell in love with her and not me. Because last year, before Shane, I was afraid of everything.

Even myself.

Especially myself.

When I hug Henry Cavendish, he goes rigid, like this is unspeakable, kind of like Shane did that first time. And I wonder if it's been since Jude died for Mr. Cavendish, too. Jude must've been a wonderland of music and magic to leave such a hole in her men when she went. Eventually, he hugs me back, and I can feel his hands shaking. He's so thin.

"Thank you," I whisper.

He draws back, eyes dark and weary. His face is a mask of grief, new lines written on the ones that came from smiling. "I can't promise anything. Shane probably hates me, and he's right to. I don't know if he'll agree to live with me, even to come back here. But . . . I'm trying."

"That's all anyone can do."

Before I can get myself together enough to ask for Shane's contact info, his dad's gone, driving his sputtering car away and down the road. Lila and Ryan surround me then, both talking at once. I'm kicking myself; that was so sudden, so fast, that I didn't find out anything I really need to know. *I wonder if he's staying at the trailer? Probably not, Shane's two hours away.* I fill the others in on the latest while I make popcorn.

Lila seems excited. "That's great news. Shane could be home soon!"

But honestly, I feel better about this for Shane than for me, because it means his dad's finally waking up from a long sleep. He cares enough to fight. I believe Shane will be back, maybe not until July, but I don't think he'd leave me forever without saying good-bye.

Whatever it is, there's a reason for his silence. I remember how he said that while he can't promise we'll be always together, he wants me in his life. He promised me silly texts and video chats, and I believe in him.

I *believe*.

And so while Ryan is goofing with Lila, I picture Shane's face and smile.

CHAPTER
THIRTY-THREE

PROM IS IN THREE WEEKS.

At the start of the year, it never occurred to me that I might go. Then, after I got together with Shane, I pictured myself in a pretty dress and him in a tuxedo. Even in my head, my weirdness about cars made it a little complicated to imagine how we'd get there because it seems unlikely that biking would work in formal wear. I walk past the girls selling tickets at the table; it's decorated in keeping with this year's theme, which is Sparkle and Shine. This means they've papered it and covered that with glitter and hung silver ribbons that flutter when people pass by.

"You should buy some tickets," Lila says.

"Why?"

"So you can go with Ryan and me."

"You're going to prom with him?" This surprises me.

"Not like that." But from her expression, maybe she wishes that was the case.

"Lila, do you *like* Ryan?"

"We're not talking about me. We're talking about you. And every girl should put on a pretty dress, so she can dance in the gym."

I smile. "You present a tempting offer."

"You could always bring Conrad. I think he likes you."

I stare at her. "Seriously?"

"It was just an idea. Look, if you can afford it, you should buy the tickets. Just in case."

"Of what?" The only person I want to attend prom with, and, well, I don't even know where he is.

Lila ignores the question, instead joining the line at the table. She's digging into her wallet. "How much?"

"Seventy per couple."

She counts out the cash and takes her packet. "Now you."

It's uncanny the way she knows I've got money on me today. Usually I wouldn't, but I was planning to stop at the P&K for groceries on the way home. I dig into my backpack for my wallet, but an arm covered in worn green fabric reaches in front of me, holding three twenties and a ten. "I've got it."

I whirl, unable to believe what I'm seeing. "Shane?"

Yes. It's him—worn jeans, black T-shirt, green army jacket, and the bluest eyes in the world. His hair is a little longer than it was, curly more than shaggy. And he's buying prom tickets? I can't even process what this means. Joy and disbelief war within me as he concludes the transaction, then draws me gently into an empty classroom. From the pictures on the wall, this is health, but I can hardly think right now, let alone speak.

"You must have questions," he says softly.

I just put my arms around him and lean my head on his chest, shaking. The tears trickle down my cheeks. It's ridiculous because

I'm *happy*, not sad, but I have no control over my emotions. He hugs me to him, resting his chin on my hair.

"Okay then, let me do the talking. I ended up fostering with this crazy religious couple. No phone. No Internet. No TV. No music. It was pretty close to hell. I think . . . it was actually worse than juvie."

"They wouldn't let you write to me? Not even a postcard?"

"I lost your address," he admits. "When my release came, I had your letter, but by the time I unpacked, I couldn't find it. I'm so sorry."

"So you're back?" I tip my head back, devouring his face with my gaze. It feels like I could never get enough of him.

He smiles at that. "It seems that somebody was pressuring my dad, making him think about me. And . . . it worked. So he contacted my social worker and started the process to get custody of me, at least until I turn eighteen. He's taken a local route with the trucking company, he'll drive a delivery circuit and be home at the end of each night."

"Oh my God," I breathe. "They approved his petition?"

"Yeah. I guess you made quite an impression on him. Says I'm lucky as hell to have you. Like I didn't already know."

"Wow. But it took a while I guess?"

"Not as bad as it could've been. Since Dad's never been convicted of a crime, never had a problem with drugs or alcohol, and there's never been any allegations of abuse, it was pretty easy for him to get me back, once he started fighting. I . . . just never expected that he would. He's better at running away."

"I bet once he offered proof he'll be home at the end of the day, it helped a lot."

"From what my social worker says, yes. We'll have regular

home visits, just to make sure things are still okay, but I don't expect any problems. And I'll be eighteen in July. So if my dad can't take living with me, then he can bail, and I'll be fine. Thanks to you."

"I'm so happy you're home," I whisper, hugging him tighter.

"I hear you started a Free Shane campaign and got me out of juvie, and then, obviously, you worked on my dad until he was willing to spring me from foster care. Damn, Sage. Is there anything you *can't* do?"

"Say good-bye to you."

"My mom believed in me like that . . . but nobody else, since. Not until you."

"It doesn't matter where we've been," I tell him. "Only where we're going."

"I have no doubt," he says, stroking my hair. "But I want to make you a deal."

"Hm?" The way I'm basking in him, I'd probably agree to anything.

"You've fought for me, figuratively, from the beginning, and I needed somebody to care. You have no idea how much. Then I lost my mind over the idea of anyone hurting you and fought for *you*, literally. But . . . we're both okay, right? Let's stand down now. And just be together. Okay?"

"Deal," I say.

He smiles with both his eyes and his mouth. "So . . . I have these tickets. And I was kind of hoping you'd go with me. Interested?"

"Try and stop me," I answer.

Then he kisses me, and all the pain and sadness slips away with the heat of his mouth on mine. I've had so many people leave, but this is the first time anyone's come back. I hold him tighter, press closer, but we're cut off by the bell.

"I'd suggest getting out of here, but I don't want to get in trouble."

So we step out of the classroom together, holding hands, and nearly bump into Dylan. Despite his participation in Green World, he's been walking around alone a lot lately, and he looks tired. He can't meet Shane's eyes. Then someone shoves him into a locker. I hear he's banned from playing baseball this spring, and the coach isn't sure he's letting him back on the football team next fall. Coach says his players need to be honorable; they need to be leaders, and Dylan let the team down. This means he has almost no shot at an athletic scholarship, so he might not be going to college. Straightening, Dylan threads his way through the crowd and continues to class.

I break away for a sec, dig into my backpack, and pull out my Post-its and my pen. I write *It will get better . . . it did for me,* and stick it on his locker. Since he offered an olive branch at Green World's garden day, I can, too. Maybe if the rest of the school sees that I can forgive him, they'll move on. This is who I want to be, the girl Shane fell in love with. She's real. She's me.

"That was nicer than I'd be," Shane says softly, watching me.

All around us, people are yelling, "Shane!" like they're happy to see him. Someone calls out, "Hope you'll be back at the Coffee Shop. Love your music."

"I'll see what I can do," he says to the girl. Then he adds to me, "I need to talk to the manager at the P&K, too. See if I can get my job back."

The rest of the day passes in a happy blur. I'm on a Shane high, giddy with relief and excitement. For the first time in weeks, the color's back in my world. No more monochrome; there are vivid swirls of red, green, and blue, all vibrant, all beautiful.

That weekend, I go shopping with Lila at the thrift store downtown. This area has mostly shut down, though a few funky boutiques, including the shop my aunt manages, are still squeaking by. I love this store; it's always got such interesting clothes.

After trying on a couple of failures, I spot a blue dress with sequins on the bodice and a layered tulle skirt. I've got nice shoulders, and this will disguise my hips, if I can wiggle into it. I peer at the size. *Looks like a ten. Maybe.* Nervously, I take it to the fitting room and it slips on like it's made for me. I don't even mind that it hits right at my knees. I step out, calling Lila over.

"What do you think?"

"It's perfect. With the right shoes and accessories, you'll look fab."

My arms are bare. I don't know if I can go to prom showing my history to the world. I fight the urge to fold them. But she seems to sense my discomfort and delivers a pair of white satin gloves. "Here. Old-world glamour."

I slip them on and feel better instantly. "Does it work?"

"Yeah. You look gorgeous. Now you need shoes and sparkle."

We find the latter in the form of a rhinestone necklace and earring set. I won't buy used shoes, so I've put everything in my basket that I can pick out here. Lila buys a slinky red dress and jet jewelry. The best part about this shop is that we each end up spending less than fifty bucks.

"Let's drop these off at the dry cleaners," she suggests.

"Good call."

Prom is in two weeks.

And they go fast. I work, I study, I hang out with my friends. I spend time with Shane. This was my life before he left, but I had to lose him to understand what a miracle this is. Now I can appreciate just how special small things can be. Every moment feels like a second chance.

Shane does get his job back at the P&K, not because they saved it for him, but because his replacement was a stoner and he kept eating things that he was supposed to put on the shelves. He's working three nights a week just like he did before, but he gets to keep more of that money because his dad is there, chipping in, buying groceries.

"Is it weird?" I ask him, one day at lunch. "Living with your father again?"

"A little. But he's trying not to get in my way. I mean, he's *there*, but he's not very . . . fatherly. I guess he feels like he lost the right."

"It's enough that he's there. It's a start, right?"

"Yeah," Shane says. "It is."

Time is. It passes. It's the best thing in the world.

Then prom's in one week. Pretty soon I'll be counting the days, which is so girly of me, but I can't help it. I'm so excited.

Since I already weakened once on the car issue, I offer to let Ryan drive us. But my friends surprise me.

Lila objects. "We don't want you to change."

"We've gotten used to your weirdness," Ryan agrees.

I glance at Shane, who's nodding. "You shouldn't compromise who you are, even for me. We'll work around it, I promise."

Then maybe someday, I'll buy an electric car. Because there are no negative associations, plus it's green. But there are no fancy restaurants close to the school. So I don't know how they're handling my quirks, and they won't tell me. Shane just says he's got a plan.

The waiting might drive me crazy.

But I'm so pleased with my life that I savor each day. I like finding Shane at our locker when I get to school. Or sometimes he's out by the bike rack, waiting for me. He often rides his bike instead of taking the bus, so it's easier for him to hang out with me after school. I love him so much. And I can't believe I never told him. He told me with my song, but I'm saving the words for prom, which is so stupid, I know. But I want it to be memorable. That should do it. I hope.

And finally, the day's here. Prom.

Aunt Gabby actually calls in a temp worker to cover the shop so she can spend all day helping me get ready. I get a deep conditioning treatment on my hair, a full manicure, then a pedicure. I'm talking the real deal, too, not a half-assed home version. In the end, my hair is silky, and I've got blue sparkle on fingers and toes. I borrow a pair of silver heels from my aunt because it would be wasteful to buy shoes that I'll never wear after this night.

Then it's time to slip into my dress and let my aunt do my hair and makeup. I could probably manage, but this seems to make her happy, and I want to be pretty for Shane. She does my hair up in an elegant twist, but leaves a few strands to curl around my face. Then she makes me up kind of old-school, heavy lips and eyes, and it so totally goes with my dress. I love the way I look. I never thought I'd say that. When I pull the white satin gloves on, I feel like a million bucks.

"Wow," my aunt breathes. "You're so beautiful."

Heat washes my cheeks. "Thanks."

She goes to get the camera. I don't even mind. Soon thereafter, there's a knock at the door, and I find Shane, Lila, and Ryan outside. She looks so incredible. Most girls couldn't pull off a red dress with red hair, but she's like a living flame, and the jet jewelry, which seemed a little dated in the shop, looks perfect on her. Ryan hasn't managed to tame his hair, no surprise there, and he's actually wearing a red plaid bow tie and cummerbund. At least he matches Lila's dress. Kind of. Actually, I think they look cute together. And Shane . . . wow. He went with classic black, so I swear we look like an old Hollywood couple. I can imagine us dancing in a musical or something. He's just staring at me, mouth half open, until Ryan nudges him.

"Say something, bro."

"You look spectacular."

Naturally, we can't get out of there until my aunt takes a hundred pictures. Then she gives us her blessing to head out. Prom doesn't start for a couple of hours, so I'm curious where we're going. Outside, the pimped-out golf cart waits. I have to be the only girl who's delighted to ride this way to prom. And I *am*, because it means they get me, even the crazy parts.

And they love me anyway.

As it turns out, we're having dinner at the Coffee Shop. But it's not the usual place. The owners, being geniuses, have brought in bistro tables, and then they sold a limited number of dinner tickets. I didn't know about this enterprise, but Shane did, because he had come in to ask about reclaiming his spot in the showcase. He bought tickets while he was in there, and so we're sitting at tables laid with white linen, candles burning.

It's surprisingly romantic, the way they've decorated the place, and the low lighting helps. There's a sign posted on the door that reads, CLOSED FOR PRIVATE EVENT. Shane and I choose the veggie option while Ryan and Lila are eating chicken. I'm nervous about dropping something on my dress. I don't say much over dinner, listening to my friends talk.

I never would've dreamed I could be so lucky.

We finish dinner and get back in the golf cart. Even though it's early May, it's a little chilly in the open vehicle, so Shane wraps his arm around my shoulder. I settle close to him. Some classes rent a hall or go to a country club, but our school has limited options and a smaller budget. The prom committee decided to have finger foods at the prom and decorate the gym. It's fine with me. Most people will have eaten before they arrive anyway.

At the door, there's a sad-looking sophomore from the student council collecting tickets. Shane hands ours over, then we step into the gym. They've done a good job converting it from its usual purpose with the flooring covered entirely in a sparkling mat, and glittery stars dangle from the ceiling. Across the room, there's a silver archway made entirely of falling stars, and a disco ball throws glimmering patterns across the dancers already moving on the floor. This is the perfect place for the queen of bright and shiny things to dance with the boy she loves for the first time. The DJ is playing a slow song at the moment, so Shane holds out his hand to me. I take it, and he leads me onto the floor.

I've never slow-danced with anyone, but it's not hard to learn with my arms around his neck. There's barely space for us to snuggle and twirl in tight circles. That's fine with me. I glimpse Gwen over Shane's shoulder, and she's dancing with Conrad of all people. I guess she spent so much time on Green World that she didn't have many options when prom rolled around. Or maybe she *likes* him; she's so driven and he's so mellow. Love is a strange and wondrous thing.

This slow song flows into the next, requiring no reaction from us. Around us, I see couples who are already tired of each other, going to look for snacks or sneaking off to drink. But I could stay

327

where I am all night. Shane's arms tighten on me, and he's gazing down into my face like he could look at me forever. A tiny thrill ripples through me.

"Sage," he starts, just as I say, "Shane, I—"

We both stop, bemused, then I whisper, "Me first."

"Okay."

"I want you to know how much I love you."

He smiles, and for me, it's like a sunrise. I love seeing the light start in his eyes and then spread to the curve of his mouth. His teeth are white but not perfect. I love that about him, too. Every flaw makes him more perfectly Shane, more right for me. I feel like we've been tested, and that we can survive anything. We're strong. We're special. We *are*. And together, we're invincible. All around us, people spin in slow circles, arms tight around each other. The DJ selects Lifehouse next, and the first strains of "You and Me" sound from the speakers. It's an older song, but it suits this moment.

"I love you too," he answers. "In fact, that's what I was going to say." He hesitates then. "I've never said that to anyone before."

"Me either."

Family doesn't count. Everyone knows that. So we're embarking on the next step together. Like before, I don't know the rules. I only know that I love him. And it's enough.

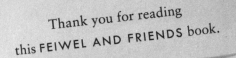

Thank you for reading
this FEIWEL AND FRIENDS book.

The Friends who made
**THE QUEEN OF BRIGHT
AND SHINY THINGS**
possible are:

JEAN FEIWEL, Publisher

LIZ SZABLA, Editor in Chief

RICH DEAS, Senior Creative Director

HOLLY WEST, Associate Editor

DAVE BARRETT,
Executive Managing Editor

NICOLE LIEBOWITZ MOULAISON,
Production Manager

LAUREN A. BURNIAC, Editor

ANNA ROBERTO,
Associate Editor

CHRISTINE BARCELLONA,
Administrative Assistant

Follow us on Facebook
or visit us online at mackids.com.

OUR BOOKS ARE FRIENDS FOR LIFE